A MIDWESTERN CINDERELLA

KRISTA LAKES

ZIRCONIA PUBLISHING, INC.

"*I* don't care that you're not royal material. You're my princess."

Zoey is hardly what you'd consider princess material. Born in flyover country, she never learned how to curtsy, let alone walk in high heels. And when she literally trips into the arms of a handsome stranger at her friend's wedding, she thinks she's finally found love.

Freddie Prescott is a charming prankster. Despite his carefree attitude, he pursues Zoey with an intensity that shows he can be serious when he needs to be. And with those rock hard abs and rippling biceps, his pursuit of Zoey is a satisfying one. Without realizing it, Zoey finds herself falling in love.

There's only one problem: Freddie is a prince.

Spending a week without Internet access or phone reception has left Zoey in a weird predicament. He certainly left enough hints that he was rich and famous, but he never outright said it. And when the time comes for him to leave their vacation getaway, he asks her to come with him to the kingdom of Paradisa.

But Zoey can't use the right fork, put her pinkie up for tea, or any of the things expected of a princess. Plus, there are those in the kingdom who don't want an American close to the throne. How can she hope to keep Freddie's love if she's a stranger to his royal world?

NYT Bestseller Krista Lakes brings you this brand new sweet-and-sexy royal romance. This standalone novel will have you cheering for an American princess's happily ever after.

"Did you go anywhere interesting?" I asked, handing him a dish to dry.

"In the army or just in general?" he asked.

"Either." I shrugged. "Both?"

"I've been to lots of places," he answered with a shrug. He glanced over at me and grinned. He was pure charm. "This one's the best so far."

I shook my head but grinned back at him. "You think you're so charming..."

He dropped his dish back into the soapy water and kissed me before I could say another word. His hands were wet on my neck, but I didn't care. My own wet hands fisted into his shirt.

His kisses lit a fire inside of me. One that burned low and hot. Tendrils of flame crept up my spine, heating my bones with desire.

"I want you," I whispered into his kiss. Our eyes met and I could see that he had that same flame inside of him.

"Zoey..."

He kissed me, his hands tangling in my hair this time. He tasted like pure lust and I had to have him.

I reached for the hem of his shirt, lifting it up. He broke from the kiss just long enough for the fabric to go over his head, but then his lips were back on mine.

My palms spread out on his chest. He was so warm. So muscular. So real that I was glad there was no way I could possibly be dreaming this. There was no way that I could imagine the solidness and the heat of him.

I pulled off my own wet shirt, tossing it to the kitchen floor.

He hissed his pleasure, his eyes looking me over with reverence. I felt beautiful when he looked at me like that. Like he'd never imagined anyone could look this amazing with their shirt off. I knew I wasn't anything special, but when he looked at me like that, I felt like a freaking super model.

I reached behind me and unhooked my bra. I loved the way his eyes dilated as he saw me. I loved the little hitch in his breath and the way his stomach muscles tightened at the sight of bare skin.

He reached out, his hand caressing the soft curve of my breast. I shivered with delight and the low chuckle he made had me shivering again.

I kissed him again, pressing my bare chest against his.

He was so warm that yet again those fires deep inside of me stoked.

"Too many clothes," I whispered. I could feel his desire pressing into my hip and I didn't want anything between us anymore...

Thank you to all the readers who have waited for this book and have kept up the excitement. You make my heart happy.

A special thank you to Andrea, Angel, Ana, Shawnna, and Kayla.

CHAPTER 1

I was falling down the aisle of the church.

I couldn't stop, despite the fact it seemed to be happening in slow motion. My feet went up in the air, my dress tangled around my legs, and my arms flailed helplessly. The bouquet sailed neatly into the third pew.

I was not made to wear high heels.

They would be the death of me.

I'd told my cousin this, but as the bride, she'd insisted.

So, now after two steps, I was tripping in the most ungraceful and embarrassing manner down the aisle. Everyone was watching. The photographer was catching every second of it.

Splat.

The whole church drew an intake of air and then went silent.

I wished there was a way to hit rewind. Or merge into

the floor. If I had superpowers, I'd be invisible right now. I'd be anywhere but here with everyone I know staring at me.

"I'm okay," I said, finding my feet. There was scattered applause, and my cheeks burned with mortification. This was my nightmare.

I wished it was a bad dream, but the tingling in my palms from slamming the floor and the ache of my butt from landing said it wasn't. I heard a soft giggle from one of my younger cousins, followed by a loud shushing, and I wished again that I could turn invisible.

I didn't like being the center of attention in the best of circumstances, and falling down the aisle at my cousin's wedding was not something I'd had on my bucket list.

I considered just running out the back of the church and hiding somewhere, but I was still wearing the stupid shoes that caused this. I'd take two steps and just crash again. So, I got up to my wobbly feet and prepared to try again.

The officiant and the groom both were staring at me, their mouths open and eyes wide. The piano player had to restart the song. At least the photographer had stopped taking pictures.

I smoothed out the satin on the front of my dress and plastered on the best smile I could manage with my entire family and the groom's entire family, all staring at me. I was never going to live this one down.

Someone handed me the bouquet. It was actually in excellent shape for having been tossed across the church. The bride's college roommate had managed to catch it when I fell. I wondered for a moment if that meant she was getting married next. Maybe since I was just a brides-maid, she'd just be a bridesmaid at the next wedding.

It didn't really matter. Right now, with my face burn-ing, my butt aching, and my pride severely injured, I just needed to get to the end of the aisle. Then I could just stand there and hope that the arrival of the bride made everyone forget my first steps into the church.

I took another step and the damn heel on my right shoe gave out. For the second time in thirty seconds, in front of everyone I'd ever known, I was going to fall again. The crowd gasped.

"Not this time," the groomsman next to me said, wrap-ping his massive arm around me. I wobbled but didn't fall. He didn't trust that a grown woman could walk thirty yards without splatting like a toddler onto the floor.

Claud was a professional rugby player for some team in Europe. He was the biggest, strongest man I had ever seen in real life, and that was the reason my cousin had paired me with him to walk down the aisle. In theory, I should have just been able to cling to him while wearing the wobbly shoes, but I'd managed to fall anyway.

He wrapped his beefy arm around my bicep and basi-cally carried me like I was a rugby ball down the aisle. My feet attempted to make the appropriate delicate steps, but I looked and felt more like a marionette on a string.

However, with Claud carrying me ninety percent of the way, we made it to the altar without me tripping again. He wasn't even out of breath.

"Are you going to be okay?" he asked before letting go of my arm.

"I can walk the three feet to my side," I promised.

Claud looked skeptical, and to be honest, he had every right to be.

I carefully lifted the hem of my skirt a little more than was needed for most people and walked on tiptoes to my spot in line. My shoes couldn't betray me that way.

My mother let out an audible sigh of relief when I made it.

The maid of honor glared at me as she came up behind me. She managed to walk the entire aisle on her own without tripping or making a scene.

Luckily, my cousin Cecelia hadn't seen a thing. She was just coming through the big wooden doors with a smile so big I was surprised the church could hold her. Everyone rose from their chairs and turned away from me to look at her.

While everyone was occupied, I slipped out of my shoes so that I could stand without falling and making another scene. No one would notice the hem of my dress pooling on the floor while the real stars of the show said their vows.

Luckily, the bride didn't notice. I was able to merge into the background, smiling, and being happy for my cousin as she married the man of her dreams.

I was throwing those shoes away as soon as I had the chance. High heels were going to be my downfall.

No wonder Cinderella left her shoe on the palace steps when she ran away. The darn things were impossible to walk in.

CHAPTER 2

*C*laud had to basically carry me back out of the church in the same manner he'd brought me in. I didn't protest. For someone as big as he was, he was remarkably gentle. Plus, I really appreciated not being the center of attention again.

I took the required photos with the wedding party, trying to stay in the background. The pictures were for Cecelia and Carlson, not for me. I looked pretty with my shoulder-length blonde hair curled softly around my face. The makeup artist had even managed to make my brown eyes look amazing, probably because she'd basically created eyebrows and eyelashes for me. My blonde brows and pale lashes were even lighter than my hair and, as such, were nearly invisible without makeup.

Even glammed up and knowing that I looked beautiful, I didn't particularly like getting my picture taken, and the fact that I was still wearing the stupid high-heeled shoes made me want to run and hide. I wobbled and nearly fell with every change of position.

The damn things were cursed.

As soon as photos were done, I ran barefoot to the backroom, not caring about the grass or the cold linoleum. I just wanted them off as quickly as possible. I carefully set the high heels by the venue's side entrance, where they'd be out of the way. They were such pretty things, sparkly and silver, but I knew they would ruin everything if I wore them for a minute more.

I'd never been able to walk in heels. My mother, aunts, and Cecelia had all tried to teach me, but it always ended in disaster. I wore kitten heels for three minutes and I nearly broke my wrist. I had crossed a room in wedges and had to use crutches for a week. Wearing pumps had required an x-ray.

I liked flat shoes. I wore ballet flats to prom. I wore delicate sandals for my college graduation. I wore tennis shoes to work and sensible loafers to job interviews. I owned exactly one pair of high heels: these. They weren't even that high. These deathtraps were going to disappear into my closet, never to come out again.

I slipped on a pair of tennis shoes and hid the cursed high heels in a dark corner by the service entrance, where I hoped no one would find them. The tennis shoes were a soft gray color, and I hoped that no one would notice my footwear change, although I suspected they would because I wasn't crashing into people.

Guests milled aimlessly around the reception room. The happy couple had been introduced while I was changing shoes, and they now walked around greeting guests. Tables were set up with little names next to each plate with where they were expected to sit. The names

"Cecelia and Carlson" were everywhere. Most of the guests were enjoying the open bar, and the beautiful June weather outside as they waited for the caterers to announce dinner was ready.

"Watch your step," my uncle teased as he walked past me to get to the bar. "You put the fall in falling in love!"

I smiled politely and reminded myself that he had been drinking all day. I really hoped no one else felt the need to make me relive the experience all night. I glanced over at the dark corner one last time to make sure that the heels were out of sight and went to join the party.

I snagged a glass of wine from the bar and wandered around for a moment before going to find my seat. My table was to the right of the sweetheart table. I could see my aunt and uncle's names to my left and the names of parents of the groom to my right with one empty seat beside me. I was alone with the parents of the happy couples for the meal.

I groaned a little and made a mental note to get more wine. It was going to be a long dinner.

Carlson's mother and my aunt, Cecelia's mother, were in a quiet war to decide which of their children had settled and which had married up. Personally, I thought both of their children were winning at life by marrying one another. Last Thanksgiving, the two women had nearly come to blows because they couldn't decide if Cecelia's mashed potatoes or Carlson's gravy was better. I'd mixed the two dishes together and ate so much that I needed to roll myself out of the house.

I had no backup tonight, either. The chair next to me was empty for the date that I had never come up with. I'd told them not to give me a plus one, but no one had listened. I sighed. I looked longingly over at the table where my parents and Carlson's aunts and uncles laughed and had a good time. No empty chairs at that table. Nowhere for me to escape.

This was going to be so much *fun*.

I sat down and took a sip of wine to bolster myself for surviving Carlson's mother's criticism and my aunt's disappointment. As cousin and friend to Cecelia, as well as a co-worker to Carlson, I was often dragged into their arguments or used as an example of how good or how bad the other child was. My love life had somehow made it into their competition for best child.

I considered leaving early or just hiding until dinner was over. In addition to dealing with the mothers, I was supposed to make a speech. It filled me with cold dread just thinking about it. But I loved my cousin. I would do anything for her. Even stand up in the middle of a crowded room and speak. It was going to be torture, but I'd do anything for the ones I loved.

I watched the room, taking in the smiling faces and happy people. Conversations flowed as freely as the wine and beer. Weddings were always amazing for people watching.

"Thank you for not pranking my wedding," the groom said to someone standing directly behind me. "I know that you wanted to."

I tried not to look obvious as I shifted slightly in my seat to see who Carlson was talking to, wishing I had a better view. Who would want to ruin a wedding? And more specifically, who would want to ruin Carlson and Cecilia's wedding?

Cecelia was my best friend, as well as a relative. She was smart and funny, and everything my mother had wanted me to be. Carlson was old-money rich, a doctor, and the kind of guy that everyone wanted their daughter to marry.

The idea that anyone would want to wreck their day was surprising.

I turned a little more, trying my best to make it look like I wasn't snooping in on the conversation. My new cousin-in-law was standing next to a handsome man wearing a cheeky grin. The other man had reddish-gold hair and perfect posture in a dark suit that looked expensive. But if he was friends with Carlson, he probably came from money. Everyone in Carlson's social circle came from money or knew people that did.

"Me? Never." I heard the male reply, humor in his friendly voice. He had a fantastic accent that made me wonder where he was from. England, maybe? "Weddings are supposed to be solemn, yet joyful occasions. I would never interrupt a wedding."

Carlson raised his eyebrows and looked skeptically at his friend.

"Receptions on the other hand..." the tall stranger trailed off with a shrug and a mischievous smile that made the groom roll his eyes.

Carlson sighed and pointed to the chair at the table next to me. "Just go sit down," he instructed. He brought the man over and greeted me. "Zoey, you know how to sedate difficult patients, right?"

I nodded. "I worked with an anesthesiologist for a whole day last year," I assured him with a playful wink.

"I'm practically a pro. I can even say some of the medication names properly."

Carlson and I worked at the same hospital, so he knew just how much of a lie that was. I could say nearly all of the medications correctly. I was a nurse, after all.

Carlson grinned. "Good. If he does anything, just sedate him for me, will you? And I do mean anything."

The handsome stranger sat politely in the chair next to me at the table, looking demure. I could practically see the halo floating over his head as he pretended to look shocked at Carlson's request.

"But what should I use? You didn't use Valium as a centerpiece." I looked around the table. Flowers and candles dotted the white linen tablecloth with little cards of paper with wedding guest names. "All I have is a serving spoon."

"I do have a rather hard head," the man replied. "I don't think a serving spoon is going to work."

"Zoey, I give you permission to knock him over the head with anything you can get your hands on. Spoons, plates, a chair- anything," Carlson told me. He gave a stern look to the man. "I'll happily pay the caterer for any damages as long as it keeps *him* from pulling pranks."

"Me? Pull a prank?" The man gave a perfect expression of innocent surprise. "Carlson, what kind of man do you think I am?"

"The kind that had bagpipes show up for the first dance at Jenkin's wedding," Carlson replied. "The kind that replaced the champagne toast with vodka at Tim's wedding. The kind that convinced the bride to wear a fake snake as a garter. The kind that rearranged the wedding toppers into a sexual theme at Dan's very conservative wedding. The kind that snuck whoopie cushions on the seats at the sweetheart table at that same wedding. *That* kind."

I couldn't help but giggle, imagining the effect of whoopie cushions at a fancy reception. The handsome man shot me a playful grin.

"I have no plans to repeat any of that," he said. He held up a hand with four fingers raised. "Scout's honor. I'll be good."

Carlson rolled his eyes again. "You were never a boy scout. And it's supposed to be three fingers, not four."

The handsome man's smile just got a little bit wider.

"Seriously, Zoey- just knock him out if he even looks sideways at the champagne bottles," Carlson told me. "And don't let him near my chair."

I reached over and picked up a large silver serving spoon resting on the table and threateningly hit the spoon into my open palm.

Carlson and the man laughed as I gave the red-haired man my best menacing look. Carlson patted his friend on the shoulder with a smile and a shake of the head before heading off to greet more of his guests.

"You'd really hit me over the head with a serving spoon to keep me from spiking the punch?" the man asked, eyeing the spoon still in my grip. "Is that medically safe?"

"Well, it's not something they officially covered in nursing school," I admitted, setting the spoon back on the table. "The hospital actually recommends using serving trays."

The man chuckled, warm and friendly. His smile was bright as grinned at my stupid joke. He had a great smile, and his dark green eyes sparkled with amusement. I loved the flutter of warmth growing in my stomach as he looked at me.

Maybe this table wouldn't be so terrible after all.

"*I*'m Freddie," he said, offering out his hand.

"Zoey," I replied, setting down the spoon and taking his hand. His hand was strong and firm. A well-practiced handshake. "It's nice to meet you."

He smiled again, and I felt a warmth rush to my cheeks, especially with my hand still in his. I pulled away and tucked some loose hair behind my ear. Little butterflies danced in my stomach, and I found myself hoping that Freddie would keep me company all night.

"How do you know the bride and groom?" Freddie asked, making conversation as he glanced around the room. The reception hall was starting to fill. It was a beautiful open room that looked out over the green grass and a small creek where Carlson and Cecelia had said their vows. White tulle and satin complemented with shades of dark blue ribbons wound through the room.

"Oh, I don't actually know them," I replied. "I just happened to have the right dress on today. I totally snuck in. I don't think anyone even noticed."

I leaned back and motioned to the dark blue satin bridesmaid dress I wore. Despite the flattering cut, there was no mistaking it for anything but a bridesmaid dress.

Freddie laughed, the sound making my soul feel lighter. His laugh was even better than his smile.

"You have excellent taste," he replied. "But I hate to tell you; three other women are wearing the exact same thing. I've been told that's a terrible thing to happen at a party like this."

"Shoot." I grinned at him, enjoying our banter, even if it wasn't my best work. "The bride is my cousin," I explained. "On my mother's side. That's why I got placed at this fancy table."

"Ah, I see." He looked around the table, seeing Carlson's parents' names as well as my aunt and uncle's names at their seat placements. "And where's your date?" Freddie asked, looking at his plate setting. "I hope I didn't steal his seat."

"No, you didn't steal anyone's spot. I didn't bring a date," I replied. I had said it enough times to my mother and aunt that I didn't stumble over the words or even feel guilty anymore.

"So I don't have to worry about 'Zoey's Date' showing up and kicking me out of my chair?" he asked, holding up the small card in front of him. *"Zoey's Date""* was clearly printed on it.

My cheeks flushed with mortification. "Nope. Don't have to worry about him at all."

"He couldn't come?" Freddie asked. He sounded nonchalant, but I thought he sounded hopeful. Or maybe it was just me hoping that he was interested in my dating status. Maybe he was still worried about someone coming and stealing his chair.

"I've been too busy with work and school to date anyone," I explained. "Plus, not having a date really annoys my mother."

He set the card back down on the table in front of him. It now looked like he was my date. I wasn't about to say anything. I was enjoying his company.

"What about you?" I asked. "Is some pretty girl or boy going to come to kick me out of my seat?"

Freddie grinned at me, and my heart sped up. I was ready to be let down, though. A guy like him, handsome and funny, had to have a dozen girls after him. Or he was interested in the other team. Guys like him were always taken or gay.

"I was only able to come at the last minute, so I don't have a date either," he replied. "Not that I had a girl to bring anyway."

Hope sprang up in my chest, and I pretended to straighten my salad fork so he hopefully wouldn't see the smile or the blush on my face.

Single and interested in females. I no longer hated this table.

"And how do you know the groom?" I asked after making sure my fork was relatively straight next to the plate.

"I was unfortunately not wearing the right dress," he replied. He winked at me. "I know Carlson from playing rugby. We played in college together."

"In Paradisa?" I asked. At Freddie's surprised look, I added, "I know Carlson played with the Paradisa Royals during his semester abroad. It would explain the accent."

"I have an accent? What accent?" he asked, face deadpan and serious. And entirely without an accent.

I fumbled for a moment, wondering if I had misheard the previous accent to his words. He didn't sound British or Scottish, but it wasn't quite Australian or South African.

He chuckled. "Just teasing," he said, with his original soft lilt on every word. "I'm actually terrible at the American accent. I can't seem to get my 'a's to come out correctly."

"I thought it was excellent. I totally believed you," I replied, liking that it made him smile. "So, you met Carlson in Paradisa. Do you still live there?"

"When the royal family lets me," he replied with a shrug. He reached for his drink and took a sip. It looked like he was drinking whiskey on the rocks.

"And what do you do there?" I asked. "I mean, what kind of work do you do? Are you in the medical field like Carlson?"

"No, not medical." Freddie looked at me, tilting his head slightly like he was trying to figure me out.

"So... rugby?" I asked. I didn't want to dig into his business, but a job seemed like an essential part of someone's life.

He looked me over again. "I was never good enough to be professional. My brother might have been. His name's Henry. Perhaps you've heard of him. He got married recently."

I thought for a moment. Carlson and I weren't especially close and I didn't know all his friends. I tried to have a good relationship with him, But other than sharing a love of medicine, we didn't have a lot in common. He grew up in New York so we didn't have the same social circles.

I shook my head. "I don't think I've heard Carlson talk about him."

A slow smile spread across Freddie's face as he set his glass down. His head cocked slightly as he looked me over. "I work in a family business."

"That sounds interesting," I said, hoping he'd tell me more.

"You'd think so." He picked up his glass and took a sip, his voice slightly bitter.

I was about to ask more when the rest of the table arrived. Loudly.

"Well, that was just about the best wedding I've ever seen," my aunt announced, flopping into her chair with a pleased look. My uncle greeted me with a pat on the shoulder before sitting next to me. The groom's parents, John and Carla, sat next to Freddie.

"It was almost perfect. Other than a few small things that got tripped up," Carla replied, giving me a cold glance. I did my best just to smile politely.

"I thought it was just lovely," Freddie said quickly. "I'm so very happy for them both."

Both mothers turned and zeroed in on Freddie, suddenly noticing that there was someone unrelated at the table.

"Are you Zoey's date?" Carla asked, looking him over suspiciously.

"If only I were so lucky," Freddie replied. He grinned at Carla. "I'm Freddie Prescott. It's a pleasure to meet you."

The man oozed charm. He smiled at Carla and then grinned at Aunt Linda, and I swear they both fluttered their eyelashes like schoolgirls. I couldn't really blame them. He was handsome.

My uncle cleared his throat softly and looked at me.

"Oh, right. Freddie, these are Carlson's parents, John and Carla," I said, realizing I should make introductions. I could feel my face heating. "And these are my aunt and uncle, the parents of the bride."

"Tim Reynolds," my uncle said, holding out his hand. "And my wife is Linda."

My blush deepened as I realized I hadn't given their names, just their relation to me. I was not made for social things like this. I always forgot the rules.

"A pleasure," Freddie assured them, not looking at all like I had gaffed. "I think I'm seated at the best table in the room."

The adults laughed, and I tried not to chug my wine. Luckily, our food started to arrive. Being at the parents' table did have some perks, like getting food first. The waiter took the silver serving spoon from our table, whispering apologies about it being there in the first place.

Freddie grinned at me, and we both chuckled.

"You never did tell me how you know the correct usage of sedating unruly guests," Freddie said, taking a bite of his meal.

I quickly swallowed my bite of chicken. "I'm a nurse."

"Our Zoey just graduated from nursing school last week. Top of her class at one of the hardest schools in the state," my aunt informed him. "She even has a job at the hospital already."

I blushed hard. My aunt was clearly bragging about me.

"Top of your class?" Freddie asked, sounding

impressed. "You must have loads of practice knocking trouble makers out."

I liked the admiration in his voice, and so I just sat there smiling like an idiot.

"We're all so proud of her. She's been a nursing assistant at the hospital for six years," my aunt decided to explain. "They practically begged her to become an RN. She'd worked there long enough that she already knew how to do everything!"

"That's not quite how it works…" I said.

"Of course that's not how it works. My son is a doctor," Carla replied. "He knows how to do everything. Nurses just help."

I smiled through gritted teeth. "That's not quite how it works either…"

"Well, maybe Zoey will go back for her MD once she's been an RN for a bit." My aunt crossed her arms. "The women in our family are certainly smart enough for it."

"Well, they are smart enough to marry well," Carla replied casually.

Freddie's eyes darted between the two women as he watched the tension increase between them. I wondered if he still thought this was the best table at the wedding.

If I were him, I probably would snarf my food and run.

"Congratulations on graduating and the new job," Freddie said quickly before one of the other women could say more. "Are you doing anything to celebrate?"

"I'm taking two weeks off of work," I replied. "My new job doesn't start until late-June, and I've been doing nothing but work and study for the last few years. I'm taking a vacation."

My aunt and Carla both opened their mouths to say something.

"It sounds well earned," Freddie said before either had the chance. He smiled at me, and I knew he meant it.

"Thank you," I told him.

"Does anyone need a drink?" Uncle Tim asked.

"I do. I'll come with you," John said quickly.

The two men darted away, leaving Freddie and me with the two women.

"She's using our cabin on the river for her vacation," my aunt said. "It's just one of our graduation presents."

I was extremely grateful for the cabin, but it was the *only* graduation present they were giving me as far as I knew. I didn't say anything, though.

"You have a cabin?" Carla scoffed. "How quaint."

"It's this beautiful place in Stevens Point, right on the river, but close enough to town to have everything a person could need on vacation," my aunt told Freddie, lifting her chin and smiling with superiority at Carla. "It's usually booked solid this time of year."

"I really appreciate the cabin, Aunt Linda--" I started to say, but Carla cut me off.

"Is it the cabin you offered the newlyweds?" Carla asked. "The one they turned down because they wanted our beach house in Florida?" She smiled at Aunt Linda, but it wasn't a kind smile. She turned back to Freddie. "I adore our beach house. We were going to go there after the wedding, but I gave it to my son because he deserves the best."

"I suppose a tiny beach apartment might be more comfortable for a couple of newlyweds who never want to leave the bedroom," Aunt Linda replied to Carla. "I'm sure when they have children, my cabin will get used every summer. It's so big and roomy. We'll all be able to visit and have adventures. I don't think you and the future grand-kids will fit in your little one bedroom beach apartment."

"It's a house," Carla corrected.

They both spoke using polite words and fake smiles, but there was no kindness. It was a war between the two of them. I thought about going to the bar with the men, but that would mean leaving poor Freddie to fend for himself.

I reached for my wine and tried not to grimace.

"Are they always like this?" he whispered as the two women argued politely about the correct way their very hypothetical grandchild should be spoiled. The two women smiled without warmth as they debated. It may have looked like smiling, but they were simply flashing fangs at one another.

"It's been nothing but competition between the two of them since the engagement was announced," I told him. "I'd hoped that the wedding would help bring them together, but..."

I shrugged and made a vague motion. I didn't under-stand their feud at all. Why couldn't they just get along?

"Well, I think two weeks in a cabin sounds marvelous," Freddie said, carefully placing his knife and fork on the plate, indicating he was finished. "What are you planning on doing there?"

I grinned. "Nothing. And it's going to be amazing."

He chuckled. "I can appreciate nothing."

"I mean, I plan on doing lots of things, but there is no

schedule and no requirements," I clarified. "It's a break from my busy life."

"That's what a vacation should be," Freddie agreed. "What kind of things are you doing without a schedule?"

I loved the way he said schedule. It sounded so much fancier than when I said it.

"There's fishing, and tubing, and swimming. There's an ice cream store with the best ice cream ever. I also plan on eating cheese curds and pizza until I can't walk, and then I'll just go float on the river." I sighed with pleasure, just thinking about it. "Or, I might just stay in bed all day and watch the river flow by and then watch lightning bugs and stars."

"Sounds like heaven," Freddie said.

"I think it will be." I grinned at him.

"Wait, you said lightning bugs?" Freddie asked. "What are those?"

"Some people call them fireflies," I explained.

"You mean the little bugs that fly around and glow?" Freddie looked confused. "I thought they made those up for cartoons."

I chuckled. "Nope. Very real. And very magical."

"We don't have anything like that in Paradisa," he explained. "Do they really glow?"

"Yes," I said with a smile. "There should be some out tonight. Would you like me to show you some? They'd be right outside."

"I'd love that." His eyes met mine, and I went breathless.

I had a feeling I would show that man anything he wanted.

CHAPTER 4

*I*t was time for my speech.

I wasn't the maid of honor, but Cecelia had asked me to make a speech anyway. She had begged me, saying that not only was I her cousin and best friend but that I worked with Carlson. I knew them both personally and professionally and that it would make her wedding day perfect.

I wasn't good at making speeches. I wasn't good at being the center of attention. But Cecelia had asked. So I was making a speech.

I stood shaking next to the sweetheart table. Cecelia grinned at me. When the MC handed me the microphone, I seriously considered just running. I was wearing tennis shoes now, so there was a much better chance I wouldn't fall on the ground if I tried to move. But Cecelia had asked. And I loved her enough to do it.

My sweaty hand shook around the microphone so hard I was sure I was going to drop it, and I knew my cheeks had to be blazing red. My stomach did flip flops, and I wished I had drank a lot more.

I stared out at the crowd, trying to remember every piece of advice from speech class. None of it was helping. I didn't want to imagine anyone in the audience naked or in their underwear. Well, no one except Freddie. And that thought made me blush even harder.

"Hi everyone." My voice shook. I knew they all had to be remembering me falling down the aisle just an hour ago. There were whispers in the crowd. "My name is Zoey Miller, and today is a great day. Today, my cousin got to marry her best friend. Well, her best friend that isn't me."

Everyone in the crowd chuckled. My confidence went up slightly since no one was making comments about me falling. Or at least they were doing so quietly enough I couldn't hear them.

"Cecilia and I have been together since birth. I'm lucky that I got such an amazing built-in friend. I'm always blessed to have her in my life. And it was even worth it to be the reason she and Carlson met."

Cecelia grinned at me and gave Carlson's arm a loving squeeze.

"We were ice-skating on the lake when I slipped. I managed to cut my hand on the ice-skate badly enough that we had to go to the ER." I held up my left hand, showing off the faint scar on the bottom of my palm. "Carlson was the ER doctor that day. I knew him from work, and I was glad he was the one taking care of me. I knew he would do a good job. He did, and six stitches later, Carlson had fixed me and gotten Cecelia's phone number."

I turned and smiled at the two of them.

"I trusted Carlson with my hands, and now I trust him with my cousin's happiness," I said, feeling emotion tightening around my throat. "And so, I raise my glass to the new couple. Hopefully, you never need to take me to the ER again."

The crowd laughed, and I escaped from the spotlight as quickly as possible. My heart pounded so hard I could barely hear anything else as I slid back into my seat next to Freddie and reached for my wine.

"Excellent speech," Freddie congratulated me.

I smiled at him and took another big sip of wine.

"It was an ice-skate that cut you?" Carla asked. She shook her head. "You and shoes just don't get along."

"What do you mean?" I asked, finishing off my glass of wine.

"Well, an ice-skate is a type of shoe, and you tripped on your shoe walking down the aisle," Carla explained. "You are just a disaster when it comes to shoes."

My face burned. I wished there was a way to melt through the floor and disappear.

"Don't worry, dear," Aunt Linda said quickly. "The speech was very nice."

"Would you like some more wine?" Freddie asked. "I need a glass myself, and I thought you could come with me."

He stood and offered me his hand. I took it like a woman drowning.

"That sounds great," I said, standing so fast I nearly tripped again. Freddie steadied me. Carla raised an eyebrow and looked meaningfully at my feet, but I ignored her.

"I must have angered a magic shoe fairy and been cursed," I said to Freddie once we were clear of the table.

He grinned. "Then perhaps all you need is a kiss from a prince to break the spell."

"If only it were that easy," I replied with a sigh as we reached the bar and ordered fresh drinks.

The lights dimmed, and a spotlight swirled the room, coming to rest on the bride and groom as they took their place in the center of the dance floor. The music started soft and romantic, with the bride and groom taking a traditional start to their dance. It stayed slow and romantic for a moment before switching to a fast swing song. Carlson had Cecelia flying through the air, her wedding dress trailing like a streamer as he swung her around the room. The crowd clapped and shouted their praise.

It was great to watch, but not something I would ever do at my wedding.

And definitely not in the spiked heel shoes Cecelia was wearing.

The song ended, and Carlson and Cecelia took bows to thunderous applause. The parent dances came next, but neither parent did anything as flashy as the spins and flips of their children.

The lights stayed low, focusing on the dance floor as servers hustled past with empty plates and dirty utensils. Freddie and I stood in line, waiting for our turn at drinks. The line didn't appear to be moving, but I didn't mind. It meant we didn't have to go back to the table.

"Do you dance?" Freddie asked, watching as the official dances ended, and free dancing began.

"Me?" I asked with a laugh.

Freddie just grinned as he held out his hand for mine.

"I have to warn you that I have two left feet," I said, hesitating slightly.

"That's never stopped me before," Freddie said, taking my hand before I could say no. We left the drink line.

I liked the way my hand felt in his as he led me to the dance floor. In a moment, we were on the corner of the dance floor, my hand in his and slowly swaying to the music.

He pulled me closer to him, the soft scent of his cologne filling my nose. He smelled terrific- like ginger and citrus. It took all my self-control not to bury my face into his shoulder and just breathe him in. I could barely concentrate on what we were doing. His hand on my hip had me very aware of just how close our bodies were right now.

And how easy it would be to kiss him.

"Ouch," he hissed softly, taking a step back. I had stepped on his foot.

"Sorry," I quickly apologized. "Two left feet. You were warned."

I fully expected him to smile and say that maybe we should stop dancing. That the cake was almost ready and he wanted a slice.

But he didn't.

Instead, he smiled and pulled me closer. His hand on my waist became more insistent, and his directions for our dancing became firm. He led the dance, giving me no confusion as to where we were going.

He raised his left hand, raising mine with it, and gently pushed with his right. I twirled neatly under his arm before coming back to him. And I didn't step on his feet in the process.

"Neat trick," I told him. "Someone might think I can dance if you keep that up."

Freddie grinned at me, joy sparkling in his eyes. "I have lots of neat tricks. It's the one thing at my job that I'm good at."

"I have a feeling you're good at a lot of things," I replied, my voice coming far more sensual than I intended. I blushed again and tried to make it not sound like I was hitting on him. "I mean, dancing. Or other things."

I wished I could flirt without feeling like a total idiot.

His chuckle vibrated through me before he spun me once again. I was getting better at following him already.

I cleared my throat, determined not to make a complete fool of myself. "So, what kind of work do you do that requires dancing?" I managed to sound almost normal.

Freddie turned his head slightly as he evaluated me.

"It's complicated," he said slowly. "But like I said before, it's a family business."

I nodded as if I understood. "I see. What do you sell?"

"Other than my soul?" he replied. He chuckled at his own joke, but there wasn't much humor behind it. "We don't really sell anything. My family works for the government."

"The government needs dancing lessons?" I asked, looking up at him.

He laughed for real this time, and I nearly stumbled. He was gorgeous when he laughed.

"You really don't know who I am, do you?" he asked, pulling me closer.

I shook my head, and a terrible thought went through me. "Please tell me we're not related."

"Definitely not related," he assured me with a laugh. "But you really don't know me?"

"No," I whispered, looking up into his eyes and losing myself to them. "But I want to know everything about you."

It felt stupid and overly cheesy as soon as it came out of my mouth. His eyes went wide, and I panicked.

"I mean, I uh...." I closed my eyes and took a quick breath. "I mean, you saved me from my aunts. And from being dateless. And I'm having a really nice time with you. And I would like to get to know you better." I smiled up at him, hoping he didn't find me too crazy. "I'm not trying to be nosey."

His face relaxed slightly.

"Well, I work for the government of Paradisa," he said slowly. "And I would love to tell you all about it, but it's top-secret."

"That sounds exciting," I told him.

"It's boring," he assured me. "It's all diplomatic embassies and brokering trade agreements. I mostly sit and look pretty while everyone around me argues semantics."

"That does not sound very exciting," I agreed. "When you said top-secret, I thought you meant more like James Bond."

"I should just say that I'm a secret agent or a spy." He grinned. "That if I told you more, I'd have to kill you. That I have a license to kill."

"I'd believe you," I replied, keeping my face serious. "You've got the suit and the accent."

"Unfortunately, I don't particularly like martinis," he admitted.

I laughed, and we kept dancing. Dancing with him was amazing. It was so easy, and I felt like I was actually a good dancer with him. Our bodies moved together as if they had always known what to do.

"Will you be in Wisconsin long?" I asked. "Or are you just here for the wedding?"

"I managed to negotiate with my brother to have a few days here," he replied. "Then I'm supposed to go to Chicago."

"What's in Chicago?" I asked, already calculating how far away he would be from me. Chicago was less than a two-hour drive away. Definitely doable to see him again.

"A conference." He sighed, and the light faded from his smile. "It's nothing important. I think it's just a way to keep me busy and out of sight for a bit."

I frowned slightly. Who would want to keep Freddie out of sight? I wanted to look at him all the time.

"I got into a little trouble with my older brother," Freddie explained, seeing my expression. "I pulled a prank he didn't appreciate. He said it was unbecoming of our station. So I've been banished from the kingdom for a while."

"To Chicago?" I shrugged thoughtfully. "I suppose it could be worse. You could have been banished some-where without decent pizza."

Freddie laughed, the smile returning to his face.

"I will say, banishment isn't bad so far," he said, pulling

me into him. I could feel the muscles of his shoulder under his jacket. I looked up at him, and all I could think about was kissing him. I wondered if he'd taste like his whiskey.

His lips were so close. All I had to do was tip my head. He leaned forward, his sweet ginger scent flooding my senses.

He pulled away from me as a camera flashed. Family laughed and posed for another picture next to us. I remembered then that I was in the middle of a crowded room with all my relatives. I'd forgotten everything but him as we'd danced. It had been so easy to lose myself to him.

An older woman bustled between us, and I scowled at the interloper before realizing it was my own grandmother.

"Now, you can't hog all the good dance partners," Grandma Betty said, stealing my dance partner away. She winked at me. "Don't worry. I'll give him back. Besides, the bride needs you. Something about her dress and the bathroom."

I glanced over toward the bathroom and could see Cecelia frantically motioning to me. She pointed to the heavy gown and then to the bathroom.

I took a step back, but my eyes went to Freddie's.

"I'll find you later?" I asked, not wanting to leave him. I could hear Cecelia calling for me.

He nodded.

"Don't worry. I won't let anyone else steal him," Grandma Betty told me with another wink. "Well, other than me. I can't help it if he falls helplessly in love with me."

"Too late," Freddie said with a dramatic sigh that had Grandma Betty laughing.

I took one last look before hurrying off to do my bridesmaid duties of holding up tulle. I hoped Cecelia could do this quickly. I wanted to get back to dancing and forgetting the rest of the world.

CHAPTER 5

I'd never had so much fun dancing.

Thankfully, Grandma Betty was true to her word and let me have my dance partner back. I was so glad I had tennis shoes on because I still managed to squash his toes several more times despite his extraordinary leading abilities.

I noticed that Freddie stayed close to me. Other guests would start to come over, particularly young women, and he would swoop me into the next dance before they could start talking to him.

I didn't mind. I liked dancing.

"All right, ladies and gentlemen," the MC called out over the loudspeaker. "It's time for the bouquet toss!"

"Single Ladies"" by Beyonce began to blare out over the speakers.

Freddie took several steps back to clear the dance floor, leaving me to join the throng of women gathering near my cousin. I sighed and considered conveniently needing to use the bathroom, but my mother and aunt were giving me the stink eye.

I had no choice. Cecelia grinned at me as I took my place in the group, and I had the horrible feeling that she was going to aim her bouquet at me. That was the last thing I wanted. It wasn't that I didn't want to get married. I did. I wanted to find someone that made me as happy as Carlson made Cecelia.

But that didn't mean I wanted to catch the bouquet and then have to take pictures. I didn't want everyone oohing and ahhing over me and making comments about how I would be pregnant within the year.

I took the spot behind my eight-year-old second cousin, and a fantastic idea crossed my mind.

I tapped on the girl's shoulder. "Brinley, do you want me to help you catch the flowers?" I asked, lowering my body so I was at her level.

Brinley's eyes went wide, and her smile grew huge. "You'd do that?"

I nodded. "If it comes this way, I'll knock it down so you can catch it. Sound good?"

"You're the best, Zoey."

I grinned at her. Suddenly, this bouquet toss wasn't so bad.

"Everybody ready?" Cecelia called out. She grinned at the women before her and turned around.

"Ready?" I checked with Brinley.

"Super ready," Brinley assured me.

We both took power stances, ready to take those flowers down.

"One, two, three!" Cecelia let the bouquet fly.

The flowers came at me like a magnet. I reached out,

ready to swat them down. Brinley was up on her tiptoes, mouth open and excited. I felt the flower stems touch my palm before a body slammed into me, knocking me out of the way.

Great, I thought as I sailed through the air toward some chairs. *Not only would I be remembered for tripping down the aisle, but also for falling at the bouquet toss.*

Somehow, Freddie managed to catch me before I slammed into the chairs.

"Gotcha," he whispered, his muscles flexing as he made sure I didn't totally eat it.

"Thank you," I breathlessly replied. I held onto him, my arms wrapped around his neck.

Good lord, did he smell amazing.

"Are you okay?" he asked, his arms still wrapped around me.

"Uh-huh," I mumbled. Then I remembered that I should probably stand on my own and not just hold onto him for no reason in the middle of a crowded room with all my relatives looking at me.

Except they weren't looking at me. They were all looking at Carlson's aunt Millie. She was doing a victory dance. Flowers stuck out of the bouquet in odd angles as she thrust her hips and flexed her arms.

I slowly let go of Freddie and went to make sure Brinley was okay. Luckily, the aunt had only taken me out in her quest to get the flowers, so Brinley was fine, if a little disappointed.

At least I didn't have to take any pictures.

"And now for the single men!" the MC called out. "Time for the garter toss!"

Cecelia blushed prettily as they brought out a chair for

her to sit on. Carlson was all smiles as he kneeled before her. Sexy music played overhead.

I looked over at Freddie, but he was gone. I found him slowly backing away from the group and heading toward an exit.

I frowned and hurried over to him.

"Are you leaving?" I asked.

"No," he said quickly. "Just getting some air."

I raised my eyebrows. "Just when the garter toss is about to happen?"

"Purely incidental," he replied. "Just need to take a breather."

I glanced toward the stage and the single men waiting next to it.

"You are single, though, right?" I asked. "There's another reason you're not over there vying for a scrap of fabric from a newly married woman's leg?"

Freddie laughed. He reached out and took my hands. "I am very single. I promise. I just don't want to catch the garter. My brother would die if he saw the pictures."

I glanced at the aunt with the bouquet waiting to take pictures with the man who would catch the garter. I had a feeling the images would be somewhat scandalous. I didn't blame Freddie one bit for trying to escape.

"Well, I think it's dark enough to see lightning bugs," I offered. "If you're still interested."

I loved the smile that lit up his face.

"Very interested," he assured me.

We both glanced back at the small crowd, cheering and laughing as Carlson's head disappeared under Cecelia's gown. No one would miss us.

CHAPTER 6

I pushed open the door to the open courtyard. Dark warm air hit us like a wet blanket. We stepped out into the night, and the sounds of the party vanished as the door shut behind us.

Frogs called out, and crickets chirped as we walked across the lawn. I still had his hand in mine as I guided us across the open space and toward a small bridge that led to a wooded area behind it.

"There should be a bunch on the other side of the bridge," I said, guiding us through the dark. "There's a small creek over there that should attract them."

I lifted my dress to cross the wooden footbridge that connected two grassy areas.

"Wait, you changed your shoes," Freddie said, noticing my footwear.

"You think I could have danced in heels?" I said with a laugh. "I can't even walk in heels. Dancing could be deadly."

"Those do look more comfortable," he agreed.

"Heels will be my downfall," I told him. "I can feel it."

"Death by shoe... sounds terrible," Freddie agreed with a soft laugh.

The two of us walked through the dark and into the forest. The sounds of summer filled the air. His hand felt good in mine.

"Is that..." Freddie pointed to a small speck of light floating above the ground.

He let go of my hand to squat in the grass, studying the lone glowing insect with childlike wonder. I let him watch it for a moment before putting my hand on his shoulder.

"You should see the ones over here," I said softly. He lifted his eyes and followed my gaze to the trees.

His eyes went wide, and his mouth opened in sheer delight.

In the trees, the grass, and the bushes, were hundreds of thousands of lightning bugs. They floated like mystical stars, hovering and glimmering in the dark of the wood.

"It's magic," Freddie whispered, rising to his feet and walking into the wooded area. I followed him, enjoying seeing someone experience the magic for the first time. It made the magic of lightning bugs real again. I hadn't felt this excited about the little beetles in years.He looked back at me, his eyes bright. "Thank you."

"I'm glad you like it," I replied with a grin myself. I stood beside him, and he took my hand. Suddenly, it was more than the magic of lightning bugs that had my heart pounding. It was standing in a romantic spot, all alone, with a handsome man.

"Thank you for showing me this," Freddie said softly, turning to face me. He was still smiling like a kid meeting Santa, and my heart melted.

If I wasn't in love with him now, I knew I would be if he kept smiling at me like that.

He reached his hand to my face and brushed a strand of hair away before softly settling his fingers on my neck. He was so gentle as he pulled me toward him, bringing my lips to his.

He did taste like whiskey. Like whiskey and wedding cake and summer dreams. He tasted perfect.

I kissed him, with lightning bugs sparkling in the sky like floating stars.

He smiled down on me as we finished the first kiss. I could feel his smile since I didn't want to open my eyes. I was afraid it might all be a dream.

"Freddie? You out here?" A voice called from the venue door. It sounded so far away.

"You don't have to answer, you know," I whispered.

"I always have to answer," Freddie replied. He raised his head. "I'm here."

"It's time!" I recognized the voice this time as Claud, the rugby player, and groomsman. I could see his silhouette in the light of the venue. Another man I didn't recognize, stood near him.

Freddie kissed my forehead. "I have to go. There's something I promised to do."

I slowly opened my eyes. "Find me later?"

He grinned. "I hope so. You might need your serving spoon, though."

I frowned, not entirely understanding what he meant. He kissed my hand and then darted off into the dark and back toward the building.

CHAPTER 7

I understood what Freddie had meant by saying I needed my serving spoon once I joined the crowd in the parking lot.

It was time for the bride and groom to leave and the party to end, but instead of a beautiful classic car or a limousine to whisk them away to their new life, there was an old rusty VW bug with cans tied to the back.

I stood in the back of the crowd, watching as everyone laughed and pointed at the car.

Freddie stood grinning next to Claud as three bagpipers appeared out of nowhere and began to play the Paradisa Royals fight song. I only knew it was the fight song because Carlson had sung it so many times.

It was even worse on bagpipes than when he sang it.

Cecelia rolled her eyes and glared at her husband. He shrugged and pointed to Freddie. Freddie went over, kissed both her cheeks, and whispered something in her ear.

When she pulled away from him, she was laughing.

She hugged him tight, and then she hugged Claus. She shook her head, took her husband's hand, and waved to the crowd.

All the guests roared their approval as the happy couple got into the tiny car. The horn made a horrible *arruga* sound, and they were off in a puff of dark soot.

I pushed my way through the crowd to find Freddie. He grinned at me.

"Too late for that serving spoon," he teased.

I shook my head and grinned at him. "You're lucky Cecelia didn't murder you."

He grinned back at me, his face shining with victory at his prank.

From the corner of my eye, I saw my aunt elbow a large man in a dark suit out of her way. I didn't recognize the man, but he looked like he could have played rugby with Carlson.

"There you are, Zoey," my aunt said, catching my arm. "We need your help. The bartender needs to be paid, and Cecelia said you were the one to talk to."

I sighed. "I have to go take care of that," I said to Freddie.

"Have fun," he said with a sly grin.

"I'm going to find that spoon," I told him and then turned to follow my aunt into the reception area. From the corner of my eye, I saw the man in the dark suit whisper something in Freddie's ear. Freddie sighed and headed in the opposite direction.

It took longer than I expected to pay the bartender. And then the caterer needed something signed, the cleanup crew needed directions to start, and suddenly, all of the guests were gone. It was just the last few members of the wedding party and me making sure things were put right.

I checked my watch to see that it was just after midnight.

I sighed and suddenly felt exhausted. My feet hurt from dancing all night, and my face felt heavy under makeup. I looked around for Freddie, but it was clear he had gone with the rest of the guests. The magic of the wedding was over.

Disappointment hung heavy around my shoulders as my fingers touched my lips, remembering his soft kiss. I had thought it was a good one, but maybe it wasn't for him. He was so handsome. He probably kissed girls all the time. It had been romantic out under the stars and lightning bugs, but we were just strangers at a wedding. He didn't owe me anything, not even a goodbye.

Still, I wished I had at least asked for his number. Freddie Prescott was a common enough name that I wasn't confident I'd be able to find him on any social media.

I went to find my heels, but one of them was missing. I looked everywhere, but one shoe was gone.

It wasn't a horrible loss. It wasn't like I was going to ever wear the darn things again. Still, I tucked the lone shoe into my purse as a memory of a beautiful night.

CHAPTER 8

The next morning was a family brunch. Apparently, it was tradition to have a beautiful family brunch with both sides of the new family the morning after the wedding.

I hadn't had as much alcohol as most of my family, but the nine AM wake-up call was far too early for comfort. I pulled my hair up into my usual ponytail and did a quick application of mascara. It wasn't much, but it at least made me look like I had eyes.

I thought of Freddie and his kiss and sighed. He probably wouldn't even recognize me without the glitzy gown and makeup. But it wasn't like I was ever going to see him again. I made a mental note to ask Carlson if he could get me Freddie's contact info.

I chose a light grey t-shirt with my school logo and a pair of khaki Bermuda shorts. I was supposed to leave directly for the cabin afterward, so I didn't want to dress up too much. I wore a dress last night. I didn't need to dress up again until at least Thanksgiving.

The morning sunshine sparkled with humidity as I walked through the quiet parking lot to my ancient car. The day was already unseasonably warm but not yet hot. The sound of insects hummed, and birds sang. It was a beautiful day. A perfect day to start a vacation.

My car was on its last legs. Any day now, I expected it to fall apart like Acme made it for Wile E. Coyote. My entire family knew it, too. There were jokes about my car at most family functions, but the old girl was the only one I could currently afford. Luckily, my grandmother was basically gifting me her old sedan at the end of the week. It wasn't anything special, but the air conditioning worked, and the bumper wasn't held on with duct tape. She had ordered a new car that was set to arrive soon and was more than happy to sell me her old one for something I could afford.

She was even going to drop it off at the cabin for me at the end of the week. Not only was I getting a vacation, but a new car. I'd basically won a game show this week.

I just had to get my current car to the cabin.

Carefully, I opened the rusty door and sat down. The car groaned like I'd eaten far too much cake last night. I rolled my eyes at my car's judgment, and I went to start the engine.

Nothing happened.

I tried it again. Again, nothing. The radio worked, and the lights were on, and the battery was the only thing in the car that was new. I took a deep breath, jiggled the gas pedal, turned off the radio, banged twice on the dash, and adjusted the rear-view mirror so it hung at a strange forty-nine-degree angle.

"Come on, baby," I begged, trying the key again. "You

just have to make it through today. Then you can retire and drink oil margaritas on the beach."

It was a lie. I had no oil margaritas or a beach. But she believed me. The engine chugged weakly and then sparked to sluggish life. I sighed with relief. I just needed her to get me to brunch and then the lake. I could walk everywhere after that. She could do this. I believed in her.

Still, I drove gently to the restaurant. I went easy on the gas and massaged the brakes. I even made the turns nice and wide. I didn't want to press my luck. I pulled into the crowded parking lot, looking for cars I recognized and found many. It looked like I was one of the last to arrive.

I turned off my car, patted it gently, and went to the restaurant.

The front door opened as I approached, and I realized that it wasn't an automatic door. It was Freddie opening the door for me.

Delight rushed through me. My lips tingled at the thought of his kiss, and excitement bubbled in my stomach. He was here.

"Well, hello." Freddie beamed at me, looking me up and down. I suddenly regretted my casual clothes and bare makeup. I didn't look like a princess today. But his smile didn't fade as he took me in. If anything, it grew warmer.

"What are you doing here?" I asked, staring up at him.

He looked even better than he did last night. He wore a dark blue polo shirt that brought out his green eyes and showed off his broad shoulders. His reddish hair was ruffled but in an attractive way.

"Wow. I feel so wanted." Freddie put a hand to his chest like I had wounded him.

I felt a blush sear my cheeks. "That's not what I meant," I quickly stuttered.

"I know." Freddie grinned, his smiling softening the teasing to something enjoyable. "Carlson actually invited me to join your family brunch. I was hoping you were coming."

A thrill of pleasure rushed through me. Had he come so that he could see me again?

"I'm glad you came," I replied. We gave our name to the hostess, and she led us through the restaurant toward the private back room.

"I secretly think he was just hoping that I'd be horribly hungover and miserable." Freddie winked at me as we walked. "Especially since I changed out his car. Did you know he was supposed to have a Tesla? With champagne and roses in the back?"

I laughed. "That was an amazing prank. You even got Cecelia to laugh about it."

"Your serving spoon sedation tricks were not enough to stop me," he replied. He stood still as the hostess opened the door to the private room, looking me over with soft eyes. "Although, the lightning bugs almost did."

I bit my lower lip, remembering his taste. I caught a whiff of his cologne, and my knees wobbled slightly.

I wanted to kiss him again, but we were about to walk into a room full of family. The hostess cleared her throat and showed us in.

There were only two seats left at the table. They were in between my aunt and Carla. The two chairs were crammed together so tightly that there probably should have only been one chair. It was a deja vu of last night, only closer quarters. I wasn't about to complain, though.

I had Freddie.

Freddie pulled the chair out for me to sit next to my aunt, and I felt like a lady. I'd never had someone hold my chair for me before. It was probably a common thing in Paradisa, but it made me feel like a princess.

We sat, our knees knocking under the table. I could feel the heat from his leg pressing against my thigh. I regretted wearing long Bermuda shorts. Even though I hated wearing tiny shorts because they made the back of my legs stick to the seat, it would have been worth it to be that much closer to him.

"I want to apologize for last night," Freddie said softly after we'd said our hellos to the table.

"For what? I'm not the one who had to drive away in that car," I replied. "You didn't do anything to me."

"I did want to say goodbye. I just wasn't able to," Freddie explained. He ran a hand through his hair, making the strands stick up slightly. "I was actually rather hoping to get your number. I don't know anyone in Chicago, and you mentioned they had good pizza. I thought you could come be my guide."

I stared at him, my heart skipping beats wildly. I blinked slowly.

"If I've overstepped, I apologize," he said quickly, mistaking my lack of being able to speak for dislike. "I don't want to impose. I know it's a long drive for you."

"Oh, no. No, no overstepping," I stuttered, shaking my head wildly. "I would love to show you Chicago. I mean, I don't know the city very well, but I'd love to explore it with you."

To be honest, I didn't know the city at all. I'd only been there two times for a concert and a high school field trip. I knew basically nothing about Chicago. But I would Google the heck out of it and become an expert if it got me time with Freddie.

"Excellent." Freddie grinned, and my heart melted just a little bit more. There was a softness to him that I found incredibly endearing. "Perhaps after your vacation?"

"I'd love that," I replied. Heck, I would add Chicago to my vacation plans if it meant I could see him again.

"Ope, excuse me," my aunt said, reaching for the syrup on the table and bumping my arm. I smiled at her and didn't feel an ounce of frustration. I was too focused on Freddie.

I barely tasted my omelet. All I could focus on was Freddie's leg touching mine and imagining the two of us in Chicago. I had no idea where we'd go or what we'd do, but some ideas were running around my head that would make my mother blush.

CHAPTER 9

Before I knew it, brunch was over, and it was time to go. I'd barely felt the minutes pass. My aunt and Carla had traded snide remarks all morning, but I hadn't noticed them at all. I was having a wonderful morning.

"May I walk you out to your car?" Freddie asked after I'd said my goodbyes to everyone.

"Sure," I said before remembering that my car wasn't exactly something I wanted to show off. But I wasn't about to miss out on a few extra minutes with him.

The sun beat down on the black asphalt as we worked our way through the rows of cars.

"Is summer like this in Paradisa?" I asked.

Freddie looked around at the sizzling pavement, the screams of cicadas, and the rising humidity and shook his head. "Not at all. It's hot, but not like this. And our insects are a bit quieter."

I chuckled. "What kind of summer activities do you have?"

He shrugged. "We ride horses, there's swimming, and the ocean is close." He smiled, his eyes going distant. "We do bonfires on the beach. The water is always cold, but it's perfect after a hot day."

It sounded like something from a movie. I could imagine him out on the beach in a preppy sweater, drinking a beer as a fire burned politely nearby.

"Well, this is me." I stopped by my car and shrugged. I opened the door to let some of the heat out, but I was going to stall for every last minute I could get with him.

He looked skeptically at my car. "It runs?" he asked. "Maybe I should have used your car for the prank."

I laughed. "Then Cecelia would never have forgiven you. And I would have been stuck at the reception hall all night."

We stood there awkwardly for a moment, neither one of us wanting the conversation to end but not having a good excuse to continue either.

"All right then." I gave him a quick hug and felt my knees wobble a little at the citrus scent of him. "You'll call me about Chicago?"

"Definitely," he promised.

I got into my car, hating the metallic groan the door made as I swung it shut.

Freddie stepped off to the side, watching me leave. I turned the key in the engine.

Nothing happened.

I tried it again. I jiggled the gas pedal, turned off the radio, banged twice on the dash, and adjusted the rear-view mirror, so it hung at that strange but necessary forty-nine-degree angle.

My car wheezed slightly, chugged twice, made a horrible sputtering sound, and died.

I stared at my steering wheel for a moment, not quite sure what to do. Not only was my car embarrassing me in front of Freddie, but now I had no way to get to the cabin.

I got out of the car and grinned bashfully at Freddie.

"Well, I think it's a good thing you didn't use my car for your prank," I said. "They would never have gotten out of the parking lot."

"To be honest, I'm surprised you survived the trip here." Freddie peered into the cabin of the car like he might see an answer. "Are you sure it's actually legal to drive that thing?"

I stuck my tongue out at him and then looked back at my car. If this were a movie, a hubcap would fall off and roll away. My car just sagged a little more in the hot sun.

"So much for getting to the cabin early today." I sighed and scrunched up my face. Frustration rolled around my chest in angry waves. I had so been looking forward to a little relaxation. Getting my car towed and purchasing a rental was going to eat up all my fun money.

"What if I took you?"

I turned and looked at him. He gave me a sheepish grin and ran his hand through his hair, the red catching the sun like a halo.

"It's a two hour drive," I told him. "It's too much to ask."

"No, it's not," he quickly said. "I'm not doing anything today. I'd much rather help you out than go back to my hotel room and watch Jurassic Park for six hours."

"The sequels aren't as bad as everyone says they are," I replied, still shocked that he'd offer to drive me.

"Oh, the six hours doesn't include the sequels. It's just the first movie. It takes that long with all the commercials the network adds in." He grinned at me. "So, really, you'd be doing me a favor by letting me drive you."

I fiddled with the keys in my hands for a moment.

Was I really going to let this man I just met drive me to a remote location? I knew nothing about him except Carlson thought him good enough to ask to family brunch.

I looked up at him, looking over his lean frame, broad shoulders, the sunlight catching his hair, his eyes green and hopeful, and his smile hopeful. He was gorgeous and sexy and kept making me laugh.

Heck yeah, I was going to do that.

CHAPTER 10

"*I* would definitely appreciate it," I said. "I'll even pay you for your gas."

He grinned wide. "No need. My brother's already expensed the car. Consider it a gift from Paradisa."

We walked back toward the restaurant, him leading the way this time.

"I just need to let my friend know I'm driving you," he said as we came to the first row of cars. "And I suppose I should let him know where we're going."

"Oh, I don't want to put someone else out--"

"No, no. You're not putting him out," Freddie quickly cut me off. "He's just staying with me at the hotel."

"Oh. Okay."

"Where are we going?" Freddie asked, stepping up on the sidewalk.

"You really want the address?" I frowned slightly. "It's in Stevens Point. I can get you the house number, but it's the only house on River Run St."

"Perfect," he said. "I'll be just a minute. Wait here."

He left me in the shade of the building as he went over to a car parked nearby. It was a very nice sedan with tinted windows so dark I couldn't see inside. The driver's window rolled down. It was the man talking to Claud during the prank that I hadn't recognized.

He didn't look happy.

He got out of the car and handed Freddie the keys. He said something to Freddie that made Freddie roll his eyes. Freddie responded with something, obviously trying to convince him. The man spoke again and then looked over at me. It wasn't just a look. It was a full-on glare.

I wasn't sure what to do. Should I pretend not to see him? Should I wave? I went with a friendly, non-threatening smile. The two men exchanged a few more words before Freddie patted the man on the back. The big man bristled as Freddie returned to me with a big grin on his handsome face.

"We're all set," Freddie said, holding up the keys.

"And your friend is okay with this?" I asked, looking over at the man. He still stood next to the car, glaring at the two of us.

"He's got a ride and will be fine," Freddie replied. He raised his voice loud enough that the other man could definitely hear him. "He's just being dramatic."

The other man just continued to glare.

"So, are you ready?" Freddie asked. He held out his hand to me.

I glanced at the man one more time, but I wasn't about to turn Freddie's offer down. I took his hand, and he grinned at my touch. The big man glared at me as we approached but left as soon as we were close enough to speak. He didn't say anything, he just went to an SUV two spots over with similarly tinted windows. He gave us one last dangerous look before getting in the passenger seat.

"He seems very friendly," I remarked as Freddie opened the passenger side door and held it open for me.

"He's just a little protective of me," Freddie explained. "He's had to pull me out of a couple of rough dates. He's a good guy, but it's in his DNA not to trust anyone."

Freddie shut my door, and I took a moment to look around the car. It was possibly the nicest car I'd ever seen. Cold air came out of the leather seats, the interior was spotless, and the dash looked like it belonged in a spaceship.

Freddie slid into the driver's seat and adjusted the mirror. "So, you drive on the right side of the road here, right?"

"Do you want me to drive?" I asked, reaching to undo my seatbelt.

Freddie laughed. "Just teasing. I have my driver's license here. It's one of the few freedoms James allows me."

"James?" I asked.

"My friend," Freddie said quickly. "Sort of."

I raised my eyebrows, wondering what kind of friend this James was. What exactly was their relationship? It sounded confusing. Was I stepping into something that I would regret later?

But Freddie was already pulling the car out of the space and driving to my car. He helped me load my suitcase into the trunk of the sedan, and we were on the road.

CHAPTER 11

Stevens Point is the small town home to the University of Wisconsin-Stevens Point. It's known as the birthplace of the creator of Mystery Science Theater 3000 and hosting the world's largest trivia contest each year. I looked forward to that trivia contest every year. My team even took third place one time.

The cabin is located a comfortable biking distance from downtown and on one of the many lakes in the area. I'd spent a week at the cabin nearly every summer of my life. It was a cute three-bedroom place with a large sunny living room. The private dock was perfect for launching kayaks, fishing, or floating on inner tubes.

The drive up to the lake was the best one I'd ever had. It was so easy to talk to Freddie. We talked about our favorite foods (he liked fish and chips best) and favorite films (Princess Bride for both of us). His impression of the Shrieking Eels had me laughing so hard I could barely breathe.

I was smitten.

We pulled up in front of the cabin. I threw open the door and sucked in a deep breath of clean air. The familiar scents of grass, water, and trees filled my lungs like liquid sunshine, and my shoulders relaxed without me thinking about it.

"It's beautiful," Freddie said, stepping out of the car and looking around. His feet crunched softly on the gravel.

I grinned at him. "Want a tour?"

"Yes, please."

I took his hand without thinking and dragged him behind me into the cabin.

The cabin wasn't fancy. It was made for kids and comfort, with the décor leaning strongly toward hunting and plaid. Every piece of furniture was made of oak, and the motifs of fishing, hunting, bears, and trees seemed to be printed on every possible surface.

Books lined every available shelf and stacked up higher than my head was a tower of DVD cases. The cabin had minimal internet, so we'd always brought our own entertainment and left it for the next season.

Not being connected to the outside world was one of the perks of the cabin.

"There's three bedrooms," I explained as he helped me carry my suitcase to the biggest one. A big wooden bed dominated the room. "But since it's just me, I'm staying in the master. It's got the most comfortable bed in the world."

"Most comfortable in the world? Do you have that in writing?" Freddie teased. He set my suitcase down and examined a carved wooden bear sitting on one of the nightstands. "How would you know anyway? You haven't been in mine yet."

"Is that an invitation?" I asked, grinning at him as I leaned against the foot of the bed. "Because I don't think we'll make it to Paradisa by tonight to check."

I watched as his cheeks pinked slightly, but he didn't look away. If anything, he smiled at me. A slow smile that promised things like kisses lit by lightning bugs.

A thrill went through my stomach, and my body heat went up two degrees. I had to look like a hot mess after being in the car for two hours, but he looked at me like I had just stepped out of a Victoria's Secret catalog.

"Do you want to stay for dinner?" I asked him. In my head, I was ready to ask him to stay forever.

"I'd like that very much," Freddie replied. He took a step closer to me, and suddenly, the bedroom felt so much smaller. My breaths were shallow as he closed the distance between us.

He reached out and plucked a small leaf from my hair, showing it to me in his fingers. He was so close that the soft citrus and ginger scent of him was everywhere. All I had to do was go up on my tiptoes to kiss him.

It would be so easy. Just a kiss, and then the bed was right there. It would be so easy to fall into it with him.

And I had a feeling he'd be amazing there.

So I kissed him.

And he was even better the second time. Today, he had a slight stubble on his cheeks, but his lips were just as soft as the night before. Just as delicious. I loved the little groan he made as he wrapped his strong arms around me.

His tongue teased at mine, and I opened for him, letting him into me. Then it was my turn to make the little groan sound. He kissed me harder at that, one of his hands tightening gently around the back of my neck.

His kiss made me see stars. They were even better than lightning bugs.

"I'm making tacos," I blurted out. It was possibly the least sexy thing I could have said. But Freddie just grinned and kept me in his arms. "Tacos sound wonderful."

And he kissed me again and I forgot all about tacos.

Until his stomach rumbled loudly enough to make us both look.

"I guess I'll have to feed you before we do anything else," I teased.

He grinned. "Good things do come to those who wait."

And he took my hand and we headed for the kitchen.

"I'm not usually the one who cooks dinner," Freddie explained. He looked down at his tomato on the counter. "And I actually lied when I said I could help. I have no idea how to dice tomatoes."

I loved the way he said *tomatoes*. It sounded fancy with his Paradisian accent. But the man had brutally destroyed one of the tomatoes. It lay bleeding in tomato paste form on the cutting board.

I pushed the mangled tomato to the side of the cutting board and put out a new one. I took the knife in my hands and showed him how to cut the slices.

"Like this?" he asked, sliding in behind me. He draped his arms over mine, resting his hands carefully on top of my own. His breath tickled my ear, vibrating straight down and activating parts of me that had nothing to do with cooking.

His heat seeped into me, and I couldn't stop my eyes from closing with a flutter. I forced myself to concentrate, holding onto the tomato like a lifeline.

"Yup," I managed to say. "And then like this."

I was lucky I didn't slice my fingers off. I wasn't concentrating on the food at all. I was utterly focused on the way his strong body pressed into mine. His hands were warm, his body firm, and I wanted to know what he would feel like pressed against me over on my bed.

We finished the tomato, and he stepped back, letting me escape.

"Do you have another tomato?" he asked, smirking slightly. "I think I need more practice."

I playfully slapped at his shoulder. "Only if you don't want to eat tonight. Our shells are about to burn."

I managed to save the crunchy taco shells from over-crisping, but it was pure luck rather than skill. Freddie struggled with the cutting board for a moment before figuring out how to dump the tomatoes into a small bowl.

When he saw me watching him, he shrugged. "Like I said, I don't usually cook. My brother likes to, but I'm more of a quick and easy kind of guy."

"Quick and easy?" I asked, raising an eyebrow. "Is that what you like?"

Freddie grinned. "Only when making food for myself," he amended. "Otherwise, I am all about attention to detail for hours. I like to take my time with things."

"Hours, huh?" Good lord, did that put ideas into my head.

We took our food out to the back porch to assemble. The sun was nowhere near ready to set, but a soft breeze from the lake made the patio comfortable. Frogs were starting to croak, but the crickets hadn't come out yet. Warm yellow light sparkled on the lake.

"So how do I do this again?" Freddie asked, poking at one of the taco shells.

"Most people put the meat, then the cheese, then whatever veggies, and salsa," I explained. "However, I like to put cheese on the bottom, then meat, then more cheese, then salsa, then veggies. I find the cheese melts better. And I get more cheese."

I demonstrated my taco layering, and Freddie copied me. He took a bite.

"This is good," he said, cheese and tomatoes dropping out of his taco and all over his plate.

"Have you never had tacos before?" I asked, watching as he managed to look somehow polite eating a taco.

"Of course I've had tacos," he replied. "I've even had them in Mexico."

"These are not Mexican tacos," I said, shaking my head. "These barely count as Tex-Mex. These are my grandmother's tacos, and she's from Germany."

"But they are delicious," he told me, stuffing the last bite into his mouth. "Even if they are messy."

"The best ones are," I agreed. I made myself another taco. They always tasted better here at the lake. It was probably just the fresh air, but the food always tasted better here.

We ate in companionable silence for a moment, both of us thoroughly enjoying the good food. It was probably my best batch of tacos, and I was incredibly grateful I had managed a good batch today.

"Those were amazing," Freddie said, helping me bring all the dishes back inside once we'd finished. "Thank you."

"I give you full credit. It was your tomatoes that made them good," I replied.

He laughed. "If you say so." He glanced down at his watch and then to the door.

I didn't want him to leave. I didn't want him to go. Even if he didn't sleep in my bed tonight, I didn't want to wake up tomorrow morning and not see him. I wanted to have coffee with him out on the porch. I wanted to take him swimming in the lake. He'd love the kayaks, and I wanted to see him light up with the fire-flies again.

"Will you stay the night?" I asked.

Apparently, my brain was done with me.

Freddie looked slightly surprised, his mouth opening for a moment.

"I mean..." I blushed a furious red. "I mean, that it's getting late. You should stay here. It's not safe to go out on country roads in the dark."

It wasn't dark outside. The sun didn't even set until almost nine PM. Not to mention that his very nice car had very nice headlights.

"I would hate to make you worry," Freddie said slowly.

"It's a long drive," I continued. "And I make amazing waffles. If you like waffles, that is."

"I do like waffles." Freddie grinned at me. He looked at his phone. "Let me make a phone call."

He took his phone out onto the porch and closed the sliding glass door behind him.

"I'm staying here tonight," I heard him say through the glass, his voice muffled and dim. I grinned and headed over to the sink to work on the dishes while he finished his phone call.

"Well, James isn't thrilled, but he'll just have to deal with it," Freddie announced when he came back in.

"Shouldn't he be happy?" I asked, looking up from the tub of soapy dishes.

"Why?" Freddie looked absolutely perplexed, and I loved the expression on him.It was absolutely adorable.

"He gets the hotel room to himself, right?" I asked, going back to my dishes. "I assumed you two were staying together."

"Not quite," Freddie replied, frowning slightly. "But close enough. Here, let me help."

He came next to me, picked up the dish towel, and began drying.

"You don't know how to dice a tomato, but you know how to dry dishes?" I asked him, watching as he dried dishes with ease.

"I got in trouble a lot as a kid," he explained with a grin. "Dishes seemed like a good punishment. Then, in the Army, it was my punishment there too."

"You were in the army?" I asked, surprised.

"47th Paradisian Battalion," he replied. He paused on his current dish. "It's kind of a family requirement."

I imagined him in an army uniform and got all kinds of hot and bothered. He looked amazing in a suit. I could only imagine how good he looked in a uniform.

"Did you go anywhere interesting?" I asked, handing him a dish to dry.

"In the army or just in general?" he asked.

"Either." I shrugged. "Both?"

"I've been to lots of places," he answered with a shrug. He glanced over at me and grinned. He was pure charm. "This one's the best so far."

I shook my head but grinned back at him. "You think you're so charming..."

He dropped his dish back into the soapy water and kissed me before I could say another word. His hands were wet on my neck, but I didn't care. My own wet hands fisted into his shirt.

His kisses lit a fire inside of me. One that burned low and hot. Tendrils of flame crept up my spine, heating my bones with desire.

"I want you," I whispered into his kiss. Our eyes met and I could see that he had that same flame inside of him.

"Zoey..."

He kissed me, his hands tangling in my hair this time. He tasted like pure lust and I had to have him.

I reached for the hem of his shirt, lifting it up. He broke from the kiss just long enough for the fabric to go over his head, but then his lips were back on mine.

My palms spread out on his chest. He was so warm. So muscular. So real that I was glad there was no way I could possibly be dreaming this. There was no way that I could imagine the solidness and the heat of him.

I pulled off my own wet shirt, tossing it to the kitchen floor.

He hissed his pleasure, his eyes looking me over with reverence. I felt beautiful when he looked at me like that. Like he'd never imagined anyone could look this amazing with their shirt off. I knew I wasn't anything special, but when he looked at me like that, I felt like a freaking super model.

I reached behind me and unhooked my bra. I loved the way his eyes dilated as he saw me. I loved the little hitch in his breath and the way his stomach muscles tightened at the sight of bare skin.

He reached out, his hand caressing the soft curve of

my breast. I shivered with delight and the low chuckle he made had me shivering again.

I kissed him again, pressing my bare chest against his. He was so warm that yet again those fires deep inside of me stoked.

"Too many clothes," I whispered. I could feel his desire pressing into my hip and I didn't want anything between us anymore.

He murmured his agreement and pulled at the waist of his pants. I pulled away from him only long enough to pull off my pants. I kicked them to the side and glanced over at him. He had his pants off and wore only dark blue boxer briefs.

And oh, good Lord, was he glorious.

He was all trim muscle. He must have played more rugby than he let on, because he was in fighting shape. A shape that made my insides turn to mush and I let out a happy little moan that made him smirk.

He kissed me again, pressing my back against the kitchen counter. His hands went to my waist, and I jumped up onto the counter. It was cold against the skin that my underwear didn't cover, but I was so hot and bothered that I didn't care.

My legs wrapped around his waist without me thinking about it. His hard heat pressed into my softness and I knew that there was no way we could stop. I was going to have him. It was like waiting for cookies to bake. I knew something amazing was coming and I was going to devour all of him.

I kissed his shoulder, tasting his skin. While he smelled of citrus and ginger, he tasted sweet. The muscle of his shoulder felt good in my mouth. Hunger for his body, to have him inside of me, made me whimper.

I closed my eyes and tipped my head back, focusing on just the feel of him pressed into me. He kissed my neck, nibbling on the delicate skin near my throat. He used soft kisses to find his way down my collar bone and down to my breast.

I gasped as he wrapped his lips around a nipple. He cupped my other breast in his hand, playing with the now rock-hard nipple between his fingers.

My hands tangled in his hair. Golds, reds, and soft browns twisted in my fingers as he sucked and played with me. I arched my back, giving him all the access to me that I could. In the process, I thrust my hips into his.

He groaned, the sound reverberating on my skin and deep into my soul

He looked up at me. The green of his eyes was vibrant and full of the fire that I wanted.

"Do you have a condom?" I asked, biting my lower lip. I wished I had thought to bring some, but I hadn't expected any guests on this trip.

The smile he gave me was the sexiest thing I'd ever seen in my life. It was slow, sensuous, confident, and excited. And all mine.

He gave me a quick kiss and then bounded off toward the living room. I sat on the counter, swinging my legs and enjoying watching his butt run. In a few seconds, I heard the sound of a luggage zipper, followed by a low curse, and the sound of another zipper.

I chewed on my lower lip, waiting for him to return. I was on birth control, but this was our first time.

He came back holding up a gold foil circle like he'd just won the Olympics.

"Found it," he announced.

"I always wanted a man who brought home the gold," I teased. He chuckled and resumed his place in front of me. My legs wrapped around him again, eager to have him between them yet again.

"Now, where were we?" he whispered, dipping his mouth into the curve of my shoulder. He traced the line of my neck with his kisses. His hands ran up and down my sides, pausing to give more attention to my breasts, but never lingering there for long.

His hand slid down to my hip and he hooked a finger around the waistband of my underwear. He found my eyes and I grinned at him before wiggling around to take them off. I grinned at him as I kicked the fabric across the kitchen.

I took the condom from him and opened it while he took off his own underwear. It was hard not to stare at his absolute male perfection. The space between my legs suddenly felt very empty without him there.

I rolled on the condom. He hissed softly as I touched him, every muscle in his stomach tightening. He let his head fall back and he groaned as I felt his entire length. A shiver of desire swept over me knowing that he liked my touch. That my touch was enough to get that kind of reaction.

His breathing was ragged as he found his way back between my legs. My stomach was a jumble of nerves, lust, and excitement as he positioned himself to take me.

I stared into his green eyes as he smiled at me. Slowly,

and with a wicked smile that told me he was going slow on purpose, he slid into me.

Both of us froze for a full breath. It was the final piece of the puzzle. A lock clicking open. A key sliding into place.

My legs tightened around his waist and I never wanted him to leave me.

He slid out just far enough to slide into me again. He groaned, his muscles tightening and straining with the effort to stay in control of himself. I dropped my head into his shoulder, and he thrust home hard.

I cried out in pleasure as he began to rock his hips. Slow and steady, but with a fierceness that made me ache. He wanted me as much as I wanted him.

Every thrust was powerful and primal. His hands were on my hips, his fingers digging into the soft flesh as he claimed me as his own.

My head fell back, exposing my throat. He nipped at it with a soft kiss.

"Zoey," he whispered. My name and the way he said it made me shudder with pleasure. "I don't want to stop."

"Then don't," I whispered back. I opened my eyes and looked at him. He was barely in control anymore. Lust flowed through him and I could see him struggling to contain himself. "Don't hold back."

His pupils dilated, the unconscious symbol of his desire.

I rocked my hips and he groaned, closing his eyes with the pleasure of it. His thrusts became faster and more frantic. My pleasure rose to meet his.

His skin was hot against mine. His muscles were strong and his body was insistent. My hands wrapped around his back, and I could feel every muscle there working to claim me as his own. I locked my ankles around him, feeling the perfect definition of his ass beneath my calf muscles.

I used my hips to draw him into me. He undulated, and his breathing became uneven and heavy.

There was so much pleasure surging through me that I wanted to explode because of it.

So I did.

The heat of desire running down my spine lit into a white hot inferno that filled my vision. I couldn't breath with the pleasure of it, the sheer pleasure of finding him within me. Every muscle from the tips of my toes to the top of my scalp clenched around him, drawing him into me.

I tingled with euphoria.

And then I heard the low male sound of his breathing. The low groan and hiss as he lost control of himself. I nearly exploded again from the shudder, the gasp, the way his body tightened and then crashed into mine.

There would never be anything in the world as good as that feeling.

It was heaven. We spent that moment, drunk on orgasm and wrapped around him, our bodies pressed together and breathing the same breath.

We stayed on that counter for a long time, waiting for our breathing to come back to something that would allow speech.

"You are... amazing," he gasped, lifting his eyes to find mine. His smile is amazed and impressed.

I grinned at him "I bet you say that to all the girls who make you tacos."

He thought for a moment and then grinned. His smile made my stomach flutter and the heat started to grow in the pit of my stomach again.

"You're right," he teased. "But only the girls who make me tacos."

I remembered that he'd never eaten tacos like mine and I chuckled.

"I don't feel that this was an accurate representation of my skill," he said, still tangled up in my legs.

"Is that so?" I asked, raising an eyebrow. "Because I'm pretty impressed right now."

"That was nothing," he assured me. "You just felt so good. I lost control. I need to earn my gold medal."

He held up the now empty gold foil package. But I was stuck on that fact that I made him lose control. That he had wanted me so badly he couldn't control himself.

"Do you have more medals?" I asked, eyeing the foil. I loosened my legs from around his waist and slid onto the floor. My knees still felt wobbly from the pleasure he'd given me already. "I'm sure we can come up with more events."

He grinned and his eyes sparkled. "I have all the medals you could want."

And my knees went all wobbly again as I took his hand and led him to the bed.

CHAPTER 13

I woke up to an empty bed.

However, the sounds of someone in the kitchen and the scent of coffee had me feeling better about it rather quickly. I brushed my teeth and hurried out to find Freddie in the kitchen.

"I ordered donuts," he said as soon as he saw me. "I wanted to make you a beautiful fancy omelet, but I also didn't want to burn down your aunt's house."

"I appreciate you not destroying the cabin," I replied. "But the coffee smells great."

"Coffee is the one thing I can actually cook by myself," he said. "That and a bowl of cereal. I'm quite good at that one too."

I grinned as he handed me a mug full of steaming caffeine. I grabbed one of the donuts from the box and took a bite of delicious sugary goodness. It wasn't on my usual diet, but this was vacation after all.

"Come sit on the porch with me?" I asked, motioning

my head to the sliding glass door. Freddie beamed and followed me out.

We sat in the morning sunshine on two deck chairs, the box of donuts perched between us on the armrest of Freddie's chair.

"Did you know that you can have clowns deliver donuts to your house?" Freddie asked, taking a big bite of donut and getting sugar on his cheek. "The company even gives you the option of scary clowns or happy clowns."

"Did clowns deliver these donuts?" I asked, suddenly worried I'd be squirted in the face by a fake flower or that I would see a red balloon floating ominously through the house.

"No. I didn't want to pay extra since you were sleeping," Freddie replied.

"I appreciate that." I reached over and wiped the sugar from his face, then sucking the sweetness from my thumb. It tasted nearly as good as he did. "Clowns before ten in the morning tend to make me grumpy."

"I'll remember that. No clowns before breakfast." Freddie nodded thoughtfully. "But how do you feel about ninjas?"

"Well, since they are ninjas and should be stealthy, they can just leave the donuts silently in the kitchen, and I'll never know they were there," I replied. "So, really, I'm fine with ninjas delivering donuts anytime."

Freddie chuckled. "I think there's a business idea there."

"Was there really an option for clowns?" I asked.

"Yes." Freddie nodded. "I must say I really hope I'm invited to a wedding again soon."

I laughed, thinking of a posse of clowns showing up to a wedding reception.

"You really are a troublemaker, aren't you?"

"I like to make people laugh," Freddie replied with a shrug. "Everyone in my family is so serious. It's all politics and manners and being proper. My mother says it's my way of rebellion."

"I suppose it's better than drugs or face tattoos."

Freddie turned slowly to look at me, a grin tugging on the corner of his lips. "You just gave me a fabulous idea."

"No face tattoos for a wedding," I said quickly. "Or the bride will have to make you wear the veil!"

He laughed. "I'm imagining my brother's face if I came home with one." He shook his head. "I don't think I'd survive three minutes. I'd probably be banished to the tower and forced to wear an iron mask for the rest of my days."

"I always felt bad for the man in the iron mask," I replied. "What do you do when you get food stuck in it? And what if your nose itched?"

"I think a face tattoo is out of the running," Freddie said ruefully.

"What if you just got one of those temporary ones?" I asked.

A crooked, devilish smile filled his face. "I like the way you think."

"We might even have some here," I said, trying to remember my childhood. "I remember my cousins and I stashing some amazing Teenage Mutant Ninja Turtles temporary tattoos in a drawer here."

"Mutant turtles? I have no idea what that is, but it sounds like a perfect face tattoo," Freddie replied.

"It's an old kids TV show," I explained.

Our conversation changed to remembering the television series of our childhoods. The man was remarkably sheltered and didn't know many of the classics. It seemed he wasn't allowed much TV as a child. I decided we would have to watch some of my childhood favorites to catch him up.

"What are you doing today?" I asked, wanting to ask him to watch old cartoons with me.

He shrugged. "James probably has something terribly tedious planned."

I chewed on my lower lip and fiddled with my coffee mug for a second, trying to muster up the courage to ask him.

"Would you like to stay here? I have enough food for you to stay for dinner." The words rushed out of me.

The smile that filled Freddie's face was brighter than the sun. His eyes sparkled more than the lake, and my heart thudded with hope.

"I'd like that very much," he said softly. "Very much."

I grinned, blushing and so very glad I had asked. "Good."

"Out of curiosity, what are we having for dinner?" he asked, sipping on his coffee.

"I have no idea," I admitted. "Whatever you want. Whatever will make you stay."

"You. You are what makes me stay," he replied, turning to look at me. His eyes found mine. "I never want to leave."

My world froze for a happy, fluttering moment.

"Then stay forever," I told him.

He grinned, leaned over, and kissed me.

It was just a simple, sweet kiss, but it made the world brighter. Joy bubbled through me, effervescent and wonderful.

"Best morning ever," I sighed happily.

"I have to agree," Freddie replied, settling back into his chair. "What else would you like to do today?"

I grinned at him and winked suggestively.

"Well, other than that." But he winked at me.

"I thought we could go out on the lake," I suggested, motioning to the lake before us. "Have you ever been kayaking?"

He shook his head. "I've been on a canoe, but never a kayak."

"Then today is your lucky day," I told him. "We have kayaks that my uncle found at a garage sale two years ago. They mostly float."

"Mostly?" Freddie raised his eyebrows.

"It's part of the adventure," I assured him. "If there's no risk, there's no reward."

Freddie looked out at the lake, a slow smile filling his face. "I love it. Let's do it."

We cleaned up our donuts and coffee, flirting as we washed dishes in the sink. It was so easy to be around him. He laughed at my sarcasm, and I giggled at his jokes. I felt like I could be me around him. It was a wonderful feeling to be myself with someone.

The doorbell rang.

"I got it," Freddie said quickly. "James is supposed to bring me some things."

He hurried over, and I could see the tall, imposing figure of James in the doorway. I gave him a small wave as I went to the bedroom to change into my swimsuit. As I left, I heard James speaking in hushed tones to Freddie, and I had a feeling that he was even less pleased than he usually was.

~

I chose my favorite tankini, the one with blue stars. When I came out, Freddie was already in his swim trunks and waiting for me in the living room. He wore a dark scowl that quickly changed into a smile as soon as he saw me.

"Everything okay?" I asked.

"It's fine," he replied quickly. "He's just a little overprotective. And paranoid. He's sure something is going to go wrong out here."

"Like what?" I asked. "You can swim, right? And we're going to wear life vests out on the boat."

Freddie smiled. "That's what I told him. There are no worries here. But he's gone. Let's not worry about him."

"How did you change so fast?" I asked, grabbing some towels from the hall closet.

"I am a master at a quick change," he confessed. "I can change my outfit in a moving car without being seen in the windows. It's handy for avoiding the paparazzi."

I shook my head at his silly brag.

"Well, Mr. Big Shot, you won't have to worry about the paparazzi much here," I told him, motioning him to the garage. "We're too out in the middle of nowhere to matter."

Freddie grinned. "Just how I like it."

CHAPTER 14

"So, you just have to move your paddles like this," I explained, showing him the scooping motion. We sat just off the dock in old leaky kayaks. The life vests smelled like last summer's sunshine and this year's mold, but we wore them anyway.

"Like this?" Freddie asked, repeating the motion perfectly. He then proceeded to turn his kayak in a neat circle, looking rather pleased with himself when he came back around.

"Yeah." I narrowed my eyes at him. "I think you've done this before."

"Not in a boat like this," he replied. "But I did do some rowing in college. The concepts are similar."

I rolled my eyes. Of course, he did rowing in college. He probably did all the expensive sports. I knew he had money. The rental car he'd driven us in hadn't been cheap. His clothes, even his swim trunks, were high end. He had gone to school with Carlson, and since Carlson was ivy-league educated, he tended to run in prestigious circles. I didn't want to pry and ask just how rich he was. But even I could tell he was loaded.

"Betcha can't catch me," I called out to him, picking up my paddle and taking off across the lake.

He caught me quickly and knocked my kayak over, spilling me into the lake.

I came up spluttering. The water was cold and tasted just a little bit fishy.

"You!" I splashed him as hard as I could. He laughed, easily dodging my attack. I tread water, relishing the cool water of the lake. "Will you hold my kayak steady so I can get back in?"

"Of course," the gullible fool replied.

I had him in the water in seconds.

"You!" This time he splashed at me. Water ran through his hair, turning the red-gold dark and rich. His green eyes sparkled brighter than the lake as he grinned at me.

I dunked him, pushing his shoulders hard under the water. His life vest kept him from going too deep, but the motion surprised him. He popped back up to the surface, spitting lake water.

"Now you're going to get it," he growled, his eyes narrowed but his mouth smiling.

"You'll have to catch me first," I called to him, swimming away through the blue water.

I used my kayak as cover, darting through the water like a little fish.

Unfortunately, he was a bigger fish and caught me quickly. I didn't mind. I rather wanted to be caught. He grabbed the back of my life vest and pulled me to him. He was about to dunk me under the water when I kissed him.

He paused, surprised. So I kissed him again. His lips

were warm after the cool of the water. He managed to make the lake almost taste good.

But then he did dunk me. I squeaked in surprise, and lake water rushed into my mouth.

I came to the surface and spat my mouthful of water at him. He twisted just in time, missing the full spray of it. I splashed him, and he splashed me back.

"Truce?" he asked after we had launched half the lake at one another. We were both breathless from laughter as we bobbed in the water next to our empty kayaks.

"Truce," I agreed. "It's almost lunchtime."

We shook hands and got back in our boats. We paddled in lazy strokes back toward the dock and our cabin. I waited until we were about twenty feet from the dock before I knocked him into the lake again.

"We had a truce!" he spluttered, spraying lake water.

I grinned at him. "I'll make it up to you."

He narrowed his eyes playfully at me. "How?"

"I'll make you lunch?" I offered.

"Not good enough." He shook his head slowly, crossing his arms. He somehow managed to not look ridiculous, even with his bright yellow life vest holding him up in the water.

"I'll..." I glanced around the lake. There wasn't another human being for miles. Still, I wasn't about to shout all the inappropriate things I wanted to do to him. "I'll do what I did last night again."

His eyes dilated, and lust clouded his features for a moment.

"I'm not sure that's enough. A truce is sacred," he replied with a small shrug. He was playing hardball.

"You're going to have to be more specific. What exactly from last night are you going to do?"

"You want me to say it?" I whispered.

He motioned to the lake. "No one is here but me. I want you to yell it."

I stared at him for a moment, unsure. It wasn't like anyone would hear us out here.

"A blow job." My voice came out soft and low.

Freddie grinned, but he put his hand behind his ear like he couldn't hear me. "What?"

I glared at him. "A blow job," I repeated, just a little bit louder.

"Still can't hear you. Probably all the water in my ears after you betrayed me," he said with a sigh.

I rolled my eyes and took a deep breath.

"I want to give you the best blow job of your life. I'm going to make you scream for me," I yelled.

"You go, girl!" came a voice from shore.

I realized that the cabin on the west side of the lake had two people sitting on the porch. I hadn't noticed them before. It looked like an older woman and her husband. My heart sank as I recognized the cabin. It was the Westons. They were my grandmother's age and went to church with my mother when she came to the cabin.

They knew my mother. They'd been at the wedding. And now they'd heard me announce I was going to give someone a blow job.

I slunk low into my kayak, Freddie's laughter ringing in my ears. He swam over to my kayak and grinned up at me.

"That's what happens when you break a truce," he informed me.

I glared at him. "What if they call my mother?"

The Westons were laughing on their porch. They didn't look like they were going to call anyone, but the idea of it mortified me. I didn't want to be a conversation piece at the next family get together.

"I'm more worried they'll call mine," he replied with a chuckle.

I splashed him with water from my oar, but he just grinned.

"I still get the blow job, though, right?" he asked, his face playful and bright.

"Only if you bring the kayak home," I told him. I snatched up his fallen paddle and took off toward the dock, leaving him to have to swim his kayak home. But he still got the blow job.

And I made sure it was the best one he'd ever had.

CHAPTER 15

"I love how peaceful it is here," Freddie remarked the next morning. We sat out on the back porch, sipping coffee and eating the waffles I'd finally made.

"Me too," I agreed. I sighed with contentment, licking the last bit of maple syrup from my fork. "This is even better than I imagined. Thank you for being here."

He flashed me a grin. "Believe me. It's been my pleasure. I think this is the first real vacation I've ever had."

"Really? You've never been on vacation before?" I frowned. "Your parents never took you anywhere?"

He shrugged. "I've been on holiday to lots of places, but it was never relaxing. It was always scheduled with tours and meetings. I had to beg for a day off to just sit at the beach or the pool, but even then, I wasn't allowed just to relax."

"Why not?"

"It's just not my family's way," he replied. "We're always on. We're always smiling and doing. I've never been allowed to sit and do nothing. There's always something that should be getting done. If you aren't doing something, then you aren't earning your keep."

"That sounds exhausting," I told him. "How do you relax?"

"I don't. I'm always working." A flicker of exhaustion crossed his face, but he quickly covered it up with a practiced smile. "It's the curse of the family business. I can never escape it."

He shrugged like it didn't bother him and popped a piece of waffle into his mouth.

"That sounds incredibly stressful." My chest tightened just thinking of it, and I shifted in my seat.

"You get used to it after a while," Freddie replied. "It could be worse. I could live in a reality show or something."

"I love my job, but it's something that I only have to do for twelve hours at a time," I told him. "It's actually one of the perks. When I leave the hospital, I'm done. I don't have people watching me all the time. I like being an hourly employee."

"That does sound rather nice," Freddie agreed.

"There are salaried options, but I like hospital nursing," I said. "But I think I like being on vacation more. I would love to have a job where I could get paid to just stay in this cabin."

"That sounds like heaven." He motioned to the lake. "This has been wonderful, though. I've never been allowed to wear pajamas all day and have absolutely no schedule. I can't remember the last time I didn't have something I had to do. It's so nice not to have someone wanting something from me constantly."

"Well, I want something from you pretty constantly." I nudged him with my elbow and winked seductively.

He laughed. "That's different. I want to give you that. All the time. It's the exact opposite of a requirement."

"Good. I'd hate to make you work," I teased him.

"Oh, you make me work. In the best possible way." His tongue licked out over his lower lip in a way that had my heart speeding up and blood rushing south. He looked me up and down, and his smile was thirsty.

I felt gorgeous with his eyes on me. Even though I wore a raggedy pair of cotton shorts and a stained t-shirt, I felt like I was wearing designer lingerie when he looked at me like that. I loved the way he undressed me with his eyes, seeing all of me and wanting every inch.

"You want to work now?" I asked, my body already excited for him.

He grinned and pointed to the food still on my plate. "I recall you saying you wanted to eat all your breakfast first this time."

I laughed. "I suppose we have time," I told him. "We have all day. No reason to rush."

The heat he ignited in me didn't disappear. It just turned to warm embers, waiting for the right time to come alive again.

And the waffles were really good. I would have hated to waste them.

"Thank you for this," he said softly after a while. He leaned toward me and put his hand gently on my arm. "I can't tell you how much this has meant to me. You're saving my sanity."

"Your sanity? You had some?" I was sure he was

teasing me, so I teased him in return. I shrugged like it was nothing. "It's just a few days at the lake."

"It's so much more than that. It's freedom." He smiled at me. This smile was warm and genuine. "I've gotten to be me for the first time in years. I *feel* like me again. You've made me feel like a person again. Like I'm more than just my name and a job I can do."

"But I haven't done anything," I told him.

"And that's what I needed. You've let me be me."

I frowned, not quite understanding. But he was happy. It was so evident in the sparkle of his eyes that he was happy. He seemed lighter. Just in the past few days, he smiled more and seemed lighter. He had played the joke-ster at the wedding, but there was an unhappy edge to him even then. That edge seemed to have dulled with us enjoying ourselves alone at the lake.

"What exactly is your job?" I asked, setting my fork on my empty plate. "Is it really that bad?"

He sighed, and a little of the light in his eyes faded. "It's not that bad. I'm not doing surgery or anything, but it's constant. I'm always supposed to say and do the right thing. You'd think the entire world would burn down when I don't."

I noticed he didn't answer my question about what his job was. I didn't push. He had said his job required a secu-rity clearance. I knew a couple of military friends with security clearances, and they couldn't say anything about what they were doing either. I didn't want to push for something that could get him fired.

"So why do you stay?" I asked him. "If it's that draining on you, why don't you quit?"

"I would if I could," Freddie admitted slowly. His eyes

went out to the edge of the lake, seeing far past the line of trees there. "But I can never quit. I was born into this responsibility. It's not something you get to give two weeks' notice on."

I thought he was being a little dramatic. Born into responsibility? Even if it was a family business, there had to be a way out. But I didn't say anything. I could only imagine the difficulty of family dynamics as well as business ones. It probably just felt like he couldn't quit, but me saying that wouldn't help him.

"Well, I'm glad I can give you a little respite," I said.

"Oh, you've given me excellent... respite." He looked me over again, his eyes dilating like I was a supermodel.

"Perhaps, I should give you more *respite* in the bedroom," I replied, liking the gleam in his eyes.

"Perhaps, you should. I did finish my waffles."

We didn't even make it to the bedroom. He got his respite on the floor just inside the sliding glass door. I didn't want to wait the ten steps to the bedroom.

CHAPTER 16

"Would you rather live in the mountains or on the beach?" I asked Freddie, my head resting on his shoulder as we enjoyed our last evening together. The days had gone so quickly and wonderfully. I had kept asking him to stay another day, and he kept agreeing. I was sure he would get tired of being out in a cabin on a lake, eating home-cooked meals, and reading books on the porch.

But he didn't. If anything, I think it soothed his soul as much as it did mine.

The night sky sparkled with stars through the window, but we were tucked under a light blanket on the couch inside. The blanket was almost too hot, even with air conditioning, but I liked the weight of it on my lap. My shoulder fit perfectly under his arm as we snuggled on the couch, just talking and enjoying the sound of crickets and frogs outside.

"I assume I get a house?" Freddie asked. "I don't have to live out in the wild?"

"Yes, you get a comfortable house with a TV and everything," I told him with a wave of my hand. "Beach or mountain scenery?"

Freddie thought for a moment, his brows coming together. "That's hard..."

"That's what she said," I immediately replied.

"Are you going to say that every time?" Freddie asked, turning to give me a gentle glare.

"Yup." I grinned up at him.

He chuckled and shook his head before settling back into his original spot. "I say mountains. We have beaches in Paradisa, but there are no mountains. What about you?"

"We don't have beaches or mountains in the midwest," I replied, buying myself some time to think about my answer.

"This is kind of a beach," Freddie supplied, motioning his head toward the lake outside.

"Then beach," I told him. "If lakes count, then I choose the beach."

"I change my answer to the beach then," Freddie said. "I want to be wherever you are."

He smiled at me, pulling me closer to him. His citrus scent was so comforting and soft. I sighed with contentment, resting my head on his shoulder. My heart fluttered with quiet delight that he wanted to be with me.

I had expected to spend my vacation alone and in quiet. Instead, I spent it laughing with Freddie. This was the best vacation I'd ever had. It had been absolutely perfect and amazing to spend every day with him.

We didn't go out. We didn't have anyone we had to

meet. We didn't do anything we didn't want to do. We just relaxed.

We had amazing, mind-blowing sex that made me glad the neighbors were too far away to hear us. And then we'd lie in bed, naked and satisfied with no concern that we had to be anywhere or do anything but enjoy the other's bare skin.

We talked. We watched old movies. There was minimal internet at the cabin, so we watched DVDs and read books. We didn't worry about the outside world or what anyone thought of us. I turned off my social media apps. My phone was only used for ordering pizza.

We talked like we'd known one another our entire lives and had just forgotten the specifics. There were no taboo subjects or things I didn't want him to know. He was comfortable and easy to talk to about everything.

"Your turn to ask a question," I said softly.

He sat quietly for a moment. "What would your ideal life look like?"

I chewed on my cheek for a moment. "Do I have unlimited money? That would change a lot of my answers."

"Sure," he said with a shrug. "You win the lottery. What do you do?"

"I'd buy a house like this one, but I'd also buy the whole lake so that the Westons can't listen to my public indecency," I replied, nudging him in the ribs. "I'd put all sorts of comfy things in it. And get cooking lessons so I can make anything, but sometimes hire a private chef."

"I suppose you'd want your house near the hospital?" Freddie asked. "So, you could keep working?"

I hesitated for a moment before answering.

"I wish I could say yes. I wish I could say that I loved my job so much that if I didn't need the money, I wouldn't do it, but..." My shoulders sagged as I shrugged. "Sometimes, the only reason I can walk into the hospital for another shift is because I have to make rent. It's not an easy job. I don't think I would tolerate being elbow-deep in someone else's body fluids if I didn't have to be."

Freddie nodded but didn't say anything.

"There are parts of my job that I adore," I said quickly. "I love helping people. I love watching people get better. I love finding ways to make life better for people. I love helping. I really do like most of my job. I wouldn't have devoted the last four years of my life to learning how to do it if I didn't like it."

"But there are parts that you don't enjoy. Parts of the job that you do out of obligation, not enjoyment," Freddie supplied. His voice was gentle. "Parts of the job that you only do because you have to. Not because you want to. And if given the chance, you wouldn't do them anymore."

"Exactly," I agreed.

I wondered just how he was able to understand me so well.

"What about you?" I asked. "What's your perfect life look like?"

Freddie took a deep breath and looked around the room. "A lot like this, actually."

"An old cabin with leaky kayaks?" I teased.

"No, freedom. The freedom to come and go as I please. To eat what I want. To do what I want. To wake up and wear what I want." He sighed. "Everyone thinks I love the spotlight, and I do. I do like the attention. But I don't crave it like they all think. I'd give it up for quiet like this."

I thought about what he'd told me about his family over the past few days.

He had told me about his brothers. He had two of them. His oldest brother, Liam, stressed Freddie out and was the demanding leader of their clan. Liam was a perfectionist that insisted everything be done according to the rules. His next brother, Henry, had just gotten married this year. Henry was almost as stuck on tradition and the family business as Liam was. Freddie did like his new sister-in-law, though. She was apparently an American and a little more relaxed about things.

Freddie's father had died a few years ago. He said his mother struggled without him. The whole family did, to be honest. His mom used tradition and duty to find the strength to carry on without her husband. Following tradition became her way of dealing with his death. As such, she'd become more insistent on Freddie following the rules and doing what was expected of him as a member of their family.

The family business. Tradition. Responsibility. It's what his father would have wanted for him. It's what his brothers expected him to now do. It's why he rebelled in small acts of stealing the spotlight. He played pranks. He partied. He annoyed his brothers in public. It wasn't the spotlight he craved. It was the power to do what he wanted.

"I still say you should just quit your job," I said, putting my hand on his thigh.

"It's just demanding," he explained. "My brother expects me to be the face of the country. To behave with decorum and always say and do the right things." His shoulders sagged, and he suddenly looked ten years older than he was. "It's exhausting. And not what I want to do with my life."

"What do you want to do with your life?" I asked. "If you didn't have to work for your brother, what would you do?"

Freddie stared at me for a moment. "You know, no one has ever asked me that. Ever."

I wondered what school he had gone to as a child. Every year I'd had to draw or write an essay on what I wanted to be when I grew up from kindergarten all the way through college. I'd answered the question so many times it had lost all meaning for me.

"So? What would you do?" I asked him.

He had to think about it. "I don't really know. It's never been an option," he explained. "I suppose I'd want to do something to help children."

"Children?" I asked.

"It's the one part of my job I do enjoy. I volunteer at the Paradisa Children's Hospital and the Child Welfare Center." There was a light in his eyes and a smile on his lips as he thought about it. "I suppose I'd work for one of those organizations full time."

I didn't tell him he should do that. That he should quit his job with his brother and do what he wanted. I didn't tell him what to do because I knew he wouldn't. I'd learned over the last three days that he loved his family and that he took his obligations to them seriously. He'd chop off his own leg before he'd let them down, even if it meant that he had to do a job he didn't enjoy.

"It's your turn for a question," Freddie reminded me, bumping me gently with his shoulder. "Maybe a dirty one this time? Something about all the things I'd like to do to you?"

I rolled my eyes at him, but I didn't get a chance to ask. The doorbell rang, interrupting both our thoughts.

"I'll get it," Freddie said with a frown, rising to his feet. He peeked out the peephole and sighed, his shoulders drooping and the light going from his eyes. "It's James."

"Is everything okay?" I asked. I wondered what James was doing here so late.

"I'm sure it is," he said, opening the door. "I probably missed a message from him on my phone, and he's making sure I'm still alive."

The door swung open, and James stood in the yellow outdoor light. He wore the same dark suit he'd worn to the wedding, as well as the same unhappy face. He glared at me, sitting on the couch.

"I'm just going to use the restroom," I said quickly, getting up and hurrying from the room to give them some privacy. I went to the hall bathroom and closed the door.

And realized that the window was open. The bathroom window was near enough to the front door that I could hear everything they were saying. I wasn't trying to eavesdrop, but I couldn't help it either. I'd hear everything just the same if I went back into the living room.

I turned on the sink, trying not to listen and failing miserably.

"You didn't answer your phone," James said, his voice low and dark. He had the same lilting Paradisian accent as Freddie. "Your brother isn't happy."

"James, it's nearly midnight. I am not working right now. I am not doing anything for my brother right now," Freddie replied. His tone was cool and formal. It didn't sound like the laughing playful man who had kissed me just moments earlier. "I don't work his hours."

"He doesn't want you here," James replied. "This is not appropriate."

"Too bad for him."

"This is not where someone of your station should be," James repeated.

"I'm staying here," Freddie replied. "I did everything you asked to make it safe enough. My brother should be thrilled. I can't get into trouble here. I'm out of his hair, just like he wanted."

"It is safe, but it's not proper," the other man replied. "Do you really want to be out here? In the middle of nowhere? Your suite at the Ritz is waiting for you. It's far more comfortable there."

"Then you can go enjoy it," Freddie replied. "I've made my decision. I'm not leaving."

"You are expected at the conference," James said, his voice growing harder. "Your brother has called me three times to make sure you are aware of your duties. He is afraid the press might find you. They are looking."

"I am very aware of my duties," Freddie replied coldly. "Officially, I don't have to be there for another day and a half. The press can find me then."

"Please, reconsider this, sir."

"No." Freddie's voice was firm. "I'm staying here until I have to leave. That's final. You can tell my brother that. I'll do what he wants, just not right now. I still have a day of freedom left, and I won't let him take it from me."

There was a beat of silence, but the big man sighed. "Yes, sir. Do you need anything?"

"No. That will be all, James," Freddie replied. He sounded so formal and cold. I barely recognized him.

But then, I wasn't sure I ever really knew him.

There was still a lot I didn't know about Freddie despite our conversations. It appeared he had more money than I suspected, especially if he had a suite waiting at the Ritz. And why in the world was his brother worried about the press? Why was it inappropriate for Freddie to be here? And who was James exactly? He was definitely more than just a friend or a worried roommate.

Who was Freddie, and what had I gotten myself into?

Suddenly, not asking any questions about his business seemed like a colossal mistake on my part. What did I actually know about this man? Just because he had told me about his family and his dreams didn't mean I knew who he was. He had told me about parts of his life, but it felt like he had also left out a lot of important details. Cold dread at what he wasn't telling me started to settle in the pit of my stomach. I didn't want to think about what I didn't know and how it could end up hurting me.

I left the bathroom and returned to the living room, trying not to panic.

Freddie closed the front door. He turned the lock, making the old wooden door creak. I couldn't remember the last time the door had ever been locked. It simply wasn't something we'd ever needed to do. No one locked their doors around here.

"I did forget to answer my phone. My brother called him all worried." Freddie shook his head and smiled. The formal tone was gone entirely, and the Freddie I knew was back. "My brother's a little overprotective."

"Everything okay?" I asked, heading for the couch.

"Of course." Freddie shrugged. "Why wouldn't it be?"

"No real reason," I replied slowly, pausing in the middle of the room. I didn't know what to say. How did I start this conversation? How was I supposed to tell him that I wanted to know who he was and what he was hiding from me? How did I ask him all of that without accusing him of lying to me?

I wanted to know, but at the same time, I really didn't. I liked the Freddie I knew.

Freddie sighed and ran a hand through his hair. He glanced over at the bathroom door, doing the mental geography of where I'd just been in relation to him. "You could hear us, couldn't you?"

"Just a little. The window was open. I didn't mean to eavesdrop," I admitted. I bit my lower lip. "James is more than just your friend, isn't he?"

Freddie sat on the edge of the couch, his shoulders drooping. "Yes."

"Is there something I should know?" I asked. I took a seat next to him. "I mean, I probably should have asked earlier, but... what do I need to know about you?"

Freddie looked at his hands, and he picked at his thumbnail. He risked a glance in my direction. "What do you know about me?"

"That you played rugby with Carlson in Paradisa," I replied. "That you are definitely wealthy. That James is probably an employee, rather than a roommate."

I paused, unsure of where to go next with this.

"And?" Freddie continued to fiddle with his fingernail, no longer looking at me.

"That I really like you." I smiled when he looked up at me. "And I'm really hoping you're not a drug lord or the son of a mafia boss."

Freddie chuckled. "Do you think Carlson would invite me to family brunch if I were a drug lord?"

"Maybe you're a *nice* drug lord." I shrugged. "It would make the face tattoo easier to decide on."

He smiled, but it was slow and kind of sad. At least it was a smile.

"I'm not a drug lord." He lowered his hands to his thighs. "To be honest, I'm not really anything special."

"Most not-special people don't have giant scary men telling them to stay safe," I replied. "Most people don't ever mention worries about the press finding them."

"True." He sighed. "James is a bodyguard. My family is very wealthy."

"Because you're drug lords?" I teased, hoping to make him smile again.

His shoulders lost a little bit of the tension in them as he shook his head. "You're not going to give that up, are you?"

I shook my head, smiling.

He took a deep breath. "To be honest, I'm kind of surprised you don't know who I am."

"I've been so busy with work and school that you could have been in the biggest blockbuster movie this year, and I wouldn't recognize you," I explained. "So, are you famous?"

"A bit."

I studied him, trying to figure out where I might know

him from. He was undoubtedly handsome, and he carried himself with confidence, but he had shied away from the cameras at the wedding. What kind of movie star didn't want their photo taken?

"You really don't know, do you?" He stared at me, wonder in his eyes.

I shook my head.

"I can't tell you how refreshing that is. How nice it is not having to be the third son. Of getting to be just me." He swallowed hard. "No one ever sees me as just Freddie. Except you."

"So, who are you, Freddie?" I asked, my voice soft.

He reached out and touched my cheek.

"My name is Frederick Archibald Charles Aster, Duke of Fernbook, Earl of Peming and Baron Highguard." He took a breath. "Prince of Paradisia."

My eyes went wide. My jaw fell open.

"What?" I gasped.

"It's a mouthful, I know," he said quickly. "But basically, I am second in line for the throne. My older brother, Liam, is the king of Paradisa. Henry is next in line, and then me. I'll drop quickly down the line of succession once they have children."

I stared at him, mouth open.

He tried to smile but failed. He ran his hand through his hair again, making it stick up in all directions. It wasn't precisely a princely look.

"I'm sorry I didn't say anything," he said, looking down at his hands again. "It's just that I don't ever get to be just Freddie. People recognize me, and they expect Prince Frederick. They expect me to be everything they've read in the papers."

He looked over at me, his green eyes afraid and hopeful at the same time.

"But you..." He smiled for real this time, his eyes darting around my face. "You didn't expect anything of me. You didn't already know every bad thing I've done or every mistake I've ever made. I didn't have to be a prince for you."

I closed my mouth. I didn't have any words to say. I was still in shock.

He was a prince.

Small pieces of our conversations fell into place. His brother being a ruler. The family business was actually running Paradisa. He wasn't a secret agent with a security clearance. He was the prince. He was who the secret agents worked for.

"Why didn't you tell me?" I asked, finally finding my voice.

"Because I was afraid of this moment. I was afraid that you would suddenly see a prince and not see Freddie anymore." His voice cracked, but he kept going. "I meant to tell you. Every day I wanted to. And then, you'd smile and say we should go do something. It was always some-thing that princes never get to do. Eat pizza in front of the tv. Use those terrible kayaks. Cook hot dogs. Swim in a public lake. Watch movies with absolutely no awards. And every time, I didn't want to ruin it."

I thought about it for a moment. If I had known Freddie was a royal, I would never have knocked him out of his kayak. I would have insisted we eat nicer food. I certainly wouldn't be wearing the ratty pajamas I had on right now.

"I didn't tell you not because I didn't want you to

know." He reached over and took my hands in his. "I didn't tell you because I am selfish and terrible. I didn't tell you because I wanted you all to myself. To Freddie. I didn't want you to meet Prince Frederick."

I closed my eyes, wishing that I could just freeze the world for a moment. I wished I had the power to give myself a moment to think. I needed more than a moment. I needed an hour or a day.

But when I opened my eyes and looked into Freddie's green ones, I didn't need more time.

"I like you, Freddie," I admitted. "I *really* like you. And this week has been one of the best weeks of my life. But..."

He swallowed hard and took a deep breath, steeling himself. "But?"

"But..." I sighed. "It's kind of a bombshell. It changes things."

He sagged. "I understand if you want me to leave."

"No, no, I don't," I said, reaching for him. "I just, it changes all the plans I had for next week."

His head rose, his eyes opening wide with hope as he looked at me. "Next week?"

"Well, I was planning on seeing if you wanted to get dinner or something with me next weekend," I replied. "I thought I'd find some seedy pizza place and get authentic Chicago pizza, but I'm now rethinking that idea."

"No, it's a great idea," he assured me. "I love seedy pizza."

I imagined a cheese pizza covered in pumpkin seeds and chuckled.

"I do have some questions, though," I said. "Actually, a lot of questions."

"I will answer anything. Anything you want," he told me earnestly.

"Do I have to call you 'your highness' or anything like that?"

He shook his head. "Not unless we're in public. And even then, I don't care. My family might, though.."

I nodded. "Okay."

"Next question?" he asked after a moment.

"I forgot all my questions," I replied with a laugh. "I'm still coming to terms with the fact that you're a prince."

"You'll get used to it," he promised. "I did, at least."

"What happens next?" As soon as the words left my mouth, I regretted them. I didn't really want to think about what came next. "Do I get to see you again?"

I knew that dating a prince had to have some serious downsides. It would be like dating someone famous. I'd had a friend that dated an actor for a few years. She'd hated it because they couldn't go anywhere. There were always fans harassing him for autographs or trying to pitch the next big movie.

They'd broken up because of it.

I could only imagine that being a prince was that and more.

Freddie took a deep breath. His hands wrapped mine in warmth and strength.

"What happens next is up to you," he said slowly. His naturally joking face was serious. "I'll be in Chicago for the next three months. I'd like to see you, but I totally understand if being with a prince isn't something you're interested in."

The idea of not seeing him hurt more than I expected.

There was no way that I could just say goodbye after this week.

"I want to see you again," I told him, loving the smile that flickered quickly across his face before he grew serious again.

"Here's the complicated part of that decision," he replied. "We have to keep it quiet."

I frowned, not understanding. "Do you not want people to know about us?"

"I would happily scream it from the rooftops that I'm dating you and feel like a king for it," he assured me. "But if I do that, if we are seen together publicly, the paparazzi will follow you. My family will expect things from you. There will be a spotlight on you. I won't ask that of you."

I hated the spotlight. I thought of having everyone watch us enter a restaurant and whisper that the prince was dating some random midwest girl.

I could just imagine my aunt bragging about me dating a prince for the rest of my days at every family function. That everyone would say that they knew me.

And that was terrifying.

"Okay. We keep it quiet."

His grip on my hands tightened. "So, that's a yes? You'll see me again?"

He was so nervous as he looked at me. A prince afraid that a commoner would say no.

"Are you sure you want to go out with *me*?" I asked. "A boring, common, unrefined, American girl?"

His smile flickered to life again. "Very much. Those qualities are part of what I find so alluring about you."

"You mean not my smile or wit?" I teased.

"I like it all," he replied. "Everything."

My heart trembled. My whole body trembled. No one had ever liked everything about me.

I leaned forward and kissed him, closing my eyes and memorizing the softness of his lips and the sweetness of his mouth. He kissed me back, his hand going gently to my hair to keep me pressed to him.

"Then, yes. I would very much like to see you again," I told him with a smile when we pulled apart.

He beamed at me, his whole face bright with pure joy. "I can't tell you how happy that makes me."

I kissed him again just as the clock in the hallway chimed eleven.

TWO MONTHS LATER, LATE AUGUST

"Hey James," I said, walking up to the hotel room.

"Did you bring it?" the large man asked, eyeing the shopping bag by my side.

"Have I ever let you down?" I handed him the bag.

He glanced around the empty hallway, as if we might be caught. Cautiously, he reached inside the bag and pulled out a flimsy plastic container. He giggled like a school boy. The sound coming out of such a big, imposing man was very strange and heartwarming at the same time.

"I love these things," he said, opening the container lid and pulling out the pasty. "Dutch letters are my weakness."

"Why do you think I bring them?" I teased. "How else would someone like me get time with the Prince of Paradisa?"

James didn't say anything as he stuffed a bite of pastry into his mouth. He stepped to the side of the door so that I could knock.

Freddie appeared in an instant. He kissed me, and for a moment I lost myself in him. His soft citrus scent filled my nose. He needed to shave, but I didn't care. I rather liked the little bit of stubble on his cheeks.

"Did you bribe him with baked goods again?" he asked, glancing over at James.

"Who, me?" I asked, doing my best to sound innocent.

James had sugar on his cheek. I motioned to him, making a wiping motion on my own cheek. If he wasn't more careful, he was going to give us away.

Freddie just shook his head and let me in, leaving James to enjoy his baked goods in the hallway. He'd follow us if we went anywhere. I'd learned he liked baked goods and had worked my way into his good graces using sugar and flour. Dutch letters made at a local bakery were his current favorite.

"Let me know when you leave," he mumbled around a mouthful of sugared dough.

I wasn't sure what Freddie and I were going to do this weekend. Most weekends, we ended up ordering food to his hotel room and staying in. Every once in a while, we were able to put a hat and sunglasses on him and go to an event. We managed to go to an entire baseball game without anyone guessing his true identity.

Other times, we weren't so lucky. Our first attempt at a fancy restaurant had us running out a backdoor without ordering a single thing. People tended to pull out their cameras if they thought they recognized the Paradisian prince.

It felt a little like dating Batman. We could only go out at night or in disguise.

I didn't mind, though. Freddie made me laugh. We loved our time cuddled up in his massive hotel room watching old kung fu movies and eating Chinese food straight from the containers. I didn't need to go out and do things. With Freddie, we could stay in and have an amazing time.

I liked it best when it was just Freddie and me. Just us without the world looking in.

I wondered if this weekend, we might try to see some of the live music. The weather was cool enough now that we could wear a hat and glasses without looking too conspicuous. I'd seen there was a band Freddie liked playing at one of the live music locations. I was hoping to surprise him with it.

He hadn't told me about the band. Like any sane person, I'd looked Freddie up on Wikipedia the moment I had decent internet. He'd told me to do as much. He wanted me to know what I was getting into.

I'd discovered that he'd dated a lot of beautiful women. I tried to feel honored rather than intimidated that he'd been with ballerinas, actresses, models, and even a professional mime. Freddie said that one was meant to be a joke, but she was actually a lot of fun to be around. The relationships had never lasted very long, but everyone seemed to love following them.

There were so many tabloids with articles about Freddie. According to one, he was actually the result of an affair with a bodyguard, while another claimed Freddie was actually the true heir to the throne because he'd been born on a Tuesday.

It was crazy. Freddie had patiently answered any and all my questions. Most of the stories about him weren't nearly as exciting as the newspapers made them seem. He was really just a regular guy that enjoyed going out to pubs and the occasional prank.

However, it did open my eyes to the level of scrutiny he was constantly under. He had an extra beer at the pub one night and the tabloids called him "Alcoholic Freddie" for two months. He once said he liked curly fries better than straight ones and they accused him of being gay. Any female photographed with him was immediately subject to scrutiny.

That made me glad we'd decided to stay quiet.

We made no promises to one another. We knew that we wouldn't be able to keep them.

I didn't tell him just how happy he made me because the longer it went on, the more I knew it couldn't last.

The weight of his title hung over us. He was a prince. I was not a princess or anything close to one. His family expected things that I couldn't deliver. I was just an average girl from Wisconsin.

We both felt the ticking of time.

We both knew the end was coming and we both pretended it wasn't happening. Maybe if we pretended hard enough, Fate would intervene. Maybe Freddie could just stay at the conference forever. Or there would be a new conference. Maybe we could just freeze time and stay in this hotel room forever.

I crossed the room and flopped onto the big leather sofa in front of a giant TV.

Freddie's hotel room was more of an apartment than a room. He had a beautiful living space with a couch, TV, and bar. There was a dining area with a table big enough to seat my entire family for Thanksgiving with room to spare.

Then there was the giant bedroom with the most amazing shower I'd ever seen. We'd spent many wonderful afternoons in that shower.

"How's the conference going?" I asked, relaxing into the leather. It had been a long week at the hospital.

"Good," Freddie replied. He sat next to me and put his arm over my shoulder. "Actually, really good."

I raised my eyebrows. He was never this excited about work. "Do you want to tell me?"

He didn't usually talk about work more than just a "Good" or "Fine" but I always asked because I cared. He listened to me talk about my work, so it was the least I could do to ask about his.

He grinned at me. "A friend just arrived today. I met him years ago when we were in secondary school. He's the Crown Prince of Navia. It's been great to see him again."

"That's cool," I said. "And definitely makes the conference better for you."

I smiled at him, glad he had a good day. And then I realized that we were discussing the Crown Prince of a foreign country like an old high school friend.

"What's really interesting is that he wants to broker a trade agreement with me. Or rather, with Paradisa," Freddie continued. His smile didn't fade and he practically vibrated with excitement.

"Very cool," I told him. I loved that he looked excited. "Isn't Navia known for some cool new technologies?"

I didn't know much about the country. Just that it was

located somewhere near Sweden and everyone wore cool sweaters.

Freddie nodded. "And since Paradisa has the largest known lithium mine, it could be a very profitable agreement. For both countries. It could be an amazing alliance."

I didn't really understand politics or governments, but Freddie was excited about this. He was more excited than I'd seen him in a while. I'd signed a non-disclosure agreement the day we'd left the cabin, so he often told me about his work. Today was the first day he seemed enthusiastic about it.

"I'm sure you'll do great," I told him.

"That's where it gets tricky," he admitted. "Officially, the nations of Paradisa and Navia have a rocky history. Think England and France. China and Japan. The US and everyone else."

"Ha ha." I smacked his shoulder. "But I thought things were good between most places. I mean, there haven't been any big wars with Paradisa since WWII. And Paradisa and Navia were on the same side."

"That doesn't mean we're friendly," he admitted. "But it's a PR nightmare.." He let out a breath and shook his head. "It's just going to require some finesse."

"You said that this Navia prince is your friend, though, right?" I shrugged. "So it shouldn't be that bad."

He chuckled and kissed my temple. "I like your optimism."

"And here I thought you just wanted me for my body," I said with a grin.

"That too," he assured me. "A trade negotiation with Navia would be amazing for my country. It would be an accomplishment they'd talk about for years. And it's something I can actually do."

The fact that he didn't switch the subject to what he wanted to do to my body told me he was very serious about this. This was important to him.

I thought about all our conversations at the cabin. About how he felt like third best in his family. How he wanted to do right by his country but never seemed to be able to measure up.

"So this would be your big chance?" I asked. "To do something great for Paradisa?"

He nodded. "It could be."

"So do it," I told him. "Make your mark."

He stared at me. "Just like that?"

"Just like that," I told him. "I believe in you. You can do it. You can do this trade thing."

The smile that filled his face was heartbreakingly beautiful. He put his hand to my cheeks and kissed me.

"Why do you believe in me so easily?" he whispered, pressing his forehead to mine.

"Because you're easy to believe in," I replied. "And I've seen you negotiate. I almost feel sorry for the flea market people."

He chuckled and settled back onto the couch. It felt so good to just sit with him. Like we belonged like this.

"This negotiation would be a little more complicated," he explained. "And I have to convince the people of Paradisa that this is the right move. They don't really trust me, given my history of pranks and such."

"But both countries will make money right?" I shrugged. "Then I'm sure everyone will be for it."

"You're such an American." He shook his head at me and rolled his eyes with a smile.

"But I'm cute. And I'm right." I grinned at him. "Money talks."

"It'll take a lot of image work. There's a lot of pieces that need to fall into place. And I have to make some calls. I have to see what the Duke of Wheaton thinks, but..." He looked over at me, excitement bright in his eyes. "I actually think I can pull it off."

"I think you can too," I told him. My good thoughts faded a little. "Wait... when would this happen?"

"Not for a little while," he said with a shrug. "Anders and I just came up with the idea today. It still needs work and approval. Even then, I'll have months of work just to prepare for everything."

The worry faded. We still had time. I knew he would have to go back to his royal life eventually. I just didn't want it to be now.

I wanted every second I had left with him.

"Whew. I thought for a moment you might be ditching me for a prince."

"Never," he promised. He kissed my forehead. "I'll never abandon you for a prince. Even one as good looking as Anders."

I went still, his words echoing in my ears. He never made promises like that. Neither of us did. We both knew this relationship was temporary.

He was a Prince. And I was a Midwestern girl with no claim to royalty.

There was no future for us. We both knew it, but we didn't say anything. We didn't want to say anything. If we stayed quiet, then we could stay happy.

It was the reason we didn't say "I love you."

If we said those words, we had to follow them up. Those words meant something. And while I most definitely did love him, I knew I was going to have to give him up eventually.

Eventually the conference would end. Eventually he would have to go back to Paradisa. I didn't have a place there. That would be it for us.

So we didn't say those words. We only felt them and pretended that it didn't matter.

He blushed, realizing how close he had come to saying something, and stood up.

"So, what do you want for dinner?" he asked, changing the subject.

"Hamburgers?" I offered.

"Are you going to ask for extra ketchup?" he asked, making a disgusted face.

"Ketchup is nectar of the gods," I reminded him. "And you don't have to eat it."

"No, I just have to kiss you and taste it." He made a gagging motion.

I stuck my tongue out at him. "You just can't admit that it's amazing and that's okay. We all have issues."

He laughed. "How about we compromise and get tacos?"

"From that place down the street?" My eyes lit up. They were real authentic tacos and my favorite.

He nodded. "You've gotten me addicted. I don't know what I'll do when I have to go back to Paradisa. We don't have any good Mexican food there."

A pang went through my chest as we both paused.

"I bet I can eat more than you," I said, breaking the tense moment.

"Such an American." He grinned at me. "I love a good challenge."

I grinned and we grabbed his hat and glasses to go grab one more batch of tacos.

CHAPTER 19

A FEW WEEKS LATER, MID SEPTEMBER

"And I already gave Jones his PRN pain medicine," I told the night shift nurse. "And that's it. Oh, and watch out for the guy in room 402. He's a little handsy and likes to put on his call light."

"Thanks for the heads-up," Susan replied, making a mark in her notes. "Anything else to report?"

I thought for a moment, and then shook my head.

"You're getting good at this," Susan told me. "I remember the first time you gave me a report. It was not this easy."

I laughed, remembering my first few days as a new-grad nurse. Despite being on the same floor I'd worked on as a CNA, it had been a whole new world for me. But three months of practice and I finally felt comfortable.

"You're doing great," Susan continued. She glanced around the room at the other nurses receiving a report for the change of shift. "I'm always glad when I get your patients. I'll take a report from you any time."

The compliment had me beaming. "Thanks."

She grinned. "So, what are you up to this weekend? It's your weekend off, right?"

I nodded. "Chicago."

"Again?" Susan narrowed her eyes at me. "When are you going to bring that boyfriend of yours around? I want to meet this guy."

I hesitated. I was probably never going to bring Freddie to the hospital.

It wasn't that I didn't want to show him off. I did. I wanted to show everyone at work my sweet, sophisticated, smart, and amazing boyfriend. I wanted to show them all the man who I looked forward to seeing every chance I had. The one that I talked on the phone for hours to. The one that made me so happy I felt like I was in a fairy tale. But I wasn't going to get to keep him. I wasn't a princess in a fairy tale. He didn't belong in my world and I couldn't bring him here without gossip and stares.

"I promise I'll bring him around eventually," I hedged. "I just have to drag him here from Chicago."

Susan evaluated me for a moment, then shrugged. "Well, have fun in the big city. I'll see you Monday?"

I nodded. "That's the plan."

We said goodbye and I did one last check to make sure I had all my nursing assignments complete. It had been a quiet day, so I had actually managed to finish my charting on time. It was basically a miracle and I wasn't about to waste it. I was off to see my boyfriend.

I waved to the nurses at the nursing station and headed out to the hospital parking lot.

I was almost off my floor when my phone buzzed.

Where are you?

I grinned. Freddie.

At the hospital. On my way.

I made it off the elevator when he replied.

The hospital??? OMG. ARE YOU OKAY?

I rolled my eyes.

Totally fine. Just finishing up my shift.

I know.. I just never get tired of the joke.

I chuckled to myself as I walked out from the hospital to employee parking. The sun was long gone and the security lamps threw long shadows. Halloween was coming and crisp fall air reminded me that winter wouldn't be too far behind it.

I liked to park at the very back of the parking lot. Since it was well lit and patrolled often by security, I felt safe parking there. My favorite spot was directly under one of the security lights which made it easier for me to find my way on dark evenings.

Tonight, a big, dark, SUV sat next to my car.

I slowed, pulling out my keys and glancing around. Several other nurses were walking to their cars, but I still considered calling for security. That was until the driver's window rolled down and I saw Freddie's grinning face.

Then I ran to his car.

"Freddie!" I shouted, laughing as he got out of the car to embrace me. He kissed me in greeting, and for a good minute I felt totally happy. "What are you doing here?"

"You were at the hospital," he explained, forcing a serious expression. "I had to make sure you were okay."

I shook my head at his terrible joke, grinning at him.

"No, really. Why are you here? I thought we were supposed to meet in Chicago?" I asked.

The joy faded from his smile.His eyes went serious and suddenly the autumn wind felt much too cold.

"I'm being called home," he said simply. "The conference is over and my brother wants me back in Paradisa. The trade negotiations have been approved. We start work on them immediately. The Navia delegation arrives in one month."

I stumbled back a step as if physically hit. I knew this day was coming. I'd known that Freddie would only be in the States for three months, but it had come so fast. Him leaving had always felt so far away. We still had another weekend. We were supposed to have more time.

I had more adventures planned. I had so many adventures planned.

And he was leaving. Paradisa was too far for weekend adventures. I didn't have the money to hop on a transatlantic flight every other weekend and I had a feeling that Freddie's brother wouldn't be keen on the idea of him coming here.

Something like despair crept around my shoulders like a dark shawl.

"I want you to come with me," he said.

I stared at Freddie for a moment, hearing the words but not understanding them. I shook my head, trying to shed the shawl of despair and millions of thoughts suddenly flying through my head.

"I want you to come with me," Freddie repeated. "I want you to be officially mine. And my family wants to meet you. Especially my mum."

He smiled nervously. That's when I noticed he was dressed nicer than usual. He wore a suit today in soft gray. He looked regal and handsome.

And hard to say no to.

"Wait, your mom wants to meet me?" I stammered. "The Queen of Paradisa wants to meet *me*?"

He chuckled. "I have told her about you," he admitted. "And it's Queen Mother since Liam is the king."

"Me, though?" I let out a shocked breath. "Why in the world would the queen want to meet me?"

"Probably because you're my girlfriend," Freddie replied, his tone light. "And probably because no one makes me feel the way you do."

"I guess it is rather normal for a mom to want to meet her son's girlfriend," I said after a moment. "But what if she hates me?"

"She won't," Freddie assured me, taking my hands. "She won't hate you because she loves me. And I love you."

It took me three heartbeats for the words to process. To realize what he'd just said. I could feel my eyes go big and my mouth open like a surprised fish.

Freddie grinned like he'd just told an amazing joke. "Yes, Zoey Miller. I love you," he repeated, full of confidence and surety. "And I'd like to introduce you to my family. I think it's time."

I blinked slowly. He'd said it. It was real now.

Our future was a real possibility.

For most people, meeting their significant other's parents is a big deal. This was bigger than just a big deal. This was meeting the King, Queen, and Prince of Paradisa. This was meeting the parents on steroids.

"Do you think I'm ready?" I asked weakly. "You've taught me some of the rules and protocol, but..." I thought I might hyperventilate. "I don't want to embarrass you. I don't know how to curtsy or which fork I'm actually supposed to use."

Not to mention, I couldn't walk in heels. Princes went

to balls. I couldn't even keep the right shoes on for a wedding.

"I can teach you the curtsy in the airplane," Freddie replied. "And I'll sit next to you at dinner and you can just copy which fork I use. I'll make sure you're doing everything right. Besides, my friend the Duke says you'll be fine."

My hands were shaking and I was glad he had hold of them. I felt better with him holding me.

"Do you think your royal family will be okay with you dating someone like me?" I asked, looking down at my scrubs. I looked so out of place next to him in his beautiful suit. "I'm not exactly princess material."

He took my chin between his thumb and forefinger, gently tilting my head up to meet his eyes. He smiled, his eyes so warm that I stopped mid-shiver.

"My family is going to love you," he assured me.

"Even though I have no idea what I'm doing?"

He smiled. "We already managed to teach one Yankee. I'm sure we can do it again," he told me, referencing his brother's wife. She too was American and was now a princess.

I stayed quiet about the fact that Ava was a senator's daughter. She'd already known proper fork usage and could probably walk in heels. She was from DC. She was used to big cities and powerful people.

I was from a tiny town in the midwest. I liked cheese and beer and being outside. I could fish and hunt, but I had no idea how to curtsy or write a treaty. I wasn't sure if I was capable of being royalty. But I didn't say anything. Freddie was staring at me with so much hope and excitement in his eyes that I didn't want to contradict him.

Maybe I could be a princess. Maybe I could learn.

"You really want me to meet your family?" I asked again, still not sure I'd heard him right the first two times.

"Yes. And I'd like to formally, and publicly, date you." He raised his eyebrows in a hopeful smile.

"Oh. So we're not only going to tell your mom, but your country too?" Suddenly, the curtsy felt like the least of my worries.

"I want everyone to see how amazing you are," Freddie explained. "I don't want these clandestine meetings and secret rendezvous, no matter how much fun they are. I want them all to know that you're with me. I want to show the world how wonderful you are and that I love you."

A primal part deep in my chest approved of being claimed. He wanted to show me off, which meant he was proud of me. He wanted everyone to know that I was his.

"You love me?" I repeated.

"I wondered when you were going to come back to that part," he said with a grin. "I think I've sprung too much on you all at once."

I just stared at him, amazed that someone like him could love someone like me. He was so gorgeous and smart and funny. He made me laugh until I cried and I never wanted to be away from him for more than a few minutes.

The idea that he loved me was so marvelous, I couldn't find words.

"I love you more than I thought possible," Freddie said, smiling as he squeezed my hands. "I love the way you think. I love the way you smile. I love your laugh and that you tolerate, and sometimes even appreciate, my humor."

I nodded, still unable to speak.

"I don't want to go back to my life without you. I hated my life in Paradisa because it wasn't my own, but if you're with me, it'll be heaven." He smiled nervously, gripping my hands just a little bit tighter. "I don't dread going back there if you're coming with me."

"But you love me?" I stammered, trying to process and remember every beautiful word he was saying.

He grinned. "Yes. I love you."

"Good. Because I love you, too."

The smile that filled his face was the most beautiful thing I'd ever seen in my entire life. There were no sunsets, no waterfalls, no beaches, no art that was anywhere as beautiful as Freddie's smile.

"And I'll go with you," I decided.

Freddie's eyes lit up like a kid getting a puppy for Christmas.

"Really?" he asked. "Because I have more speech to convince you. I have flowers in the car, and a special restaurant and--"

I kissed him just to make him stop talking.

"You already convinced me," I told him, whispering the words with a smile. "Because I love you."

CHAPTER 20

I hesitated, plane ticket in my hand, staring down the passenger boarding ramp of an airplane.

It wasn't that I wasn't excited. It wasn't that nerves had finally gotten the best of me.

It was that I wasn't sure this was real.

The flight attendant at the gate smiled and scanned my ticket. She didn't call security on me or ask to see some identification. She didn't ask Freddie to show ID or to take a selfie. She just smiled and motioned us forward as if this were totally normal.

As if getting on a plane with a prince was totally normal.

Granted, Freddie was traveling under his alias, Fred Prescott. He wore dark sunglasses, a baseball cap, and an oversized sweatshirt that hid his identifiable features. I wore something similar, but mine was for comfort, not for disguise.

Freddie squeezed my hand as we walked down the

ramp and to the plane. We found our seats, which were more like private couches than seats. Not to mention the fact that our two seats were able to completely seal off from the rest of the plane. It was like having a tiny private room.

"Window or wall?" Freddie asked, pointing to the two "Chairs" in our first-class "Room."

"My ticket says aisle," I replied, looking down at the piece of paper in my hand.

"Take the window," Freddie said, giving me a gentle push. "That way you can see Paradisa from the air."

"Are you sure?"

"I've seen it before," he replied with a shrug. "It's not nearly as exciting for me."

I took the window seat, grinning like an idiot as I peered out the window. All I could see was the lit up tarmac with various luggage carts and blinking lights, but for a moment, I imagined the dark green coast of Paradisa like I'd seen in all the pictures.

I swallowed hard, trying to keep my excitement in check. I still had a nearly eight hour flight to wait.

I played with everything. My chair had the ability to turn into an actual bed. I had a TV with new movies on it. The flight attendant brought me freshly baked cookies. There were actual blankets and pillows. I even had slip-pers and an eye mask with a lavender scent.

It felt luxurious. I'd never left the States. I'd only flown economy. This was lots of new all at once. But we were all alone in a dark room. The engines hummed and the lights were low. The flight attendant had left us now that we were airborne.

"Do you think she's coming back soon?" I asked Freddie, trying to keep my voice low and seductive. I put my hand on his thigh and licked my lips.

Freddie's jaw tightened. "Yes. They have a tendency to show up at the most inopportune times," he replied. "We can't."

"Oh." I tried to keep the disappointment off my face as I pulled my hand away.

He sighed. "It's not that I'm not interested," he explained. "It's that I am now the Prince again. I have to maintain decorum. I can't be caught snogging on a plane. It'd be in the papers before we even landed."

"But nobody knows it's you," I replied. I could hear the pout in my voice, even though I was really trying to keep it in check.

"The pilot knows. I suspect a flight attendant or two do as well." He grimaced. "I still have to behave myself. I don't want the tabloids hearing about you like that. I want to introduce you to my family with no bad press hanging over your head. We have to make a good first impression."

I imagined meeting his mother with the news that we'd been caught canoodling on the plane. That would definitely be awkward and not a good way to meet a queen.

"Okay." This time, there was no pout in my voice. "I'll behave."

Freddie grinned at me. He leaned over and kissed my cheek. "Don't worry, though. I'll make it up to you."

I matched his smile. "I look forward to it."

For a moment, Freddie looked like he might change his mind. That he might kiss me more than just on the cheek. But then he shook his head, his shoulders sagging slightly.

"Try and get some rest," Freddie advised, turning his chair into a bed. He flashed me a quick grin, and pulled the mask low over his face. I watched him for a moment before turning back to my own chair.

I turned it into a bed and pulled the mask down over my eyes. I tucked the blanket up around my chin and fluffed my pillows until I was comfortable.

We would arrive in Paradisa at ten in the morning Paradisian time once we'd crossed the entire Atlantic Ocean. Theoretically, sleeping now would minimize jet-lag. I tried to take nice, deep, even breaths, but my mind was going faster than the plane.

I'd quit my dream job to get on this plane.

Well, it wasn't my *dream* job, but it was a job that I had dreamed of and worked really hard to get. I liked my job. I had liked my boss and my coworkers, but there was no way I could take two weeks off. And that's if this trip only lasted two weeks. There was a very good chance that I'd be staying in Paradisa longer than that.

My roommate was excited that she'd have the apartment to herself for a while. I had more than enough to cover a couple months rent. My parents were holding onto my car for me.

It was actually rather frightening how easily I was able to escape my life. I was able to run to Paradisa in under a weekend. I'd just put everything on pause.

I'd packed my best clothes and even borrowed a couple of nicer things from Cecilia. I'd told her I was meeting Freddie's parents and she'd practically foisted her closet on me. Unfortunately, not much fix, but there were at least a couple of items that weren't thrift store purchases now in my suitcase. I wasn't quite at "Meet the queen" fashion ready, but at least I wasn't at "Embarrassing poor Midwest" either.

I had no idea what my future was going to be at this point.

And that terrified and excited me.

I lifted my mask and peeked over at him. He was passed out, snoring softly. I envied him. He was going home. He knew what was coming, and I was mostly not ready.

I put my mask back down and tried to go over the frantic lessons the past two days. How to curtsy. How to speak to the queen. How to dress. How to eat politely.

There were so many rules.

It felt like trying to learn a foreign language without anyone to practice on. I had the lessons, but no experience. I'd always thought I had nice manners. My mother prided herself on the fact that I never put my elbows on the table, used ma'am/sir, and always said please and thank you.

Yet, that wasn't going to be enough. I had to be more.

Meeting a partner's family was stressful. Meeting a royal family was stress on steroids.

I wanted Freddie's family to like me. I wanted to make Freddie proud. I knew it mattered to him. He pretended that what his family's traditions and rules didn't matter, but the fact he upheld them showed that wasn't true. He didn't like them, but they were important to him.

Not to mention there was a lot riding on this. Freddie was going back to Paradisa to start brokering the trade agreement between Paradisa and Navia. The next month would be critical for not only drafting the deal, but also gaining and bolstering enthusiasm from the Paradisian people. It was going to take a lot of effort. I needed to support him.

I took a deep breath and tried to remember the rules for addressing the queen. If I couldn't sleep, the least I could do would be to prepare. Freddie had taught me as much as he could, but I needed real world practice. Thankfully, Freddie assured me that his friend the Duke would help me and that it wouldn't be too hard.

I was going to make Freddie proud.

No one was at the airport to greet us.

Well, there was a chauffeur and a car, but none of Freddie's family or friends.

We changed into nicer clothes in a private bathroom. I wore the suit I usually wore for job interviews- black dress slacks with a matching blazer and a conservative dark blue silk blouse. I'd managed to get two jobs wearing it, so I figured it was good luck.

Freddie changed into a suit that had me feeling self conscious. His dark gray suit was impeccable. Mine suddenly felt a little threadbare. My slacks were slightly worn on the hems. The style was obviously dated. I fiddled nervously with a loose button on the cuff of my jacket I'd never noticed before.

"You look great," Freddie assured me, but I didn't believe him. It sounded more like he was trying to convince himself more than me.

I reached for his hand. He gave me one quick squeeze before pulling away.

"We can't remember?" he said softly. "My mother has to accept you into the family before we can be seen together as more than just friends."

I sighed. We'd gone over this.

The oldest royal of the family had to approve of everyone. Royals often started dating before official approval, but it was always kept very quiet. If a couple wanted to be able to go out in public, they had to do something called the "Stair Walk."

Basically, the Royal Family would invite the lucky man or woman to a party. At the end of the night, they would be invited to walk down the stairs with the Royal Family at the end of the party. It was symbolic of allowing someone into their home.

Every royal couple had done it. Even Henry and Aria. It was tradition.

As such, Freddie and I weren't allowed public displays of affection until I'd had my Stair Walk. Freddie assured me that it would happen quickly and that we could still be dating in private.

We followed the driver out to the car and still no one was there. No one was waiting in the car with hugs and smiles. It felt strange.

The last time my mother came home from a two week trip, we greeted her at the airport with signs and balloons. Heck, even the couple of times I picked up my cousin, I'd been excited to see her. There was no one here excited about us coming back.

"It's not you," Freddie explained as we settled into the back of the big black town car. "It's actually a good thing. They're not involving the press. You get to meet them on regular terms. If they'd shown up here, the whole place would be a circus."

"But no one?" I motioned to the giant empty backseat of the car.

"I promise, this is normal," he assured me.

I nodded. Just because it was different than my family didn't mean that it was bad. It probably was better to meet them in a quiet setting than at an airport.

There was so much to see as we drove to Freddie's home. Paradisa was a small island off the coast of Western Europe. In ancient times, they'd been explorers and known for their trading abilities. In recent history, they were known for advances in computer technologies and a recent discovery of massive lithium deposit. As such, the island country was prosperous.

Green trees and ancient buildings were the two things I noticed most. There were castles just chilling by the side of the road like regular buildings. Ancient castles older than my country sat easily next to buildings from this century.

It was beautiful.

With every mile closer to Freddie's home, he grew tenser. It had started on the plane, but his jokes were fewer and more forced. His posture went from casual to rigidly upright. He fidgeted.

Even his palms were sweaty. Although that could have been me. My palms were sweating buckets with nerves.

The car stopped and waited for two huge wrought iron gates to swing forward on silent hinges. Guards with very dangerous looking rifles eyed us carefully as we passed. I swallowed hard, but Freddie hardly noticed.

Gravel crunched softly beneath the tires as we drove to what I realized was a castle. A long winding road up to a freaking castle. There were parapets and gargoyles. Stained glass windows added color to the gray stone walls in addition to bright green vines. When the car stopped, I sat staring out the window, my jaw open and barely blinking.

"You coming?" Freddie asked, waiting for me to come out of the car.

I snapped my jaw shut and exited the car. The smell of recent rain, cut grass, fresh flowers, and old stone filled my nose. I breathed in deep, soaking it all in.

"We're staying here?" I gasped, still in awe.

"For a few days," Freddie replied with a shrug. "I don't want to overload you with protocol yet, and this is the most private house. We'll be able to get you up to speed on all the rules here."

"It's beautiful," I replied, still staring at the stone architecture. "I've never seen a castle before. Isn't there supposed to be a moat?"

"No moat," Freddie replied. "But we do keep a catapult on hand for invasions."

"Really?" I asked, almost believing him.

"Of course not. I forget you Americans don't have these," Freddie said, a smile flickering on his face for a moment. "It's just a castle. Nothing special."

"*Just* a castle," I repeated, shaking my head. "Even if it doesn't have a moat, or a catapult, I'm impressed. Do you really live here?"

"This is Remington Castle. It's the private residence of the Queen. The King lives at the Royal Palace of Breckshire." Freddie explained. "I don't live at either. Technically, I have Kanire Castle in Fernbook, but I prefer the flat in Westshire."

I stared at him for a moment. I had read about his landholdings and titles, but this was the first time that it hit me that he actually had them. He had a castle. And apparently a flat in the capital city.

"Well, I do hear the upkeep on a castle is atrocious," I finally replied. "And the resale is just terrible."

Freddie laughed, losing his tension for a moment.

"The heating and cooling is astronomical. The arrow slits just let all the cold air right out," he replied.

We walked up the giant stone steps to an oversized wooden door. Two guards stood in fancy wool uniforms of gray and green on either side. I half expected Freddie to reach up and use one of the massive knockers, but a smaller door cleverly hidden inside of the bigger one opened first.

Freddie led me in. A tall man in a black suit bowed as we entered.

"Your majesty," the man said, rising slowly. "It's wonderful to have you here again."

"Thank you, Mr. Irson," Freddie replied. "Are our rooms ready? I'd like to rest before dinner."

The man's face twitched slightly. "The Queen Mother has requested that you and Ms. Miller join her and the King for tea. Now."

I felt Freddie's entire body stiffen for just a fraction of a second.

"Of course," Freddie replied. He turned to me, green eyes serious. "Are you ready?"

I wanted to say "Not really." I wanted to tell him that I

hardly slept on the flight and I was so nervous I thought I might puke.

"You're going to do great," Freddie told me, leaning over and kissing my temple. "They will love you at least half as much as I do."

"Which I'm assuming will still be a lot?" I asked, smiling as I looked up at him.

He grinned. "More than a lot."

A little bit more confidence crept into my bones.

"Do I look okay?" I asked him.

He took a step back and evaluated me. He licked his thumb and brought it toward my cheek. I pushed him away with a laugh.

"Yes, you look beautiful," he said with a smile. He held out his hand and I took it.

I was shaking. He gave me three quick squeezes and he nodded to Mr. Irson.

We walked down lushly carpeted hallways filled with oil paintings. I assumed they were relatives of Freddie's. Some were in regal armor, others on thrones, and others in heroic poses. None of them were smiling. If anything, I felt like they were judging me as I walked past them.

As if this American girl were anything but unworthy of a Prince of Paradisa.

Mr. Irson brought us to an ornately gilded wooden door. He knocked twice before entering.

"Prince Frederick and Ms. Miller," Mr. Irson announced in a booming voice as he stepped to the side of the room to let us enter.

I'd heard of sitting rooms. I'd heard of parlors. This was the first time I'd ever actually been in anything that fit the description. The big windows had heavy burgundy velvet curtains held back with golden ropes. Oil paintings of men and women in flowing robes sat in golden picture frames. The carpet matched the drapes and looked soft enough to sleep on. Everything seemed to be gilded and ornate as possible.

In the center of the room were four gilded chairs around a gilded table. Two seats were occupied by the King and Queen Mother of Paradisa.

My mouth went dry and my palms were sweaty. My stomach twisted and I considered just running for the door. Unfortunately, Mr. Irson was already closing it behind us. I had no escape.

"Hello, mum," Freddie said, letting go of my hand and crossing the room. He kissed her cheek and she smiled at him. "Hello, Liam," he said to the King.

Liam stood from his chair and the two brothers shook hands.

"I'd like to introduce you to my girlfriend, Zoey," Freddie said when they'd finished. I appreciated that he called me his girlfriend.

Both the Queen Mother and King now looked directly at me. Freddie favored the Queen Mother in looks. They shared the same kind eyes, although hers were blue to Freddie's green. They had similar smiles, although Freddie had a much more masculine jaw that I assumed favored his father. Her graying blonde hair was pulled into a neat bun at the back of her head.

King Liam was a slightly different version of Freddie. Where Freddie was all grins and bright eyes, Liam was stern and powerful. He was taller, paler, thinner, and much more serious than his youngest brother. They shared the same reddish light-brown almost blond hair, although King Liam had his trimmed and neatly arranged.

Freddie cleared his throat and did a slight knee bend, reminding me that I was supposed to be doing something.

"Oh, right," I whispered, dipping into a low curtsy. It was probably one of my best ones. "It's a pleasure to meet you, your majesties."

Technically, as an American I didn't have to curtsy. But I wanted to show respect. I wanted to show Freddie's family that I would be willing to do what was needed to fit in here. To be an asset to Freddie, rather than a liability.

Besides, curtsying was the easy part. It was the manners and rules that sounded hard.

When I rose back to standing, neither monarch looked impressed.

"It's lovely to meet you," the Queen replied warmly. "Please come join us."

I glanced at Freddie, making sure that was actually what I was supposed to do. He gave me a small nod and motioned with his head to the chair furthest from the King.

I sat carefully, suddenly very aware that I was not dressed nearly as well as the other people in the room. The Queen Mother wore a beautiful long sleeved blue dress and patent leather shoes that shone. Her hair and makeup were perfect. Liam wore dark blue slacks and a dress shirt with a tie.

Freddie cleared his throat. "We weren't expecting introductions until dinner."

"Mother didn't want to wait," Liam explained, picking

up his tea. He sipped at it delicately before setting it back down. "And, we both agreed that letting you have a private dinner would be more comfortable. This seemed the easiest solution."

"Well, thank you for that," Freddie replied. "Although, it might have been nice to know so we could dress the part."

"Oh, don't be angry with Liam," their mother chided. "I was the one who suggested tea. I don't mind what you're wearing."

I fiddled nervously with the loose button on my left jacket cuff.

"Do you like milk or sugar, dear?" the Queen asked me.

"Um..." My mind went totally blank. "Uh, sugar?"

She raised her eyebrows, unsure if I was asking her a question or if I actually wanted tea.

"Sugar, please," I repeated, trying to sound confident and knowing that I was failing miserably.

"None for Freddie," Liam said before Freddie could reply. "We have things to discuss."

Freddie glared at his older brother.

"Besides, you don't even like tea," Liam continued. He took one last sip of his own cup and set it down. "Ms. Miller, it was lovely to meet you. Mother, thank you for a lovely tea. Freddie, you're with me."

Freddie sat in his seat for a breath.

"Matters of state, little brother," Liam said, rising from his chair. "There is actual work for you to do."

Freddie looked at me. "Will you be alright?"

I smiled, trying to look confident and completely at ease. "Of course."

"Go with your brother, Freddie," the Queen told him.

"I'll keep the monsters away from Zoey. Besides, I have a feeling she's hungry. I know I always am after a flight. I had some sandwiches made."

My stomach rumbled giving me away as she motioned to beautiful little triangle sandwiches neatly arranged on a plate next to the tea set.

Freddie stood and kissed the top of my head. "I'll be back as soon as I can," he promised.

I smiled again.

I didn't want him to leave. I did not want to be alone with the Queen Mother of Paradisa. I didn't want to be alone in this place without him. I didn't know the rules. I didn't know what was actually expected of me. But I did know that I couldn't panic. I had to stay calm. I would just be ridiculously polite. It would be fine.

Freddie grabbed two small triangle sandwiches off the plate, taking a bite out of one as he followed his brother out the door. He looked back at me one last time, giving me an encouraging smile. The door clicked shut.

CHAPTER 23

Suddenly, I was very aware of how quiet the room was. And how I wasn't saying anything and neither was the Queen Mother. But I couldn't remember if I was allowed to say something first. All Freddie's lessons on proper etiquette all muddled and combined into blurry rules in my mind.

"So, you're the girl that finally stole my baby's heart," the Queen Mother said, handing me a cup of tea.

I nearly dropped the delicate china. "I, um... I... uh..."

She waved her hand and smiled. "Did you know you're the first girl he's brought home as a 'girlfriend'? The first girl he's ever actually *wanted* me to meet? The first girl he's ever asked to consider for the Stair Walk?"

I shook my head no and her smile widened.

"I believe he's absolutely smitten with you," she said, taking a small sip of tea.

"I'm smitten with him," I blurted out. My cheeks flushed and I frantically took a sip of tea. It scalded my mouth, but I managed not to make a complete fool of myself by just swallowing the burning liquid.

"I'm glad for that." The Queen set her tea on the table, the china clinking softly. "I'm told you're from a small town in the Midwest?"

"Yes, Ma'am," I replied quickly, glad to have a topic I was confident on. "I brought you a gift... they're in my suitcase. I meant to give them to you at dinner."

Instead of looking disappointed, the Queen looked overjoyed.

"Thank you, my dear," she said warmly. "I do so love local items."

"It's just some local jams and cheese," I quickly replied. I didn't want to oversell the gift. She was a Queen. People usually gave her jewels or elephants. My cheese suddenly seemed stupid. "It's not much."

"I have heard wonderful things about the cheese from Wisconsin," she said. "And I'm sure my son has told you of my fondness for jam."

I smiled. "Yes. He actually helped me pick out the flavors."

"Oh, thank you." She grinned at me, picking up her teacup and for a moment, I didn't feel so terribly out of my depth.

A knock came from the ornate doors that I'd come in through what felt like forever ago. I hoped that it was Freddie coming back. His mom seemed nice, and this wasn't going terribly, but I really wanted him back.

Mr. Irson stepped into the room, his back ramrod straight.

"The Duke of Wheaton," Mr. Irson called out.

The Queen's expression didn't change, but her posture

stiffened slightly as she set her teacup down with a soft clink.

A handsome man, probably a little older than the Queen Mother, walked in. Or rather, sauntered in. He walked like he owned the place. Like we were the interlopers. He smiled as he walked to the table and gave a beautiful bow.

His bow was elegant and practiced. It made me realize just how bad my curtsy had been before and I tried not to wince.

"Your Majesty," the Duke said. He had the Paradisian accent, but there was something fake about it, as if he were exaggerating it to demonstrate just how Paradisian he was. "I hope I'm not intruding. I happened to be in the area and was hoping to speak with King Liam."

"Duke Orwell, it's always lovely to see you," the Queen replied smoothly. "I'm afraid the King is not with us."

"Ah, I see. Then I shall have to be content with your beauty," the Duke replied.

I watched the Queen carefully, trying to figure out if that kind of flattery was normal here.

Her smile was tight lipped. "I'm afraid I don't have a tea set for three."

My eyes widened a little. Even I knew that was a dismissal, but he seemed to shrug it off as he took the seat next to me.

"Tea isn't necessary. Although, I do appreciate the thought," the Duke said, smiling broadly at her. His smile was too wide, as if he thought a smile was just his lips baring teeth. "I am merely saying hello."

"And perhaps getting a glimpse of our guest?" The Queen smiled politely, but her eyes were cold. "I'm sure it's what everyone is talking about. The young prince's new love story?"

"You wound me."He placed a hand to his heart, still wearing the too wide approximation of a smile. He turned and looked me over. "But since she is here. I am Orwell Stansberg, Duke of Wheaton."

He tipped his head, finally acknowledging me. His hair was so blond it was practically gray. He wore it combed over to hide that it was thinning, even though I don't think it actually fooled anyone. His dark suit looked expensive, but he needed a better tailor. Even I could see that it needed to be let out around the waist and taken in at the shoulders.

I had no idea what I was supposed to do. We'd only gone over how I was to introduce myself to the King and Queen Mother. I was to always say "No comment" to the press. My backup plan was just to watch Freddie and do what he did, but since he wasn't there, I had no idea what I was supposed to do.

"It's very nice to meet you," I said slowly, doing a semi head-bob-seated-curtsy thing. "I've never met a Duke before."

His eyes looked me over and I felt very small.

"Obviously." He flashed that fake smile at me. "For the future, it's traditional to stand when someone of higher ranking enters the room. Not that I'm a stickler for protocol. Don't worry about it today."

Shame flared on my cheeks, red and hot. "Thank you. I'll remember next time."

He leaned back in his chair, crossing one well-dressed leg over the other. "How do you like Paradisa?"

"It's so beautiful," I told him. "I've seen pictures, but it's so much better in person. This castle, for example. The pictures don't do it justice. It's absolutely stunning."

His mouth smiled, but his eyes remained cold. They were a pale blue that had no depth or warmth, as if no one had bothered to color them in. He turned to the Queen. "How quaint."

Anger flared to life next to shame in the pit of my stomach. I was not a small child to be spoken to like I wasn't there. Yet, there wasn't anything I could do about it.

"Was there something you needed, Duke Orwell?" the Queen Mother asked. "I'd like to resume my tea with my guest."

"No, Your Majesty," he said, not rising from his chair. Liam's chair, I realized. He'd taken Liam's spot.

The Queen raised her eyebrows and smiled pointedly at the door.

He rose gracefully to his feet, as if that had been his plan all along.

"Oh, Miss... I'm afraid I didn't catch your name." The Duke focused his pale eyes on me and I wanted to squirm.

"Miller. Zoey Miller, sir," I replied.

"Ah. Well, Ms. Miller, I do know how difficult learning all this court protocol can be," he said. "For instance, you should also stand when I leave the room. But don't worry about it today."

I felt foolish still sitting in my chair, although I had a feeling I'd feel just as foolish if I'd stood up just then.

"Duke Orwell, she is my guest," the Queen said softly, her voice low and dangerous.

"Of course, Your Majesty," he quickly said, bobbing his head toward her. "I meant no offense. I simply wanted to offer my daughter's services. She's about your age and knows all the court protocols. I'm sure she'd be delighted to help you if you'd like a tutor."

His eyes went up and down, stopping on the shabby hems of my pants and the loose button on my cuff. I shrank slightly, knowing that I definitely needed his daughter's help. Or someone like her.

"Thank you, Duke. That's a kind offer," the Queen said, speaking for me. "We'll be sure to discuss it."

The Duke smiled his strange empty smile at the two of us like it was the most charming smile we'd ever seen.

"Good luck, Ms. Miller. The court here is a difficult place. I'd hate for you to see how difficult it can truly be here," he said. His smile vanished, his cold eyes hard on me. "I hope you find your place."

I stared at him, feeling like his words were a threat rather than polite words. There was no warmth on his voice or in his eyes. He very obviously did not want me here. I glanced at the Queen Mother, but she was sipping her tea.

"Your Majesty." He bowed low to the Queen and then turned and left. He didn't say goodbye to me.

I sighed with relief when the door clicked shut behind him.

"I hope he didn't scare you," the Queen Mother said, handing me the plate of sandwiches. "He really is quite important around here. His trade negotiation ability is unheard of. I'm not a fan of his interpersonal skills, but his business ones do help the country. He is very necessary for Freddie."

I took one of the small triangle sandwiches. It looked to be egg salad. It tasted amazing and it took all my willpower not to stuff it down my throat and reach for another.

"It's fine," I told her. I glanced toward the door again. I really didn't want that man to come back. I shivered a little and looked back to the Queen Mother.

She nodded. "Now, back to our original conversation. I wanted to tell you that my son hasn't said such wonderful things about a girl in a very long time."

"Really?"

She nodded again. "I believe the last time I had such a glowing review from him was in the first grade. Shelly McStar gave him a drawing of a purple dragon."

I grinned. "Ah. I will have to work on my drawing skills then."

The Queen laughed, removing all the tension the Duke had brought with him.

"I've never seen him so happy," she told me. She shook her head. "Apparently, all my boys need to be happy is American girls."

"We are pretty amazing," I replied. I froze, wondering if I'd been too cheeky.

She laughed again. "I see why he likes you," she said, her voice warm and light. "You'll have to meet Aria. Henry and Aria are in Tunisia at the moment, but I'm hoping you'll get a chance to meet them."

"I'd like that." I tried to keep my excitement in check. Meeting Aria? That was a dream. She was a senator's daughter who married a prince in her own magical fairy tale. It felt absolutely surreal.

And even more so when I realized that I wasn't so different from her.

"I'd like to invite you to a small event tomorrow," the

Queen continued. "It's a small fundraiser in the garden. I would very much like you to come. It would be a nice introduction to the inner circle of Freddie's world here."

Panic rose in my throat, but I forced it down. "I'll have to speak with Freddie."

"I'm sure he'll agree," she replied. "But I do hope you'll come. It's not quite a Stair Walk, but it is a way to introduce you to our world here."

"Thank you."

"Of course." She smiled. "Now, if you'll excuse me, I have an appointment. Mr. Irson will take you to your rooms. Freddie already asked the cook to bring you both dinner in his room. I'm sure he'll show you where that is." She looked pointedly at me. "I know that my son is a grown man, but please respect the rules of the house. There is no sleeping together under this roof until you are married. And certainly not before the Stair Walk."

"Of course, ma'am," I replied quickly, a blush finding my cheeks again.

"Not that Freddie will obey it," she added under her breath. She looked at me. "But I'm hoping you're made of better stuff."

"Of course, ma'am. I promise to follow the rules," I replied.

"Good." She paused, her mouth stern. "I need to inform you of something."

I imagined the worst. Freddie was betrothed. She hated another American coming to the family. She'd discovered that my ancestry wasn't good enough. She didn't like me.

"Freddie has chosen you as worthy to be seen with the royal family. We don't just give out the Stair Walk to anyone that comes along." She looked me over, her eyes pausing on the hems of my pants. "We have certain standards. I need you to uphold them."

"I want to," I said quickly.

Her lips thinned.

"I mean, I want to, Your Majesty," I quickly amended.

She sighed. "It is important that you do not bring shame to the family. Do you understand? Especially with Freddie's trade negotiations, his image must be impeccable. He must show the country that he can be trusted with Navia. If the people do not believe he is past his partying and silly days, they will not be in support of his affiliation with Navia. You are now part of his image, do you understand?"

I nodded. "Yes, ma'am."

"This is a hard family to join. This is not an easy life you are choosing, if you can survive it." She raised her chin, looking like the queen she was. "We have more rules than most. We have less freedom."

I nodded slowly, feeling the weight of a dynasty all around me. "But you have Freddie."

She smiled then. "Yes. We do have Freddie."

"Then, I will happily follow your rules," I told her. "Or at least, I will try very hard. I will do anything to support him."

"Anything?" she asked, raising one perfect eyebrow. "Even if it is the hardest thing you have ever done?"

"Anything," I promised.

"Good," was all the Queen Mother said before she turned and left the room.

Everything was going wrong.

My dress was wrinkled, my feet too swollen for my shoes, and to top it off, I was running late.

I hadn't thought about the fact that my power cords for my phone wouldn't work in Paradisa since they used a different kind of plug, so my phone had died. My curling iron didn't work. I didn't have a hair dryer.

The party was starting out in the garden and I wasn't anywhere near presentable, especially not to a queen and her friends.

I was going to bring shame to the royal family and I hadn't even done anything yet. So much for helping Freddie's image.

It didn't help that now I was crying, making my makeup run. I stood in front of the beautiful bathroom mirror and wished I was anywhere else. Why had I agreed to this party? I should have just waited until I was more ready to be in public.

"It's fine," Freddie assured me, putting his warm hands

on my shoulders and smiling at me in the mirror. "Just take your time."

"But I want to be good!" I sobbed. "This is not the first impression I wanted to make."

Freddie smiled. "Do you know how often I am late? Or Henry? Henry is always late."

I sniffled. "Is Aria ever late?"

He opened his mouth and then shut it.

Aria wasn't late, then.

"Don't worry," Freddie said instead. "Just finish up and come out when you're ready. I'll say it's my fault."

"You're mom made it very clear we're not supposed to be sleeping together in the house," I replied, although I wasn't sure that calling the castle a house was the correct phrasing.

"I was going to keep it innocent, but I like that's where *your* mind went." He chuckled. "Fine, it can be my fault and I'll make it very clear that you were the dutiful virgin."

I glared at him in the mirror. "You're not helping."

"I'm sure no one has even noticed. This isn't a party for you, it's a fundraiser that you happen to be going to," he explained. "If you're a few minutes late, no one will even notice."

"Except your mom."

"Who won't mind. She may be Queen Mother, but she's actually human most of the time," he replied. "She'll understand. She likes you."

I tried not to sigh.

"I'll go run interference. It'll be fine. I promise." He squeezed my shoulders.

"Okay." I nodded and took a deep breath as he flashed

me a smile and headed out to the garden. I could hear soft music and I hated that I was going to be late.

I was only ten minutes late, but it felt like I was hours behind. I knew that I looked swollen from flying and there were bags under my eyes that no amount of concealer could tackle. But I'd managed to iron my dress and my eyeliner was actually even.

My dress was one of Cecelia's. It was a beautiful dark blue with a flared skirt that fell just below my knees. I knew shorter wasn't approved, so I'd checked to make sure it was long enough. It was tight through the waist with a black leather belt and then up to a square neckline. The straps were wide enough to cover the majority of my shoulders.

Cecelia had worn it to her work meetings and even a couple of weddings. It was fancy without being over the top. I thought it was perfect for a garden party. I wore my favorite dressy sandals. They were black with black ties around my ankles that matched the black belt of the dress. Plus, they showed off my pedicure. My toenails matched the dark blue of the dress.

I don't think I'd ever been so color coordinated in my life. I even had on blue underwear that matched, although I doubted the Queen Mother would care about that.

I hurried down the stairs, going over the rules for how to address the Queen Mother in my head. I was supposed to curtsy and always end my sentences with a "Your Majesty." I needed to keep my drink in my left hand so I would never have a clammy handshake. I was only supposed to nibble on the food, and not if I had a drink because then I wouldn't have any hands to greet people with.

The soft sounds of music and people chatting wafted through open windows as I hurried down the corridor toward the garden entrance. It was a surprisingly warm day and the castle had as many windows open as possible to let in the autumn sunshine and warm breeze.

I smoothed my dress, checked my hair, and did a quick mental checklist. I was ready. I put on my best smile, pushed open the door, and stepped out into the garden.

It took a moment for my eyes to adjust to the bright sunlight. The neatly trimmed grass was bright green under fallen yellow leaves. It looked like everything was painted with natural gold with the way the leaves swirled and landed on chairs and stones. Fall was here, even if it was warm enough today that it didn't feel like it.

A flash went off in my face and I was glad I'd been wearing a smile. I shook my head, trying to clear the surprise of the photo as I looked around for Freddie.

A gloved hand grabbed my wrist. I turned, expecting to see Freddie but it was Mr. Irson with a very annoyed look on his face.

"Come with me," he hissed, tugging me back toward the door.

I glanced around, unsure of why he wanted me to leave.

"I'm supposed to be here," I told him, not fighting, but not going easily either.

"You are not dressed appropriately," he whispered, glancing around nervously.

I frowned and looked down at my dress. "What?"

He pushed me toward the garden door, shoving me through it before I had a chance to object.

"My dress is fine. It's designer. It's nice," I told him,

trying to keep my voice low so it wouldn't echo on the stone walls. "I don't even have any cleavage showing."

"It's very lovely," he agreed. "But it's shoulderless. You cannot have bare shoulders."

"Oh." I brought my hands up to hug my bare arms. "I didn't realize."

"And, your shoes." Mr. Irson shook his head. "Closed toe shoes are required. And no nail polish."

He said it gently. There was no reproach in his voice, no shaming, or chiding. He wasn't being mean. But it still hurt. I had dressed up as best I could and I had messed it up. I wished I could just melt into the stones. Shame and embarrassment weighed heavy in my stomach.

"What do I do?" I asked him, blinking back tears. I would not mess up my eyeliner. That was apparently the only thing I'd gotten right.

"Do you have a cardigan? Or a wrap?" he asked, looking me over.

"I brought a white sweater," I replied. "I didn't wear it because it's so warm today."

He nodded. "Put it on. Different shoes? Heels, perhaps?"

I shook my head hard. "No heels. But I have nice black ballet flats."

His mouth twisted as he considered it, but then he shrugged. "That should be acceptable."

I nodded and ran upstairs as fast as I could go.

"WALK!" Mr. Irson shouted after me. I switched to my hospital speed walk, which was almost as fast as a jog. There was a no running rule at the hospital, but sometimes you needed to move fast.

Now I was really late.

Mr. Irson was waiting for me at the door. He looked serene in his black tuxedo and white gloves. His gray hair was neatly swept back without a single one out of place.

"Better?" I asked, slowing to a stop in front of him.

He looked me over with a critical eye.

"Much," he said after a moment.

I sighed with relief.

"It's still barely passable, but it will work," he corrected. His bright blue eyes narrowed. "Did Prince Frederick go over dress protocol with you?"

"He said I should dress nicely. Like for a wedding," I replied. "Considering this is what my cousin wore to several weddings, I thought I was safe."

Mr. Irson sighed. "It's a little more complicated than just 'dress nicely.' I'll print you a copy of the dress codes. I'm not surprised the Prince was unaware of the rules for females."

I shifted my weight and glanced to the door.

"Go on out," he told me kindly. "You look fine now. You're not too late. The Duke's car just arrived a moment ago, so you're not the last one here."

"Thank you," I told him. "I really appreciate it."

"You are very welcome," he replied, his face stern. He didn't seem the type that smiled much or at least for very long. "I'll endeavor to make sure you are prepared in the future."

I nodded. "I'd appreciate that. Anything I should remember?"

"No one eats before the Queen Mother. Even if it doesn't make sense," Mr. Irson counseled. "She often finds it an amusing game to wait for the last possible moment, just to keep things interesting. She's a bit of a trickster at times."

"Well, at least Freddie comes by it naturally," I said.

Mr. Irson chuckled, but quickly schooled his face back to seriousness.

I took a deep breath as I faced the wooden door to the garden.

Time to try again.

CHAPTER 25

It felt like everyone in the garden was whispering as I stepped out.

This time, I was ready for the bright sunshine. I was ready for the beautiful trees and the careful lawns. I was ready for the photographer to flash a light at me.

"There you are," Freddie said, crossing the lawn to greet me. "Why did you disappear back inside?"

"I needed a sweater," I replied lamely.

He frowned. "But it's so warm. Are you not feeling well? We can leave if you need."

I sighed. "Apparently, I'm not supposed to have bare shoulders."

Freddie's eyes went wide and his cheeks went red. It made the red in his hair stand out even more than usual.

"I'm so sorry, Zoey," he said softly. "I didn't even think... I didn't realize...The Duke had said to let you dress yourself..."

I waved him off. "It's done," I told him. "Now I know.

And Mr. Irson is giving me a copy of the rules so I don't do it again."

Freddie sighed and ran a hand through his hair. "I am sorry. It's my fault."

I shrugged. "It's okay. It's not the end of the world. I'm just glad I had a sweater that matched my dress."

Freddie's smile started to come back. "And you look beautiful. Let me introduce you to some people."

He offered me his arm and I took it, feeling like a princess for a moment.

But only a moment.

No one was dressed like me. All the other women wore light colored dresses. Their chiffon skirts ruffled in the breeze. They wore see-through long sleeve tops that fluttered like the autumn leaves. They wore hats. They wore heels.

I stuck out like a sore thumb. Wrong color. Wrong dress. Wrong shoes. No hat.

I seriously considered just running back inside, but a photographer snapped my photo again. And Freddie was so excited for me to join his world.

I resolved to do better next time.

I was going to have Mr. Irson help me. No repeats of this mess again.

"Zoey, I'd like you to meet some friends of mine," Freddie said, bringing me to a small group of people. He pulled his arm away. I'd only been able to hold it as he escorted me. "This is Count Marcus, Lord Fyron, and Duchess Stansberg of Wheaton."

The first two men were within a few years of Freddie and me. One was heavyset and the other thin, but their smiles were polite.

"Oh, please call me Sophie," the young woman replied, holding out her hand. She was perfect. Perfect straight blonde hair. Perfect makeup. Perfect pale pink chiffon dress. Perfect matching pink heels and demure hat.

She didn't have a problem picking out the right clothing. Her eyes were a soft blue, but she looked slightly familiar.

"Are you the Duke of Wheaton's daughter?" I asked, hoping I got the title right.

She laughed, a soft sweet sound. "I am. My father mentioned he met you."

Good grief. Even her accent was perfect.

"It's very nice to meet you," I said, dipping my head in what I hoped was customary enough not to cause offense. I had no idea how I was supposed to address minor nobles. She didn't have any of the coldness her father did. They shared the same eyebrows and chin, but her blue eyes were warm and her smile genuine.

Sophie cleared her throat and I saw her dip into a low curtsy. I turned and saw the Queen Mother approaching us. She wore a long, pale yellow, pleated skirt and diaphanous yellow blouse with an oversized hat.

I managed to stumble into a clumsy curtsy before the Queen Mother reached us. It was nowhere near as graceful as Sophie's bow. Dipping my head, I stared at Sophie's pink heels. They were tall and slender. I would have died just standing in them, but she managed to not only perform, but hold a perfect curtsy in six inch heels.

I waited for Sophie to rise before standing again. `

The Queen Mother smiled at both of us. Her eyes went up and down my outfit. Her lips held her smile, but the light flickered from her eyes. She was not impressed.

My heart sank just a little bit more. So much for an appropriate coming out.

"We are glad you came," she said, using the royal we.

"Your Majesty," Sophie replied, dipping her head. I mimicked her as best I could.

The Queen Mother nodded politely to both of us. She gave Freddie a look I couldn't read and then continued walking. I let out a sigh I didn't know I was holding in.

It wasn't that I thought the Queen Mother would scold me in public. I didn't expect for her to point out that my dress was incorrect and my shoes didn't quite match the belt. She didn't have to. I knew it. I knew she'd looked me over and seen everything wrong with me.

I wasn't a princess. I wasn't even princess material.

It was blindingly obvious, especially with Sophie standing next to me. *She* was princess material. She looked the part. She knew what to say and what to do. There was no way she ever showed up with a wrinkled dress and bad nail polish.

"Is this your first garden party?" Sophie asked once the Queen Mother was out of ear shot.

"Is it that obvious?" I asked, looking down at my dress. I smoothed at wrinkles I had missed with the iron.

She touched my shoulder. "You look lovely. The dress would be perfect for tea or an indoor party. Garden parties are traditionally lighter wear. Chiffon, light silk, lace- anything that breathes and stays cooler, typically in light reflecting colors. It's a holdover tradition from before air conditioning."

"Oh. That makes sense," I replied. "I didn't know."

"And I'm sure Freddie didn't tell you."

I shook my head. I glanced over to see him talking to

the two men. He wore light gray slacks with a pale yellow shirt that reflected his mother's outfit. He looked perfect.

"It's not entirely his fault. Freddie doesn't know what to wear to these things, and he most certainly has no idea what a lady should wear. He has someone that lays out his outfits for him," Sophie explained. "He was never good at deportment, and it's not like he pays attention to the rules anyway."

I nodded. I wished someone had laid out my outfits.

"Don't blame Freddie too much," she advised. "But you do look very nice. I like the dress very much."

"Thanks," I said, not really believing the compliment, but appreciating it anyway.

"Do you like Paradisa so far?" she asked, changing the subject.

"It's beautiful," I told her. "We're supposed to go on a tour tomorrow so I can actually see more than just this castle."

"Be sure to stop at Whymore Pub," she advised. "They have the best fish and chips. Freddie says that they're the only thing he misses from home. He once paid a valet to bring him a box all the way to his college dormitory."

She giggled with the memory. Her familiarity made a small patch of jealousy rise to the surface.

"How long have you known Freddie?" I asked.

"Oh, forever." She shrugged. "We went to primary school together. My father has worked in the Paradisian government for ages. I can't think of a time we weren't together, to be honest."

I could feel jealousy starting to wrap green tentacles around my chest.

"So, you two are close?" I asked.

"As friends," she quickly clarified, her blue eyes coming to mine. "We tried dating once. While it thrilled my father, it was a disaster. It was terrible. We are good friends, but a terrible romantic match. Awful, really."

She shook her head and made a disgusted face.

"That bad, huh?" I asked. I couldn't see how this beautiful woman who understood Freddie's world and Freddie could be anything but perfect together. They seemed like they would make a picture perfect couple.

She laughed. "He's wonderful. Funny, sweet, and smart. But he drives me absolutely bonkers. He doesn't want to go to parties, and if he does go, he wants to wear something completely inappropriate. He hates politics and I think if he could be a normal, regular person with a normal, regular, *boring* job, he would jump at the chance."

"And you wouldn't?"

"I love politics. Well, I love the intrigue of them," she explained. "The parties, the politics, the intrigue, the public- I love being in the center of all the action. Everyone was watching me and seeing what I could do. The drama of it all is like candy for me."

Being in the center of political action sounded terrible. I much preferred my quiet and peaceful life. I didn't need that drama. I hated drama, but Sophie didn't.

I raised an eyebrow at her. "That sounds like the opposite of fun to me."

"And neither does Freddie. That's why you are so perfect for him." She smiled at me. Her pale blue eyes looked me over, but she looked pleased with what she saw rather than disappointed. "You love Freddie. I can see it when you look at him. And he loves you. He's smiled more today since you came out than I've seen him smile in a year."

My first real smile of the day crossed my face. Maybe I had found a friend here.

"I know my father offered my help if you need it," she said after a moment. "He specifically asked me to remind you of it."

My real smile faltered.

"I'd like to offer my help on my own," she continued. "I want you and Freddie to succeed. And I know how hard this place can be. If you need someone to help you with outfits or anything, I'd love to help."

"Thank you," I replied, unsure if I would actually take her up on it. While I appreciated the offer, it felt forced since her father had also mentioned it. It would be too easy for her to set me up to fail, and I had the distinct feeling that her father wanted me to fail.

"I want you to succeed here," she said. She glanced around. "I just want Freddie to be happy."

She was so earnest. I believed her.

"What should I wear tomorrow?" I asked. "For the tour."

She looked me over thoughtfully. "Do you have light slacks? And a button shirt. And heels, of course."

"I have nice gray slacks and a dark blue silk button-up shirt," I replied. "But no heels. Heels and I are not a good combination."

She pursed her lips. "I suppose you can wear flats. There's no real regulation that it must be heels for informal events. If you come to a formal event, you will have to wear heels. That's required."

"Have they scheduled your Stair Walk yet?" she asked.

"Um, I don't think so."

"That's alright. I know they scheduled Aria's for the day she arrived," Sophie said with a soft laugh. "That one felt very hurried. It's better that there's time for you to prepare."

I smiled weakly. "Right."

"I was just a girl when I did my Stair Walk. Perk of being the Duke's daughter is that I did it before I even knew what it was." Her smile grew. "Oh, I can just imagine you and Freddie for your Stair Walk. It'll be like Cinderella." She grinned. "Please let me help you pick out your dress. You would look stunning in pink."

"Don't plan her whole wardrobe yet," Freddie interjected.

"Only because you won't," Sophie replied. She frowned at him. "Really, Freddie. I'm a little disappointed in you."

He flushed at being called out.

"Zoey, would you like to go shopping with me after your tour? Or the next day?" Sophie asked, turning to face me. "I'd like to help you get set up."

"That would be nice," I replied. "I'll probably need at least another sweater."

I glanced over at Freddie and he flushed harder.

"Excellent." Sophie smiled at Freddie and me. "Now, I see my father has arrived. I should go say hello."

She gave my arm a friendly squeeze and walked away.

"She will make sure you are perfect," Freddie said softly, coming to stand by me.

"Really?"

He nodded. "She's really good at this stuff. Dresses, dining, etiquette, protocol. She's as good as mum at it."

I looked out at Sophie as she greeted her father with a

demure head bob. She laughed at a joke someone said, looking completely at ease in a circle of powerful men.

"I should have asked her to help you in the first place," Freddie said softly. "She would have made sure you had the right dress. I didn't even think about the fact that you might need help. You always seem so confident."

I looked over at him surprised. "Maybe at home. But I have no idea what I'm doing here."

"I'll fix it then," he said. "Go shopping with Sophie. I'll give you the money. I want you to look, and feel like you belong here."

My mouth opened but I didn't have anything to say.

"What are the perks to dating a prince if he doesn't take you shopping?" Freddie asked. "You should look like a princess. Because to me, you should be one."

My heart stuttered in my chest. Was he talking about making me a princess? I wasn't sure I was ready for that. I loved him, but the idea that he might want to marry me made my head a little woozy in a good way. He did want me to do the Stair Walk after all.

He grinned at me. "Want to get out of here?"

I nodded vigorously. I was hot in this sweater and I hated that it felt like everyone was looking at me.

He grabbed my hand and pulled me through the garden door. The last thing I saw was Sophie frowning after us.

CHAPTER 26

"Well, that went better than expected," Freddie said, wiping some dirt off his hands.

His beautiful gray slacks were brown at the knees and a smudge of dirt lay swiped across the bridge of his nose.

I raised an eyebrow at him. "Seriously?"

He leaned over and wiped some dirt off my cheek. "We made it, didn't we?"

He motioned to the forest just past the small meadow we were currently walking through. I dusted my hands together, trying to get the mud off. I'd managed to keep most of the dirt from my dress, but I wasn't much cleaner than Freddie.

Behind us, trapped in the cultivated gardens of the castle, music still played. A tug of guilt found my middle, but I pushed it away. I didn't want to be at the party. I didn't want everyone looking at me and whispering.

I wanted to be out here.

Instead of a proper moat, the castle had carefully

manicured lawns. Freddie and I had crossed those easily. The neat grass was held close to the castle by a waist-high rock wall. We'd scrambled over it, giggling as he'd helped me up and over. The wall was filthy and covered with dust and mud.

But I didn't care. We were free now.

A wild meadow, full of tall grasses and the last of the yellow daisies surrounded the wall. Once we were over, I'd finally let out a sigh of relief.

There were no crowds here. It didn't matter if I had dirt on my cheek or the proper dress. I would have preferred better shoes, but I was glad I wore flats instead of heels. Bright sunshine and the sound of birds filled the air.

Freddie grinned at me. "You look happier." His smile was as bright as the sun.

"So do you," I replied. I sighed with contentment, breathing in the scent of wild grass, earth, and sunshine. "Is this what you wanted to show me?"

He shook his head. "It's over here," he said, motioning to the trees.

He took my hand in his. I loved the safe, warm feeling that washed over me at his touch. Things were better when he was around.

"You aren't going to lead me into the forest like a big bad wolf?" I asked as we walked to the edge of the trees.

"I do have something that's nice and big," he replied, flashing me a devilish grin.

I realized that it wasn't actually a forest that we were walking into. It was the ruins of a castle surrounded by trees.

The stones clearly formed the shape of rooms and

hallways. The roof was made of sky and tree branches now, but the building had once been elegant. Grass grew instead of carpet and flowers peeked out of doorways long since fallen away.

"This is the Ruinous Castle," Freddie explained. "It used to be my favorite place as a kid."

Ruinous certainly fit the place, yet there was a magic I couldn't deny to it. I could easily see a young boy running around the stones, pretending to be a knight protecting or invading.

"King Edward the Third built this place for his mistress," Freddie explained. "His mother lived in Remington Castle. This is close enough that he could 'visit' his mother, but spend the night with his mistress."

The trees hid Remington Castle from view, but every once in a while a small snippet of music would float down.

"When she died, the castle fell into disrepair. It's said that King Edward's grief is what destroyed the place, making the castle fall faster than it should have," Freddie continued. "It's said that he loved his mistress more than life itself. He died in this castle not long after his mistress. That it then crumbled around him, needing love to stay built and finding none."

"Is it haunted?" I asked, wondering if the King and his mistress walked the ruined stones.

He looked around and shook his head. "The truth is that the stones were used to fix Remington after the second World War." He shrugged. "I've never seen a ghost here, and I've been here a million times since I was a kid."

"Even at night?" I asked. We walked a corridor of crumbling stone to what was once a room. The walls were high enough to still be walls. A tree grew in the center of the room, providing a fluttering roof. I took off my sweater, carefully setting it on top of a large stone near the base of the tree.

"A couple of times," Freddie admitted. "I used to come out here anytime I wanted to escape my duties. Which was a lot."

He pointed to a corner of the room where a shaft of light flickered through what was once a window.

"I used to read there," he explained. "And I had a tarp draped across that spot over there so that even when it rained, I could escape out here. No one ever bothered me out here. I know Mum knows about this place, but she always let me be out here. It was my safe place." He turned and smiled at me. "I wanted to share it with you."

A soft breeze fluttered his hair. His green eyes were bright in the warm sunshine that filtered through the leaves of the tree. His smile was unguarded as he stood before me.

I kissed him, tasting the last bits of summer warmth on his lips. His hands came to my neck, warm and soft as he tangled them in my hair.

"I love you, Zoey," he murmured, voice sweet and heavy.

It didn't matter how many times he said it, each time gave me a thrill. He loved me. Freddie loved me.

I was the luckiest girl in the whole world.

"I love you," I whispered back, kissing him harder this time.

He kissed me back with just as much enthusiasm, pushing me back until my back touched the stone wall. It was cool and hard, especially compared to the warmth of

Freddie to my front. I loved the way he felt pressed against me, holding my body to him.

He kissed me like he couldn't get enough. I ran my hands up his chest, feeling the muscles under his shirt. His hips pressed against mine, his attraction hard and obvious against my hip.

I looked up into his eyes. "I want you," I whispered.

He grinned. "You're willing to risk my mother's wrath?"

I smirked. "We're not under your mother's roof right now."

His eyes darkened with desire as he looked me over, his smile changing from mischievous to incredibly turned on. He licked his lower lip, his eyes going to my own mouth. His gaze was hungry and something primal and deep inside of me responded.

His hand went to the hem of my skirt and he slid upward, the soft blue fabric hiding his fingers. My breath hitched as he passed my upper thigh. I whimpered as his fingers caressed the soft blue satin of my panties.

He chuckled at my gasp, his smile curling his lips as he touched me through the fabric.

The naughtiness of it was such a rush. Knowing that we shouldn't be doing this, that being together like this was very much against the rules, made it so much hotter.

We shouldn't be doing this, I thought to myself. *Someone will catch us.*

But I didn't want to stop. I couldn't stop. His touch was so tempting. Too tempting.

He slid his fingers under the elastic of my panties, humming his pleasure as he touched my skin.

"So wet and perfect," he growled in my ear as he slid a finger inside of me.

My knees buckled, but he held me up against the wall. His thumb caressed me as his fingers explored my depths. I kissed him just to keep from moaning too loud.

Sunlight flickered through the evergreens. The breeze hummed over the stone remnants of the castle. All I could smell was Freddie's citrus and ginger scent that drove me crazy. His fingers found a tempo that had me rocking my hips for more.

"Come for me," he whispered, flicking his thumb just a little bit harder. "Come for me, Zoey."

The rough hoarseness of desire in his voice is what did me in. The blatant need in his words was my undoing. My entire body shuddered. My knees went weak and it was only Freddie that kept me from falling to the ground in an orgasmic puddle.

The prideful smirk on Freddie's face when I opened my eyes was sexy as hell.

I reached for his belt, undoing the leather and metal easily. I didn't pull down his pants. I just reached for the hard erection straining against the cotton of his briefs. I slid it free, feeling his heat and desire in my hands.

The small groan of pleasure at my touch made my core heat to melting.

I grinned up at him, stroking him with my fingers and watching the way his eyelids flutter as his head tips back in pleasure. We've been together long enough that we both trust my birth control to be enough.

I glanced around, making sure that we are as alone as I think we are. There was nothing but the sound of Freddie's heavy breathing and the wind.

He braced himself with a hand on the wall behind me, his jaw tight with concentration. I raised my leg, wrapping it around his waist. He pushed my underwear to the side. That smirk, the one that made me feel like I'm in on the greatest joke in the world, crossed his face as he pushed forward and slid into me.

We froze when he was in me all the way to the hilt. I whimpered, my body shaking with desire and sensation. He felt so damn good, even with all our clothes still on that I thought I might explode right there.

When he began to thrust, it took everything I had not to cry out in pleasure. Just because we didn't see anyone didn't mean that no one was around. I didn't want anyone to hear me and come to investigate.

My leg tightened around him, begging him for more. His hand grasped at the wall, his fingers going white at the knuckles as he held onto the stone and searched for his release inside of me.

"My turn," I whispered, my breath coming in shallow pants. "Come for me."

His pupils dilated. I could feel the muscles in his stomach tighten and he thrust into me so hard I whimpered.

He sped up his thrusting. I closed my eyes, reveling in the feeling of him filling me. The feeling of him needing me to find his release. I craved his release more than I wanted my own.

His breath caught, his eyes closing with concentration and his brow furrowing. I felt his need inside of me and I want it all.

He exploded, grunting with his effort. A flock of birds startled out of the trees behind us at the sound. He groaned, and it made every muscle in my body tighten around him. I wanted to draw him into my soul.. He dropped his head into the arch of my neck, his breath hot on my skin.

We're both still breathing hard when he looked up at me. He kissed my cheek and pulled away. I whimpered with the loss of him. My legs were still shaky as I pulled my dress down from my waist.

"Do you have any idea how many times I have fantasized about that?" he asked after he'd buckled his pants back up.

I raised an eyebrow at him. "Sex in general or sex outside?"

"No. Bringing a girl here. Showing her this place." He motioned to the wall we'd just banged against with a grin. "Doing that."

I could imagine a horny teenage Freddie in this place. I could imagine him sitting in these stone walls and dreaming of the day he'd have a girl to bring here.

"So how many girls have you brought here?" I asked.

"You're the first." He brought his hand to my face, his eyes soft and full of warm love. "I've never had anyone I've actually wanted to bring here before."

My stomach did the familiar happy flip flops that only Freddie could create. The ones that made me feel special and loved. The ones that made me believe in happily ever afters.

"I love you, Zoey," he whispered, running his thumb gently along my cheek.

He kissed me, sweet and soft. The need was still there, but in the background this time. I sighed with pleasure, feeling satisfied but knowing I would want more later. I would always want more of Freddie.

"Will you show me more of this place?" I asked, biting my lip flirtatiously. "I don't want to go back yet."

He grinned at me and adjusted his belt. The knees on his pants were still muddy from us climbing through the meadow and his shirt was wrinkled where I'd held onto him without realizing it.

"I'll show you everything," he promised.

CHAPTER 27

"How do I look?" I asked Mr. Irson. "Better this time?"

I wore the slacks and button-up silk blouse just like Sophie instructed. My hair was loose around my shoulders, but neatly curled. My makeup was light and sensible.

Just like the fifty-page rule book said to be.

Mr. Irson's eyes went up and down, evaluating every fiber of my clothing. I tried not to wiggle or fidget.

"Perfect," he said after a moment. "Just the shoes. You really don't have heels?"

I crossed my arms. "No. No heels. I can't walk in them and I guarantee it would be a worse disaster than if I wore a bikini out on the tour."

Mr Irson's eyes went wide and he looked utterly horrified by the idea that I would even propose such a thing. "Then, the flats will do."

I grinned, feeling pleased. I was going to get this. I was going to follow all the rules the palace asked and I was going to do it well.

"Thank you for helping me," I told him. "I know it's not really your job, but I really do appreciate it."

"My job is to keep the Queen Mother's house running smoothly," he replied. His face was solemn but his eyes smiled at me. "If I keep you out of trouble, then the house will run smoother."

It was pure impulse, but I hugged him. He smelled like peppermint candies.

He let out a surprised huff of air and gently patted my shoulder. When I pulled away, he looked more surprised than anything. I supposed hugs weren't exactly common around royals.

"There you are," Freddie said, coming around the corner of the hallway. He wore a dark blue suit with a dark green shirt underneath. I pushed images of me taking it off of him in the car out of my head.

I smiled at him. "Just making sure I meet requirements."

"You look perfect," Freddie agreed, giving a nod to Mr. Irson before crossing the hallway to greet me. "I have some bad news though."

"Did something happen? Is everyone okay?" I asked, immediately imagining the worst situations. "Is someone sick?"

"No, everyone is fine," Freddie assured me. He ran a hand through his hair. "I have to work with the Duke on the negotiations today. The time table shifted."

"But you'll do that after we go on our tour, right?" I asked hopefully, already suspecting the answer.

Freddie shook his head. "I'm really sorry, Zoey. The Duke says it has to be now."

Anger heated his voice, though he quickly tamped it down.

"It's okay," I told him. "We can go on a tour another day. You have a lot of work to do to prepare for the Navian delegation. Don't worry about me."

"I did have a possible alternative," he offered. "What if you and Sophie go out today? It won't be an official tour, but she can help you shop so that you don't have to worry about what to wear for a while. And, the press shouldn't be all over you yet."

"I guess I could do that," I said. I shrugged. "I mean, I'd rather hang out with you, but it would be nice to have all my clothes taken care of."

"I promise, I'll make it up to you," Freddie said, taking my hands. "The Duke can't expect me to do everything right away. He now owes me at least a full night off."

I grinned at him. "Okay."

Freddie smiled, but there was stress around his eyes.

"Are you okay?" I asked.

Freddie sighed. "I'm fine. It's just being back here. The responsibilities never end around here. The trade negotiations and all the image work is a little bit more intense than I first thought. The Duke wasn't kidding when he said this would be hard work."

"Can I help at all?" I asked.

He kissed my cheek and Mr. Irson tutted. Freddie wasn't supposed to kiss me, even though we weren't exactly in public.

"I love that you would even ask," he said, his voice soft in my ear. "But no. There's nothing you can do to help me."

I turned and kissed him full on the mouth. It wasn't a

long kiss, but he grinned at me when he pulled back. Poor Mr. Irson was beet red and looking everywhere but at the two of us. That was very definitely not allowed.

"Dinner?" Freddie asked me, taking a step back. "I had the kitchen order you some ketchup."

"Really?" Excitement rose in me.

"The cook is furious, but I got it," he replied with a smile. "You have your own bottle. And it is entirely yours because no one else in the castle even wants to smell it."

I giggled. "I look forward to dinner then."

He flashed me a devilish grin. "Maybe we can go for a walk afterwards. There's still other rooms of the Ruinous Castle we need to explore."

My core heated and my returning grin was very sexual.

Mr. Irson pretended to ignore us both.

"I love you," Freddie said one last time, his eyes meeting mine.

"And I you," I replied.

He grinned, the smile on his face the same one as he'd worn at the cabin. Pure happiness. He winked once at me before turning around and disappearing down the hall-way. I watched him go, my silly joy fading with his every step.

"You know, I don't think I've ever heard him say that," Mr. Irson said, watching the Prince disappear.

"Everyone keeps telling me I'm the first official girl-friend," I replied with a shrug. "The first girl he's requested to do the Stair Walk."

"No, it's not just that," Mr. Irson said with a frown. "I've never heard him say that he loves someone. Not to his parents, not to his siblings, not even to his stuffed toys."

My brows came together as I looked at Mr. Irson.

"I've known that boy since before he could walk, and I've never seen him smile the way he just smiled at you." The corner of Mr. Irson's usually stern mouth flicked upward into a half smile.

For him, that was practically a full out beaming smile.

"Ms. Miller, I do believe you make him happy," he told me.

My heart lightened. "I'm glad. He makes me happy too."

"Good. But please don't kiss him like that again before the Stair walk." Mr. Irson looked down the empty hallway and shook his head slowly. He looked back at me, his eyes going up and down my clothing once again. "What you're wearing is appropriate for a shopping outing with Ms. Stansberg. Perhaps different shoes?"

I glared at him and he shrugged.

"Just thought I'd try," he said softly.

I rolled my eyes at him, ignoring the ghost of a smile I saw on his face.

CHAPTER 28

Shopping with Sophie was an experience unto itself.

She was a force to be reckoned with. Sophie made shopping into an Olympic qualifying sport. We visited three stores, tried on over thirty dresses, twenty different kinds of slacks, thirty-seven skirts, and more types of shirts than I could keep track of.

"With your hair and skin, you should wear pastels," she advised, holding up a pink gown that shimmered in the light. "Some darker colors will work, but I think we need to stick with the lighter things. They will also give you an air of innocence."

"Are you saying I'm not innocent?" I asked her, putting back a deep burgundy sweater.

She grinned at me. "Not in a million years. You're dating Freddie."

"He's not that much of a bad boy," I replied. I held up a blue shirt.

"Too low cut," she said, shaking her head at the shirt.

"And I know Freddie isn't all bad. He's just got the reputation."

"So why do I have to dress innocent?" I asked. I held up a long sleeve pale green shirt that Sophie nodded at. "Why do I matter?"

"You matter because you will be seen as an extension of Freddie. If you're sweet and demure, then that means that Freddie has changed his ways and the monarchy is safe once again." She held up a purple skirt, wrinkled her nose, and put it back. "Everything you do from now on out has meaning. What you wear has meaning. What you don't wear has meaning. Everything will be evaluated, examined, and displayed to the public."

I quickly put back the sparkly tank top. "Can I just wear my hospital scrubs?" I asked. "Those are professional, conservative, and show that I am a good person."

Sophie looked over at me. "You know, that could work. But not really. Only if you were working. Maybe a photo at the hospital, though. I know the president of Saint Mary's..."

She trailed off, mumbling to herself as she made a note on her phone. I sighed and shook my head. I'd been mostly teasing.

"You said 'the monarchy would be safe again,'" I said, holding still while she held up a teal sweater set to my body. "What do you mean by that? Freddie is second in line for the throne. Less if Liam or Henry have kids."

Sophie put the teal sweater set into the pile to try on. I tried not to look at that pile. It was huge. She glanced around the store, but no one was paying any attention to us.

"Freddie thinks that he's not important to the monarchy," Sophie explained. "But he is. He's very important."

I frowned. "Why?"

"He's an amazing trade ambassador," Sophie replied. She glanced around again. "My father says that Freddie walks into a room and everyone relaxes. He's good with people. You've seen him, Freddie can charm the pants off of anyone."

I nod, thinking of how easily he'd charmed the pants off me. "But he doesn't think he's important."

"He has the ear of the throne. Liam listens to Freddie. A lot. I don't think Freddie realizes just how much Liam depends on Freddie for advice," Sophie replied with a shrug. "I mean, where is Freddie right now? You were supposed to be doing a tour thing, right? But instead, he's helping Liam. He's the one that convinced Liam to do this trade treaty with Navia."

I frowned thoughtfully. "I guess Liam is always asking Freddie to do things. I always thought they sounded important, but Freddie always thought they were dumb."

"Freddie always complains about how his brother is coming up with unnecessary tasks, but it's not true," Sophie continued. "Liam is usually asking Freddie to do the tasks that Liam isn't so great at. The interpersonal stuff."

"Like talking at a conference to bolster trade relations," I offered.

"Or meeting with heads of state and showing them around. Freddie makes people comfortable. He's funny and sweet. He has no idea how useful that is to the crown. This trade treaty will be proof of his skill." She looked at the pile of clothes. "We should go try these on."

"Liam should tell him," I said, walking to the changing rooms.

Sophie laughed. "Liam? Say something nice to his brother? Have you met him?"

We went into a giant changing room. Sophie handed me the teal sweater set and turned her back so I could change. It made more sense for her to just stay with me than to have to go out the door every time. It saved a lot of time this way too.

"Liam seems nice enough," I said, pulling the skirt up and smoothing the sweater. "What do you think?"

Sophie turned and round and made a face. "Too frumpy," she said. "Darn. It is a great color for you." She handed me a pink skirt. "And Liam is nice. He's just too stressed out about being a good king to think about anything else. Or anyone else."

"Doesn't that kind of make him not a good king?" I asked. I froze with the sweater half over my head. "And I mean that in a totally non-treasonous, totally hypothetical way."

Sophie snorted. "We're a free country. You can say anything you want about the King," she replied. "And that pink skirt works. Put it in the keep pile."

I dutifully stepped out of the pale pink skirt and set it neatly on the bench. Sophie handed me a lilac dress that would have been perfect for the garden party.

"So, *is* Liam a good king?" I asked, putting on the dress.

Sophie took a deep breath. "I think he can be. He's trying too hard to be his father, but he only sees his father's successes and none of his failures. King Albert had years of experience that Liam doesn't have yet. Even

King Albert struggled with telling Freddie he was doing a good job."

I nodded. A tingle of jealousy flittered over my skin and settled like a knot around my chest. Sophie knew Freddie and his brothers. She'd grown up with them. There was a history and friendship there that I would never have. But it was nice having someone to talk to. Someone who could explain the sibling dynamic, because Freddie certainly didn't want to.

"I shouldn't say anything, but I think you should know," Sophie said, still looking away from me while I changed. "There are big plans for Freddie. My father says that he could end up more powerful than the King if he tried. This trade idea just proves it."

"Freddie would hate that," I said, recoiling at the idea.

"Yeah, but that doesn't change the fact that Freddie has a lot more power than he thinks." She shook her head as she looked at the lilac dress. "Which is why we have to make sure you're perfect. You now represent him at all times."

"I want to help him," I told her. "I really do."

Sophie smiled at me. "I know. And I think you're great for him. He's happy with you. I'd rather he be happy than powerful."

"Me too," I replied. We shared a smile.

"But enough about that," Sophie said. "We have other things to go over. Like how to address nobles and the correct way of getting out of a car. You can't just fling your legs out like you're in the wild west."

I sighed as she handed me a sea-foam green blouse.

"Teach away, Master," I replied.

Sophie grinned.

CHAPTER 29

"Are you sure this is okay?" I asked, feeling incredible guilt that I was going to spend so much of Freddie's money. The simple scarf in my hands was priced more than I had ever paid for an entire outfit.

Sophie frowned. "There are higher end shops," she said slowly. "I suppose we can find things there, but I really do like the color palette we found here."

"Higher end?" I squeaked out.

She looked at me confused. "That's what is the matter, right? That these may not be nice enough?"

I stared at her. "No, no. That this is too nice. This is so much money for... clothes. And just clothes."

"Clothes are what people base their opinions on," Sophie replied. "And this is nothing. Remember, Freddie is a prince."

I looked at the pile of clothes. I didn't even want to know what they were going to cost.

"I already have permission and this isn't even going to

put a dent in the limit," Sophie told me. "We could buy twice this and still have funds left over."

I stared at her.

"Go wait outside if it makes you uncomfortable," Sophie said, rolling her eyes. "I'll pay for it and tell you a beautiful lie on the price."

I hurried to the big glass front doors, leaving Sophie with the pile of clothes and the royal credit card.

Late afternoon sunshine filtered through the bright store windows. Outside, people walked briskly past. Some stopped to admire the clothing in the windows, but most people were on their phones or obviously in a hurry to get somewhere.

I pulled open the heavy glass door and stepped outside.

It was colder today than yesterday. Gray clouds filled the limited sky I could see between tall buildings. I took a deep breath in, smelling car gas and street vendor food. I wrinkled my nose, missing the soft scent of grass and stone from the castle.

Westshire was the capital and biggest city in Paradisa. The city had stonework that predated the US mixed with new buildings. Ancient and modern architecture mingled and combined with castles merging into skyscrapers.

A car pulled to a stop in front of the shop. I frowned at it as the driver hopped out and ran around to open the back door.

Out stepped Freddie and I grinned.

"Freddie!" I shouted, running across the sidewalk and throwing my arms around him. I kissed him, glad to see him. He kissed me quickly before pulling away.

"Well, hello," he said, smiling at me. "Not that I don't like the kiss, but it's not exactly standard."

"Oh, right." I winced. "I just saw you and forgot. Old habits die hard."

"I did like it though," he said, grinning at me. "Did you find anything you liked?"

"Sophie was amazing," I told him. It was hard not to reach for him. I wanted to touch him. I didn't like having to stay away from him. "Here, come look."

I turned and hurried to the front door of the shop, pulling it open and holding it open for Freddie.

He stopped midstep, looking at me and then the door. His face paled and went emotionless.

I frowned, and then remembered that females weren't supposed to open doors. They were supposed to wait for the nice chivalrous men to open them and opening them myself was considered rude and an affront to someone's manhood.

"Sorry," I said, dropping the door. "I'll remember the rules one of these times."

Freddie's face didn't change. That's when I noticed the people with cameras.

The people with cameras that were now frantically taking pictures of me holding the door open for the prince. The people with cameras that had to have just caught me kissing him just a few moments ago.

My face burned and I wanted to melt into the sidewalk. I wanted to turn invisible and run as fast as my legs could carry me. I squeezed my eyes shut, my chest constricting and my stomach about to hurl.

"It's okay," Freddie said quickly, opening the door and escorting me inside. "It's fine."

But I knew it wasn't. I knew it wasn't by the way the cameras pressed to the glass of the store. I knew it wasn't fine by the way Freddie made eye contact with Sophie. The thin press of her lips as she glared everywhere but at me said it was anything but fine.

I could already imagine the Queen Mother's disapproving look. I remembered how tired Freddie had looked after James' visits and I understood completely. I was trying to do right by the royal family and failing.

"Get her away from the windows," Sophie hissed. "This is going to make the evening news. And she's not even dressed properly yet."

Freddie gently guided me behind a wall of clothing, hiding us both from the photographers outside. I couldn't believe they would be so interested in me holding a door open.

"I'm sorry," I whispered. "I didn't mean any harm."

"I know," Freddie said with a soft smile. "You're trying."

I knew he meant it as a compliment, but it only made me feel worse.

I was trying and I was failing.

Freddie deserved someone better than someone who was just *trying*. He needed someone who didn't accidentally break all the rules. He needed someone that wouldn't accidentally open doors or wear the wrong thing. Someone who made him look good.

He needed someone better than me, especially if he was half as powerful as Sophie seemed to think he was.

I sighed.

"Don't worry," Freddie said with a shrug. "It'll be fine. I'm sure they're just happy to see me back in country."

He didn't say it like he believed it. He sounded like he was trying to convince me that the apocalypse wouldn't be so bad. That there were going to be perks of a hellfire landscape.

I looked down at my shoes, trying very hard not to panic or cry. The last thing I needed was to leave the store with streaky mascara and blotchy skin.

"Hey, Zoey." Freddie's voice was light and friendly.

I didn't look up.

Suddenly, his face filled my vision. He was down on his knees, looking up at me with a playful smile.

"Boop." He reached up and booped my nose. When my eyes widened in surprise he made a silly face. His eyes crossed and he stuck out his tongue, screwing his face up to the side.

I couldn't stop the snort. I couldn't stop the smile.

He grinned at me. "There. That's better." He rose back to his feet, putting his hand under my chin and raising my gaze with him.

"Did you really just boop me?" I asked. His hand was warm under my chin and I liked the touch.

He leaned forward and kissed the tip of my nose. "Yup."

I didn't know what to say. The Prince of Paradisa had booped my nose.

But it had made me smile. It had made me feel better and I no longer felt like the world was collapsing. So what if a couple of people had pictures of me opening a door? Or kissing his cheek? It wasn't like I'd done anything really wrong.

I was overreacting.

I took a deep breath.

"Thanks," I told him. Freddie smiled. His beautiful eyes met mine. Warmth flooded me. There was no way I could be sad when he looked at me like that. I was beautiful. I was perfect. He loved me. Those eyes loved me.

For a moment, I believed that it would be okay.

"You two should go out the back," Sophie announced. "I'll bring the clothes to the palace."

Freddie squeezed my hand before breaking eye contact with me.

"Thanks, Sophie."

She grinned at him, a real smile of pleasure. For a split second, I felt jealousy flitter across my skin.

"I'm actually enjoying it," Sophie replied. She turned to me, her smile still bright. "I'll come by this evening. We'll go over what to wear, how to wear things, and what to do if you have a wardrobe emergency."

"A wardrobe emergency? Like my dress falling off?" I thought of the infamous Super Bowl Halftime where Janet Jackson's pasty was revealed.

"Is that a common problem for you?" Sophie asked, looking slightly concerned. "I meant if your hat falls off while you're walking. Or you get mud on your shoes."

"Oh. That would be more likely."

Freddie snickered. "Unless I'm involved."

Sophie glared at him. He grinned at her, putting an arm over my shoulder and pulling me close to him.

"Dinner is at seven," he told her.

"I'll be there," she replied. "Now get going. Don't let them see you."

She made a shoo-ing motion with her hands toward the back of the store.

Freddie grinned and pulled me closer to him. I loved

how much safer I felt with him touching me, and even though I knew we weren't supposed to touch in public, this didn't feel like public.

"Can the cameras see you?" I asked, glancing over the tall clothing rack at the windows. We were still alone in the store. None of the photographers had come inside, something I was grateful for. It probably was because James was standing guard at the door looking incredibly intimidating.

"I don't care," he told me. "They're going to find out that I'm dating you. And heaven forbid they find out I like to put my arm around you."

"Back exit, please," Sophie called out.

We threaded through racks of clothes, weaving our way to the back exit. A man who could have been James' twin was waiting for us.

Freddie nodded to the man and we escaped out the back door and into a waiting car.

I let out a huge sigh of relief once we were on the highway and heading back to the castle.

Maybe no one would even notice my little mistake.

CHAPTER 30

"… *And* did you see what the American was wearing?"

I cringed as a photo of me popped up on the TV screen. It was from the garden party. My shoulders were bare and I wore the stupidest smile.

"We here at "Royalty Watch" can not believe that the Queen Mother finds this appropriate. It is an affront to Paradisian values," the commentator continued. "Add in her lewd behavior toward the prince, and I'm not sure that this American is going to be welcome in the royal household. Kissing before a Stair Walk? The scandal!"

The screen flashed to a video of me kissing Freddie's cheek and holding the door open.

I stuck out my tongue at the TV. "It wasn't lewd," I said.

"Lewd would have at least included tongue," Freddie agreed, settling into the couch next to me. He put his arm over my shoulder and handed me a bowl of popcorn. "Want to get lewd now?"

I looked over at him and grinned. We sat in a comfortable sitting room with a huge TV. In any other house, I would have called it a living room, but this was a castle.

"Can you not?" Sophie asked, taking the chair to my right. She curled into it like a cat, tucking her legs delicately underneath her. She had her own bowl of popcorn. "When I agreed to movie night, I did not agree to you two pretending to be in the back of the theater. And Zoey, no popcorn. You're on the royal diet now."

I put one last piece of popcorn in my mouth before handing the bowl back to Freddie. He put it on a table far from both of us, taking away the temptation.

"No popcorn I can handle." He pulled a blanket up onto our laps. "But I guess we'll just have to be sneaky with the other thing I desire." He snuck his free hand under the blanket and squeezed the top of my thigh.

Sophie rolled her eyes and made an annoyed sound. "Why are you watching this trash anyway?"

"It's what came on when I turned on the TV," I explained. I shrugged. "And then I was curious."

"Well, that show is absolute rubbish," Sophie informed me. "Just gossip and meanness. You don't need to watch such things."

I knew I didn't, but I couldn't help but wonder how popular the show was. Were thousands of people watching it right now? Were they all commenting on my bare shoulders and lack of basic decorum?

I hated that I wasn't perfect. That I had tried and failed. I hated being on the TV and all I wanted to was to just hide in this castle and be with Freddie. I didn't need garden parties or fabulous balls. I just wanted Freddie.

"And don't worry," Sophie assured me. "We have protocol practice all day tomorrow. I've cleared both our schedules. We're going to have you princess worthy in no time. When I'm done training you, they'll think you were born knowing the rules."

I sighed, already dreading tomorrow. It would be full of curtsies and proper speaking etiquette. Sophie was going to try and teach me to wear heels. She was a nice person and a decent teacher, but I wasn't looking forward to a day of being told I was doing everything wrong.

"Will you turn on the movie?" I asked, forcing cheerfulness into my voice. At least we could enjoy this evening.

"Anything would be better than this rubbish," Freddie agreed, reaching for the remote. He'd barely picked up the remote when Liam walked into the room.

"Ah. Good. I see you've seen the news," Liam said. He wore a perfectly tailored black suit with a dark purple shirt underneath. He was perfectly groomed and handsome- not a single hair out of place. Contrasted with Freddie's unbuttoned shirt, wrinkled pants, and messy hair, the two bothers couldn't have been more different.

"If you call that news," Freddie retorted. He clicked the TV off. "What of it?"

"What of it?" Liam's voice came out calm, but his eyes looked like they were about to bug out of his head. "It's a disaster."

"Disaster?" Freddie scoffed. "Earthquakes are a disaster. Hurricanes are a disaster. That-" he motioned to the dark screen- "Is *not* a disaster."

I shrank down into the couch. Maybe I could just

disappear into the couch cushions before Liam realized I was there. This was not a conversation that I wanted to be a part of.

No such luck. Liam's blue eyes found me and he glared at me like I'd kicked his favorite puppy. His eyes were the color of a winter's sky just after dawn and not much warmer.

"Do you have any idea of the scandal you're causing? How much this could hurt your appeal in the negotiations? How much damage she is doing to you?" he asked, his voice cold and impersonal. It reminded me of when I'd overheard Freddie speaking with James at the cabin. There was no friendly smile or gentle teasing. Just professional and impersonal words.

I opened my mouth, but I didn't know what to say.

"Leave her alone," Freddie growled at him.

Liam turned his glower onto Freddie. "She is the talk of three news stations. Everyone wants to know about the American. Unfortunately, all they know is that she doesn't know how to behave. Pictures of inappropriate footwear. Kissing, Freddie. *Kissing.* That is completely uncalled for and strictly against protocol. She hasn't even done the Stair Walk for heaven's sake."

My cheeks went hot to the touch. It hadn't even been much of a kiss. Just a peck on the cheek. Maybe I could pretend I was French and doing a traditional greeting.

"It's not that bad," Sophie told him. "The press is just curious. They don't have much to go with, so they're focusing on what they do have."

"Which isn't proper for a royal family," Liam replied. He shook his head. "I can't believe how badly you've botched this. I'll have to fix everything."

"Isn't that your job?" Freddie asked his brother. "To make sure everything is prepared and perfect? I'm the screw-up, remember? I'm just following the job you laid out for me. I obviously planned this just to make you look bad."

For a split second, Liam's cold demeanor flashed into something red hot. He smoothed his jacket lapels, taking a moment to regain his composure.

"Frederick, you need to make sure that your romantic liaisons are appropriate for the monarchy." Liam's tone was so frosty I swore I could see his breath in the air. "That hasn't happened."

"And it isn't her fault," Freddie shot back. He rose to his feet, standing toe to toe with his older brother. "Zoey has done nothing wrong. I will not have you attack her. She is anything but inappropriate. I take responsibility. You will stop this. Now."

Liam took a step back, surprise on his face as he stared at his younger brother. A beat of silence grew between them, awkward and uncomfortable.

"Liam? You said the press is hungry to know more about her?" Sophie asked, untangling her legs from underneath her. She rose gracefully to her feet, crossing the room with a ballerina's grace, and put herself between the two brothers.

"Yes," Liam replied, his gaze still locked on Freddie.

"Then we should give her to them," Sophie replied.

Both brothers and I stared at her.

"What?" I whispered. "I'm not press ready. I can't do an interview or something."

Panic started to curl in the pit of my stomach. I hated public speaking. I hated having everyone's attention on me. What if I messed up the interview? It would be on tape. Liam hated my innocent mistakes now, and I could only imagine the mistakes I could make in an interview.

"Oh, not a live interview," Sophie assured me. "Something that shows the people the real you. And it will benefit Freddie's negotiations."

I sat confused. Somehow, I didn't think me in fishing gear eating donuts or throwing a backyard barbecue with a cooler of beer was going to help Freddie's trade work.

"Zoey, you're a nurse, right?" Sophie continued. When I nodded she turned back to Liam. "So have her go to the hospital."

A million problems with this idea flew into my head. I wasn't accredited here. I didn't have a Paradisian nursing license. I'd looked up how to get one, but it took months and I hadn't studied for any of the tests. Besides, I didn't bring any scrubs.

Liam's mouth thinned, but he didn't frown. "Go on."

"Zoey, were you trained for adults or children?" Sophie asked me.

"Uh, adults," I stammered. "But Sophie…"

"Then Westshire General," Sophie said. "She goes in. Looks at the facilities. Greets some pre-selected patients. She gets to see some of the new technology Freddie already negotiated for the hospital from Navia. We'd have an American nurse praising Paradisa and Navia."

"Hmm…" Liam raised an eyebrow.

"I make sure her outfit is perfect," Sophie continued. "Freddie makes sure she follows protocol."

"Good luck with that," Liam mumbled under his breath.

"The press gets their look at Zoey, but we get to

control the narrative," Sophie continued as if she hadn't heard Liam's snide comment. "It's a great way for us to give Zoey good press coverage. They'll see the lovely American girlfriend taking an interest in Paradisia's well-being. We get to praise our connection with Navia. It's a perfect way to officially introduce her and start to create some goodwill toward Navia. Everyone wins."

Liam didn't look pleased, but he didn't say no either. "It could work."

"Are you okay with that?" Freddie asked, turning to look at me. "You can always say no."

I looked from Freddie to Sophie to Liam.

I wanted to say no. The last thing I wanted was to go out in public and have my picture taken. We would be in a hospital, but that didn't mean I had a clue as to what we were doing. I could already see disaster looming ahead of me, but I didn't see a way around it either.

Freddie pleaded with me using only his eyes. He wanted to make his brother happy. I could do that. All I had to do was go to some stupid hospital and smile and wave. Maybe push a couple of retired volunteers around in a wheelchair a few times.

I sighed. "I'll do it."

"Excellent!" Sophie clapped her hands and smiled at me. "Don't worry. I'll have you looking perfect."

"I want only positive press from this," Liam warned. His eyes went to Sophie. "Fix things with the social media representative. Make this look good. Make *her* look good. Make the Navia deal look good."

"Yes, sir," Sophie replied. She was practically vibrating with excitement.

I was already swimming in dread.

Liam faced me. "I'm not pleased with the current media around you. This is your chance. Do not let us down."

Freddie was suddenly between us, his arms crossed and eyes fever bright.

"You don't get to talk to her like that," he said.

Once again, Liam took a small step backward. It looked so awkward that he nearly stumbled, but Freddie didn't flinch.

"I'll do my best," I said, peeking my head around Freddie. Suddenly, I remembered that he was the King and I was supposed to get up and curtsy and...

I didn't get up. It was too late now. I'd messed that up. If I did it now, it would only draw attention to the fact that I didn't do it in the first place. I didn't want Liam more unhappy than he already was.

Freddie glared at his brother as he resettled himself on the couch. He flung his arm protectively over my shoulder, pulling me into him. His strength comforted me. He was my knight in shining armor as he turned on the TV and put on the movie.

"It'll be fine, Liam," Sophie promised. "You look like you could use some rest."

He nodded, suddenly looking tired. Sophie touched his shoulder and even from the couch I could see him stiffen. She pulled back, realizing that she'd touched the king.

She ducked into a quick curtsy and hurried back to her chair.

If Freddie had a normal relationship with his brother, I would have offered to have Liam stay and watch the movie with us. But Liam wasn't a normal brother.

Before I could offer to let him stay, he turned and walked out of the room.

CHAPTER 31

"You did well today," Sophie said, picking up her purse and carefully tucking it over her shoulder. "Well, other than the whole walking in high-heels part."

"I did warn you," I replied. I sat demurely on a high-backed chair in my room. I was waiting for her to leave so that I could slouch and flop into bed. I was exhausted.

Princess training was hard work.

"I thought you were kidding," Sophie said. She shook her head. "Well, it's something for us to work on tomorrow."

"But tomorrow we're going to the hospital." A small ripple of fear went through me. I wasn't ready for our hospital visit, but Sophie and Liam both wanted it done as soon as possible. They wanted the good stories about me coming out instead of just more pictures of my scandalously bare shoulders.

"Yes. We're going to practice in the morning before we leave," Sophie replied. She looked over at me. "Don't worry. You'll be wearing flats to the hospital. I want this to go well, remember?"

I wanted to stick my tongue out at her, but that was decidedly not royal.

"I'll see you at seven. We're going to go over breakfast protocol while we eat," she said.

"Do I get actual breakfast?" I asked hopefully.

"You get egg whites and a superfood smoothie," she replied. "You have to look like a princess, and that requires sacrifice."

I sighed. I had expected as much. I wasn't a fan of my new diet. It was all low carb, low fat, healthy stuff that I knew I should be eating.

I missed my cheese curds and beer. I missed barbecue and desserts. But I could do it if it would help Freddie's image. If I could look the part that he needed me to play, I could eat egg whites.

Sophie paused with her purse in hand by the door. "You really did do well today. It's a lot to learn."

For the first time all day, I didn't feel like a total failure. Sophie was a tough master. She didn't let me slide on anything. It reminded me a lot of nursing school. There were many correct answers, but Sophie wanted me to pick the *most* correct one.

"Thanks." I smiled at her.

"Get some rest. I need you looking your best tomorrow," she said. She made sure her hair was smooth and she left the room. She didn't look like she'd spent the last twelve hours making me into a princess. "Oh, and there's something I wanted to tell you."

I raised my eyebrows, already expecting the worst. "Oh?"

"I want you to know how important what Freddie did yesterday was," Sophie replied. She fiddled with the strap of her purse.

"What Freddie did?" I mentally went through yesterday, trying to pick out something important.

"Standing up to Liam," Sophie explained.

"He defended me," I replied. "That's kind of what a boyfriend is supposed to do."

"He defended you to *Liam*. He always let Liam win. Liam is the King, Zoey. He's the most important person in the building, this city, this country, and possibly this entire corner of the world." Sophie fixed me with her gaze. "And Freddie told him to back off."

"Oh." Warmth rose in my chest and a small surprised smile crossed my face.

"Not only that, Freddie didn't back down, and Freddie always gives in to Liam." Sophie paused, making sure I understood just how important this was. "And he didn't yesterday. He was ready to punch Liam if needed. I don't think I've ever seen him do that. Ever."

My heart pressed hard against my ribs as love for that man grew inside me.

"I didn't realize it was a big deal," I said. I now understood the strange step back Liam had done. The surprised look on his face when Freddie hadn't backed down.

Freddie had fought for me.

Sophie shrugged. "For most men with older brothers, standing up for a girlfriend would be sweet. But for Freddie and Liam... For them it's a big deal."

"Thanks for telling me." I wrapped my arms around myself, keeping all the happy feelings safe inside of me.

"I figured that since it's my job to tell you what the

monarchy is doing, I should explain that too," Sophie replied with a wink. "Anyway, never doubt that man loves you."

"I don't," I assured her.

She smiled. "Anyway, I'll see you tomorrow. Have a lovely evening."

As soon as the door clicked shut behind her, I let myself slump into a puddle on the couch. It wasn't even a comfy couch, but it felt so good not to sit perfectly straight. I didn't realize how many muscles it took to have perfect posture or just how bad my posture was until I had someone reminding me of it every ten seconds.

I groaned as I stood up. I kicked off my shoes and slid out of my clothes, pulling on the most comfortable pair of sweatpants and a t-shirt. I had forgotten how nice it was to just wear comfy scrubs all day. Dress clothes were not comfortable.

I knew I should hang the skirt. I knew I should pick up the silk shirt and at least throw it over the back of the couch, but I was too tired. I crawled into bed, pulling the heavy covers up around my chin. I sent a goodnight message to Freddie and set my phone down. The lights were low and I was ready for sleep. It was barely past dinnertime, but I was ready to call it a night.

There was a knock at the door. I opened one eye and glared at the door, hoping that it was just my imagination.

The knock came again.

I sighed. Sophie probably forgot something. Or she wanted me to practice one last thing.

I padded over the soft carpet and slid the door open. "No more curtsies, Sophie. I'm tired."

Freddie's smile filled the room.

"Shhh," he hissed, slipping through the doorway. "Mum saw me in the hallway and she thinks I safely tucked into bed for an early evening."

I glanced down the empty hallway, making sure that no one saw him sneak into my room. He wasn't supposed to come to my room unsupervised per royal decorum. We were supposed to meet in a sitting room or at least keep the doors open. Freddie's shoulders relaxed the moment the door clicked shut.

He reached for me, pulling me to him in a sweet kiss that made getting up for the knock worth it.

"You're already in pajamas?" Freddie asked, looking down at me.

"What? You don't like my PJs?" I asked, crossing my arms and narrowing my eyes at him.

"I'd like them better on the floor," he replied with a cheeky grin. "But on you is a great second."

I rolled my eyes, but smiled as I headed back to my bed.

"Come join me," I said, patting the bed beside me.

"I'm not supposed to," he reminded me. He wore casual pants and a soft t-shirt. It was loungewear, but a step up from pajamas. Royals didn't even sleep in regular pajamas.

"Since when do you follow the rules?" I asked him.

He grinned and hopped into bed. The light went out, wrapping us both in a blanket of early evening shadows.

I snuggled into his shoulder, his arm wrapped around me. I loved the way our bodies fit together like pieces of a puzzle. His warmth seeped into me, soothing aches I didn't even realize I had. He completed me. I felt whole when pressed into him. The world wasn't quite so scary and I didn't care quite so much what anyone else thought.

"How was your day?" he asked, his voice rumbling through his chest under my head.

"Hard," I replied. "I think I'm starting to get it, but then there's random rules that don't make any sense."

"Like no blue on Tuesdays?" Freddie asked.

"Wait, I can't wear blue on Tuesdays?" I lifted my head, looking at him.

He winked at me, grinning at his joke. I rolled my eyes and smacked him gently in the shoulder.

"The worst part is that it's believable," I continued. "I'm really afraid of messing things up tomorrow."

He tightened his embrace around me. "You are going to be perfect tomorrow," he assured me. "I know it. Because you're already perfect."

I felt like I was made of sunshine.

"How about you?" I asked, changing the subject. "How was your day?"

"Better now that I'm here," he replied. He sighed. "The negotiations are difficult. The Duke wants to stay three steps ahead at all times. I don't feel like I'm making any real progress. It's all just talk right now. There's still so much to do before the official delegation arrives. I'm not sure I'll get it all done in time. Especially with all the small boring things."

I thought of what Sophie had said. That Freddie was more useful than he realized.

"Maybe the small talk is important. It makes people feel comfortable," I told him. "It's good for building trust and that's what this deal needs, right?"

Freddie smiled down at me. "I'm sure it does help. I'm

sure it's useful. It just doesn't feel like it. Especially with my brother breathing down my neck to do more."

"Let's not talk about Liam," I said.

"It does feel strange to talk about my older brother while I'm in bed with you," Freddie agreed. He nuzzled the top of my head, giving me three quick kisses. "What do you want to talk about?"

"Um, global warming? Politics?" I offered. "You know, something to keep our blood pressure down."

Freddie chuckled and the sound went straight to my bones. It resonated deep within me, bringing joy and happiness.

"Hey, I love you," I blurted out.

Even in the pale, flimsy light, I could see him smile.

"I love you," he replied. He kissed my head again. "I can't tell you how much it means that you're here."

"In bed with you?" I teased. "Because I'm not taking these sweats off no matter how much you sweet talk me. I'm already in trouble with your brother. I don't need your mom after me as well."

Freddie chuckled again. "I'm just glad you haven't gone running. My family... this place..." He sighed. "It's a complicated place to be."

"I'm not going to lie and say I didn't consider running," I told him. "Especially when Sophie made me practice correct etiquette for holding a spoon for two hours."

Even in the dark, I could see the handsome curve of the smile on his lips. The way his hair flopped carelessly yet perfectly onto the pillow. He was warm and strong beneath me.

"But I'm not running," I told him. "It'll take more than a lesson with a spoon to scare me off."

Freddie's muscles relaxed underneath me. His hand found mine, our fingers interlocking in the dark.

Lying together in the dark felt more intimate than sex. We were exposed to only one another. We could pretend there was nothing beyond my wooden door. That the stone walls held only the two of us. That we were the only people that mattered in the entire world.

He was bare to me in the dark, despite being fully clothed. Just as I was bare to him. There was nowhere to hide in the dark. And nowhere I'd rather be.

"I love you," he whispered again, his voice heavy with sleep.

I knew we should get up. That he should sleep in his own bed, but I didn't move. He was too warm, too comforting, too wonderful. I didn't want to be in this bed alone.

I snuggled into him, listening to his breath slowly even into sleep. I loved that I made him feel safe enough to rest. With me, he was comfortable and relaxed.

Because that's how I felt with him.

We were just ourselves.

CHAPTER 32

"It's too bad no one needed CPR," Sophie lamented as we walked down a corridor of the hospital. She wore a pristine cream dress with matching heels. I wore a light blue pant suit that made me think of super fancy scrubs. I was fairly sure that had been Sophie's intent when dressing me this morning.

"Right... too bad," I agreed, sarcasm dripping off my voice.

"Oh, I didn't mean..." Sophie went a pretty pink. She even blushed prettily. "I meant, it would have been some great press to have you save someone's life."

I smiled and nodded politely. I knew she meant well, but it just showed me the disconnect between our worlds. I would never wish for someone to have an injury, especially one requiring CPR, just so I could get a good photo.

It probably made me a terrible celebrity, but a good person.

Overall, the day was going well. I had followed all of the rules the royal family sent out and I had even gone above and beyond what they expected. Everyone was happy with me. I was happy with myself. I was proud of how hard I had worked today.

We walked down the hallway, Sophie's heels clicking on the tile floor. My own flats made no sound as we walked. Light flowed in through big windows on the sides of the hallway. It was a beautiful hospital made out of an old church that was renovated into something new and old at the same time.

I imagined working in a place like this. I imagined coming to work every day and basically being in a castle. I imagined hundreds of years of women and men coming to work here. The lives that had started here. The lives that had ended here.

It was so different from the hospital at home. That hospital had been built in the 1970s. The linoleum floors were scratched and worn. The elevators creaked and groaned. That hospital smelled like a hospital. It smelled like sanitizer and bleach.

This hospital smelled like old stone. This hospital didn't smell old- it smelled ancient. But a clean ancient. It wasn't bad, just different. Despite being a hospital, it didn't feel like home.

We walked down the wide stone hallway until we came to a series of doors. Sophie opened one and I found several of the camera men that had been following me all day. They were seated with computers open and footage already going.

I could see myself smiling and laughing on the video and for the first time, I didn't think I looked stupid. It was a testament to the skill of the photographers that they made me look so regal.

"I'm going to check some of your video," Sophie explained, pausing at the doorway. "You head down to the courtyard. Freddie will meet you there."

I nodded and my heart sped up. I couldn't wait to see him.

"There will be members of the press waiting for you," she continued. "You'll answer some pre-approved questions and take some photos. Remember to mention how new technology is changing healthcare for the better."

I nodded. I'd made sure to mention how impressed I was at everything in the hospital, but especially the new improvements due to increased trade with Navia."

"Also, no holding hands with Freddie or anything romantic," Sophie reminded me. "You're supposed to be just friends. He's here as a courtesy. And remember to smile."

She made a cheesy grin at me, moving her hands to enforce the motion.

"Am I not smiling enough?" I asked, trying to remember what my face had been doing all day. It hurt like I'd been smiling.

"You're doing fine," Sophie assured me. "Just, smile *more*. We want good pictures. We want everyone to like you and think of you as the pretty angel on Freddie's shoulder."

I screwed my face up into an overly happy grin. I smiled so hard the muscles in my face hurt with the effort of it.

"Too much," Sophie said, shaking her head. "You know what I mean."

I let the smile fall. I did know what she'd meant. I was just tired. We'd been at the hospital for over two hours. I'd pushed wheelchairs and talked to patients. I'd brought cookies to every nurses' station on every floor and then smiled with the nurses.

I'd talked to everyone, ignoring the existential dread of being the center of attention. Everyone wanted to talk to me. Everyone wanted to be in the pictures.

Everyone wanted to meet the Prince's girlfriend, even if it wasn't official yet. It was like getting a sneak peek into the future. A chance to say, "I knew her before she was famous" and no one in the entire hospital wanted to miss the opportunity.

The camera was always on, looking for good images and video clips.

It was exhausting.

I left Sophie in a dark room to review the current footage. I hoped we had enough. I didn't want to go back and shoot more. I wanted to go home, take a shower, and hide under the covers for the rest of the day. Preferably with Freddie.

I followed the hallway down and to the left. I'd seen the courtyard from a window upstairs, so I knew there had to be an entrance around here somewhere. The hallway was quieter and narrower here. I wasn't sure I was going the right way, but I found an exit door and stepped outside.

And ended up in a parking area.

I sighed. My internal compass appeared to be malfunctioning. I'd been sure that this door would lead me to the courtyard. I tried to go back through the door, but it had locked shut behind me. I had no way to get back inside.

Great.

At least the weather was nice. The afternoon sunshine felt good as I walked across the parking lot. I could see a gate with trees behind it on the other side of the lot. I'd just go in through the gate, find Freddie, answer the questions, do my best to smile, and then we could go home.

I reached the gate, and just as I opened it, two people came up behind me. The woman wore a smart blue blazer and the man held a TV camera. They both looked out of breath. They were probably one of the reporters I was supposed to talk to and were running late.

I smiled politely, holding the gate open. "Are you one of the reporters I'm supposed to talk to?" I asked.

"You could say that," the woman replied with a huge smile. "You're Zoey Miller, right?"

I smiled back, trying not to look at the camera. Sophie had told me not to look at the camera for these interviews. Look at the interviewer. "I am."

"What do you have to say about these photos?" the woman asked. She thrust out several 8x10 glossy pictures, forcing them into my hands.

"What?" I fumbled with the photos, letting go of the open gate. It clanged shut, startling me with the sound.

"Is that you in those photos?" she asked, pointing to the top one.

I nodded, flustered. The top photo was an older one, taken in front of my freshman dorm. I beamed out from the photograph, my blonde hair loose around my shoulders and wearing a university T-shirt I'd won at orientation that morning.

"What do you have to say about the rest of the pictures? Since you just confirmed that's you." The woman grinned at me.

I frowned, and looked down at the other pictures in my hands.

They were all of me and they were all bad pictures. I was drinking. A lot. I was doing a keg-stand in one. I had a red solo cup in another and was obviously drunk. A third had me asleep on a dirty couch, my makeup smeared, an empty beer bottle in my hand.

They were not flattering. They were not the pictures of a perfect angel keeping Freddie on the right path.

And they were also several years old. They were images from my first college party. Sweet little freshmen me had gone to a fraternity house rager. I'd gotten far too drunk and fallen asleep on a couch. My roommate had woken me up shortly after the last image and made me go home.

I stared at the photos in my hand.

"That is you, right?" The woman asked, a cruel smile filling her face. "You already said it was."

Panic set in. These were not the reporters I was supposed to be talking to.

"Where did you get these?" I gasped.

"So, you admit these are you?" The woman's eyes glinted with malicious delight.

I froze, every muscle in my body going absolutely rigid. My heart rate went out of control. My vision blurred. This was bad.

Sophie was going to kill me.

Liam was going to kill me.

"No comment," I stammered, reaching for the gate. I had to get inside to the courtyard. I had to get to Freddie. I had to get away from them.

"Do you routinely drink to excess?" the woman pressed. "Do you have a problem with alcohol?"

The gate handle slipped in my sweaty fingers. My heart pounded so hard in my chest I thought I might explode. My vision blurred, either from panic or tears, I wasn't sure. I tugged and pulled on it, struggling to get away. It wouldn't open.

Suddenly, the gate swung out, nearly knocking me off my feet. Freddie stood on the other side.

His smile was brittle and cold as he looked at the woman and the cameraman.

"There you are," he said warmly to me, motioning for me to join him. I scrambled inside. I wanted to hide behind him. "The real reporters are waiting."

Freddie slammed the gate in the face of the woman with the blue blazer. The metallic clang rang out harsh. It seemed to echo for a long time.

"Are you okay?" Freddie asked, slowly turning to face me. "I heard the gate close, so I came over. Those are the reporters for that trash "Royalty Watch" show. Did you talk to them?"

I was shaking so hard I couldn't answer.

"Please tell me you didn't talk to them." Freddie's voice was quiet and had a grim warning in it.

"They had photos," I whispered. I realized they were still in my hands. I thrust them out at him. Freddie had to tug them gently out of my fingers. "I didn't mean to talk to them."

He let out a long sigh as he looked through the pictures. Frustration crossed his brow, his shoulders drooped, and a little bit of the light left his eyes.

"These are from years ago," I explained, frantic that he

understand. "I don't know where they got them. I thought they were the reporters I was supposed to be talking to. She just handed these to me and... and..."

And I'd ruined the entire day's work in two seconds. It didn't matter that these were old. There was no footage of me verifying them.

All our hard work today wouldn't matter. A keg-standing girlfriend was far more interesting than one walking around a hospital.

Maybe Sophie was right. CPR might have been a better option.

And I hated myself for thinking that.

Freddie pulled me to him, wrapping his arms around me. I buried my face in his chest, willing myself not to cry. I didn't want to get makeup all over his beautiful suit. I didn't want to make an even bigger fool out of myself. He wasn't supposed to be holding me, but I clung to him like a lifeline.

"It'll be okay," Freddie promised, his hand gently smoothing my hair. "It's okay."

I knew that it wasn't. Not really.

"I'm sorry," I whispered into his chest.

He sighed. "It'll be fine."

He sounded like he believed it as much as I did. Which meant, neither of us believed it at all.

CHAPTER 33

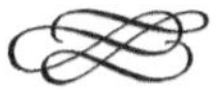

I hid in my room for as long as I could. I didn't want to come out and go to dinner, but I didn't really have a choice. Dinner was already scheduled to be a celebratory meal in the dining room. The king and queen mother were to be there.

Except we didn't have anything to celebrate. I'd failed my job today.

I put on clean clothes. Sophie had laid out a tea length dark blue dress with lace overlay and long sleeves this morning. I wore it with stockings, as per her instructions. I put my hair up in a neat bun, hoping that the simple style would be acceptable. My makeup was light and natural, just the way Sophie had taught me.

At least I could do that right.

A knock on my door summoned me to dinner.

"It's time, Ms. Miller," Mr. Irson's voice called through the door.

I hurried over and opened it.

"Thank you," I told him. "I'm mostly ready."

He smiled and looked me over. "You look lovely," he said. He frowned slightly at my feet. "No heels?"

I shook my head. "Not if I don't want to embarrass myself more than I already have."

He glanced down the hallway and then back to me. "I heard what happened," he said softly. "I'm sorry that they tricked you like that."

He reached out and patted my shoulder.

I almost cried. It was such a kind gesture. My lower lip trembled and I swallowed the huge lump in my throat.

"Thanks," I managed to whisper. I sniffled, despite my best effort. "I'm really trying."

"I know. I see it," he replied. He squeezed my shoulder. "And for what it's worth, I think you're doing well. This is not an easy world to jump into."

"You can say that again," I replied. I sighed. "Do I really have to go down to dinner? They're all going to be so disappointed in me."

"You have to go." He gave me a stern look. "You'll survive. You're made of strong stuff."

I didn't feel like I was, but the way he said it made me believe that it might be true.

"What if I'm not, though?" I asked. "I'm not like Sophie. She is so much better at all of this. She wouldn't wear the wrong dress. She wouldn't have talked to that reporter. What if Freddie picked the wrong girl?"

Mr. Irson stood quietly for a moment. His eyes narrowed and he looked me over, inspecting me once again.

"Freddie chose well," he said after a moment. "He picked the right woman for *him*."

I tried not to roll my eyes. "But I am terrible at this."

"So?" he asked.

"Freddie needs someone who can navigate his world. Someone who doesn't set the press into a feeding frenzy every time she steps out the front door." I shrugged. "That's not me."

"Freddie needs someone who understands him. Someone who makes him smile and laughs at his jokes," Mr. Irson countered. "He needs you. Not Sophie."

Again, the way he said it had me believing it could be true. That he could be right.

I sighed. "Well, hopefully the royal family agrees with you. Wish me luck that I'll survive dinner."

"If the Queen Mother gives you any trouble, you just remind her of the night in '63," Mr. Irson advised.

"The night of '63? What happened?" I asked, raising an interested eyebrow.

Mr. Irson gave me a wicked grin. "Something much worse than a few college photos. If she gives you any trouble, you come find me."

I hugged him. This time, he was a little less surprised, though still quite stiff.

"Thanks again," I said, pulling back.

"You are quite welcome. Now, go downstairs. You have five minutes before you're expected and being early can only help your case. Punctuality matters."

I nodded and quickly headed down the ornate hallway and down the beautifully carved stairs. I passed several maids in their black and white outfits. They all pretended not to look at me as I passed, but I could feel their eyes on me anyway.

It wasn't unfriendly, but it wasn't welcoming either. I

was very clearly an interloper in their world. Even the maids knew this place and its rules better than I did.

I breathed a sigh of relief when I found the dining room doors still shut. Two big heavy wooden doors with elaborate carvings of stags and trees barred my path. It meant that I wasn't late. At least I hadn't screwed this up.

I chewed nervously on the inside of my cheek as I paced a small space beside the door. There was a bench I could sit on, but I was too nervous.

How angry was Liam going to be? His mother?

How much had I let Freddie down? I knew that he pretended like it didn't matter, but it did. So much depended on him. His family was the most important thing to him. Sure, he complained about them, but he never let them down. He followed their rules, even if he didn't like them.

He already felt like the Prince of Failure. His oldest brother was king. His middle brother was a talented politician and beloved for finding an American senator's daughter to marry. He thought he was the last in line for everything.

This trade negotiation was supposed to change every-thing for him. He needed me to hold up his image and make him look good. He needed me to support him and give him good optics.

And I'd confirmed keg stand pictures instead.

I wondered if maybe this was a sign. All my mistakes were a sign from the universe that we weren't' supposed to be together like this.

On the other hand, he made me happy. Freddie's smile was sunshine and I was a plant. I only grew when he was around. He made me laugh and giggle. When he grinned at me, my world felt right.

I thought he felt the same.

But since we'd come here, he hadn't grinned much. If anything, he'd been grumpier. I'd thought it was just the stress of coming home, but maybe it was me. Maybe it was the stress of having to deal with someone who had absolutely no idea what they were doing. .

"Waiting for dinner, Ms. Miller?" A male voice asked, distracting me from my thoughts.

I turned, grateful for any excuse to get me out of my thoughts only to find the Duke leering at me.

I swallowed down bile and tried not to let distaste show on my face. I don't know what it was, but there was something smarmy and unlikable in his face. Maybe it was the hollow smile. Maybe it was the ice cold way he looked at me like I was a pebble about to get in his shoe. I managed to remember my manners and dipped a small curtsy.

"Punctuality is important, Your Grace," I replied, keeping my voice light. "And I am famished."

"Well, don't let it ruin your American figure," he replied.

"I'll do my best," I said. I couldn't decide if he meant it as an insult, so I just smiled politely.

"Did you have a nice trip to the hospital?" he asked.

"I did," I replied. "It's an absolutely beautiful building. I love the way they merged the old building with new technology there."

I glanced around, hoping that the dining room doors would open. I could escape into the dining room and at least with others around I wouldn't be his main focus.

He nodded slowly, a neutral agreement noise coming from him. I smiled politely, glancing again at the door. His cold eyes unnerved me. They had no light to them. No joy resided inside this man.

"I also saw the pictures."

"Oh?" I replied. "I didn't know they had approved them yet. Although, I suppose since Sophie is your daughter you would have access to them before anyone else."

"Not those pictures," he replied. He smiled at me, but it was a shark's smile. A cruel smile. "The other ones."

"Oh?" My heart pounded in my chest. How in the world had he possibly seen the photos already? It had only been a couple of hours. Surely the "Royal Watch" hadn't released them yet, right?

He shook his head and made a soft tsk sound. "It's a shame. I did have high hopes for you," the Duke said. He watched me, his eyes unblinking as he waited for me to break.

"Those were very old," I explained.

"It doesn't matter," he replied. "What matters is that they are out there now. What matters is what the people think. Freddie is a beloved prince. They will want what is best for him."

"And what if I'm what's best for him?" I asked, feeling a hot anger rise in the cold shame of my chest.

He shrugged. "I know he thinks you are, but his life is not his own. It is the curse of royalty. They do not get to choose their own lives."

"Freddie has chosen me." I said the words with conviction, but somewhere deep in the dark of me, I wasn't so sure. There was nothing concrete to say that he hadn't. He'd brought me here to Paradisa, hadn't he?

"He's done a poor job of preparing you," the Duke scoffed. "Or are you just struggling? I did offer to help if that is the case."

"Sophie is doing just fine," I growled.

"Of course she is," he agreed. "She is my daughter, after all. *She* doesn't fail things."

The insinuation hurt, but I ignored it.

I raised my chin, unwilling to back down now.

"I'm afraid I've gone about this all wrong," the Duke said. He sighed. "I didn't mean to offend you, Ms. Miller. I simply may be the only one willing to tell you the truth."

"The truth?" I asked, crossing my arms.

"The older princes won't say it. They love their brother too much. The Queen Mother won't say it for the same reason. And young Prince Frederick is too in love with you to see a single fault," he replied. He held up his hands like he was warding off an attack. "Again, because he loves you. There is nothing wrong with that."

"What won't they tell me?" I pressed. Anger bubbled under my skin.

"That you don't belong here." The Duke said it in the same tone of voice someone would talk about the weather. Or a baseball game. Like it was normal and not at all unkind.

"Excuse me?"

"You are an American. You are lovely and very sweet, but this place..." He motioned to the gilded and ornate walls all around us. "This place is not meant for you. You stick out here. You are attempting to try, and it is commendable, but overall, not worth the effort."

"So, you're telling me to leave?" I asked, my tone cool.

"Not at all, sweet girl. I would never say that," he said, another one of his flat smiles crossing his face. A politician's smile. "I'm simply giving you perspective. The prince is needed here. You aren't. They had to make a special trip to a hospital to provide some basic reason for you to even have a reason to leave the castle."

I swallowed hard. He was right. But I wasn't about to say that to him.

"I'm trying to save you some heartache," he continued. "I'm trying to be honest with you. I tell people the truth. I don't play games like most politicians. And I'm telling you that despite your best efforts, this isn't the place for you."

"I love Freddie," I said stubbornly.

"I know you do. And he loves you," he replied. "But that doesn't mean that this will end in a happily ever after. What happens in a month when you fail again? What happens when you tell someone a state secret? What happens when Freddie needs you, and you don't have Sophie to tell you what to do? When you accidentally insult the Prime Minister of Japan and lose Paradisa another trade contract?"

I hated every word coming out of that man's mouth. I wanted to punch him. I wanted to sock him right in his chubby jaw and send him flying into the wall.

But that didn't mean he was wrong.

"Wait, what do you mean *another* trade contract?" I asked, suddenly noticing his words.

"It's not important. Freddie managed to pull it out of the fire," the Duke replied. "But Navia is unsure of working with a man so loose with his morals. You don't follow the country's traditions of Stair Walk. You party to excess. What kind of person is Freddie if he associates with you? Is that someone that Navia wants to do business with?"

I stood stuttering. Did I really have that kind of power?

"As I said, I don't mean to tell you this to be unkind," he said. I realized suddenly that his hand was on my shoulder. I did my best not to recoil. "I tell you this for the exact opposite reason. I do not wish to see you or Prince Frederick harmed. He managed to convince Navia to continue the trade, so it was not a problem. This time."

I dropped my shoulder out from under him, taking a step back. I still felt his touch on my shoulder like he'd covered me in grease.

"I'm here to help," he said. His ice eyes met mine. "If you wish for my help, I will give it. If you wish to leave, I can get you home. There is no shame in giving the Prince what he needs."

"I have no intention of leaving," I informed him, raising my chin like all the princesses in movies did.

"Of course," he smiled that reptilian smile again that made my skin crawl. "Just know that should you ever need me, I am at your disposal. I hate seeing you fail."

I bristled. "I am trying my best."

"And what if your best isn't enough?"

I stared at him, unable to come up with a reply. That thought haunted me a lot recently. That I wasn't enough. That I wasn't good enough for a prince.

"Have a wonderful dinner," he said. He bowed slightly, and I wondered if he was mocking me. "I hope the princes won't be too hard on you."

He turned and walked down the hallway. He fit in with

the opulent artwork and plush rugs. I rubbed at my arms, suddenly cold and exhausted. What little energy I'd regained after the trip to the hospital, he'd drained.

I didn't want to think about his words. I didn't want to think about how he was right. I didn't belong here. I wasn't sure I ever would.

Luckily, the doors to the dining room opened and I was able to go inside. It wasn't the ideal distraction, but it was better than thinking over what the Duke had said.

CHAPTER 34

*D*inner was a quiet and terse affair.

Liam pointedly never looked at me. The Queen Mother watched her sons with sad eyes. She attempted small talk twice, but when no one helped her continue the conversations, she quickly stopped.

Freddie tried to answer his mother, but Liam shot him such deadly looks that he quickly stopped talking at all.

I had nothing to say. What could I possibly have to say?

"I'm so sorry I went to a kegger once in college. If I had known those pictures would come back to haunt me, I would have stayed in my dorm room and never left."

It wouldn't have fixed anything.

So, we ate our delicious food in the awkward silence of silverware and chewing.

"Freddie, I would speak with you," Liam announced, setting down his knife and fork on the empty plate.

"I'm actually rather tired," Freddie tried to say, but Liam cut him off.

"We have things to discuss." There was no arguing with the King.

Freddie nodded, his face pale. He carefully placed his silverware and waited for Liam.

Liam stood. We all did. That was protocol. Everyone does what the king does. If he stands, we stand. When he sits, we sit. We had to wait to leave until King Liam was ready to leave.

Liam stalked out the main doors, leaving a cold trail of wind behind him. The room suddenly felt far too large and drafty. Outside, the wind howled with a storm about to hit.

"I'll come find you," Freddie whispered to me, putting a hand on my shoulder as he passed. He nodded politely to his mother and followed his brother out of the room.

I waited for the Queen Mother to take her seat again before sitting.

"You're getting better," she remarked, picking her fork back up. "Would you like dessert? The boys abandoned us before the pudding came out."

I wanted to run up to my room and hide for a week.

"Pudding sounds lovely," I replied, trying my best to smile.

The Queen Mother motioned to a steward waiting by the kitchen doors. Those doors were cleverly carved to blend into the paneled walls. Within seconds, a waiter emerged with two beautiful chocolate puddings on a silver platter.

My mouth watered. I hadn't been allowed to eat anything sweet since I got here. My diet was closely regu-lated so that I would look like a lithe perfect princess.

I'd lost three pounds already, but I missed food. I was

tired of salads and quinoa and simple chicken breasts. My only concession was ketchup. That was the only thing that I was allowed to have with my egg whites at breakfast that wasn't considered "Healthy."

The pudding called to me with the sugary goodness I craved.

I waited for the Queen Mother to take her first bite before tasting mine.

It was heaven. I've never been big on pudding, but this was pudding. It was thick, creamy, and decadent as sin. This was no instant mix pudding. I suddenly understood the Christmas songs about pudding.

"This is very hard for Freddie," the Queen Mother said. She dipped the tip of her spoon into the pudding and nibbled on the smallest of bites.

I sighed inwardly. Here it came. Here was the lecture.

"I'm not going to chastise you," she said, reading the look on my face.

"You're not?"

She shook her head. "What would it accomplish?" she asked. "I'm sure Sophie already laid out exactly what you should have done."

I cringed. Sophie had laid it out. She'd taken me to a quiet hallway and spelled out exactly how much those images could ruin everything.

"But the way I see it, there's nothing you could have done about it," the Queen Mother continued. "It does put a speed bump in our plans to accept you into the family, though."

My shoulders sagged and I played with my now empty pudding cup. I'd devoured it in three bites and wished I could have more. "I'm so sorry," I said softly.

"Oh child, Heaven knows that Freddie has had worse pictures," the Queen Mother replied, waving a hand through the air.

I looked up at her, surprised that she wasn't more angry.

"The problem isn't you. The problem is image. Our family is the face of the entire country. We must present an image that is strong, respectable, and untarnished. It is the price of the monarchy to always be on display, to always have to show the country the correct behavior," she explained.

This sounded very much like what Sophie, Liam, and Freddie had all told me. This is why I had to be perfect.

"We can't have any hint of scandal or drunkenness tied to the family," the Queen Mother explained. "Even if it is the truth. The truth doesn't matter to the public. Only what we show them."

I frowned, not quite following what she was saying.

"My point is, your infractions have been minor, my dear. They will be quickly forgotten, but at the moment they are causing problems," she explained. "Given the trade deal that Freddie is working on, they are problematic. He needs to appear scandal free and changed from his old ways."

I didn't know it was possible for my shoulders to sag lower, but they did. I was a failure. Freddie needed me to be perfect and I wasn't even close. I was actively hurting him. All he'd ever wanted was to make his family proud. This trade deal was his chance and I was in the way.

Maybe it would be best for me to just leave.

We could do a long distance thing. I loved him. He

loved me. We could make it work. Then I wouldn't be such a distraction to him here.

"Do I need to leave?" I asked. My voice caught on the words, not really wanting to say them out loud.

"No," she quickly told me. "If anything, you are a good influence on Freddie. Since he's met you, he's been happier than I've ever seen him. No, you can't leave him now."

"What do I do then?" I asked, raising my chin to look at her. "I promise I am trying."

"I *can* tell," she assured. "These photos are a speed bump, not a roadblock. Today was not the end of the world, despite what Liam might have you think."

"I feel like it is," I replied, so softly I'm not sure she could hear me.

"Bare shoulders, a kiss, and some college photos are nothing in the grand scheme of things. Those are all easily smoothed over," she assured me. "It just will take some time."

I didn't want to take time. I wanted Freddie to be happy now. I wanted to fit in here now.

"There is to be a ball in two weeks," she informed me. "It is to greet the official delegates from Navia."

I perked up, my shoulders raising slightly.

"It will be your chance to truly be introduced to Paradisa society. Your Stair Walk. By then, the video and photos you created today will be out and circulating. We will no longer have a party girl dating Freddie, but a respectable nurse," she told me.

Excitement and dread bubbled in my stomach.

"Would it be my official Stair Walk?" I asked, my voice tight.

"If things go well the next two weeks," she replied. "I see no reason not to have you walk the stairs with us."

I nodded, feeling a bundle of nerves clench and unclench along my spine.

"Thank you," I said softly.

"For what it's worth, I would give you a Stair Walk today if I could," she replied. When I looked up in surprise she continued, "Freddie loves you. In any other family, that would be more than enough. In any other family, approval wouldn't even be needed. But this family requires extra steps. Literally, in fact."

She smiled at her own joke about stairs and the Stair Walk.

I stared at her for a moment, unable to say anything. She approved. Even though she couldn't say so publicly, she didn't hate me.

The Queen Mother pushed her barely half eaten pudding away. "I'm sure that's been more than enough time for Liam to chastise Freddie." She stood slowly, using the table for support. "I recommend you go rescue the poor man."

I smiled at her, copying her standing motion.

"Thank you, Your Majesty," I said, remembering to dip into a curtsy at the last second.

The Queen Mother smiled and waved me off to go find Freddie.

CHAPTER 35

*W*ind shook the windows and promised rain when I found Freddie leaning against the wall next to the door to my room. His back was pressed against the wall, his long lean legs angled into the middle of the hallway. His shoulders slumped and he had his head leaned back against the wall with his eyes closed. He looked as exhausted as I felt.

"Hey." I took the spot on the wall next to him, close enough to touch. The hallway was dark with the incoming storm. The lights hadn't yet been turned on, giving us the illusion of privacy in the gloom.

"Hey." He didn't move his head off the wall or open his eyes.

"You okay?" I asked, moving my hand to find his. All happy thoughts of my Stair Walk vanished. He looked so pale and exhausted. Sad and overwhelmed.

"We should run away," he said. He opened his eyes and stared at the ceiling. "We should just leave. Just get in the car and go."

I had to admit that I liked the idea, but I knew it wouldn't work. The trade deal, Liam, and his responsibilities here wouldn't just disappear because we got in a car and left.

"I think that would cause even more scandal than we've got now," I replied. I gave his hand a squeeze that he didn't return.

He slowly turned and looked at me. His beautiful green eyes were dull. Usually, there was a sparkling light that danced in his gaze, but this evening, it was gone. The color was there, but none of the spark. The playful smile that always teased at his lips was lost.

"Are you okay?" I asked again. Outside thunder rumbled.

He sighed and turned away. "I wish we hadn't come back. I wish I hadn't done this trade negotiation with the Duke helping."

I had to agree. We'd been so happy in Chicago. We'd laughed. We'd smiled.

We didn't do either of those things here. Freddie was always off with Liam or the Duke. The Duke seemed to command all of his time. Freddie always seemed to be repeating the Duke's words.

I was always walking on eggshells to make sure I was following the rules. I could tell that Freddie was too. He was so stressed here, forced back into his familial role in addition to the stress of his new one.

"What if we leave soon?" I offered. "We stay long enough to make your brother happy, and then we go back home. We go back to the way it was before."

"We can't go back. This is home," he informed me. "And I can never leave. He says I'm too crucial."

I frowned. "What do you mean?"

"These trade treaties will always need me," Freddie explained, still staring at the far wall. "Apparently, I'm crucial for their continued success. I'll be needed for more of these deals. I am the grease that keeps the cogs moving. The leaders trust me because I am the third son and not likely to rule. I am an important part of the system now. It won't stop. It won't ever stop." He scoffed. "First time in my life I'm actually needed and it's the only place I don't want to be."

My chest tightened around my heart. It was a cruel trick to make Freddie think he wasn't needed for his country until the moment he found happiness elsewhere. For years he'd tried to find his place in the royal world, only to find he wasn't needed. Now that he had other things to make him happy, the royal world wanted him back.

I let go of Freddie's hand and gave him a full on hug instead. He held perfectly still for a moment before tucking his face into the curve of my shoulder and wrapping his arms so tightly around me it hurt.

His breathing was shaky and I wasn't sure if I was hugging him, or if he were just holding onto me for dear life.

"Come inside with me," I whispered, kicking open the door to my room. He nodded into my shoulder before straightening.

I closed the door behind us with a soft click. I locked it. One yellow lamp illuminated the bed like a spotlight, drawing both of us to it.

I knew what he needed. What we both needed. Something that would ground us and connect us back to one another.

I tugged on his hand, leading him to the bed. He hesitated, his green eyes going to mine.

I put a finger to my lips and tugged again.

A hint of a smile began to twitch on his lips.

"Are you sure?" he whispered.

I looked him over. His long, lean figure was so elegant. He wore dress slacks and a pale blue button-up shirt. He'd taken off the tie and jacket he'd worn at dinner and undone the top two buttons of his shirt. Not enough to see anything, but enough that he looked more relaxed.

"I already broke a rule today," I said, sashaying over to him. I reached up and undid the next button down on his shirt, loving the way his breath caught at my touch. "Might as well break another."

My hand settled on his chest, feeling the heat seep through the expensive fabric. I itched to touch his skin. How many days had it been since I'd been with him?

Too many. Even when we were separated by miles, we'd still been intimate. We'd talked on the phone or video called when I couldn't be in Chicago.

But here, even though we were steps from one another, we'd barely touched.

I missed him. I missed the Freddie that kissed me in the middle of a lake. I missed the Freddie that always called from his hotel room with naughty things for me to do in the middle of the night.

I missed us.

He licked his lower lip as I reached behind me and undid the zipper to my dress.

"Pull it," I whispered.

He did. The dark blue lace slid from me, pooling on the floor. I wore only a pretty lace bra and panties. His pupils dilated and his breath caught.

"Zoey…"

God, I loved the way he said my name. I loved the hoarse need that reverberated through him. I loved it when he looked at me like I was the most beautiful and sexy creature he'd ever seen in his life.

He didn't bother with the rest of the buttons. He tore the shirt open.

Buttons scattered and pinged off the bed frame. The sound of icy rain smacked the windows as I reached for him.

The wonderful ginger and citrus scent filled my mind. I'd missed smelling him. I'd missed being close enough to smell him. I wanted to bury my face into his shoulder and breathe him in like I was breathing in life.

My hands were on his chest, feeling his skin. Warm hard muscle greeted me and I moaned slightly in anticipation. His movements became frantic at the sound as he kicked off his shoes and pulled free of his pants.

He wanted me to the point of distraction.

His hands were on my lace panties, ripping and tearing. I didn't care if he ripped them off me. I wanted them ripped off. I wanted him inside of me more than I wanted to breathe. I needed to feel him. I needed to know that he was still mine. I craved our connection.

I reached for his briefs, tugging on the elastic. His length sprang free. He was hard and ready for me. I licked my lips as I feasted my eyes on him.

Good lord was he glorious and I was starving for him.

I gave his shoulder a gentle shove, pushing him to the

bed. He sat on my fancy four poster bed, his green eyes dark with desire as I stripped bare before him.

I knelt to the floor, moving between his legs. I loved the way his pupils blew as he realized what I was doing. I loved the way his breath caught. I loved the way the muscles in his stomach tightened in anticipation.

One lick. One lick from stem to tip to make him whimper and groan.

I grinned as I did it again. He let out a ragged breath, letting his head fall back and eyes close to the pleasure only I could give him.

I licked again, this time lingering at his perfect tip and then flicking my tongue against the smooth skin there.

He groaned, low and masculine. Every muscle in his stomach and chest tightened. His hands clenched the bedsheets.

His legs started to shake as I took him into my mouth. I could feel his pleasure surge through him. The soft whimper of pleasure as I sucked nearly made me lose control. I loved having the power to give the man I loved this kind of pleasure.

I felt like a freaking sex goddess.

"Stop," he gasped, putting a hand to my shoulder. I looked up at him, seeing a sheen of sweat already starting on his chest. "You keep that up and I'll lose it."

I sucked just a little bit harder, flicking my tongue at a spot I knew made his toes curl.

"I want you first," he whispered. His eyes met mine. They shone with lust and desire and love. "I need to have you."

My own heart trembled at the stark need in his voice. The way his voice cracked just a little.

I stood and as soon as I was up, he grabbed me, pulling me to him. My knees went to the bed on either side of his lap. I straddled him, feeling his skin against mine.

He kissed me, his mouth insistent. His tongue found mine, and I reveled in his taste.

It was then that he thrust upward and found me. I was ready for him. I'd wanted him inside of me since the moment he'd walked in my door. He slipped into me, completing me. Filling me.

We both gasped at the sheer pleasure of it. Of being filled. Of being wrapped up in warmth.

I rocked my hips, slow and sensual, and feeling every inch slide of him slide home.

His fingers ran down my back, feeling my skin. He kissed my shoulder and nibbled on my neck. Slowly, we rocked against one another, finding our rhythm once again. We'd been apart for what felt like forever, and now we were finding we still fit.

There was a sweetness that made my heart ache. A slow sensual burn that I knew would never die flared in the pit of my stomach. Our eyes met and held.

Slow lustful fire filled every motion.

But I needed more. I craved more.

And so did he.

I rocked my hips harder. He thrust up, filling me and making me gasp. Still, I needed more.

I slid to his left, aching at the sudden emptiness without him inside of me, but knowing that something better was coming. His hand caressed my butt and down my leg as I moved further onto the bed. He licked his lips, enjoying the show of me moving around him.

I crawled to the head of the bed and then looked back at him. I waved my ass, enticing him to come claim me.

He growled like a caveman as he rose to his knees and found his way behind me. I loved the heat of his hands on my hips. I loved the easy way he slid inside of me. I loved how this felt carnal and primal. This wasn't refined sex. This was animalistic.

Our bodies collided with wonderful ease. He grunted as he thrust, and I arched my back, trying to take every inch of him as deep as I possibly could. His fingers tightened around my hips, and I slammed into him.

I cried out, unable to control the lust and pleasure rising inside of me. It was uncontrollable and overwhelming.

"Shh," he whispered, pushing deep and holding himself there. I whimpered, wiggling my ass against him. If we were too loud, we'd be caught.

He pushed on the small of my back, forcing me to the bed. I let my legs slide out and my arms go to the side. I buried my face in my pillow so I could scream out my lust and pleasure without worrying about being discovered.

His hand splayed on my back, pinning me to the position that gave him the most pleasure. I undulated beneath him, finding my own pleasure as he found his.

His thrusting sped up as he began to lose himself to my body. I could feel him swell inside of me. I wanted him to explode. I wanted to be the reason he let himself lose control. I wanted to be his release.

His breath came in quick pants and then he stilled, his hand pressing down hard. I loved that I was his release. I was able to give him this.

He was able to lose himself to me.

So I let myself go with him. I let go of all the stress, the angst, the worry, and the fear. I let myself tip over the edge of pleasure with him.

My Freddie.

We tumbled through perfect oblivion together, finding sweet release.

We were both panting, our hearts pounding and bodies shaking. He rolled to the side, and I instinctively curled into the hollow of his chest with his arm wrapped protectively around me. His hand caressed the bare skin of my shoulder in lazy circles. It was the most peaceful and simultaneously erotic feeling to have him touch me.

Our heartbeats thundered together as rain lashed the windows. I clung to him and him to me like we might get lost in the mist outside.

All around the storm raged outside, wind beating at the windows and rain pelting the roof. Thunder rumbled somewhere distant.

But we were safe. We were together.

CHAPTER 36

I was glad for that stolen night. I didn't care that we'd broken the rules. I'd held onto him, feeling his warmth seep into me and give me strength. Strength to get through this. Strength to know that we loved one another enough to get through this.

I didn't get to have five minutes alone with Freddie for the rest of the week.

The Duke pulled him into every meeting, every information gathering session, every new change no matter how small, everything. Suddenly, Freddie was integral to everything. He had no spare time. Not even in the evenings when he was supposed to be with me.

Freddie ate dinner with the Duke so they could plan their negotiations. Those first few nights where we'd eaten in his rooms felt far away and long ago.

The few times he ate meals with his family, he looked tired and worn. The conversations were never personal, especially not with Liam at the table. I'd look across the table and he'd smile, but we'd never get more. He'd kiss my cheek and disappear back to the office with a smiling Duke always close behind him.

I sent him messages, but his responses were always clipped and short. The few evenings that he managed to get free, the Duke would come and claim him. I often snuck down to his rooms only to find he was still with the Duke or that he was already asleep so he could wake at dawn and begin again.

The amount of work he was doing was unbelievable and constant.

I was kept nearly as busy. Sophie was determined that I would be perfect for the ball. I needed to be able to dance, talk to everyone, recognize and name everyone, and she wanted me to wear heels.

The dancing, talking, and memorization sounded intimidating, but doable. The heels sounded like torture and completely unobtainable. But she was determined. I would wear heels for the Stair Walk.

My nights were lonely. Without Freddie, I had no one in the castle. Most evenings, I curled up in my bed and tried to sleep. I couldn't even call my family during my lonely nights because of the time difference.

Once Sophie left me for the day, I felt terribly alone in a foreign place. The massive bed with hanging drapes and fancy wallpaper only reminded me more and more of how much I didn't belong here.

I didn't even look forward to meals since Freddie wasn't there. My baked chicken breasts with plain spinach were just to keep me alive. I missed hamburgers and tacos. I missed not only my favorite foods from home, but just enjoying my meals.

Butthe dress had to fit and I had to look the part of a princess.

One night with a week to go, Sophie, Mr. Irson, and I were in one of the numerous sitting rooms. We'd pushed all the furniture to the walls, giving us a space to practice dancing. Mr. Irson had been stolen from the hallway to be my dancing partner for the third time this week.

"And-a one, and-a two... no, no, no, your elbow needs to stay up," Sophie chastised. She hurried over and lifted my sagging elbow so my arm stood parallel to the floor.

"Perhaps a break is in order?" Mr. Irson suggested. "I need to rest for a moment."

I had a feeling the old man could dance all night. He didn't look tired. He did the waltzing steps with practiced grace and never complained when I stepped on his feet.

Well, maybe considering how many times I'd stepped on his feet, he did need a break.

"No breaks," Sophie replied. "She has to be perfect."

A knock on the door made us all turn to look.

"Come in," Sophie called.

Hope surged in my chest that it was Freddie. I desperately wanted to see him. I wanted to show him how much better my dancing had become since the wedding where we'd first danced. Between Mr. Irson and Sophie, I was getting pretty good.

And I wanted to see him. It felt like an eternity since we'd had even an hour together without the Duke interrupting us.

A woman with dark hair opened the door. She had a huge garment bag draped over her arm.

"Is this a good time, Ms. Stansberg?" the woman asked. Her accent was not Paradisian. It was Russian.

Sophie glanced at my sagging arm and the stalwart Mr. Irson.

"It's perfect timing," she replied. "Mr. Irson, thank you for your assistance."

He bowed slightly. "The pleasure was mine." He turned to me. "Ms. Miller."

"Thank you for dancing with me, sir," I said, dipping into a slight curtsy with a demure head bob. It was what I was supposed to do when dancing with someone from a higher station than myself.

Mr. Irson flushed slightly and I realized that I'd just paid him a compliment. I'd just thanked him not as a servant, but as a superior.

Sophie motioned the woman inside the room while Mr. Irson headed out.

"Zoey, this is Claudia Rigel," Sophie said, motioning to the woman. "The best designer in Paradisa."

"Oh, you flatter me," the woman replied, but she did not blush. Instead, she turned and looked me over. "Strip, please."

I blinked twice. "What?"

"Take off your clothes," the woman repeated.

I glanced over at Sophie, my eyes wide.

"Well, do it," Sophie told me. "I'll even turn around if you want." She spun on her heel so that she was no longer looking at me. "You American's are so prudish sometimes."

I blinked twice. Apparently not stripping in the middle of a room in front of strangers made me a prude.

This was definitely the weirdest part of my day. The woman gave me a "Hurry up" motion and I reached for my shirt, pulling it up and over my head. I slid out of my skirt, carefully folding my clothes onto a nearby chair.

The cold air against my bare stomach made me shiver. The sound of a zipper caught my attention.

"Good. I was afraid you'd be more... American," Claudia said.

"I've been on a diet," I told her, wrinkling my nose at the memory of the tiny salad I'd had for lunch. With no dressing.

She pulled out a dress from the garment bag, and suddenly I understood what was going on.

This was a dress fitting.

I nearly laughed with relief. Claudia held up the dress and my laughter faded into astonishment.

The dress was gorgeous. Pink lace with a fitted bodice and cap sleeves caught my eye immediately. Claudia helped me into the dress, her hands cool against my skin.

The square neckline accented my collar bones and the keyhole cutout on the back gave a hint of sexiness to the dress. It was classy and elegant with just a touch of sexiness. It was perfect.

"Not bad," Claudia mumbled. "Stand up on here, please."

She pointed to a small step stool that seemed to have magically appeared out of thin air. I did as she asked and she quickly began pulling and tugging on the dress. Small pins appeared in her fingers and she only looked away from me to write numbers down on a small pad of paper.

"Oh, it's perfect," Sophie gasped, turning to look at me. She grinned. "Freddie will love it."

I felt a nice warmth run through me. I wished there was a mirror so I could see the full effect, but I could wait until tomorrow. Besides, my hair was up in a ponytail and I had only minimal makeup on.

"Only a few minor alterations," Claudia announced. "Now, the hem. Do you have the shoes?"

"Oh, right. Here." Sophie hurried over to the corner where she had bags of things for us to practice with. She pulled out a pair of pale pink heels that we'd been practicing in all week.

I nearly fell off the stool. "No."

"Yes," Claudia and Sophie said at the same time.

I sighed and put them on. Luckily, I didn't fall and rip the dress doing so. I even managed to stand still while Claudia adjusted the hem so that I had a lovely lace train that I knew I would trip on at some point tomorrow.

"You've been practicing in these shoes all week," Sophie told me. "They're broken in and you haven't fallen once today in them."

"I also wasn't wearing a gown," I reminded her. "And I tripped plenty yesterday."

Sophie rolled her eyes. "You'll do fine. Besides, this is what is expected."

"You need heels for this dress," Claudia chimed in. "You have a nice ass, but heels make it nicer. This dress, it needs that. You need the length in the skirt." She motioned to the skirt of the dress. "See, the shoes give you the illusion of long legs. Men like long legs."

I tried not to sigh. "I just don't think it's a good idea."

"You'll be fine," Sophie assured me. "And you look like a million bucks."

"Better than a million bucks," Claudia disagreed. "You look like a princess."

A princess is exactly what I needed to look like.

"Now, remember, you're going to have to dance in this," Sophie told me. "And I can't have you hiking it up like some cowgirl. I need you to actually be good at this."

I fixed her with a glare. "Seriously? I can't enjoy looking pretty for two seconds without you reminding me that I don't belong here and am probably going to screw things up?"

Sophie didn't even blush. "It's for your own good. You've already made enough mistakes that I'm just looking out for you."

I wanted to give a sassy retort, but I didn't have one. I did make mistakes here. There were a million things to mess up on- which spoon, which hand to hold a drink, the difference between a marquess and an earl, the appropriate height of a curtsy...

She was right. I was as out of place here as a cowgirl.

"Take off the dress," Claudia told me in her heavy accent.

I kicked off the shoes so I wouldn't die trying to take the dress off. I could just see myself catching the beautiful pink lace on the heel of one of the shoes and ripping the delicate dress to shreds. I had my shirt on and was reaching for my skirt when a knock came on the door.

"Just a minute," I called out, but Claudia was already opening the door.

"Your Majesty," Claudia said with a head bob as she hurried out with the dress in her arms. I turned, afraid it was the Queen Mother or the King, but it was Freddie.

"Is there something I need to know about going on here?" Freddie asked, eyeing the skirt in my hands. My shirt just grazed the tops of my underwear. He eyed me up and down, a seductive smile playing on my lips. "Because I'd really like to join in."

I stuck my tongue out at him. "You're only invited if you wear a dress," I said.

"Done," he replied. "I'm a size eight."

"What are you doing here?" Sophie asked, crossing her arms. "We're working."

"Looks like it," Freddie replied. He crossed the room and kissed me. "I've wanted to do that all day," he whispered. For a minute, it felt like the old us. The real us.

I giggled, a girlish delight rising up in me. My bare legs had goosebumps and I considered removing my shirt again.

"Hello? I'm still here," Sophie reminded us. I blushed hard.

"What? You want to join in?" Freddie asked, his hands still on my waist. One palm had slipped under my shirt, his hand on my bare skin.

Sophie made a disgusted sound. "We're working."

Freddie glanced down at my bare legs. "If you say so."

I smacked his arm playfully. "We are. I was trying on the dress for tomorrow."

"Oh."

I had been expecting him to smile. I had expected him to be excited, but his shoulders stiffened and his face went hard.

"Oh?" I asked.

"I'm just tired," he replied. He smiled, but it was his courtier smile. The one he wore around his brother or when I knew he was working. "Long day."

"Can you put your skirt back on?" Sophie asked, pointing to the skirt still in my hand. I blushed hard. "You know what? Take a five minute break. But please, have clothes on when I come back." She looked at Freddie. "Both of you."

Freddie made a "Who me?" innocent face that Sophie rolled her eyes at. She picked up her phone and left us alone.

reddie kissed me before the door had even clicked shut. His kiss was hungry.

"God, I could just take you here," Freddie groaned, his hands tightening on my waist again.

"We only have five minutes. You're not that fast," I told him. I pressed my half naked body into him, feeling the heat of his desire against my bare hip. "Although I am really tempted to try."

He chuckled, the sound low and rumbling. He sighed, not letting me go, but not instigating further.

"You should put your skirt on or I'm never going to be able to stop," he said after a moment. He kissed me again before forcing himself to take a step back.

I slid on my skirt and he sighed as I settled it around my waist.

"I never would have caught anyone but you like that," he said, looking at me wistfully.

Something about his words pricked at me.

"What? What do you mean?"

He shrugged. "I don't know anyone that would let themselves be caught without a skirt."

"What?" I asked, going still.

"It's just that no Paradisian royal would ever be naked in a room like you," he said with a shrug. "My mother would flip."

Anger flared in my chest and my jaw tightened. "I didn't exactly have a choice. You just walked in. The door was closed for a reason."

"Whoa, don't get defensive," he said, taking a step back.

"I'm not," I retorted, definitely sounded defensive. I forced myself to take a breath. "It's just that everyone keeps blaming me for things I don't have control over."

"Like not wearing clothing?" He meant it as a joke, but I wasn't laughing.

I felt my face go flat and my mouth tighten into a thin line. All day I had been chastised. "Zoey, keep your elbow up. Zoey, suck in your gut. Zoey, you're not walking right. Zoey, that's inappropriate. Zoey, that's wrong."

Freddie's words were the straw that broke the camel's back. Something inside of me broke, filling my stomach with anger. He hadn't seen me all day, but he felt fine poking holes in what I was doing.

"I didn't mean it like that," Freddie said quickly, seeing the immediate danger in my face.

"But you did," I countered. My angry switch was definitely flipped now. "I have done my damn best. But it's not good enough. I have tried, Freddie. I've done everything I can to follow your stupid rules. Rules you didn't even bother to teach me!"

My voice was rising to screech levels but I couldn't stop. Suddenly all the hurt, the anxiety, the failure, the frustration, and the anger rose to the surface. All the lonely nights. All the hours of waiting for him to return a message.

I had nothing here. And everything I did seemed to be wrong.

"I can't help it that you aren't succeeding," he snapped back. "I have been working my ass off. I can't be expected to bottle feed everything to you."

"Which is why you haven't had a single minute to give me more than a two second reply to a single message?" I asked. "I didn't realize picking up a phone was that hard."

"I have more responsibilities than you realize. You have no clue what it takes to survive here," he shouted back at me. His cheeks were pink and eyes feverish. I wondered when the last time he'd actually slept a full night had been.

"I have been fucking doing my best and it isn't enough for you," I spat at him. "I'm obviously not good enough for you!"

Freddie's face went white. Then red, then white again.

"That's not fair," he said. His voice was low and soft. It was a dangerous voice. It was the kind of voice you used when speaking with a crazy person or a wild animal. A wild animal that was totally out of control and obviously needed a lesson.

It made me even madder.

"You're right," I sneered. "It's not fair. Nothing about this place is fair. A little warning on the way over might have been nice."

"I did warn you. I told you my family was different," he growled.

"You did. But you didn't tell me that I couldn't wear

sleeveless dresses. Or that it wasn't okay to wear freaking sandals," I replied. "You didn't prepare me for any of this." I motioned around the room. "All you gave were vague 'my family is weird' speeches."

"And you can't handle any of it," he snarled. "Every girl I've ever met has wanted to be a princess. Except you. And you don't have a freaking clue what you're doing."

"Bingo," I told him, a mean smile crossing my face. "I'm not princess material. Poor choice on your part. Seems to be a hobby for you."

As soon as the last sentence left my mouth, I regretted it. The hurt that crossed Freddie's eyes cut me to the core. He stumbled back a step as if I'd physically hit him.

"Freddie, I'm sorry," I said quickly, but I knew it was too late. "I shouldn't have said that."

"No, you shouldn't have." His face lost all emotion and he wore the Prince mask that I hated. The one that showed no joy or any hint of the wonderful funny man underneath it. "But that doesn't mean you aren't right."

All the fight went out of me. I felt like a candle without a flame, sputtering and wallowing in sticky wax. I was so tired. So very tired.

"I'm sorry, Freddie," I said, quieter this time. My eyes fell to the floor. "I'm just frustrated. And tired. And I shouldn't take it out on you."

He sighed and from the corner of my eye I could see him run a hand through his hair.

"I'm tired too," he admitted. He sighed, his shoulders drooping. "This wasn't what I wanted to happen. I just wanted to see you. To touch you for just a moment."

The room was quiet between us. My heart ached now that it wasn't full of angry venom any more.

Slowly, I looked up at him. "Can we try this again? I liked the beginning part a lot better than the middle."

He didn't smile, but he lost the Prince mask. "Yes. I agree."

I took a deep breath, smoothed my clothing, and put on a smile.

"Would you like to dance with me?" I asked, holding out my skirt the way I would a gown. I flashed him a smile. "I could use the practice."

A smile flickered on his lips. He nodded his head, just as a prince should when agreeing to a dance.

I grinned and did a happy wiggle.

That at least made him chuckle. "I don't think Sophie taught you that," he said, the familiar smile creeping into his voice once again. "But I like it."

"Nope, definitely not Sophie approved," I agreed. I hurried over to the pink heels and slid them on. "But she has taught me this."

I walked the seven steps back to him without tripping, spilling, or stumbling.

"I am impressed," he admitted. He still wasn't fully smiling at me. I'd swiped too deep with my claws to have him trust me again so quickly. But at least he was holding out his arms for me to dance with him.

He hummed a soft waltz as he spun me around the room. I didn't trip on a single thing. I didn't step on his feet.

"You have been practicing," he said, pleased surprise filling his face. "And in heels no less!"

"I know. Sophie might make a lady out of me yet," I replied. I made sure to catch his eyes. "But I will still flip your kayak."

He smiled at me then. It wasn't a grin or one of his smiles that knocked me off my feet, but it was genuine. It was one that said he was on his way to forgiving me.

It was one that made me feel like normal was possible. Happiness was possible. That *we* were possible.

We just had to try our best.

"Is it safe to come in?" Sophie called from the doorway. She had a hand over her eyes. "Please tell me you both have pants."

"Well, I do," Freddie replied. He winked at me. "Zoey isn't wearing pants."

"I'm dressed now too," I added, giving his shoulder a gentle shove. "Skirt on and everything."

"Thank goodness." Sophie lowered her hand and shook her head at the two of us.

"I should be going. I still have so much to do, and I'm sure the Duke will be looking for me. I'm supposed to be working," Freddie announced, taking a step away from me. I instantly missed his touch. I'd missed him so much recently. "I just wanted to stop by and say hello."

"It was nice to see you." I meant it. I wished he didn't have to go. I hated that we'd fought. That we seemed to be taking our stress out on one another, and not in the bedroom where it would at least be fun.

He kissed me softly on the cheek. It was so soft that I barely felt it. He did a polite bow, the kind he was supposed to do after finishing a waltz, and then left the room. I chewed on the inner corner of my lower lip.

I hadn't meant to hurt him. I hadn't meant to be mean, but I'd just finally snapped.

Too many nights of being alone. Too many days of not being myself and following the rules of protocol. I missed hugs. I missed ketchup. I missed people smiling and talking to me like I was a human being and not some mythical princess.

"You two okay?" Sophie asked. Her blue eyes were like eagle's eyes, watching Freddie and I's every move.

"Fine," I replied. It was mostly true.

She pursed her lips but didn't say anything.

"Do you mind if we quit for the night?" I asked. "I'm really tired. And I think some sleep will help with the bags under my eyes."

"That's what makeup is for," Sophie replied. "Let's look through the binder and make sure you know all the names. Then we'll practice the stairs a few times. You need to be prepared for the Stair Walk."

I sighed as Sophie picked up the heavy white binder full of names and pictures of people I'd never met but was expected to know.

It was going to be a long night.

The ball was tomorrow and I was about ready to puke.

Tomorrow, all my hard work would pay off. Tomorrow, I would do my Stair Walk and officially be accepted into the Royal Family's inner circle. Tomorrow, I could kiss Freddie on the cheek in public. We could hold hands and go on dates again.

I clung to the idea that we could go back to normal, even though normal in this place would still be very strange.

I practiced walking down the stairs in my pink heels for two hours straight just after lunch. The surprise benefit was that my butt was in the best shape ever from the constant up and down of the stairs. I hadn't tripped once so far and actually felt semi-confident.

Sophie had me wearing a bedsheet as a dress so that I could practice without ruining the actual dress. I didn't blame the florists setting up flowers for staring at me as I went up and down the stairs wrapped in a white topsheet.

I felt like an American ghost haunting the Paradisian Palace- out of place and completely ridiculous. But I could go up and down without tripping on the hems or tangling the skirt around my feet.

I wished I had thought to do this for Cecelia's wedding. It would have made that day go a lot smoother.

"I think you're as ready as you're going to get," Sophie informed me after yet another successful stair run.

"You think so?" I grinned at her as I took the bottom two steps without tripping. For the first time in my life, I felt confident in the high heel shoes. Or at least not about to die.

She nodded. "There isn't much more we can do with only a few hours left. You're as good as you're going to get."

It felt like a backhanded compliment. Like one her father would give me. Sometimes I forgot that this sweet girl was related to the Duke. Although they both had shrewd minds, Sophie actually seemed to care about others. The Duke was just good at pretending he cared.

"But the ball isn't until evening," I countered. "I have all day tomorrow too."

She shook her head. "Tomorrow will be busy with getting you ready. We have to make sure you're camera ready tomorrow. Hair, makeup, all of it. It will take all day."

"Oh." I visibly sagged. "It's like Prom without the corsage."

Sophie frowned. "Do you want a corsage?"

I shook my head. "No. I'm good."

"Okay." She shrugged. "I think that you should take the rest of the night off. Go to bed early. Makeup can do wonders, but a good night's sleep is better than any concealer."

As if I was going to be able to sleep tonight.

"Thanks." I untied the knot holding up the bedsheet and unwrapped myself from it.

Sophie took it from me. "You'll do great tomorrow," she promised. "You've worked really hard. I'm actually quite proud of you."

I stared at her and a pleasant lightness filled my chest. Sophie rarely gave compliments, so this felt like a win.

"Who are you and what have you done with the real Sophie?" I asked her, playfully suspicious.

She rolled her eyes at me. "You are an American. The only way you had to go was up. You couldn't possibly get worse."

Now it was my turn to roll my eyes. "You just wish you could be as cool as me. You wish you had my amazing accent and love of hamburgers."

"The love of hamburgers is universal." She grinned at me. "But I will never understand your love of ketchup. Blech." She made a disgusted face that made me laugh.

"I forgive you for your lack of good culinary taste," I told her. "Not even Freddie likes my ketchup."

"Maybe you could go find Freddie." She said it offhand, but she didn't look at me. She pretended to be busy folding sheets. "I imagine he might enjoy the taste of ketchup tonight."

I raised my eyebrows.

"Are you telling me to break the rules?" I asked, feigning innocence.

Her eyes came up to meet mine and she shrugged. "As far as I know, and I do know all the rules, fraternization is just not allowed *inside* the palace." She winked.

I shook my head at her with a grin. "Well, you know I am trying very hard to follow the rules."

She grinned. "I know. Now, get out of here. Take the night off and get rid of those worry lines around your eyes before they turn into wrinkles."

She flashed me one more smile before heading up the stairs with the bedsheet and back into the main palace. I stood, feeling strangely naked without the sheet, at the bottom of the grand staircase. I closed my eyes and tried to imagine tomorrow.

I could do this. I would do a good job.

My thoughts were interrupted by my stomach growling. An idea came to me.

What if I surprised Freddie with dinner? I didn't hold out much hope that the Duke was going to give Freddie the entire night off, but maybe I could at least get thirty minutes. It wouldn't be enough to take Sophie's suggestion and leave the castle, but it would be better than nothing.

I pulled out my phone to message Freddie and see what he wanted to eat. The last message from Freddie was over three days old. I stared at the phone screen and tried to remember the last time I'd seen him in person.

It was even longer than three days.

When we were in different cities, we'd at least texted every evening. Most of the time it was just a simple goodnight, but we hadn't even done that here.

We'd been closer to one another with miles between us than we were sleeping in the same building.

The thought cut like a rusty knife, leaving me uncomfortable and a little sad.

"He's just stressed. We both are," I told myself, putting the phone back in my pocket. "I'll surprise him with his favorite. It'll be good."

I grinned at the idea. I imagined walking into the study with a box full of tacos and the smile that would light his face. I knew he wouldn't be able to stop work for long, but everyone had to eat. I loved the idea of making him smile.

Finding decent tacos in Paradisa was an impossible task. I found lots of Indian and Italian restaurants, but the few Mexican restaurants didn't have what I wanted for Freddie.

Then I remembered that Sophie said the Whymore Pub made Freddie's favorite fish and chips. His favorite food before he'd discovered tacos. I called them and ordered enough for three people with the plan to give the Duke a bag of food so he could disappear into another room for a little bit.

A courier arrived with three bags of fried food, still hot from the fryer. I grinned as I paid the man and hurried down the hallway to Freddie's office. This was definitely not on my diet and I didn't care.

I'd only been inside a couple of times, but I knew where it was. My footsteps were soft of the plush carpet in the middle of the stone floor. The last bits of orange sunlight flickered through the windows like magical sprites to guide me.

I paused in front of the heavy oak door. The smell of delicious fried fish and potatoes wafted around me like perfume and I grinned at the thought that no man would be able to deny me smelling like this. No woman either, to be honest.

I grinned and knocked politely, but soundly.

Freddie's face appeared with a frown.

"Zoey?" He took a step back, the frown still creasing his brow. "What are you doing here?"

I held up the bags of food. "I brought dinner."

He looked at the bags of food and his frown deepened. He rubbed at his stubbled jaw.

"I already ate," he replied. "I wish I had known."

Defeat hit me hard. My shoulders sagged.

"I messaged you," I said, thinking of how I had wanted to surprise him.

"And I didn't reply because I was busy," Freddie replied in a tone that made me look up with surprise. It wasn't a nice tone. "I haven't even seen the message. The Duke had my phone."

"I didn't want to wait until it was too late," I explained. I shook my head slightly, trying to clear my thoughts. I was hungry now and trying very hard not to get annoyed because of it.

"You should have thought this through more carefully," he chastised me. "I am very busy, Zoey."

"Um, maybe we could still have a couple minutes together?" I offered. "Just take a break? Have a couple of french fries with me?"

I held up the bag of delicious smelling food.

"Now is not a good time," Freddie replied. He glanced back into the office before looking back at me. "What were you thinking?"

"I just wanted to do something nice," I replied, my voice small.

Freddie sighed. "It's just not a good time right now."

"Who is out there?" the Duke asked. He came into the doorway. "Oh. It's you."

I tried not to take affront at the way he said "You'. He said it like I was a stray dog or beggar on his doorstep.

"Your Grace," I said, dipping a quick curtsy. His sneer remained despite my manners.

"You're timing is terrible," the Duke informed me. "As usual."

I tried not to wince. I wished I hadn't bought the food. I wished I had just gone back to my room alone. I regretted trying. It hurt all the more because I had thought this would make Freddie smile. I had wanted to make him smile and feel the glow of his love.

"I'll go," I said. "I'm sorry I bothered you."

"Oh no, no." The Duke pushed the door open. "You've interrupted us now. Might as well get your five minutes no matter the inconvenience to Paradisa. No matter the harm you cause in the process."

"I really don't...." I mumbled as the Duke pushed past me and into the hallway.

"Have your five minutes," he told me. He looked me up and down and obviously found me wanting. "I insist."

I watched him saunter down the hallway. How did that man make me feel like such a child? How did he make me feel so small?

"I'm really sorry," I said, turning to face Freddie. "Do you want to go in and sit down?"

"You aren't allowed in here," Freddie reminded me. At least he didn't sound unkind about it. There was sensitive information about the treaty in there. He shut the door behind him and locked it. I knew he was supposed to do that, but the fact that he didn't trust me hurt a little. "We can just sit in the hallway."

"So, how are things going?" I asked, taking a spot on the floor against the wall opposite the door. I sat criss-cross-apple-sauce like I used to in kindergarten. Freddie stayed standing, his arms crossed like he was guarding the door from me.

"Busy. There's still so much to prepare," Freddie replied. He took a deep breath and I could see the exhaustion wearing at him. He rubbed at the bridge of his nose like he had a headache coming on. "The delegation arrives tomorrow and the next few days will be spent going over the final modifications. I have a lot to work on right now. There's a lot riding on me finishing this on time."

I got the message that I was disturbing him loud and clear. "Right," I said. "You are on the final stretch and can't have interruptions."

Silence filled the hallway. I looked down at the paper bag full of food. It was probably getting cold by now. I felt stupid and small. Especially since he was still standing. He couldn't have been clearer that he wanted to go back in and go back to work.

"I'll just go. You don't want me here." I rose to my feet.

"It's not that I don't want you," Freddie said quickly. "I always want you."

A little warmth crept back into me. He didn't hate me at least. How had we gotten to the point where I thought he even might hate me? Two weeks ago, I had been so sure in our love. Now, we were stretched to the breaking point.

"Are we okay?" I asked. "I didn't mean to interrupt you."

"After the Duke told you not to?" he asked. I frowned, confused. The Duke hadn't said anything to me. But before I could say anything, he kept talking. "On the night before the delegation arrives? What did you expect to happen?" he asked with a frustrated sigh.

"What did I expect?" I repeated. The little bit of warmth dissipated. "I expected my boyfriend to be able to take five minutes to tell me how his day went. I expected the one person I know in this country, the person that I came to this country for, to want to see me. I don't think that's that crazy."

"I have responsibilities," he growled. "I can't just take care of you all the time."

"Then how about just a little bit of time?" I asked. "You haven't said three words to me all week. You don't even message me anymore. I saw more of you when we lived in different cities. You had responsibilities then, too."

"You have no idea what I'm responsible for right now," he scoffed. "I don't get to sit around eating bonbons and chatting about shopping all day like you."

I took a step back. "Is that what you think I've been doing?"

"Well, you're obviously not planning a multinational trade negotiation."

There was so much venom and bitterness in his voice that I didn't know how to respond. I'd spent every waking moment learning how to be around Paradisian royalty. It wasn't easy work to learn a lifetime of posture and speaking patterns in a week.

"You have no idea what I've been doing because you haven't asked me once," I told him. "I haven't had a freaking bonbon since I got here. I'm not allowed to have bonbons. I'm not allowed to have anything."

He looked surprised at me. "The Duke didn't say anything about that."

"Yeah, well, why would he? I'm on a diet. Thanks for noticing the weight I've lost," I said, motioning to my body. "Thanks for noticing all the work I've done so that I can fit in here. So that I can be with you. So I can help you."

"Help? I'm not seeing a lot of help from you," Freddie replied. "I barely see you even try to fit in here. If Sophie didn't dress you, you'd wear a bathrobe all day. If I didn't remind you, you'd forget to curtsy to the Duke every time. It irks him that you disrespect him. And that irks me. I just wish you'd try harder."

Red flashed in my vision. I was trying harder than I had ever tried in my life. I wasn't perfect, but I was trying. I tried to remind myself that he was under a lot of stress. We both were.

"You sure you haven't eaten?" I asked. "Because you're being shitty and I'm hoping it's just because you're hungry."

"Maybe I'm just not impressed with what you've done," he replied. "Maybe the Duke is right and you're not the person I need right now."

I stared at him, open mouthed and dumbfounded. Silence filled the space between us, heavy and awful. I took three deep breaths, trying to clear my head.

"Do you want me to do the Stair Walk tomorrow?" I asked point blank.

"Of course I do."

I sighed a little in relief. He did still want me.

"It's already been announced," he continued. "If you didn't, people would talk."

The relief went cold in a heartbeat.

Where was the man I loved? Where was the man who made me laugh and played jokes? Because the person standing in front of me wasn't him. The Duke had replaced my wonderful Freddie with someone else.

"I'm so glad that's your reasoning." I crossed my arms. "Makes me feel all warm and fuzzy. Loved, really. I feel fucking wanted."

"Classy, Zoey." He shook his head in disbelief. "I can just see all your hard work at being a lady."

I wanted to hit him. I wanted to throw the bag of food at him.

"You know what?" I took a deep breath. "You don't seem to be in a good mood right now. I am a little hangry myself. So, I'm going to go cool down."

"Probably a good idea," he agreed with a sneer.

"Here." I slammed one of the bags into his hands. "I don't care if you eat it. But I bought it for you. I bought you your favorite food from your favorite restaurant because I wanted to do something nice for you. Even though I'm an incompetent idiot who can't do anything right, at least I know how to order from Whymore Pub, so I'm not a complete idiot. Just a dumb one."

He looked down at the bag and his face twisted with regret and confusion. "This is from Whymore Pub?"

"Yup." I glared at him. "Paid for it myself."

"I didn't realize." he sighed and ran a hand through his hair. "I thought you just got something from the kitchen. I didn't think..."

"Obviously you didn't think," I agreed. "I'm not even

hungry anymore so I'm just going to toss what you don't want on my way out."

It was a lie. I was ravenous and going to swallow my entire bag of food the minute I was alone. I just didn't want to be in this hallway anymore. I didn't want to fight anymore.

"Zoey, I'm sorry. I'm just..." he sighed. This time the apology at least sounded sincere. "The Duke's been in my head. I'm just so stressed. I feel like I might break."

He sounded so defeated and tired that my heart ached for him. I wanted to hold him to me, but I was still angry and hurt. Just saying that he was stressed didn't make up for his antagonizing tone and careless words.

"I'm sorry," I said softly. I hated that he looked so worn. I hated that we were both so tired we were ready to fight. This wasn't us. I wished I knew what had poisoned us against one another. Who could have whispered words into our ears to make us dislike the other?

We stood in the hallway for a moment with neither one of us actually looking at the other.

I waited for a real apology. For my Freddie to hug me and tell me that we should sit and eat the stupid fish and chips. That he was sorry and that everything was going to be okay. That this wasn't normal.

But he didn't say anything. He just stared at the floor, stubborn in his self-righteousness and anger. His jaw tightened. He sighed about to say something, but the sound of the Duke's footsteps coming back down the hallway stopped him. Our five minutes was up.

Despite the fact that we were still next to one another, I felt alone in the world.

"Have a good night," I finally said, giving up on my

nice surprise. I started walking back toward my own room. I didn't want to see the Duke again if I didn't have to.

"You too," he said softly after me. He watched me walk away and then went back into the room to do whatever the Duke said he should do next.

"Miss Zoey Miller of the United States of America."

My name echoed out over the staircase. It sounded so strange to have my country listed after it. I wasn't competing in the Olympics. I wasn't even really there to represent the US, but it did mark me as different.

The beautiful gold and marble steps led to a rounded lobby. Two huge white wooden doors stood open across the space, showing off a massive ballroom. The ballroom glittered with silk from a hundred dresses. Candles flickered in alcoves and the sounds of music filled the air.

It was everything I had imagined from watching Sleeping Beauty, Cinderella, and Beauty and the Beast.

I took a deep breath and stepped forward.

I had imagined that everyone would stop and stare. That the music would falter and the dancers would turn from their partners and gaze up at me. That I would see the Prince and we would make eye contact and the world would watch in a loving glow as we found one another.

No one looked. Freddie wasn't even in the room. I pushed away the small hurt. He had other responsibilities.

I kept a neutral pleasant smile on my face as I glided down the stairs, my hand resting delicately on the handrail just as Sophie had taught me. No one watched me. I stepped off the last step into a room full of glittering jewels and murmured conversations.

A few courtiers glanced at my direction, smiled politely, and continued their conversations. I was not important here. This was only my introduction to the party. The Stair Walk was still to come.

Still, this moment had seemed like it should feel important. But instead, I felt small and inconsequential.

A feeling I was becoming all too familiar with.

Another name boomed out from the top of the stairs and a young woman around my age descended the staircase just as I had.

Again, no one but me looked.

It was normal here. To be announced and to glide down the stairs into the world of princes and courtiers.

"Excellent job," Sophie congratulated me, coming across the lobby. Her voluminous skirts rustled on the marbles floors, and she didn't walk. She glided.

Sophie looked beautiful. She had her blonde hair curled and styled up on her head, showing off her long slim neck. Her dress was so pale blue it was nearly bridal white. The cut was modest, yet showed her hips and curves to their full effect.

I had felt beautiful in my pink lace with my hair in a simple chignon near the nape of my neck. Next to Sophie, I felt plain and, yet again, inconsequential.

"I didn't trip," I replied with a smile. "So far so good with these shoes."

My feet already ached from the petite heels. They weren't very high, but I missed my flats. Sophie had already confiscated the pair of flats I'd tried to sneak in and hide for later.

"Good. Now you just have to do it again in a few hours," Sophie replied.

I nodded. At the end of the night, the Queen Mother and her family would greet her subjects at the top of the stairs. She would call me to her. I would walk up the stairs and then walk down them with the royal family. It was ceremonial of me being accepted into the family.

I hoped that it would mean I could have time with Freddie again.

That things could change for the better. Tonight was when all my hard work would pay off. I took a deep breath, readying myself for the night ahead. I could do this. I could make everyone in Paradisa love me.

Even Freddie.

"Come with me." Sophie turned and I followed her into the ballroom.

It was so beautiful. Music filled the air and dancers spun and circled. Silk, lace, jewels, and laughter were everywhere. I could see why so many fairy tales had balls as part of their magic.

I finally saw Freddie near the throne dais at the far end of the ballroom. He stood talking with the Duke and a man I could only assume was Henry. They were both of similar height and build, but Henry's hair was lighter and his nose and jaw favored their father. They both wore the Royal Family's colors with sashes across their chests and medals and tassels pinned everywhere cloth could be seen.

I grinned, hoping to catch his attention. I started to raise my hand to wave to him before remembering my place.

I couldn't just wave at the Prince. I couldn't dash across the dancers and hug him. This wasn't a backyard barbecue or a family reunion. I had to be on my best behavior.

I stared at him, willing him to look up and see me. I hoped that he would sense me and at least acknowledge my presence with a smile or head nod.

But Freddie didn't see me and Sophie kept walking. I kept my disappointment to myself.

"Zoey, I'd like to introduce you Princess Aria," Sophie announced, coming alongside a young woman with a bright smile.

Aria had beautiful black hair loose around her shoulders. Her gown of dark green satin looked royal and lovely. She was exactly what a princess was supposed to look like. It was no wonder to me that the Paradisa public adored her. She stood with such poise and elegance that only came from being born into high society.

Once again, I felt out of place. She was a senator's daughter. I was the daughter of a farmer.

I dipped into a curtsy. "Your Majesty."

"So you're the one Freddie keeps talking about," Aria said, reaching out a hand to greet me. It was so strange to hear an American accent I nearly froze. It sounded so friendly and welcoming.

"It's nice to meet you," I replied, still holding the curtsy. She was a princess after all.

"Oh, please stand up," Aria said, sounding flustered. "And don't worry about titles. Please, just call me Aria."

I rose out of my curtsy, feeling a smile start to form on my face.

"I'll leave you two to get acquainted," Sophie said. She didn't curtsy. "Excuse me."

Aria nodded her head and waited until Sophie was out of earshot. "It's so nice to have another American in the family," she said with a giggle. "I can't tell you how excited I am to have someone in the castle that at least understands the appeal of ketchup."

I stared at her for a moment. "Ketchup?"

"You are the reason there's ketchup in the kitchen, right?" Aria asked. "No one else around here eats it."

"I like it on my breakfast potatoes," I admitted. "Apparently Freddie had to bribe three people just to order it."

"They all are crazy. No one here eats it and they all seem to think it's sacrilege to put it on anything," she explained. "I stole some for my lunch today. I hope you don't mind."

"Not at all," I replied with a grin. "I am more than happy to share my ketchup."

"Thanks." She grinned. "How are you adjusting to all this craziness?"

I looked around the room. There was so much elegance and I didn't feel like I belonged here for a second. "Um, it's coming?"

"Don't worry. It gets easier," she promised. "The hardest part is getting used to the food."

"It is different here," I agreed. "I miss burgers. And tacos. And eating in general."

"They are a little stingy with portions here," she agreed. "And they like their princesses to eat healthy."

"I'm so tired of salad," I admitted.

"I will have to take you to the best taco place in the city." She grinned. "It's this little hole in the wall off Timberelm Square that's owned by an American. It's the only place I've found that makes a decent taco. Took me months to find it. We'll sneak out and eat enough for three college guys."

My mouth watered. I'd barely eaten anything for dinner tonight so that I would fit comfortably into my dress. I'd been too nervous to eat much anyway, but a taco sounded amazing. And the fact that she'd found a taco place here in Paradisa was great.

"I think I'd like that," I replied, hungry for more than just food. She was offering friendship. I didn't have very many friends here. Freddie was always busy with work. Sophie treated me like I was her job, and I basically was. It would be nice to have someone who would enjoy having some ketchup in the fridge and could talk about tacos.

"Princess Aria, you look lovely." The Duke's voice cut through our conversation as he slid into the space next to me where Sophie had once stood. He bowed low to Aria.

"Ah, Duke Orwell." Aria's smile flattened. "How nice to see you again."

"I wanted to congratulate you and your husband on your successful return," the Duke replied. "It will be nice to have Prince Henry at the palace again."

"I agree," she said with a nod. She motioned to me. "Have you met my friend, Zoey Miller?"

He looked at me like he finally noticed I was there. "I have."

I dipped into a curtsy. "Your Grace," I replied.

He turned back to Aria, ignoring me completely. "I was hoping I might have a moment of your time, Your Highness."

"In a moment," Aria replied. "Ms. Miller and I were having a conversation."

"It's rather important," the Duke said. "It's not something Ms. Miller needs to be a part of."

The presumption of his words galled, but I was in no place to say anything. I was the low man on the totem pole here. And he was probably right. There was little here that I actually needed to be a part of.

"It's fine," I said, not wanting to make a stink. "I'd love to hear more about the taco place later."

Aria frowned. "I'll find you again later," she promised.

The Duke took her arm and guided her off away from the dancing without a word. I didn't even get a backward glance from the Duke to acknowledge I'd said she could go. I didn't matter to him. I wasn't important or even worthy of a moment of his time.

I glared after them, wishing that I had had some witty comeback or pithy reply. But there wasn't much I could do. This wasn't my world and I was just learning the ins and outs of how to interact in it. I sighed.

"That's a big sigh."

I turned to see Freddie grinning at me.

"Freddie." I grinned at him. I wanted to throw my arms around him and kiss him. He looked so handsome in his dress uniform. His light brown hair was swept back and neat from his face. The red and gold highlights added dimension and beauty to him. My fingers itched to touch his smooth face and linger on the strong line of his jaw.

But I couldn't do any of that.

I curtsied.

"Rise," he said, a smile in his voice. He looked me over. "You look amazing."

"So do you," I told him.

I hated that there was several feet of space between us. That until the Stair Walk was complete, there would have to be several feet of space.

"May I have a dance?" Freddie asked, holding out a hand. He looked exhausted up close and I wondered how much time he'd spent working with the Duke before the ball.

"Are we allowed to?" I hesitated taking his hand. I needed to be perfect tonight, but when he smiled at me, I thought I could be.

"Yes," he assured me. "As long as it's just a waltz. I am allowed to dance with anyone I want."

His hand felt warm in mine. My heart fluttered with nerves.

Just be perfect, I told myself. *No big deal.*

CHAPTER 40

Freddie brought me out to the side of the dance floor. He didn't bring me to the center though, but to a small space off to the side. It almost felt like we were hiding. Freddie was supposed to dance in the center where everyone could see him, but he'd taken me to the side of the dance floor near the edge and against the wall.

Like I wasn't good enough to be seen with him. Like I didn't matter enough to take center stage.

We'll have more privacy this way, I told myself, trying not to see the worst. *Besides, you hate being the center of attention.*

It felt good to be in Freddie's arms. Soft music drifted around us, changing from a waltz to a foxtrot.

Foxtrot was my worst dance, but I didn't want to pull away from Freddie. I didn't want to disappoint him. I'd already disappointed him last night. I didn't want to do it again. I managed thirty seconds of terrible dancing before I stepped on Freddie's foot.

He winced, gasping hard enough that the dancers next to us glanced over. The heel of my shoe was not kind to his feet.

"Maybe dancing isn't the best idea," I said, taking a step back and promptly bumping into another couple. They glared at me and I held up my hands. "I'm so sorry."

"What are you doing?" Freddie hissed, glancing at the couple I'd bumped. They looked important and I was sure that me saying, "Sorry" wasn't exactly the correct ballroom etiquette.

Everything seemed to be spinning. I couldn't take a deep breath, not in this dress. The ballroom that had felt so big a few moments ago suddenly felt crammed and far too populated.

"Excuse me," I whispered and I fled the dance floor, my face hot. I hurried out of the ballroom, every step starting to hurt. Maybe I could find a glass of champagne or wine. Something to soothe my nerves. I found a waiter and grabbed a flute of champagne from his tray. I sipped at it, trying to catch my breath.

"What are you doing?" Freddie asked, catching up with me outside the ballroom. We were in the lobby near the stairs, but off near a wall. His green eyes were hard.

"Calming down," I told him. I took a sip of the champagne. It took effort not to gulp it. "I'm trying to do what I'm supposed to. I can't dance and I panicked. I don't want to mess this up."

He took the champagne from me. "No drinking," he admonished. "Not in public."

"But..." I sighed, my shoulders sagging at yet another thing I had done wrong. "Sophie said I could have one glass."

He handed the flute off to a waiter. I sighed as I watched it walk away.

"There are pictures of you doing a keg-stand all over the internet right now," Freddie reminded me. He glanced about the room like he thought everyone was listening in on us. "The last thing you need is a picture of you drinking."

I crossed my arms, feeling petulant. He was right. I could imagine the news report of me being drunk now. That didn't make me not want the champagne less, though. If anything, it made me want a glass even more to steady myself.

"I still want one," I said, peevish and annoyed. I hated being treated like a child and taking away my champagne made me feel underage.

"Are you even trying?" Freddie asked. "The Duke is concerned you are going to ruin tonight with your care-lessness."

My eyes cut to him, going wide. "What?"

"Are you even trying to do well tonight? You nearly bowled over the Earl of Wistmarsh and you're out here guzzling booze," he chastised. "So, I'm asking if you are trying to sabotage tonight. Do you want to be here?"

My arms fell to my sides and my jaw opened. I had to shake myself.

"Of course I'm trying," I replied, my voice shaking with effort.

Freddie looked me over like he didn't quite believe me. "You know how important this is to me."

"Do I?" I asked him. I motioned to the beautiful room. "You said you don't like this life. That you'd rather be out on a lake in the middle of nowhere. That you don't need the constant watching eyes, yet, you're asking me to do this."

"I'm asking you to follow tradition," he said. "I'm asking you to follow the rules of my family. To honor Paradisa."

"And I am trying," I told him. "I am doing my best."

"And what if your best isn't enough?"

I took a step back. The Duke had asked me that same question. I didn't have an answer then and I didn't have one now.

Freddie looked like a prince. He stood like a prince. He sounded like a prince. He stood straight and tall, handsome in his uniform and completely without the playful smile I loved. He looked imposing and perfect.

I felt like a girl from a flyover state that didn't know which fork to use playing dress-up in clothes that weren't mine.

"Do you want me to leave?" I asked, looking up at him and trying to see the man that had tried to knock me out of a kayak. That had stared in wonder at lightning bugs and laughed with me so many times. "Do you want me here?"

"Don't do that," Freddie said, his voice hard and royal. "I asked you here, didn't I? I've done everything I can to make you comfortable here. I'm not the one who has to prove herself tonight."

I swallowed hard. That wasn't the answer I was hoping for. I thought about leaving. About just going back to my room and going to bed.

I was too stubborn to quit, though.

"No," I agreed. "You're just supposed to be the one supporting me doing it."

He rolled his eyes. "The Duke said you would do this to me. That you would do your best to ruin things."

I ignored him. I could see Sophie in the ballroom, obviously looking for me. I was going to finish out this night. I was going to be strong enough to see the sunrise tomorrow. Hopefully, tomorrow things would be brighter. Less stressful.

I curtsied, putting my hands out in a flourish. "Your Majesty." I said it with as much acid as possible.

When I rose, I walked around him and headed back into the ballroom with my head high. I kept expecting to feel his hand grab for mine, or to hear my name, but nothing ever came.

"How are you doing?" Sophie asked me several hours later.

"My feet are killing me, and I nearly tripped on my dress," I admitted.

Her eyes went wide. "What?"

"I'm fine," I assured her. "The lace on the train of my dress is just a little loose."

I turned, showing her how the very edge of the gown was worn. The beautifully worked lace kept catching in my shoe if I raised the heel of my foot too high.

She sighed with relief. "That's something we can deal with. I thought you might have had a real problem. Did you make conversation with anyone?"

"I spoke with the King of Navia." I pointed to a man around my father's age wearing a very elaborate uniform.

Sophie's eyes nearly bugged out of her head. "And? Please tell me it went well."

"He was very kind. He just arrived here today for the official delegation," I explained. "He said that I looked so lovely and that I made him laugh. He offered to introduce me to his son because he would love a daughter-in-law like me."

I took a perverse sense of satisfaction in that conversation. *That* monarch thought I was good enough for his son. Although, it was a little strange that speaking to kings didn't feel overwhelming anymore.

"I'm glad to hear it." Sophie nodded with a sigh of relief. "Anything else go wrong? Other than the hem of your dress."

"Why do you assume it would?" It hurt that was the default question.

"Did it?" she asked, crossing her arms.

"No." I raised my chin. "I've been perfect. I've curtsied and smiled. I've remembered everyone's names and talked about the weather or the Paradisa Royals. I haven't had a sip of champagne, I haven't eaten so I can't have crumbs on my dress, and I've stayed away from dancing."

"Good." Sophie looked pleasantly surprised. "Are you ready for later?"

I nodded. "All I have to do is walk down the stairs and not die," I replied. "I already did it once today, so I should be fine."

She cocked one eyebrow and I resisted the urge to smack her. Why did everyone assume I was going to fail tonight? Why did they all think I was incapable of walking and being polite?

"Go rest your feet," she advised. "There's some seats in the atrium. Relax for a little bit so that you're fresh for the exit."

I nodded. That sounded wonderful. I left Sophie in the ballroom and returned to the atrium. I found a small embroidered couch nearly hidden behind a tropical plant. It was wide enough that I could sit without crinkling my dress and the plant gave me a semblance of privacy.

I couldn't help but moan once I sat. My feet ached to the point of distraction. Even though I could now walk in these shoes, it didn't mean that I liked heels or that I was used to them. I glanced around, making sure no one could see me, and I slid my shoes off.

I was sure someone was going to look at the moan of relief this time. My bare feet and shoes were hidden under the skirt of my dress, so I was safe. But with the shoes off, I was now afraid that I might not have the strength to put them back on again. It felt like now that my feet were free, they were swelling and might not fit back into their beautiful heeled prisons.

I relaxed back on the chair, letting myself have a moment of relief.

"Have you seen the American?" A woman's voice caught my attention. I followed it and found two elegantly dressed women older than me within earshot.

"The Princess?" the second woman asked. She wore a scarlet red dress while her friend wore light purple. "She looks lovely."

"Not her," the Violet woman replied. "The other one."

"The other American?" Scarlett asked. She tilted her head slightly. "Oh, the one in pink that is supposedly dating Prince Frederick."

"That's the one," Violet said, nodding her head.

"Her dress is lovely," Scarlett said.

I smiled, feeling my confidence going up.

"That's the only lovely thing about her," Violet replied. "She's a drunk. Earlier, the Prince had to take her drink away. She was so drunk she nearly knocked over the Earl on the dance floor."

Scarlett's hand went to her throat. "No! What a disgrace!"

"I saw it," Violet assured her. She shook her head. "Our poor Frederick. He's such a troubled soul. He needs someone better than yet another American."

"I think it's just a cry for attention," Scarlett replied. "The boy is always looking to make people laugh. Perhaps this girl is just some kind of joke?"

Tears stung at my eyes as I jammed my feet into the heels and stood.

I left the couch, ignoring the surprised gasps of the two women as I passed. I didn't spare them a backward glance. I kept my head high, even though all I wanted to do was run to my room.

You are a strong, independent woman, I told myself. *And it doesn't matter what they think. You are not a joke. They don't matter. Freddie loves you. That's what matters. He makes you happy and you make him happy.*

I kept my chin up and managed to keep the tears at bay. I needed to find Freddie. Our earlier disagreement still stung and I wanted to fix things. I needed to fix things.

And then I saw him.

He was in the center of the dance floor, his arms cradling Sophie as they twirled in a complicated waltz.

The steps were more complex than anything I knew how to do, but the two of them performed flawlessly. She laughed, the sound bell-like and beautiful as he spun her. Her pale skirts flared out and the lights caught the jewels in her hair, making a natural crown.

Every eye in the room was on the two of them.

Freddie was grinning as they spun. His eyes were bright with laughter and his grin wide and infectious.

I hadn't seen him smile like that since we'd arrived.

He wasn't smiling because of me. He didn't even know I was in the room. He was smiling and happy because he was dancing with Sophie.

"Don't they look perfect together," the woman in front of me murmured to her husband. She rested her head on his shoulder as they watched the dancing. "Ah, to be young and in love."

The husband wrapped his arm around his wife and kissed her cheek. "They do match one another well."

I couldn't disagree.

Sophie was elegant and perfect. She knew how to dance and just what to do. She knew what to wear and how to wear it. Her best was enough. She'd grown up in this world with Freddie. She knew him in a way I never could. She was making him laugh right now while I was only making him angry.

I imagined Sophie in my place. No one would be afraid of Sophie falling down the stairs. No one would question her having a glass of champagne. No one would assume her best wasn't good enough.

The music faded as the song ended. Applause filled the ballroom. Freddie grinned, basking in the limelight. Sophie stood beside him, perfect and regal. They looked like a romantic movie. They were so beautiful.

Freddie's eyes met mine. I smiled, trying not to show any hurt or anger that he was dancing with someone else. He was allowed to dance with whomever he wanted. I raised my hand in a silent wave, just to say hello. It wasn't boisterous or big. Just a raise of my hand and a smile.

It wasn't exactly princess-like, but it wasn't something I was expressly forbidden to do either.

His smile disappeared. All the light and excitement washed out of him as if he'd been doused in cold water.

His reaction hurt like a physical punch to the gut. My hand dropped and I turned away, not wanting to see more. I turned and ran directly into the Duke.

The man must have been standing directly behind me. There was no way he had missed Freddie's sudden change of expression and then the fact that I was trying to get away.

"Your Grace," I murmured, dipping into a quick curtsy. I'd spilled some of his drink, but he didn't seem to notice. "My apologies. I didn't see you there."

He shrugged. "They're a handsome pair, aren't they?" He moved his mouth into the shape of a smile, but yet again I was struck by how it wasn't an expression of joy. "I always thought it would be the two of them together."

I made a noncommittal noise. I tried to keep walking, but he put out an arm, keeping me in place within the crowd. He smelled strongly of scotch. He watched as Freddie and Sophie began dancing again. It was another dance that I was completely incapable of doing.

"In the old days, they would have been betrothed." His eyes left the Prince and Sophie and came back to me. "How much easier his life would have been then. How much easier this all would have been."

"Excuse me?" Indignation swelled in my chest and I took a step back in surprise.

"I know that he loves you," the Duke replied, waving

my affront off. "But think of the ease. You can't deny that my daughter would make a better princess. Not because you aren't princess material," he sneered slightly, "But simply because she knows what is expected of her. She knows what to do."

I didn't really have a good argument for that. To be honest, it was frighteningly close to my own thoughts. Sophie *would* make a better princess than me. It was just that Freddie didn't love her like that.

"Just imagine the two of them," the Duke continued, his eyes going distant. He sipped on his drink and I wondered just how many he'd had tonight. "Freddie with his trade negotiations, and Sophie hosting state dinners. There would never be an out of place fork or a bare shoulder to be found."

I ignored the dig at my expense. "But would they be happy?"

"They wouldn't be stressed," he countered. "Can happiness bloom where there is constant turmoil? Is it possible to be happy when all the world is against it? When one person simply cannot seem to fit into the other's world?"

"Yes," I said, feeling my stubbornness rise to the challenge. "Love can survive."

"For a time. I suppose it is romantic. The star-crossed lovers is a popular trope for a reason." The Duke shrugged. "But it never lasts. The star-crossed lovers always die in the end."

I looked back to the dancers. Sophie and Freddie were laughing again as they spun. The crowd was smiling. No one looked displeased or unhappy. No one looked at the two of them the way the crowd looked at me. Like I wasn't enough.

I couldn't ignore Freddie's easy smile. I couldn't ignore the fact that Sophie wasn't stepping on his feet. No Earls were being run over. He didn't hide her off to the side of the dance floor. He stood out in the center with her. Proud of what she could do for him.

Sophie would have had instant family approval. She'd done the Stair Walk as a child. Liam would be thrilled to have Sophie making sure Freddie followed the rules and did as he was told.

Angst and unhappiness started to drape around my shoulders like a gray shawl.

"But true love conquers all," the Duke said. He focused his cold blue eyes on me once again and I felt like squirming. I didn't want to stand here talking with him anymore.

"That's what they say." I tried to smile, but my face didn't want to work. "May I get by you?"

I tried to dart around him again, but there was no space with the other guests around us.

The Duke didn't move his body. If anything, he managed to block my path more. "You look like you just want to go home and leave the young Prince here to dance with my daughter."

I tried not to flinch. That was exactly what I wanted to do. For the first time, the Duke seemed to look happy. He took a deep swig of his drink.

"Did something happen between the Prince and you?" he asked. I didn't like the excitement in his voice at the idea that Freddie and I were fighting.

"I'm just a little tired and want to go sit down," I admitted. "I'm not used to these crowds and all the dancing."

"Ah, yes." The Duke nodded. He smiled, but it made

my skin crawl. He was happy at my misery. "But this is what Freddie's life is. He is so good at diplomacy. I think he could put the King out of a job if he wanted."

I frowned. "Freddie wouldn't want to be king," I told him.

"Everyone says that," the Duke replied. "But no one means it. Power is everything. Freddie has power. He just has to realize it. I have already helped him so much. There's still so much more he can do."

His eyes went back to the dance floor and I was grateful I no longer held his gaze.

I didn't like the way the Duke looked at Freddie. He looked at him like the Prince was the Duke's next meal. But there was nothing I could do.

I was a nobody with no power. It didn't matter what I thought.

I took a step away from him, trying to see if there was another way out. Unfortunately, it was either cut through the dance floor or get past the Duke. There were too many people in my way otherwise.

"My daughter doesn't even have to try," the Duke said softly. "Unlike some who will never succeed no matter if they try their very best. I keep telling Freddie that, but he doesn't seem to listen."

I flinched at his words. I looked back at the dance floor just so I wouldn't have to look at the Duke's smug face anymore. Freddie was smiling again. Happy. Sophie giggled as they did a particularly complex step and he spun her in a beautiful arc. Her dress swished like Disney himself had animated the scene.

I knew the Duke didn't like me. But that didn't mean

he was wrong. Maybe I was one of those people that would just never succeed.

"Excuse me," I said, finally seeing an opening to the Duke's left. I took it, nearly knocking over the guest to his left in the process. I didn't care. I just wanted to leave.

The Duke watched me for only a second before turning back to watch his daughter dance with the prince and the applause of the crowd that followed.

CHAPTER 42

I didn't cry.

I told myself it was nothing. That Freddie was just enjoying a dance with a friend. I didn't think about the way his fingers had splayed on her hip. I didn't think about the graceful curve of her lips as she smiled up at him.

I didn't think about his laugh.

I didn't think about how Sophie was so much better at being a princess than I was.

Of how much easier Freddie's life would be without me. Of how much happier he could be here if he didn't have to deal with me and my mistakes.

I left the ballroom and found a balcony. The night air was cold and sharp after the heat of the ballroom and it felt so good. Out in the darkness, I could imagine that I was alone. That I was back at the lake.

I closed my eyes and thought about home.

Home where I was allowed to have a drink in my hand at a party. Where I was allowed to dance. Where I didn't have to curtsy. Where I wasn't on the news all the time. Home. Where I fit without trying.

Home was where I belonged.

Homesickness struck hard and steady. And there was no Freddie to push it away. There was no one that actually wanted me here.

I missed working in the hospital. I missed helping my patients and knowing that I had a purpose. Every day I walked into the hospital, I knew what I was doing.

Here, I had no clue.

I closed my eyes and took a deep breath. I just needed to get through tonight. Things would be better once I was allowed to officially date Freddie. We could go on dates again. We could travel together. It wouldn't be like at the lake, but we would have ourselves again.

At least, I hoped we would.

I knew the press would still be interested in me. I knew that I would still have to always be on my best behavior, but once I was officially dating Freddie, I would at least have the protection of the Queen Mother's blessing. Maybe even Liam would come to like me eventually.

There was a chance I could make things good again. That Freddie and I could go back to the way things had been in Chicago. I clung to those bright days.

I just had to get through tonight and everything would be good again.

I took a seat on a stone bench and stared out at the night, listening to the quiet and letting my thoughts and worries about Freddie drift. I went through the days, trying to remember the last time he'd smiled at me like he'd just smiled at Sophie.

It was farther back than I cared to admit.

"What are you doing out here?" Sophie asked, surprising me from my thoughts.

"Just getting a breath of fresh air," I replied. "Did you have a nice time dancing with Freddie?"

I managed to keep all bitterness out of my voice and I was rather proud of myself.

"We haven't danced in almost an hour," she replied. "It's nearly time for you to climb the stairs."

I blinked at her. I'd lost time out here in the dark by myself.

She touched my shoulder. "You're freezing. Are you okay?"

I forced myself to smile. "I'm fine. I'm used to colder than this."

She frowned but didn't say anything. "Come inside. It's just about time. You need a good spot by the base of the stairs."

I followed her inside, suddenly blinded by the bright lights of the ballroom after the dark of the balcony. Every step was fire. Sitting had let my feet rest for a bit, but now they were complaining. I wanted to limp, but I knew that would only make Sophie yell at me.

I took my place at the base of the stairs near one of the banisters. A crowd made of guests gathered around me, everyone wanting to see the Queen Mother's address.

It was tradition. The Queen Mother or the King would stand at the top of the stairs and bid their country a good night. Those who were to join the family would be called up the stairs. The entire family would then come down the stairs, exit through the ballroom and go off into the night.

My hands shook with nerves.

The Queen Mother could still change her mind. She could still decide not to call me up the steps. The King could countermand her. Freddie could contradict her if he wanted and call Sophie.

I pushed that thought away.

The doors opened at the top of the stairs and the Royal Family emerged. Liam wore a jet black military uniform. Henry and Freddie wore matching uniforms that had only slightly less medals and tassels hanging from their shoulders. Aria looked resplendent in her green satin dress.

The Queen Mother came out last. She wore a gown of deep blue and I realized I hadn't seen her at the ball at all. She hadn't been on the throne dais watching the dancers in the ballroom. I couldn't recall seeing her at all.

"Paradisa," King Liam boomed out from the top of the steps. "We thank you for coming out tonight. We thank you for joining us in celebration of the return of my brothers."

"And your new sister!" someone in the crowd yelled out.

Liam chuckled. "Yes. And my new sister. Thank you all for coming."

I held my breath. This was when the Queen would call me up.

It seemed the entire room held their breath. I knew I was.

"Will Zoey Miller please join us this evening?" The Queen Mother's voice was soft but confident.

A little of my overzealous nerves faded. I hadn't been forgotten yet again tonight.

A murmur went through the crowd as I stepped onto

the bottom step. My hand rested lightly on the handrail, and I held my head high as I climbed the stairs.

I hated that I could feel every eye on my back. I could feel their judging glares and cold looks. I knew that every inch of me was being evaluated. Was I good enough for their beloved youngest prince?

I arrived at the top of the stairs after what felt like an eternity. Luckily, I wasn't out of breath and I managed a deep curtsy.

"Walk with me," the Queen Mother said.

A gasp went through the room.

This wasn't what usually happened. Usually, the King or one of the princes would take her arm and guide her down the stairs. Usually, the person being accepted into the royal circle came last. After every other member of the royal family.

Aria grinned at me and I hoped this meant something good. I hoped this meant that I was truly invited into the inner royal circle. That Freddie and I would get our happily ever after.

I went to the Queen Mother and offered her my arm. She held onto me, and for a moment, I didn't use the courtier training Sophie had taught me. I used my nursing skills. I was walking the Queen Mother like a patient.

Except I'd never walked a patient while wearing heels before.

The room was silent as we made our way down the stairs.

Then, with only three steps left to go, disaster struck.

~

I was falling down the stairs.

I couldn't stop, despite the fact it seemed to be happening in slow motion. The long lace of my dress train had finally caught on the heel of my shoe and I was now tumbling down the stairs.

With the Queen Mother on my arm.

The marble floors rose to greet us. Shrieks filled the air.

I was not made to wear high heels.

They would be the death of me.

I managed to wrap my arms around the Queen, and pivot, putting myself in her path so that I would land first.

And *splat*.

My back hit marble with a thud.

The whole room drew an intake of air and then went silent.

The Queen Mother was on top of me. My back was cold against the marble of the floor. My head thunked hard and I saw stars.

Everything went crazy.

Someone grabbed the Queen Mother. Someone grabbed me. Lace hung from my dress in a long strip, showing the soft pink satin underneath. It felt like I was more exposed than if I were naked.

My pale pink high heeled shoe sat on the bottom step looking like Cinderella had left it there for the prince to find.

CHAPTER 43

We sat in yet another sitting room somewhere deep inside the castle. This one looked like it had been stolen from the Downton Abbey set, complete with turn of the century furniture and oil portraits. I fully expected Dame Maggie Smith to walk in wearing full costume and yell at me for trying to kill the Queen Mother.

I figured I probably had a slight concussion from hitting the marble floor with my head.

The Queen Mother sat on the center sofa. The on-call doctor was speaking softly with her. So far, they hadn't found any injuries. She seemed to be alert and oriented. She answered questions and moved without restriction. The doctor didn't look worried.

Liam sat beside his mother holding her hand. Aria sat on her opposite side with Henry on the couch across from them. Freddie stood by the window, his arms crossed. Sophie stood near him, her expression unreadable.

I sat in a high backed chair in the far corner of the

room. It was as far away as I could get from everyone without leaving. The doctor hadn't looked me over yet. Other than someone dumping me into the room, no one had cared much about me.

"You okay?" Freddie had asked when we'd first entered the room. When I nodded, too dazed to do much else, he'd left me to go check on his mother. He hadn't come back to me yet.

Sophie's phone rang and she fluttered by the window. She spoke quietly, yet forcefully. Even without being able to hear her, I knew she was talking about me. About what had just happened.

I shivered and it made everything in my body hurt. The room was ice cold and my ripped dress provided little heat. I could already feel the bruises forming all along my back. I had one on my calf from the bottom step that was already a nasty purple and bigger than my palm. I didn't think I'd broken any bones, but I would be purple and blue from head to toe by morning. My head throbbed and a goose egg the size of Manhattan was already forming.

Two big tears dripped down my cheeks. I wiped them away, trying not to smudge mascara all over my face.

I wasn't crying because of the pain. The pain was secondary to my shame at this point. I actually preferred the pain because it was something I could focus on that didn't make me want to curl into a ball and die. The pain would pass eventually. The shame would remain forever.

I couldn't have failed more if I'd tried.

I'd tripped and nearly killed the Queen Mother. The beloved symbol of the country of Paradisa. The mother of the King. I'd practically pushed her down the stairs.

It was supposed to be my moment, the moment where the Paradisian country would accept me, where Freddie's family would accept me. This had been my chance to make things better for Freddie. For us.

And I'd tripped.

I'd ruined everything. I had no idea how I could possibly salvage any of this.

I wrapped my arms around me, trying not to shiver. Shivering hurt the twisted muscles in my back. I wished I was home. My mother would have gotten me a blanket. Someone would have at least checked on me by now.

Sure, I had screwed up. The Queen Mother needed to be looked at first, and I was very okay with that.

But no one seemed to care that I had fallen too.

Not even Freddie.

I'd never felt so alone in my life.

"Well, I don't see any damage," the doctor announced. "Just a few bruises. Less than I'd expect after a fall like that, to be honest."

That's because she'd fallen on me. At least I'd managed to do something right.

"I'll check on her in an hour and make sure things are still going well," the doctor continued. "I see no reason for concern, though."

"Thank you, Doctor," Liam said, rising to his feet and shaking the doctor's hand. The doctor nodded. He bowed to the King and Queen Mother and left the room.

I guess I need to figure out my own medical care, I thought to myself. I hoped I had some pain meds in my travel bag.

The room was quiet for a moment except for the soft *tick tock tick tock* of the clock.

"Let's get you to bed," Aria said, rising from the sofa. "You should rest."

"I'll be just fine," the Queen mother replied, but took Aria's arm to steady herself as she stood. "It really wasn't that bad of a fall. Zoey managed to take most of the fall herself."

The room went quiet and everyone's eyes went to my chair.

I shrunk down, wishing that I could just blend into the embroidered armchair and disappear.

No one said anything. Liam's glare was daggers in my direction.

"Let's get you upstairs," Aria repeated. Henry and Liam fluttered after the two women like worried mother hens, leaving Sophie, Freddie and me in the room.

The heavy wooden door to the sitting room closed behind them. I could hear the sounds of servants and whispers outside, but in the room was silence again. Just the soft ticking of a clock somewhere over the mantle stayed constant.

Sophie sighed, pulling my attention from the door. "It's all over the news," she announced, putting her phone down. "I've managed to keep the tabloids from calling it an assassination attempt, but it's not great. The video is already out there."

I didn't know it was possible to feel worse about things than I already did.

"Thanks for doing that, Sophie," Freddie said. His voice was low and in perfect control. It was his royal voice. The one he used when he didn't want to show emotion. The one he used when there was too much emotion.

"I'll keep trying," Sophie said. She looked over at me. She opened her mouth like she was going to say something, but promptly snapped it shut. "I'm going to go make some more calls."

She hurried out of the room. The door slid shut again, leaving Freddie and me alone with only the sound of the clock.

Tick-tock. Tick-tock. Tick-tock.

It was almost midnight.

"Mum's okay," Freddie said, breaking the long silence between us. He still stood by the window, looking out into the night. Every line of his body was rigid. "The doctor says no damage."

"I heard." My voice shook, although I wasn't sure with what emotion. Pain? Fear? Anger? Uncertainty? All of them? The fact that he'd basically forgotten I was there was a dull knife in my heart. Bitterness tainted everything. "I think I'll be okay, too. Thanks for asking. I know the doctor didn't even look at me, so I might be wrong though."

I didn't do it in a nice way. I knew I sounded bitter and snotty. But I hurt. And I wanted just a little bit of sympathy. A little bit of comfort.

I had fallen down the stairs too.

Freddie's eyes flared. "You're twenty-five and not a beloved monarch. You'll be fine."

I recoiled as if he'd thrown something at me and then I froze in the chair.

"Thanks for your concern." This time I knew the reason my voice shook. Heartbreak was the emotion this time.

I wanted to get up and walk away, but I didn't have any

strength left in my body. I was so cold and stiff. Besides, I only had one shoe on.

Shame weighed on me. Loneliness crushed me.

Freddie sighed and ran a hand through his hair. The perfect prince look was gone. His uniform was wrinkled and his hair a mess. "That came out harsher than I meant," he said, still sounding like royalty. "Sorry."

The apology felt more like a slap than apology.

I didn't say anything. I didn't look at him. I stared at my torn dress and missing shoe.

Tick-tock. Tick-tock. Tick-tock.

"Tell me what happened," Freddie said. It wasn't a question. He didn't say it with malice, but it didn't feel like he was on my side either.

"I tripped. My heel caught in the lace of the dress," I explained. In my head, I relieved the memory. How the loose piece of lace on the hem of my dress and my high heeled shoe had tangled. How I'd fallen forward. How I'd twisted my body so that I would take the brunt of the fall.

I lifted the hem of my dress. "Here's where the step hit my leg," I said, showing him the growing mark on my leg. "I also hit my head if you want to feel the knot that's growing there."

He didn't move from his spot by the window.

"And you couldn't have caught yourself?"

I stared at him.

"Sure. I decided that falling down the stairs with your mother and injuring myself was the better option. I wanted to make a complete fool of myself."

He rolled his eyes at my sarcasm. "I just don't understand how this happened."

"My heel caught in my dress," I said, slowly enunciating every word. "I tripped. Luckily we were at the bottom of the steps. I don't understand why that's not clear."

He shook his head, crossing his arms and looking out the window again. "I don't understand how you could be so careless."

"What?" The question came out more breath than words.

"You knew this was important." He turned back to me, his eyes cold and fierce.

"It was an accident," I replied. I shifted my weight, wanting to stand. I whimpered with the movement and stopped.

"It always is with you," Freddie replied.

"What's that supposed to mean?" I asked, freezing in place.

"It was an accident that you wore something inappropriate. It was an accident that you kissed me. It was an accident that you talked to the reporter." He narrowed his eyes and glared at me. "It was an accident that you fell down the stairs. At some point, you need to take responsibility for your accidents."

"Do you think I'm doing this on purpose?" I asked.

He sighed. "No one else seems to have this problem," he replied. "Just you. Even the Duke sees it."

I nodded. "That's because I'm the only one who has never done this before." My voice rose in anger with every word. "I'm the only person in this entire castle that has never been to a garden party. I'm the only person in this entire city that isn't allowed to kiss her boyfriend in public. I'm the only person in this country that the reporter wanted to catch. And apparently, I'm the only person in the entire world who has ever fallen down a step."

"Oh, come on, Zoey." He rolled his eyes.

My throat tightened. I wanted to add, "I'm also the person you're supposed love," but I couldn't seem to get the words out. The room went quiet again.

Tick-tock. Tick-tock. Tick-tock.

"I am not being judged fairly here," I told him after a moment. "I'm not perfect, but I am trying."

"No, you're not trying," he snapped at me. "Don't be dramatic. It's not that hard to go down a step. And don't blame the dress. Sophie has done those steps dozens of times. The Duke told me you were going to ruin tonight and you most certainly did."

Anger bubbled up hot inside of me. For a moment I didn't feel cold. I felt dizzy with heat.

"You're right," I sneered. "I'm obviously not trying hard enough. That's it. I just didn't try hard enough on the stairs."

"Sophie does it without trouble every time." He glared at me. "I don't see why you can't either. I need a partner not a liability."

His words splashed over me like a bucket of cold water.

The anger and fire went right out of me. I'd used up all my stubbornness and fight just to stay at the party. To keep dancing and smiling.

I didn't have any energy left.

I was empty and tired. I hurt. I ached. The cold enveloped me again.

I was a liability.

"Just imagine the two of them," the Duke had said.

"Freddie with his trade negotiations, and Sophie hosting state dinners. There would never be an out of place fork or a bare shoulder to be found."

"A liability?" I repeated, my voice catching on the word. With every muscle screaming in my body, I stood. I took an uneven step and kicked off my remaining shoe so I stood barefoot on the floor. I left it there as I limped the few steps to the door, wincing with pain every step.

"Zoey." He didn't say my name with love or tenderness. He said it like I was a small child running away from a punishment. He said my name with annoyance and disdain.

"Then be with Sophie since she's so perfect." With my hand on the doorknob, I turned to look at him. "Because it's pretty obvious you don't want me anymore."

I left the room as the clock struck midnight.

CHAPTER 44

I'm not sure how I made it back to my room.

I just know that I stumbled through the hallways, tears streaming down my face as I forced my aching muscles to move. No halls were empty as I walked along with cold bare feet.

I opened the door to my room, expecting to find it dark and empty. Instead, a warm light shone by the bed. Mr. Irson was pulling the drapes of my room shut and humming as he prepared the room.

"My apologies, Ms. Miller. I wasn't expecting you to return so early tonight," he said, tugging the drapes tight. He turned with a smile on his face that quickly faded the moment he saw me. "Oh my. Are you alright?"

He rushed to me, his eyes full of concern. He touched my shoulders gently, moving down my arms and checking for injuries with kind hands.

"Is anything broken? Do you need a doctor?" he asked. Worry filled his voice and wrapped me like a warm blanket. I wanted to sob into him.

"I fell," I stated. "And I nearly killed the Queen Mother in the process."

He stared at me for a moment, trying to figure out if this was another of my strange American mannerisms.

"I'm sure you didn't nearly kill the Queen Mother," he said, putting his hands gently on my shoulders. They felt so warm and kind and for the first time all night, I didn't feel like a horrible burden.

Sobs caught in my throat. "You should tell Freddie that."

He frowned, and without warning, hugged me to him. I didn't expect it, but I needed it. I leaned into the man, sobbing as he patted my back. For someone as formal as Mr. Irson, he was strangely good at the soothing gesture.

"There, there," he whispered. "I'm sure everything will be fine."

I shook my head, but I was crying too hard to disagree with him.

He let me cry. He didn't ask me questions or try to pull away. He just held me and let me cry into his shoulder as he rubbed my back and made soothing noises. He smoothed the back of my hair, pausing when he felt the lump growing there. His touch was so gentle it didn't hurt more than a mother's touch.

"Thanks," I said when I finally had a little control over myself. "I'm sorry."

I wiped at my nose and moved away from him. I felt like such a child.

"Nothing to be sorry for," he assured me. "Now, go take a hot shower. I'll get you some tea and medicine. An ice pack for your head."

I nodded meekly.

"Do you need a doctor?" he asked.

"I don't think so," I replied. I had enough medical training to know I was okay. I didn't need a doctor. "Maybe just someone to check on me in a couple of hours and make sure I wake up and can answer questions. Just in case of a concussion."

"I will do that. I did it once or twice for the princes after rough rugby games," he said with a gentle smile.

"Thank you."

"Now, go on to the shower," he urged, pointing me toward the bathroom. "It will do you good."

I did as he instructed. The hot water poured over me and I cried again, but at least now I felt warm. I cried until there were no more tears left in me and the room was filled with steam.

I came out of the bath to find a set of satin pajamas laid out on the bed. Sophie had bought them for me with all the other clothes. That day felt long ago. On the nightstand, a small teapot steamed with a cup ready beside it. I could smell chamomile and lavender. Two chocolate chip cookies sat on a plate next to a bottle of Advil and an ice pack.

The kindness of the gesture made me cry again.

I slid into the pajamas, glad that the soft satin of them didn't hurt on my bruises. I poured a cup of tea and climbed into bed.

I didn't care that I got crumbs on the pillow when I ate the chocolate chip cookies. My stomach rumbled with hunger and I devoured them both. I sipped on the tea, finally feeling warm despite the ice pack on my head.

I knew I should turn off the lights and go to sleep. That I needed rest.

But my heart was broken. I didn't want to turn off the lights and be alone in the dark. I didn't want to be alone with Freddie's voice repeated over and over in my mind.

"Don't be dramatic. It's not that hard to go down a step. And don't blame the dress. Sophie has done those steps dozens of times."

"You're twenty-five and not a beloved monarch. You'll be fine."

"You're not trying."

"I need a partner not a liability."

Fresh tears rolled down my cheeks.

Despite it all, I still loved him. I loved his playful smile. I loved the small moments of the two of us together. I wished that we could go back to how things were before we came to Paradisa. Before he'd locked himself up in the office with the Duke for days on end.

Back when he was still mine.

I kept looking toward the door, hoping that Freddie would come in. That he would knock and come in with a bottle of ketchup as a sign of peace between us. That there would be some sign from him that he didn't mean the things he had said.

That he had forgiven me, at least a little. That he at least wanted to check on me.

But the door stayed shut. One message on my phone from him.

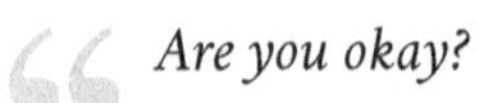

Are you okay?

 **Fine.**

I hadn't wanted to say more. There hadn't been another message. There were dozens from Sophie, but I didn't want to look at them.

My phone dinged with a new message.

It was from Cecelia.

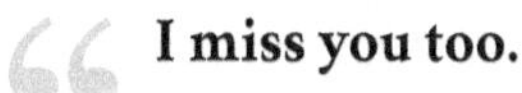 *How is Paradisa? Is everything as wonderful as I hope? I miss you!!!!*

I stared at the message for a long time. I typed back:

I miss you too.

The phone dinged almost immediately.

When are you coming home? Carlson says your boss misses you.

Homesickness rushed through me hard enough to knock me over. Another message came through.

> *You doing okay? I saw some weird stuff on a tabloid the other day. They were all shocked that you wore a dress. I love that dress and have worn it to tons of fancy things. I have no idea what their problem was.*

Fresh tears trickled down my cheeks. I missed home.

> **Freddie and I had a fight. I'm having a rough night. You have perfect timing.**

Not even two seconds went past before I had a reply.

> *That bastard. You okay? Do I need to hop on a flight? I don't care that he's a prince, I'll make him be nice to you.*

I imagined I was home for a moment. I would go to Cecelia's apartment and she'd hug me and tell me that Freddie was being an ass. She'd threaten to have Carlson beat him up. She'd bake me cookies and pour me whiskey.

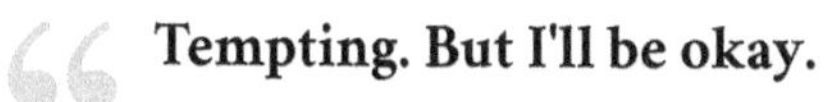 **Tempting. But I'll be okay.**

It was false bravado. I wasn't sure I was going to be okay. But there wasn't anything Cecelia could do for me right now. Right now, just knowing that someone was in my corner made me feel a lot better.

Not everyone thought I was a liability.

I looked up flights. It's actually cheap for you to come home. There's a sale on flights to Chicago.

You'd come pick me up, right?

I'd never leave you hanging. I want you home!

I stared at the screen, feeling my broken heart mend on

the edges. It was nice to have someone have my back. It was nice to feel wanted. My phone dinged again.

> *Crap. I just realized what time it is there. Go to bed. Call me in the morning, okay? He'll realize you're the best and it'll be all good.*

I replied back that I would call her.

I hoped that what she said was true. That Freddie would come to his senses and everything would be all good again.

But in the middle of the night with my head aching and his harsh words echoing, I wasn't sure.

What if I went home? I thought. *What if I left all of this behind?*

Without Freddie, there was nothing for me here. He clearly didn't want me here. I wasn't even sure he even really liked me right now. I did supposedly push his mother down the stairs.

I pulled up a flight finder website on my phone. Cecelia was right. It was cheaper for me to fly home than I expected. There was even a flight available for tomorrow.

My finger hovered over the flight information. What if I did go home? What if I left all this craziness behind me?

No more diets. No more media. No more curtsies. No more perfection.

I could go back to normal. To my job where I knew what to do. My life would be easy again. No one would bother me for interviews or care that I wore a dress twice. No one would care about what I wore.

I didn't know what the future looked like here. The Stair Walk was supposed to be the approval Freddie and I needed to publicly date, but I wasn't sure we had it. The Stair Walk hadn't exactly gone as planned. Would Freddie and I just stay in this hidden not-dating world that we both hated?

What was I supposed to do here? I had absolutely no idea what was expected of me right now.

I had no idea what I was supposed to do.

Going home sounded safe.

But I still loved Freddie. Even with our fight, I loved him. I didn't want to leave. I didn't want to go back to my life without him. He was part of what I considered to be normal. I wanted to make things right between us, even though I wasn't sure how. I hadn't done anything wrong. I didn't have much more I could give him.

I needed to know that I wasn't alone in this relationship.

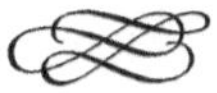

CHAPTER 45

I pulled up his name in my messages and froze. I had no idea what to say.

There was a knock on my door that made me look up. It wasn't Mr. Irson's gentle three beat knock.

Freddie?

My heart sped up, fueled by hope.

Maybe there was a chance I didn't need to send this message.

"Come in," I called, throwing off the blankets.

The door opened.

But it wasn't Freddie.

It was Sophie and the Duke.

"What are you wearing?" Sophie asked, looking completely shocked.

I stood in the center of my bedroom, and looked down at my pajamas and bare feet. Everything was covered. She'd picked these pajamas out for me. They were long pants and long-sleeved dark satin and covered everything appropriately. I was suddenly glad I hadn't worn the tiny cotton shorts and tank top I often did.

Sophie made an exasperated sigh and stalked over to the bathroom. She handed me a white cotton robe. "Please cover up. Try to be appropriate."

I slid the robe over my shoulders.

"Honestly, I know we went over this," Sophie continued. "I know we went over how to answer the door and appropriate dress. Especially with a man in the room."

She glared at me, her eyes darting over to her father.

"I'm sorry. It's one in the morning and I didn't expect anyone," I growled. I didn't bother to curtsy or greet the Duke. It was the middle of the night and this was my bedroom. "What do you want?"

"There's a problem," Sophie replied. She still wore her dress from the ball. She'd pulled her hair out of the pretty updo and into a tight ponytail. Despite being one in the morning, her makeup was still perfect.

"Is the Queen Mother okay?" I asked, suddenly worried.

"Oh, she's fine," Sophie assured me. "Doctor checked her and she's asleep."

I let out a small sigh of relief. "Good."

"But..." Sophie paused. "There is a problem with what happened."

"What?" I knew I should feel dread, but I was so tired and overwhelmed that there wasn't room for any more dread inside of me. I was already too full of emotion to hold more.

Sophie chewed on her lower lip. She glanced over at her father.

"Somehow the press is saying that this was an assassination attempt," the Duke said.

"What? That's ridiculous," I replied. I looked back to Sophie. "I thought you said you'd taken care of that."

"I did." She looked frustrated. "But somehow it didn't stick. The video is out and there's comments that you pushed her."

I stared at her, frozen to the spot. "People think I pushed her?"

"Only a few," the Duke said. "But enough that it's a concern. Enough that the authorities are looking into it."

"I don't know how this is happening," Sophie told me. She held her arms like she didn't know what to do with them. "I really don't know how this is happening. There's nothing in any of the videos that look like anything but a simple fall."

I guess you're not perfect at everything, I thought to myself.

"This is a big problem," Sophie said. "I'm trying to fix it, but..."

Her phone began to ring.

"Let me get this," she said. She brought the phone to her ear and went to the hallway. I stared after her.

I had thought there was no way this night could get worse. But apparently I was being accused of trying to assassinate the Queen Mother? It felt ridiculous.

"I can't believe this," I said softly. I sunk into a chair near the foot of my bed. "What does Freddie say?"

The Duke took a step toward me. "He's still angry."

"He can't think that I tried to hurt his mom."

"No, no. Of course he doesn't think that," the Duke assured me. "But it does hurt his public image. The accusation will always be there now. It puts him in a difficult position."

I buried my head in my hands.

"So what do I do?" I asked him, lifting my head. "Who do I talk to? Do I write a letter? Do I do a TV interview?"

"Those are options, but not good ones," the Duke replied. He crossed the room so he could stand before me. "My daughter asked me to come here because I can help you."

"I'd really appreciate any help you can give me," I said. I looked up at him, feeling completely hopeless.

"Go home," he advised. "Leave Paradisa as soon as you can."

I didn't say anything. I didn't know what to say.

"But how do I make things better?" I asked.

"You can't." He said it calmly. "You can't make this better. You can just leave and let us clean up your mess."

I thought I had cried all my tears in the shower. I hadn't. I didn't want to cry in front of the Duke, though, so I swallowed them down hard.

"So I just leave?" I asked. "Just pack my bags and get on an airplane?"

"Yes."

I covered my face in my hands again.

"What about Freddie?" I asked. "I need to talk to him."

I stood up and the Duke caught my shoulder.

"He doesn't want to talk to you right now," the Duke advised. For a moment, pity flashed in his blue eyes. "I'm very sorry, but he asked me to make sure you don't see him. He made it very clear that he doesn't want to see you right now. Do not talk to him." He sounded almost panicked that I would.

Something deep inside me shattered. Pieces of my heart ricochet around inside my ribs like tiny jagged knives.

"Oh." Was all I could say. My knees gave out and I sat back down into the chair with a thud.

My bedroom door opened and Sophie came back in.

"That was the lawyer," she explained. "No one is pressing charges. The investigator says it's very clearly an accident. So, no legal trouble right now. Just a lot of damage control."

"Good," the Duke replied. He didn't look pleased at the news, but I didn't care. "But Ms. Miller has decided to go home."

"She has?" Sophie sounded surprised. She looked over to me and her shoulders sagged as she found my face and saw the defeated expression there. "Oh. You have decided."

"It's for the best," the Duke assured his daughter. "It's not wise for her to stay here right now. She's not a good fit for the family's needs at the moment."

I swallowed down hard tears. I'm not sure I was ever a good fit for the family's needs.

"Do you mind if I have a moment with Zoey?" Sophie asked her father.

"Of course. I'll see to your flight arrangements," the Duke said. He looked back over at me, his blue eyes cold and glittering with victory. They were so different from his daughter's, despite being such a similar shade. "Good night, Ms. Miller."

He walked calmly to my bedroom door and left. Sophie stood staring at me from the center of the room.

"I really appreciate all your help," I said softly. I looked up at her. "You've been wonderful."

She just looked at me like she couldn't believe I would give up.

"Your dad says that it's best if I leave." I looked down at my hands. "There was a flight tomorrow. I mean, today I guess. I'll be out of your hair by lunch."

"You were looking up flights?" Sophie asked. She sounded surprised. "I know that this stair thing makes things really hard, but you don't have to leave. We can work through this."

"It's not just the fact that I fell down the stairs." I gave her a weak smile before staring at my hands again. "Freddie and I had a fight. A big one."

"People have fights all the time," she replied.

"Things haven't been... good." I wiped at my cheeks. "I don't think he likes me very much right now."

"He loves you," Sophie said. "I know he does."

"Then why did he not care that I was hurt?" I asked. I pulled at the leg of my pajamas and showed her the bruise. Sophie gasped when she saw it. I let my pant leg fall back. "He didn't care. He just cared that I wasn't trying. That I made him look bad. That I was a liability to him."

The words tumbled out of me, harsh and bitter. I couldn't stop them. Raw emotion and pain colored every syllable.

"But... I thought..." Sophie shook her head. "I thought things were good. I knew it wasn't easy, but I didn't think it was this bad."

"He hasn't spent time with me all week. We haven't had more than five minutes together, and that's when I made him." I said softly. I hated the ache in my chest at all the lonely nights the past few weeks. "He's been too busy for me."

"I thought he came by when we were done," she admitted. "I always made sure to leave at least a little bit of time in the evenings so you could have some time together."

"And he was always too busy with the Duke," I replied with a shrug. "He hasn't kissed me since that reporter tricked me. I think he's been avoiding me. I think he's realizing that bringing me here was a mistake."

I hated that I said the last part out loud. But I couldn't stop now. Now that I had said it out loud, it was true. The fact that Sophie didn't immediately contradict me said she thought so too.

"I thought that tonight would fix things. I thought that once I had family approval, we could have time together again. But..." I trailed off. I closed my eyes, the pain in my heart hurting so much I wanted to hide under the covers.

Sophie stared at me, open mouthed and wide eyed. "I didn't know."

I shrugged. "I think it's just too much to ask of both of us. I'm not meant for a place like this. I'm not designed to fit in his world."

I thought of all the ways I didn't fit in here. It was more than just the little mistakes. It was the way I carried myself. The food I liked. The way I walked. I could handle blizzards but I didn't know how to survive the court.

"But... I know he loves you," she repeated. She said it like a mantra. Like it could fix everything if she just said it enough times.

"Star-crossed lovers always die at the end," I told her.

She frowned. "That's what my father says."

"Well, he's right."

"Are you sure you can't work things out?" Sophie asked. She came over to where I sat. "Do you really want to run?"

I thought for a moment.

"I'm so tired, Sophie," I admitted. "I'm so tired of doing everything wrong. I'm tired of remembering to curtsy. I'm tired of trying to figure out what I'm supposed to wear and what I'm supposed to say. It's exhausting being perfect. Especially when the person I'm doing it for tells me that I'm not even trying."

"I'm sure he didn't mean it like that," she replied. "He's just been under a lot of stress. Tonight he saw his mother fall down the stairs."

"He just saw me fall down the stairs too," I reminded her.

She slumped into the seat next to me.

"I really thought you two were going to make it," she said after a moment.

I tried not to scoff. "Have you seen me? I'm not doing so great."

"You were doing your best," she replied. "I guess Freddie's more like Liam than he thought."

I glanced over at her.

"Liam is single because no one is ever good enough for him," she explained. "He won't let anyone close. I thought Freddie had found a partner in you. I thought he was happy enough to keep trying. I guess not."

We sat in silence for a few minutes.

"Do you want help packing?" she asked. "I don't think I'm going to be able to sleep tonight."

"That would be great," I told her. I slowly came to my

feet. "And thanks again for everything. I'm sorry I wasn't a better student."

"You were a great student," she replied. "I shouldn't have made you wear the heels. You probably would have been fine if you'd been wearing shoes you were comfortable in."

"I was supposed to wear heels," I reminded her. "And I agreed to it."

"Still, I'm sorry."

I hugged her. She froze for a moment, as all Paradisians seemed to. They weren't big on physical affection here.

I let her go and went to find my suitcase.

"I want to record you saying what happened," Sophie said. I stopped and turned to face her. "I know that you aren't staying, but I don't want anyone saying you didn't try either."

I don't want anyone saying you didn't try. If only that were possible.

"Sure," I agreed. It wouldn't hurt. "I can do that."

Sophie gave me a sad smile.

"Then let's get to work one last time."

CHAPTER 46

My hand trembled and I pulled back.

My whole body shook and I thought I might be sick.

"Just talk to him," I whispered to the empty hallway. "He loves you. It'll be fine."

I counted to ten and forced my hand to move. I knocked. It was clear and loud and I glanced around the hallway, sure that heads were about to pop out of every room and yell at me.

No doors opened.

Silence hung in the hallway. The pale light of the coming dawn flickered like a ghost in the windows as I waited. I thought of running away. I thought of just going back to my room and hiding under the covers until I had courage again.

But it had to be now. I would be on a plane in an hour.

Unless Freddie stopped me.

If he said I should stay, I would cancel my flight. I

would stay here with him and deal with the consequences of the Stair Walk. I would do it for him.

My heartbeat thundered in my chest, too fast and completely unsteady. *I should probably see a doctor about that*, I thought. *Or have a little less caffeine.*

A possible concussion didn't help either.

The door cracked open. Freddie's sleepy face peeked out. "What are you doing here? You're not supposed to be near my room."

I felt like a kicked dog. *You're not supposed to be near my room.*

"I wanted to talk to you," I said, keeping my voice neutral.

He rubbed at his face and groaned. "Now? Can't we do it when the sun is up and I'm not hung over?"

I hadn't realized he'd had that much to drink last night.

I crossed my arms. "I can't do it later."

He sighed, annoyance in the angle of his jaw. "I don't have time for this, Zoey. I was sleeping. I have a big meeting today."

He started to close the door.

"I have an airplane ticket home in an hour."

The door stopped moving. "What?"

"I bought a ticket home," I repeated. "The Duke says that it's not a good idea for me to be around right now."

He stared at me for a moment. "You're leaving Paradisa?"

I swallowed hard. I searched his face, looking for some hint that he wanted me to stay. "The Duke says I should. That it's for the best."

He thought for a moment, and for a brief second, I thought he was going to tell me to stay. But he didn't.

"Then we should listen to the Duke. He's been right about everything." His voice was flat and his expression unreadable. It was the Prince mask. "He's always been right about you. Everything you've done, he predicted. I should have listened to him in the first place."

I took a step back, my heart reeling once I'd processed his words. "Oh."

He sighed and pushed his hand through his messy hair. "Zoey..."

"No, I get it," I said quickly. My voice cracked as I attempted to contain all the horrible emotion filling up my chest and about to drown me. "It's not a good time. You're busy. I'm sorry to have bothered you. Go back to bed."

I took another step away from the door, wrapping my arms around myself. My head hurt again and everything felt shaky and surreal.

"Zoey..." Frustration filled his voice. "This just isn't a good time..."

"Good luck with your negotiations today. I hope you get everything you want." I turned and started walking down the hallway, blinking hard to keep from crying.

I heard him call my name again, but he didn't leave the safety of his room. He didn't chase after me.

My tears were hot and heavy as I left his room. I was exhausted. Bone weary in more ways than one. Suddenly, I wanted to be home more than anything.

"How'd it go?" Mr. Irson asked as I opened the door to my room. He set my suitcase by the door and looked up with a smile that quickly faded. "Oh."

"I should probably get to the airport." I wiped at my nose, determined to keep a stiff upper lip in front of him.

He sighed. "I was hoping you wouldn't be leaving."

"Me too," I told him.

"The Duke is downstairs in a car waiting for you," he informed me. "I told him it wasn't necessary, but... at least you'll get to skip security if you go with him."

I thought about taking off my shoes and pulling out my laptop while everyone stared at me and whispered. There's the girl that nearly killed the Queen Mother.

"That'll be nice."

He crossed the room and hugged me. "Good luck, Zoey."

"Thanks." I hugged him back, leaning into his strength. I breathed his peppermint candy scent in, knowing that he at least cared. "Thank you for helping me."

He gave me one quick squeeze before pulling back.

"Get going or you'll be late." He frowned at me. "Punctuality matters."

I wanted to laugh. Punctuality didn't matter. Nothing did.

"Thank you," I said. I went to the nightstand and pulled out a small envelope. "Will you give this to the Queen Mother? It's just an apology letter. I don't want to wake her up."

He took the letter and carefully tucked it into a hidden pocket. "I will make sure she gets it."

I nodded and looked around the room one last time.

It never felt like home here, but I was still sad to leave it.

But it was time for me to go back where I belonged.

~

"You're making the right decision," the Duke told me.

I nodded, not really listening.

Rain hit the window on the car. Gray clouds and mist fogged my view. Outside, the airport loomed.

Home loomed.

My head still ached. I hadn't slept for more than thirty minutes all night, but I figured I could sleep on the plane.

Sophie had helped me pack. Somehow, everything I owned fit in two little suitcases.

I didn't bring the clothes Sophie had bought that day back when everything still felt full of hope. It didn't feel right to take them. They were never really mine to begin with. They were doll's clothes. Something to play with, but never really meant for me.

I fiddled with the straps on my bag, pretending to check them, but really just looking for something to keep my hands busy.

I didn't want to check my phone again.

I didn't want to see that there were no missed calls. That there were no unread messages.

"Just let him be," the Duke counseled. "This is what needs to happen. The hurt will fade with time. You'll both move on to better things."

I pretended not to hear him. Who could be better than a prince?

"This is what needs to happen," the Duke continued. "Things will turn out as they should."

I nodded again.

"I'll tell him you said goodbye," he said. He motioned to the driver. "It's time for your flight."

"Thank you, Your Grace." I gathered my things. "Thank you for the ride to the airport."

I got out of the car and a security officer escorted me directly to the terminal. I walked past onlookers, but with my sunglasses and scarf, no one even pointed. I was invisible for the first time.

I waited by the door of the plane, hoping against hope that Freddie would show up at the airport. I kept imagining him running through the airport, eluding security and catching me before my flight could leave.

I waited for the last possible second to board the plane. I waited until the flight attendant told me I had to go in or they would take off without me.

But he never came.

The flight home was uneventful.

I didn't cry. I slept, if you can call it that. My dreams were filled with restless anxieties. I woke up every fifteen minutes. My body still ached from the fall and I struggled to find a comfortable position. It was a very uncomfortable flight.

But true to her word, Cecelia was waiting at the airport for me.

She had a sign that read, "WELCOME HOME" in big bold letters. She had three helium balloons in bright colors attached to the sign.

For the first time in a month, I felt loved. Wanted.

"Welcome back," Cecelia said, wrapping me up in a hug. Hearing her lack of accent was so strange. I'd grown accustomed to the lilt of Paradisa.

"Thanks for coming to get me," I replied. "I know it was kind of last minute."

"Well, you did promise me a present." She winked at me. This was fun banter. There was no actual expectation.

"Airport chocolate, just as promised." I told her, handing her a duty-free bar of Paradisa chocolate..

She gasped and pretended like I had given her solid gold. She grinned and wrapped her arm around my shoulder.

I smiled. For the first time all week, I smiled.

Cold, crisp autumn air greeted us in the parking lot. The air here felt different. Younger. There were no castles here. The wide open sky was a different color. I wondered why I had never noticed that before.

"You okay?" Cecelia asked, tossing my bags in the back of her car.

"Just tired," I told her.

She paused, looking me over. "Right. Tired." She sighed. "I saw your fall. It was pretty epic. Do you want Carlson to look you over?"

I rubbed at the back of my head. "I'm okay."

She pouted.

"But if it will make you feel better, I'll get checked out," I told her.

"He's waiting for you at home," she said, getting in the driver's seat. "You're staying with us for a few days."

I didn't object. I hadn't warned my old roommate that I'd be coming back and I didn't want to just walk in and surprise her. Besides, I wanted to be around people that loved me. That liked me for who I was. I needed some moral support.

"Were you wearing heels?" Cecelia asked, glancing over at me once she'd started the car.

"Yes."

She nodded. "You really need to stop wearing those shoes."

"No kidding," I agreed. "I have decided to never wear heels again. No matter who asks."

She put the car into reverse and we were on our way. "Good."

"Can you imagine me wearing them at my own wedding?" I asked, wanting to make conversation. Making fun of myself seemed like something I could do. "I can just imagine myself going head over heels in a frothy white gown."

Cecelia chuckled. "Your poor husband would have to catch you."

I sobered quickly, my stomach going cold. The person I imagined waiting for me at the end of the aisle was Freddie. I swallowed hard. I didn't want to make conversation anymore. I just looked out the window at the buildings going by. I stared at them like they were the most interesting things I had ever seen in my life even though I wasn't actually seeing them.

My mind was far away.

"Do you mind if we stop for food?" Cecelia asked, breaking into my thoughts after a long time. She didn't wait for an answer as she turned into a fast food restaurant parking lot. "I'm starving."

The scent of hamburgers and french fries hit me like a familiar hug. My stomach rumbled.

"I want a ButterBurger, fries, and a salted caramel concrete mixer. And extra ketchup."

Cecelia looked over at me, eyebrows raised. "Did they not feed you over there?"

I laughed. "It was a long flight!"

"Extra ketchup?" Cecelia asked. "Really?"

"They don't believe in ketchup in Paradisa," I replied. "I want all of it."

She shrugged and shook her head. "Sure, weirdo. You can have all the ketchup you want." But she said it with love.

We swung through the drive through and I loved that Cecelia ordered sweet potato fries as well as onion rings. I wasn't going to be hungry for long.

"Oh, I have missed you sweet grease," I moaned, taking a bite of my burger. Ketchup leaked everywhere.

Cecelia giggled. "Since when are you so polite?"

"What?" I asked.

"There is no grease dripping down your chin. Or ketchup," she said, pointing to my food. "You're holding that thing like a princess."

I looked down. I had the burger still neatly wrapped so I wouldn't drip any juice. I even had a napkin draped across my lap.

"Oh. I guess they did manage to get some manners to stick," I said. I took another bite, still keeping things neat and polite.

Even though I ate it differently, it tasted like home.

CHAPTER 47

I checked my phone. No messages. No missed calls.

Nothing for two days from Freddie.

Several from Sophie, but nothing that made me rethink my decision to leave.

"You okay?" Cecelia asked from the kitchen. I tucked my phone back into my pocket and tried to smile at her as I walked into the living room. The smells of spaghetti filled the air. "Have a seat. Watch some TV. Dinner won't be ready for another twenty minutes or so."

I sat down on the comfy leather couch and pulled a quilt over my lap. It was such a different couch experience than what was in Paradisa. I couldn't imagine a worn quilt made by the Queen Mother on a worn leather sofa with soft throw pillows. This couch was made for comfort and family, not for looking pretty.

I turned on the TV.

And saw Freddie.

"In world news, Paradisa and Navia have signed a

historic trade agreement. Paradisa, known for their lithium deposits and Navia, known for new technology signed the agreement this morning. The two countries have had a contentious relationship, so this partnership is a huge step for both kingdoms."

On screen, Liam, Freddie and the Duke stood next to the Navian King and his son. They were smiling and waving to cameras with the paperwork signed in front of them. Freddie shook the Navian Prince's hand and they grinned at one another.

The trade negotiations were a success.

I knew I should change the channel and stop staring. I tried not to look at Freddie's sweet smile. I tried not to see how tired his eyes looked even though his grin was big. How he looked out in the crowd like he was looking for someone but not seeing them. He was probably looking for Sophie.

I was happy for him, even if I was still sad. I wanted Freddie to succeed. I had tried so hard to do my part that even though I wasn't there, I was still happy for him.

The screen moved to the left of the Duke to where the Queen Mother stood smiling and clapping. She seemed well, if a little pale. Henry and Aria stood on either side of her. I was glad to see she was doing well.

"But the real question is where is Zoey Miller, the girl-friend of Prince Frederick?" the female newscaster asked. "Americans and Paradisians alike are asking where the royal love interest is."

A picture of me and Freddie popped up on the screen. It was from our day at the hospital. I was laughing at something he'd said and he was looking at me with so much love. We looked so happy and in love. I wanted to sob.

"She was not in attendance at today's event, but the Royal Family says that she suffered no serious injuries after the regrettable Stair Walk incident. They give no comment on the status of the Prince's relationship," the reporter continued.

A clip of my fall down the stairs came on the screen. Pink lace flying, the Queen Mother's eyes going wide, the thud as we hit marble. I winced.

"The Queen Mother is said to have made a complete recovery after the regrettable Stair Walk incident," the TV reporter continued. "Despite outlandish claims the fall was an attack on the Queen Mother, most Paradisian's feel a connection to the young American."

The screen went to a young woman.

"I don't know how anyone can say that Zoey pushed the Queen Mother," the woman said, her Paradisian accent strong. It looked like she was in the crowd celebrating the signing. "It's very clear she just tripped. If anything, I relate to her. I'm always tripping and falling over things. If anything, it makes those royals more relatable."

My heart warmed. Someone out there liked me.

"I don't know about another American coming into the Paradisian Royal Family," a young man said. He too spoke with a Paradisian accent. "But I like her. The girl can take a fall better than most footballers."

I grinned, feeling vindicated. The screen switched to a new woman. She looked to be in her forties with dark hair.

"I hope she never comes back," the woman said with a

sneer. It sounded so much crueler with the Paradisian accent. "She can't even walk down stairs properly. What kind of wife is that for a Prince? We deserve better. We deserve someone that can bloody walk."

My good mood faded. I stuck my tongue out at the TV.

"Zoey Miller was not seen at today's signing, leading many to speculate that the Prince's relationship may be on the outs," the female reporter continued. The screen went back to the studio. "I know we're all interested in this love story."

"We wish them both the best and hope for a happily ever after," the male anchor agreed. He turned and smiled into the camera. "In other news, do you know what chemicals are in your fire extinguisher?"

"I'm still impressed you didn't break anything," Cecelia said, flopping onto the couch beside me. "I've seen that video hundreds of times and I'm always impressed."

"Hundreds?" I asked, looking over at her.

She shrugged. "It's become kind of epic," she replied. "I saw one version of it put it to the *Titanic* theme song and slowed down to fit. It's Oscar worthy."

I sighed. And then giggled a little. If you can't laugh at yourself then you'll be miserable.

"I guess the upside is that I will always be internet famous for this," I replied. "There is now a hilarious video of a Queen falling down the stairs. I will be on jumbotrons at every sports game for decades any time someone trips."

"You should probably write a book. That's how all the internet famous people make money these days," Cecelia agreed.

"'How to Ruin Your Life by Falling Down Stairs.'" I shrugged. "I guess it has a nice ring."

"Hey, you didn't ruin your life." Cecelia lost the gentle joking tone and faced me. "And I really am sorry about how things turned out."

"Yeah. Me too." My eyes felt hot. I blinked away tears I didn't want. "How long until dinner?" I asked, wanting to change the subject.

"Not long," Cecelia assured me. "Carlson should be home any minute and the bread is nearly toasted."

I nodded. "I'm going to go clean up."

"Okay."

Cecelia watched me rise from the couch and head to the bathroom. I didn't really need to do anything, but I felt shaky and wobbly since seeing Freddie. I wasn't over him. I probably never would be. I knew that for the rest of my days, my heart would break a little every time I'd see him on the TV.

Without thinking I texted him.

Congratulations. I saw the signing on the news. I'm happy for you.

I immediately wished I hadn't sent it, but it was too late.

"Stupid, stupid," I said to myself. I looked up at the mirror. "Why did I do that?"

"Because you have to be nice to everyone," I answered my own question. "Because it's what a princess would do. Because you're an idiot."

I sighed and wished that I didn't miss him. That I didn't care.

I washed my face, splashing cool water on my cheeks. I tried not to think about Freddie.

I stared at my splotchy cheeks in the mirror and wondered what he was doing right now. Was he celebrating with Sophie? Was he finally relaxing? Did he miss me?

I sighed. It wasn't my problem anymore.

In a few months, all that would be left of our relationship would be a funny video clip for football fumbles. In a few months, no one would remember me and I could go back to normal.

I heard the front door open and quickly finished up. I was hungry for dinner.

"Hey," Carlson greeted me as I joined the small table. Cecelia was busy loading up plates with noodles and sauce. "It's a good thing you're staying here."

"Why?" I asked him, taking a seat.

"There's a bunch of reporters at your apartment," Carlson replied. "And several showed up at the hospital. They heard you were back in town."

I sighed. "Great."

My gut twisted at the idea of being on TV again. Of being the center of attention. I didn't want it at the beginning and I didn't want it now.

"Write a book," Cecelia advised, taking her seat. "Lots of good publicity right now."

I rolled my eyes. "Well, hopefully it will all blow over soon. I'm not that interesting. I'll just go back to work and be boring again. Everyone will forget about me."

Carlson and Cecelia looked at one another.

"What?" I asked.

"It's just that it might not be that fast," Carlson explained. He winced and shrugged apologetically. "And the hospital is on a hiring freeze."

"Of course they are," I muttered. I sighed and shook my head. "So much for going back to normal. So much for paying bills."

"Oh honey, it's not that bad," Cecelia quickly assured me. "I'm sure something will open up."

"Maybe I should write that book," I said. I stabbed my fork into my spaghetti. I wasn't all that hungry, but it smelled good and I knew it was something I'd never have been allowed to have in Paradisa. So I wanted it. "But after dinner."

Cecelia and Calson made small talk as we ate, but my thoughts were on my future. No job at the hospital. Reporters at my apartment. Nothing was ever going to go back to normal.

I couldn't escape what his world did to me. I couldn't escape the effects of him.

It didn't help that my heart still ached for him. That I still craved his touch. That I dreamed about him at night and woke up alone and angry.

"Do you think they're hiring in Des Moines?" I suddenly asked.

Carlson looked up surprised. "What?"

"Or another city. What if I moved?" An idea was forming. I could move somewhere. Go by my middle name for a while. Start over. I could find normal again.

While there would always be the video of me falling down the stairs, I didn't have to cling to it. I could move on. Find a new life. Remake myself without Freddie even though it would break my heart.

"Um, I guess?" Carlson swallowed a bite of spaghetti. "I know a doctor in Madison. He needs a good office nurse."

"Give me his contact info," I said.

Carlson and Cecelia shared another look that I couldn't understand.

"I'll get it for you after dinner," Carlson replied.

I nodded and took another bite of spaghetti. I was going to have seconds just because I could.

CHAPTER 48

"Thanks. I'll send you my resume," I said into the phone.

I sighed as I ended the call. The job in Madison was decent. There was nothing wrong with it. The pay was good, the benefits fair, and I had a friend in Madison that would be happy to rent me a room.

I sat down on the guest bed and pouted.

It just wasn't what I wanted.

I wanted Freddie. I wanted normal.

But those two things didn't go together.

"Zoey."

I turned at the sound of my name to see Cecelia standing in the doorway to the guest room. Soft morning light filtered around her. Her face was drawn and pale.

"What's the matter?" I asked, rising quickly. Something in the pit of my stomach went cold. I'd seen that face on Cecelia before. It was when she'd told me that our Grandmother had died.

"You have to come in here." She swallowed hard and

glanced toward the living room. "There's something on the TV you need to see."

Fear whirled dark in my stomach as I walked through the short hallway.

The big TV was on a news station. The view was from a helicopter circling over a car accident.

I frowned. The cars were on the wrong side of the road.

"Prince Frederick of Paradisa has been air-lifted to Westshire General Hospital. His condition is listed as serious, but the Royal Family has not made any public announcements," a male news reporter announced. The helicopter continued to circle over the accident.

Everything inside of me went numb.

"Sit down," Cecelia whispered, guiding me to the couch. At least, I think she whispered it. I wasn't sure about the volume of the world. It was too loud and too quiet. There was a rushing in my ears and numbness in my hands.

I stared at the TV, watching but not really seeing.

"Details are just coming in," the reporter continued. "While this is the vehicle customarily used by the King, the only passenger was Prince Frederick. It appears as though the Prince and his driver were turning off the highway and were headed toward the airport when another vehicle collided with the left side of the vehicle. At this time, it appears to be an accident."

The words faded. Everything faded. All I could see was mangled steel. A tire fallen to the side of the road. Glass sparkling on dark asphalt. Flashing lights.

Freddie.

My Freddie.

A low scream started in the bowels of my core. I opened my mouth, but no sound came out. Just a small whimper. The worry, the emotion, the pain was too great. It was too big to escape me.

Instead, horror and fear writhed in my chest like restless snakes, squeezing my organs and making it hard to breathe.

"Zoey, your phone's ringing." Cecelia's hand was on my forearm.

I looked down in surprise.

Sophie.

My fingers felt leaden as I tried to press the button. I couldn't seem to move them properly. Finally, I managed to answer the call before it went to voicemail.

"Sophie?" I managed to whisper, my eyes still glued to the TV. "What's going on?"

"You need to come home," she said, her voice so sad a tear slid down my cheek. "You need to come home right now."

"I'll be on the next flight," I promised.

And I ran for my car.

"Do you think it's her?" the flight attendant whispered to her friend. They both peeked over the drink cart, trying not to be obvious as they looked at me and failing miserably.

"Why's she in coach?" the second replied. She shook her head. "Can't be her."

The first sighed. "Yeah. She looks really similar though."

"It's hard to tell without her falling down," the second replied with a snicker.

I pulled my hood further down my face and turned up my music, ignoring them both.

This seat in coach was the first flight I could get. It was also the only seating I could afford. I didn't have access to the Royal Treasury to buy flights anymore.

The man to my right was snoring softly. The woman to my right was writing furiously on her laptop, which she had carefully turned away from me so I couldn't see what she was writing. Every so often she would stop, think, tap her fingers on the keys without typing, glance over at me, and then begin typing again at a furious pace.

I hoped she was some kind of romance author and not a reporter.

I tried not to look up information on the accident. It was like not scratching an itch.

The car was usually used by the King. The other driver ran a red light and smashed into the left rear door then took off. The police were looking for him, but they didn't have much to go on. It felt strange how little information there was.

Freddie had luckily been sitting on the right side of the vehicle. If he'd been on the left, he would have been dead. As it was, he was still in the hospital in critical condition.

Sophie was waiting for me at the airport. Or rather, she had a driver meet me at the gate with a sign who then brought me out to a waiting dark-windowed limousine.

I chuckled darkly at the thought that this time there was a sign greeting me.

"How is he?" I asked, sliding into the car. Sophie sat across from me, petite and perfect. Not a hair out of place or a wrinkle on her clothes. I looked like I'd just spent twelve hours on an airplane and was far from petite or perfect looking.

For once, I didn't really care.

"Stable," Sophie replied. She looked like she'd been crying. "He woke up a couple of hours ago. He's been asking for you."

I nodded, my voice catching and making it impossible to talk.

Sophie reached across the space and put her hand on my knee.

"What happened?" I asked. "I've been listening to the news, but nothing has been released yet."

"He was coming to see you," Sophie said. Her voice was soft.

"What?" I nearly fell over as the car started moving. "What do you mean?"

"He felt awful about what happened," Sophie explained. "He used Liam's car and…"

"But he's okay?" My voice trembled.

"The doctors think so," she told me. "Zoey, he wants you to know he's sorry. He wanted to come and apologize. He didn't know what the Duke was doing to him."

I shook my head, confused. I was more jet-lagged than I thought. "Your father?"

"My father is not a good man. He's manipulative and power-hungry." She looked out the window, her face pained. " I thought Freddie knew that, but I think he forgot. I think he forgot just how much my father wants power."

I thought of the Duke. Manipulative and power-hungry were kind ways of describing him.

"But he's very good at what he does," Sophie continued. "Probably because of those attributes. He has a lot of sway over things. And in Freddie, he saw the perfect opportunity to grab more power. He saw his way to the throne in Freddie."

I think he could put the King out of a job if he wanted. The way the Duke said it had bothered me even then. The hungry way he'd looked at Freddie.

Sophie slowly pulled her eyes from the window and back to me. They were big and blue and so full of tears. "He poisoned Freddie against you," she explained. "He told Freddie that you weren't trying. That you were a failure. That he would ruin the monarchy by being with you."

"Freddie wouldn't believe that," I said quickly. "He's smarter than that."

Sophie wiped at her cheek. "Usually. But my father is really good at making you think his ideas are your own." She swallowed. "He had weeks to whisper in Freddie's ear about how you were failing."

Power is everything. I remembered him saying at the ball. *Freddie has power. He just has to realize it. I have already helped him so much. There's still so much more he can do.*

Maybe it wasn't so crazy to think about it after all.

"But why turn him against me?" I asked.

"Because Freddie loves you," Sophie explained. She looked down and her cheeks went red. "And not me."

"But you don't love Freddie..." I said it slowly. The ache of her loving him would kill me. "Do you?"

She looked up quickly. "No. Not that kind of love," she agreed. "But my father didn't care. If I were a princess, his status goes up. He gets the power he wants by marrying me off like we're in the fourteenth century."

In the old days, they would have been betrothed.... he'd said. You can't deny that my daughter would make a better princess.

"I'm still confused," I told her.

"My father lied to Freddie. He said you were a terrible choice. That all you wanted was his money and fame. That you would only fail him. That you would ruin everything he had worked so hard on," Sophie explained. "And Freddie listened to him."

"Well, he wasn't entirely wrong," I replied. "I did fall down the stairs and nearly kill the Queen Mother."

"And guess where the rumor that you tried to assassinate her came from?" Sophie asked. I looked at her with wide eyes. "And why I couldn't seem to get rid of it."

"Your father?" I whispered. "He was responsible for those rumors?"

"It was an easy way to get rid of you," she explained. "To get you out of the way. He'd already called them and given them your college pictures. It wasn't hard to convince them to run with the allegations."

"The college photos?" I repeated. "He gave them to the reporters?"

"I couldn't figure out how they got them. You aren't the type of girl that posts that on Facebook," Sophie continued. Anger tinted her voice. "He convinced Liam's social media manager to give him the photos. And then he leaked them. He knew you'd be at the hospital and what time you would be scheduled for interviews. He set you up."

I stared at her in shock.

"He made you look bad. And then kept badgering Freddie about how you weren't good enough. He then made sure to break Freddie's heart. And he hoped that with Freddie's heart broken, he could convince Freddie that what he needed was me."

"And that you would be a perfect princess for him. Easy. Low stress," I said, remembering the Duke's drunken words about how his daughter was a better fit for the Prince.

Sophie nodded. She looked miserable.

"How... how did you figure this all out?"

She looked down at her hands for a moment before looking me in the eye. "He asked me to help."

I swallowed hard. Angry butterflies roiled in my stomach. Had she been sabotaging me all along? Had she been working against me the entire time?

"And did you?" My voice shook despite my best effort to stay calm.

"God no!" She shook her head hard enough a strand of blonde hair came loose from her bun. "I love Freddie like a brother. I don't want to seduce him. I didn't want to mend his broken heart."

She said the words with such disgust that I thought she might be sick.

"You're my friend. Freddie is my friend. I wouldn't do that to either of you." Her eyes went hot with anger. "He asked me to go help Freddie get over his heartbreak after you left. He made sure you were on a plane and far away before putting me into play."

The angry butterflies quieted. She hadn't betrayed me.

"I didn't tell him a flat out no," she said, her eyes flickering with guilt as she looked at me. "I let my father believe that I was going along with his plan. And I went to Freddie and asked him what my father had told him."

"And?"

Her eyes went hard with cold fury. I could see the resemblance to her father then. "My father worked Freddie to the bone. He lied and said that you didn't have time for Freddie. That he found proof of you just wanting to use him. That you were stringing him along. That you were going to break his heart and sell it all to a tabloid. That you set him up from the beginning."

I stifle a gasp. "Never!"

"I know." She touched my leg again. "But my father made sure that he was the only person talking to Freddie. That he thought my father was his only friend. That my father loved him like a son. Like Freddie always wished his own father had loved him."

I ached for Freddie. I wanted to kill the Duke. He had used Freddie's insecurities and fears perfectly. "That's why he made him work so much. I knew the trade negotiation didn't need that much work. It was to isolate Freddie."

Sophie nodded.

"When he asked me to seduce Freddie, I suspected something was up and started looking into things. That's when I found the reporter, the pictures, all of it." Sophie continued. "I should have seen it earlier, but I was so busy making you perfect that I didn't suspect my father was trying to ruin it all."

I sat in stunned silence. All this time, I thought I had been doing something wrong. That I had failed Freddie not just as a girlfriend, but as a partner, and as a friend.

But it had been the Duke. He'd sabotaged me at every turn. No wonder Freddie thought I wasn't trying. No wonder he thought I was a liability. It was all the Duke, the man he'd trusted like a father, had told him.

"I am so sorry, Zoey." Her voice quavered and her eyes

came to mine. Tears streamed down her face. "I would never hurt you. Or Freddie. Ever."

I took her hand in mine and squeezed.

"I believe you, Sophie."

She took a deep, shuddering breath. "Thanks."

"But what does the car accident have to do with any of this?" I asked. Panic rose in my chest again thinking about Freddie. Now that I knew he didn't hate me, I had to see him. I had to tell him that I loved him.

"I told Freddie everything two days ago," Sophie explained. She closed her eyes. "He was devastated." She opened her eyes. They pleaded with me to understand. "He loves you. He felt so terrible about what he'd done. He wanted to make things right."

I held my breath. He loved me. He still loved me. I wanted to stick my head out the window and scream it to the city. Freddie still loved me.

"He came up with this elaborate idea to buy this house on a lake. He called seven different Weston's until he found one with a house on the river near your aunt's cabin," she explained. "He was going to buy it and have you come out there. He was going to apologize and make a grand gesture."

My heart thudded in my chest and my mouth went dry. "He was buying the Weston's cabin?"

"Something about not having to deal with neighbors and shouting inappropriate things?" Sophie shrugged. She shook her head. "And I've ruined the surprise of it now."

"No, it's not ruined," I assured her. I remembered that day on the lake.

. . .

"A blowjob." My voice came out soft and low.

Freddie grinned, but he put his hand behind his ear like he couldn't hear me. "What?"

I glared at him. "A blowjob," I repeated, just a little bit louder.

"Still can't hear you. Probably all the water in my ears after you betrayed me," he said with a sigh.

I rolled my eyes and took a deep breath.

"I want to give you the best blow job of your life. I'm going to make you scream for me," I yelled.

"You go, girl!" came a voice from shore.

I realized that the cabin on the west side of the lake had two people sitting on the porch. I hadn't noticed them before. It looked like an older woman and her husband. My heart sank as I recognized the cabin. It was the Westons. They were my grandmother's age and went to church with my mother when she came to the cabin.

"He had a meeting set up for this morning," Sophie continued. "He was on his way to the airport. He took Liam's car so he could get there faster. He was on his way to come find you and make things right."

Her eyes met mine, full of tears and regret.

"And then the accident happened."

CHAPTER 49

My brain went fuzzy.

Thoughts and images flitted around my skull like caffeinated hummingbirds, never settling down long enough for me to see them clearly.

Freddie was coming to see me. Freddie still loved me. Freddie was buying the cabin. Freddie was in the hospital.

The car turned off the highway. Sophie sat quiet, letting me process everything.

"How bad is it?" I asked once I was in control of myself again. I forced my brain to go into nursing mode. Forced it to turn scientific and clinical. "What are his injuries?"

She hesitated.

"Tell me," I urged. "Or I'm just going to imagine the worst."

"He shattered his femur and his right arm. Three skull fractures, two broken ribs, and a punctured lung."

Once again my breath caught. I thought for a moment I might die, but then my heart started again.

"They've stabilized him. They don't think there's any

damage to his brain and they said his lung will be okay," she quickly assured me. "They already performed some surgery. He asked for you the moment he woke up."

"I need to see him," I told her. My hands were shaking.

"Then it's a good thing we're at the hospital," she replied as the car came to a stop. I looked out the windows to see Westshire General.

Sophie led me inside the hospital. She knew what floor to go to and where his room was. I saw James standing guard outside. He smiled when he saw me.

"Zoey," he said as we approached. "Did you bring me a dutch letter?"

I laughed at the absurdity of it. He gave me a small hug.

"He's waiting for you," James said, stepping to the side of the door.

"I'll wait out here," Sophie said. She leaned against the wall near James looking exhausted. She wrapped her arms around her chest. I wondered if she'd slept in the last few days. James shrugged out of his jacket and put it around her shoulders. I saw her smile warmly at him before I went into the room.

The room was dark with the curtains drawn. The smell of antiseptic and hospital linens hit me. IV machines chugged and a motor for the chest pump hummed. I mentally did the medication list and care plan in my head without thinking.

Freddie lay on the hospital bed. His eyes were closed. A bandage was stark and white across his red-gold hair. The traditional blue speckled hospital gown didn't hide his broad shoulders, but it did make him seem so much smaller. Fragile.

I took a seat next to him and lowered the rail between us. I wanted to be as close to him as I could. I didn't want to wake him, so I just stared at him, my eyes hungry for every detail.

His arm was in a cast. I could see the heavy outline of another cast under the white knit blanket covering his legs. A tube ran under the chest of his gown, hissing like a small snake. Bruises mottled his beautiful skin. He had a black eye.

I wanted to sob. I wanted to wrap my arms around him and heal him with my love. Instead, I just took his hand.

"Did I die?" Freddie asked, opening his good eye. "Are you an angel?"

"Oh, Freddie." I leaned over the bed and kissed his forehead on a bare patch of skin that I hoped didn't hurt.

"Yup. I died and went to heaven," Freddie said with a smile.

I choked back a laugh. "You better not die. I'd hate to have to use all my nursing skills to bring you back."

"Did you bring a silver serving spoon?" he asked. "Or did the staff provide you with a serving tray?"

I wanted to kiss him. He was back to his old self.

"I heard you were coming to visit me," I said, wiping at my cheeks. Somehow, I'd started crying.

"So Sophie ruined my surprise?" He smiled at me. "I'll have to have words with her."

"Eh, I think the driver of the other car ruined the surprise," I told him.

He looked down at our still entwined hands. IV tubing ran up his wrist, but I held onto him like he might run away, IV pole and all.

"I was an idiot," he said softly. His eyes left our hands and came to find mine. They were so beautiful. Green like summer trees with flecks of summer sun shining through them filled my world. "I'm so sorry. For everything. For not believing in you. For not fighting for you."

Both pairs of our hands were shaking. We clung to one another, our trembling steadied by the other.

"It's okay," I said.

"No, it's not." He frowned at me. "I wasn't good to you, Zoey. I said that I loved you, but I let the Duke say terrible things about you. Things that I started to believe, even though I knew that you would never do anything to hurt me. That you were amazing and perfect."

The lump in my throat threatened to explode.

"You are so perfect, Zoey," he continued. "And I don't deserve you. Sophie showed me how much work you did. I see now how blind I was. How cruel and callous I was. And I am so eternally sorry."

Tears ran hot down my cheeks. I didn't bother to wipe at them. I didn't want to let go of Freddie's hands.

"And I wanted to surprise you." His trademark half-smile played on your lips. "I wanted to give you a piece of what we had at the beginning. You said that your dream was to buy a house like your aunt's, but with the whole lake so that the Westons couldn't listen to your public indecency. I was going to buy their cabin. So you could still be close to family, but have the lake, too."

I didn't know it was possible to love someone so fiercely after being so angry with them. Perhaps the hurt of losing him made my heart bigger and gave me more room to love him. I wasn't sure. All I knew was that I did love him.

I'd forgiven him the moment I'd seen him. I'd loved him more with every breath he took.

"You don't have to buy me a cabin to apologize," I whispered, my voice cracking with emotion. "A card probably would have worked."

He reached up and touched my cheek with his finger. "You deserve far more than a card," he replied. "Not even a cabin is close to what you deserve."

"How about just you?" I asked.

Hope bloomed on his face, beautiful and stunning. "You'd take me back?"

"Nah, I thought I just fly across an ocean to turn you down," I teased.

His smile brightened at my teasing. He knew it meant that I'd forgiven him.

"Well, if I'd have known that nearly dying would have brought you back, I could have saved a fortune," he replied with a teasing grin of his own. "Real estate prices are higher than ever."

I sniffled. "Do you know that I flew coach to get here? That's how much I wanted to be here."

"You did?" He touched my cheek. "I suppose that's a true measure of love."

I laughed. "No, but I do love you."

His face brightened and he smiled at me. Truly smiled. One of his rare smiles that he only used when he was truly happy. And this time, it shone with love.

"I love you, Zoey Miller," he said softly. "And I don't want you to ever leave me again."

"I love you, Freddie Prescott," I replied. I leaned over the bed and kissed his lips. His lips were gentle and sweet.

I was a reverse Prince Charming, waking up my Sleeping Beauty with a loving kiss.

I sat back in my chair and he smiled at me. Already the color had returned to his face and he looked better. More alive.

"Well, I'm not flying coach home, so you don't have to worry about me running off anytime soon," I teased.

He grinned. "I still haven't shown you *my* castle," he said. "And I don't mean to brag, but it's much better than my mother's."

I chuckled. "Do we have to sleep separately?" I asked. "Or is that only under your mother's roof?"

"You completed the Stair Walk. Mum has no complaint with me dating you." I loved the way he looked at me. With love and reverence, and just a touch of desire. "I think as long as we don't publicly flout our carnal adventures, no one will mind. It is my house after all. Not hers."

"Then I'm in," I told him. "I'm yours. I always have been."

"And I was a fool not to see it." He took my hands again and kissed them. "Thank you, Zoey. For coming back for me. I don't want to live this life without you. The past few weeks were the worst of my life. The car wreck wasn't as bad as not having you. I need you, Zoey."

"I need you, Freddie." My voice shook so hard I was surprised I was able to speak at all. "I never want to leave you again."

I leaned over and kissed him again, closing my eyes against the tears.

My Prince. My Love.

CHAPTER 50

"Is the Queen Mother not in residence today?" the Duke asked Mr. Irson as he walked through the hallways. "I don't see her standard hanging outside."

"The Queen Mother is visiting her son, the King, in Westshire," Mr. Irson replied smoothly. "Would you like me to tell her you asked after her?"

"No, no please," the Duke replied. He smiled his lizard-like smile. "This is supposed to be a secret meeting."

"Of course, Your Grace." Mr. Irson dipped his head politely. "I am the model of discretion."

Mr. Irson led the Duke through the empty stone hallways to the sitting room attached to Freddie's bedroom. He knocked smartly three times and then opened the door.

Freddie sat on a comfortable couch with his injured leg elevated. The cast was hidden by oversized pants. A comfortable chair sat opposite of him with a small table between them. A black expensive looking box sat on the table. The TV on the far wall was dark, but soft classical music played. Freddie turned off the music as the Duke entered.

"Your Majesty," the Duke purred, bowing low.

"Thank you for coming on such short notice," Freddie replied. "Please come and sit with me. We have much to discuss."

"I didn't know that you had been released from the hospital," the Duke said, taking the seat opposite of Freddie. "I'm glad to hear you are healing quickly."

Freddie took out a bottle and popped two white pills into his mouth.

"They released me this morning," Freddie explained once he'd swallowed the pills. "I must say, I was glad to come home. A week, three surgeries, and enough metal that I can pick up radio stations."

"Three surgeries?" the Duke asked. "What did they do to you?"

"They put all sorts of metal pins and disks to fix my femur," Freddie explained, pointing to his leg. "My arm required another set of hardware. And then I had to get the chest tube taken out, but the doctors say that I won't need it anymore."

"And the skull fractures?" the Duke asked.

"So you did check up on me," Freddie said with a chuckle. "I have a hard head. The doctors said they'll heal just fine."

"I am glad you are feeling better," the Duke replied.

"The pain medications help," Freddie admitted, tapping his pocket where he kept the white pills. "But it was your daughter that got me through the worst of it."

Beside me, Sophie snorted.

"Shh," I chastised her.

"She came and visited me everyday," Freddie continued, oblivious to Sophie and me. "I realized what an invaluable asset she is."

"Well, obviously," Sophie said.

I shushed her again. "I can't hear them when you talk," I growled at her, pointing to the TV screen.

Sophie, Liam, Henry, Aria, and I were all in the security office down the hall watching everything going on. Multiple security cameras in addition to the ones we'd hung in Freddie's sitting room gave us all the angles we needed.

"I did see that she came home smiling far more often than usual," the Duke replied, leaning back in his chair.

I had no doubt that she'd been smiley. Sophie had visited every day Freddie was in the hospital. And every time she came, she always brought James a pastry. She'd say hello to Freddie and me and usually go back out in the hallway with James to "Give us our privacy." Somehow, she always managed to only come visit when the big man was on duty.

I made sure to tell her about dutch letters.

"I have a proposition for you," Freddie said, bringing my attention back to the screen. "It concerns you and your daughter."

"I give you all my blessings," the Duke replied. "I have always wanted the two of you to find one another."

Freddie's eyebrows raised. "I didn't even ask the question."

"You didn't have to," the Duke replied, full of self-confidence. "There's a bottle of my favorite whiskey on the table and you're talking about my daughter and her happiness. It's not a difficult leap."

"I don't love her." Freddie says it without rancor or passion.

"Who says marriage needs love?" the Duke replied, not missing a beat. He narrowed his eyes slightly. "Although I am surprised to hear that from you."

"This past month has taught me much," Freddie replied with a slight shrug. "I've seen what I can accomplish. And I've seen how much love can hold me back."

The Duke's eyes began to twinkle with greed. He sat up straighter, his interest piqued.

"Let's have a drink, shall we?" Freddie pointed to a side table behind the Duke. "There's scotch and glasses behind you."

The Duke stood and turned. He grinned as he saw the scotch. "The good stuff, eh?"

"I don't go cheap," Freddie told him. "Two fingers, please."

"This stuff is my weakness," the Duke said. The room was quiet as the Duke poured out two glasses. He gave Freddie the requested two fingers, and himself three.

"I'm going to be blunt." Freddie leaned back in his chair, cool and relaxed. He sipped on his scotch, but barely had any. "I want to marry your daughter for political reasons."

"That's not unheard of for the monarchy," the Duke replied with a shrug.

"But I need to make sure that our goals are the same. I need to make sure that I have read the room correctly. I am going to lay my cards out on the table." Freddie's eyes focused on the Duke. "And I need to make sure that you are exactly what I think you are."

"Go on."

"I want the throne." Freddie wore the Prince mask. The one that showed no emotion.

But the Duke's face lit like a candle as he grinned at the prince.

"And how do you mean to get it?" the Duke asked. "Nothing treasonous, I hope."

"I would never harm my brother," Freddie quickly assured him. He shrugged and settled the glass of scotch on his good knee. "Liam has expressed a lack of interest in ruling. After seeing my success with the trade negotiation, he is unhappy and is thinking of abdicating."

Greed flickered so fast across the Duke's face that I nearly missed it. "What about Henry? He's next in line."

"He's married to an American and we all know how they are," Freddie replied with a sneer. "Besides, Henry's a thick footballer. He wouldn't know how to write a treaty unless you gave him a crayon and a color by number page," Freddie replied.

"Hey, just because I prefer non-toxic washable markers does not mean I can't write a treaty," Henry said in mock anger as he watched through the camera. "I color inside the lines at least fifty percent of the time!"

"It's really more like ten percent," Aria informed him, patting his shoulder like he was a small child needing something explained. Henry narrowed his eyes at her.

"And only when it's a picture of a puppy," Liam added with a sad shake of his head.

I giggled.

"Shh, I'm trying to listen." Sophie glared at all of us.

"So, you're saying you want to be king?" the Duke asked, looking thoughtful. He took a long sip of his scotch.

"I can only do it with your help," Freddie replied. "And therefore, I'm asking for your daughter's hand in marriage. To secure your help."

"And the Queen Mother? The King?" the Duke asked.

"Why do you think they're not here right now?" Freddie replied, motioning to the empty room. "I can't exactly tell my mother that I'm bypassing my older brothers. That I'm the better king."

"But you are the better king," the Duke replied, his voice smooth as silk. "And I'll be there to help you."

"How do I know that you will?" Freddie asked. He sipped casually on his scotch, his eyes boring into the Duke.

Everyone in the security office held their breath.

"Because I've already been helping you." The Duke shrugged. He finished the glass of scotch. He stood and poured himself another.

"We need more than that," Liam said softly, his eyes glued to the monitor. "Get him to brag, Freddie. Do that thing you're so good at."

I watched Freddie settle into the couch. I watched him roll his shoulders, the muscles flexing slightly under his shirt. I noticed the way his face held no judgment. The easy smile. He looked comfortable and relaxed and like nothing in the world mattered.

"Such as?" Freddie asked. "Perhaps how you saved me from that American bitch?"

"Hey!" I glared at the screen. I knew he didn't mean it, but that didn't mean I had to like hearing it either.

Sophie gave my shoulder a gentle squeeze that told me she understood.

"She was holding you back," the Duke replied. "I simply helped you see that."

"While I greatly appreciate you showing me her true nature, that doesn't inspire confidence that you'll actually help me take the throne," Freddie told him, his green eyes going just a little bit harder. "I need proof to trust you, Duke."

The Duke looked thoughtful. He sipped at his drink, emptying it by half.

"I was the one that gave the reporters the photos and told them what time to be at the hospital," the Duke admitted.

"Very clever." Freddie looked slightly impressed, but then shrugged. "But that's child's play. My secretary could do that."

Indignation sparked in the Duke's face. "I was the one who got the rumors going that she'd pushed the Queen Mother as an assassination attempt."

Freddie leaned forward. "That's a little bit better. Definitely more of what I was expecting out of someone like yourself." He took another sip of his scotch and leaned back. "But again, still not impressive."

I chewed on my lower lip. What else did the Duke have to admit? That he'd sent Sophie to seduce him? That wouldn't help his case. That he'd slowly lied and convinced Freddie that I was horrible and not attempting to help him?

The Duke swirled the last few golden sips of his scotch around in the crystal glass.

"You have something, don't you?" Freddie asked. He

set his own crystal glass down on the table between them. I noticed that there were still two fingers of drink in it.

"Your accident," the Duke said slowly.

"Yes?"

"I was the one who planned it."

Freddie stared at him confused. "That's not exactly a ringing endorsement of why I should trust you."

"That car was meant for the King," the Duke explained. He drained the last of his scotch. "He was supposed to be the one in that car."

A gasp went through the security office. Sophie's hand went to her mouth and she stared at her father's face on the screen in horror. Liam's jaw was so tight I was afraid he might break a tooth. Aria clung to her husband.

I started to shake.

Freddie's face went pale. He glanced at the camera before he looked down at his feet. When he looked back up, it was with the Prince's Mask. There was no emotion, negative or positive.

"That accident was meant for Liam?" he asked. His face was neutral, but his tone sounded impressed. "Which is why the car ran into the left side. That's where Liam usually sits."

"I never meant to hurt you, Freddie," the Duke assured him. "I would never hurt you. I just want you on the throne. With you in charge, this country would be unstoppable."

"But why now?" Freddie asked.

"Because Sophie said you needed her," the Duke replied. "And with the success of the trade negotiation, you are unstoppable right now. The timing was perfect."

Freddie forced his lips into a smile. "Well, I am extremely impressed. Thank you."

"You are most welcome... King Frederick." The smile the Duke gave Freddie made the hair on the back of my neck stand up. It was cold and cruel and calculating.

"We should celebrate," Freddie announced. He reached for a small silver bell and rang it. "Pour another glass, Duke."

The Duke continued his predatory grin. He thought he'd won. I turned away from the monitor in disgust and went to the hallway.

"That swine," Liam growled. His handsome face was flushed and his hands clenched. I touched his shoulder and he spun to me. "That man almost killed my little brother. He could have killed Freddie."

The anger in Liam wasn't regal. It was brotherly and far more dangerous.

"I'm glad it wasn't you," Henry said, coming up beside him. "Not that I'm glad it was Freddie. But that accident would have killed you."

"It nearly killed Freddie," Liam shouted. "I will see that man hang for what he did to my family."

I looked back to the security monitor. The Duke was a dead man.

"To the new King," the Duke said, raising a glass.

Liam's eyes bored holes into the screen, watching as the Duke drained his glass in his treasonous toast.

Enjoy your moment, I thought. *You will never have another.*

The King took a deep breath, and his eyes went so cold and hard I nearly took a step back. "Arrest him."

We watched the Duke's face turn from exultant, to

confused, to angry as the police barged into the room and arrested him.

"What's going on?" the Duke yelled when they went to put handcuffs on him. "Do you have any idea who I am?"

"They know very well who you are," Freddie said quietly. He stood, balancing on his good leg. "And now I do as well."

"Freddie, my boy." The Duke's eyes suddenly held fear. "You know I would never hurt you. That accident was never meant for you."

"No. It was just meant for my brother," Freddie growled. "And you tried to ruin the woman I love."

"For your own good," the Duke cried.

Freddie took a step toward him, wincing in the process. He leaned over to whisper in the Duke's ear. I could still hear him due to the microphone on Freddie's shirt.

"I will marry Zoey," the Prince whispered. "And I will make sure you have a live-feed from your jail cell. If you live that long. Traitors don't live long in Paradisa."

The Duke went deathly pale as Freddie returned to the couch.

Sophie stayed in the security office when the police walked her father out to the waiting police car. I stood in the hallway with Liam beside me.

"You!" he snarled when he saw me. He thrashed against the two police officers holding him. They didn't let go, although I could see the muscles in their arms strain to hold him.

"Yes. Me." I held my chin up. "Goodbye."

I didn't curtsy. I didn't use his title. I just turned and walked into the room where Freddie sat waiting for me.

CHAPTER 51

Two months later, Early December

"I'd carry you across the doorway, but I don't think that's a good idea," Freddie said as he hobbled up to the doorway of the castle. His crutches crunched slightly on the white crushed gravel.

"That's only when you get married," I told him. "So you have time."

I winked at him. He grinned at me.

We'd already spent two weeks at his mother's castle. Freddie was slowly on the mend, but doing well. It would be weeks yet before he no longer needed the crutches. Femur fractures take a long time to heal.

I wasn't in a rush though. He was officially on vacation.

And we were going to enjoy it at his castle.

Freddie's castle was stunning. It was bigger than his

mother's, but more modern. Freddie's castle was only built in 1831, making it one of the newer castles of the country. The Romantic architecture made me think of Pride and Prejudice. I could easily imagine Mr. Darcy striding across the perfectly kept hedges.

Inside, the massive hallway was breathtaking. White marble, high square windows, and peaceful fabrics reminded me of spring.

Mr. Irson stood waiting for us.

"Your Majesty," Mr. Irson greeted Freddie with a bow. He dipped his head to me in a formal greeting I didn't deserve. "Ms. Miller."

I ran over and hugged him. "What are you doing here? Did the Queen Mother lend you to us?"

"She did," Mr. Irson replied with a smile just for me. "She thought you might need someone to keep the Prince in line."

"Whatever do you mean?" Freddie held the hand of his unbroken arm to his chest in mock surprise. "I am the model of a perfect patient. I am strictly following doctor's orders. I even got a nurse to look after me full time."

I rolled my eyes but grinned at him.

"Would you like me to show you to your room, Ms. Miller?" Mr. Irson asked, pointedly ignoring Freddie. That just made Freddie grin wider. I could already see the gears turning in his mind on how to prank the older man later.

But I knew Mr. Irson would take it in stride. And probably come up with a revenge prank of his own.

"Actually, I was hoping to take her to South Garden," Freddie informed him. "There's something I'd like to show her."

"Very good, sir." Mr. Irson bobbed his head. "I will bring your bags to your room."

The older man took my things and headed off down a brightly lit hall.

"The South Garden?" I asked. "What do you want to show me there?"

"Something good," he replied. He glared at the crutches as he tried to cross the marble floors. "It's going to take me a moment to get there."

"I'll help," I told him. "You just show me where to go."

I loved the warm smile Freddie flashed at me. I loved the way my body tingled and my heart sped up just from his gaze.

I loved everything about him.

We walked down a wide hallway. Freddie pointed out the conservatory filled with plants, the ballroom, and the library. I could already imagine grabbing one of the beautiful leather books and going to the plant filled conservatory on a rainy night. It would be perfect.

"Come outside," Freddie said, motioning to a large white wooden door.

I tugged the door open and we stepped out onto a large stone patio. Huge stone planters stood empty against the late fall winds. I imagined that they would be full of flowers in every color come spring. Empty flower beds flanked the stone steps leading down and away from the patio.

And to the ocean.

I stared out in wonder at the pale green sea. The wind tasted salty and cold. Gray and white clouds skimmed and danced in the pale blue sky. It looked like a storm might come this evening. Pale sand strewn with gray rocks and green seaweed contrasted against the green of the waves.

It was cold and crisp, but absolutely beautiful. Like a painting. The sea in autumn.

"It's beautiful," I whispered. I didn't want to blink. I didn't want to look away from it.

"Just like you," Freddie replied.

I grinned at his cheesy line, turning to look at him.

But he wasn't standing.

He was down on one knee.

With a ring.

The wind caught his red-gold hair, tossing it around his nervous eyes. Eyes the color of the sea.

"Zoey Miller, I love you," he said. His voice trembled slightly and I loved him all the more for it. "I love you more than I ever thought it was possible to love someone. These past few weeks have shown me just how much I need you."

He looked up at me, his green eyes bright.

"Will you marry me?"

I didn't have to think.

"Yes." I grinned at him "I love you, Freddie."

His eyes sparkled and his laugh of joy made me dizzy.

"I'm going to need you to help me back up," he said. "I think I'm stuck."

I ran to him, wrapping my arms around him and kissing him as we both fell back onto the rock patio.

"Here," he said, pulling himself into a sitting position. He held out the ring.

A huge square blue sapphire surrounded by smaller diamonds glittered in the black satin of the box. I gasped.

It didn't belong on my hand. It belonged in an art museum.

"And then there's this one for everyday," he continued. He held out another box. In this one was a silicone ring in ocean green. The color of the ocean behind us. I'd seen nurses wear these rings because they wouldn't get caught on patients and could easily be cleaned.

He slid them both onto my ring finger. First the silicone one and then the art-magazine worthy one.

"Thank you, Freddie," I whispered, staring down at them.

"No, thank you, Zoey." Freddie reached over, his fingers gentle under my chin as he raised my face to look at him. He took my chin with his forefinger and thumb and brought me in for a kiss.

"She said 'yes,' guys!" I heard Cecelia's voice cut through.

I pulled away from Freddie's kiss to see my family coming out the door.

Cecelia and Carlson stood hand in hand grinning at me. Sophie, James, Mr. Irson, Liam, Henry, Aria, and the Queen Mother stood beside them. My own mother and father were alternating between grinning at me and staring at the royals.

And then three bagpipers came out onto the landing.

I turned back to see Freddie laughing.

"Got ya," he yelled over their music. "How's that for a surprise?"

"That's quite enough of that," the Queen Mother announced, shushing the bagpipers. "Off with you."

The three bagpipers grinned, bowed, and headed back

inside. The Queen Mother shook her head, but she was smiling.

"You did say 'yes', didn't you?" Sophie asked, sounding just a little bit worried.

I held up my hand to show off my ring and everyone cheered.

CHAPTER 52

"You look perfect," Mr. Irson told me.

"Thanks," I whispered, making sure I had a good grip on his arm. Even though I was wearing flats, I wasn't taking any chances in this dress.

Organ music echoed down the stone hallway of the giant cathedral. The sound of a full choir faded in and out, mixing like angels in the distance.

It was time.

"You'll do great," Mr. Irson whispered, handing me off to my mother and father.

"You look so beautiful, baby," my father whispered, his eyes full of tears.

"I'm so proud of you," my mother said, wiping a tear from her eye before taking my arm.

We stood at the main doors to the inner sanctum. The heavy wood muffled the sounds of the music, but I knew what was waiting for me on the other side.

Or rather who.

Freddie.

My Freddie.

I swallowed hard as the big doors swung open and the music surrounded me. It looked like the entire kingdom of Paradisa had crowded into the church. Every pew was filled to bursting. All I could see were smiles.

I clung to my parents. They in turn, had iron grips on me. There was no way they were going to let me fall. My satin gown slid across the stone floor, but I didn't trip.

And even if I did, I had all the people in my life who loved me to catch me.

I couldn't see Freddie. I knew he was there, but there were so many people in the huge church that I couldn't see him.

I found Cecelia and Sophie. They stood at the altar, waiting for me with grins as bright as the sun.

And then I found Freddie and he outshone them both.

He stood with his two brothers, dressed in his military finest. He stood tall, with no sign of injury. His golden hair gleamed. His sea-green eyes filled with happy tears as soon as he saw me.

And then I heard the bagpipes.

I began to laugh. I wanted to run to him. To laugh with him.

This was where I belonged.

I didn't trip. I didn't stumble.

My father and mother gave me to the man I loved.

"Dearly beloved, we are gathered here in the sight of God...."

I heard the words, but I felt them in my bones.

Freddie was mine. He was my happily ever after.

And no shoe in the world was going to take that away.

Escape With Me: A Midlife Love Story

"I gave it all up to be happy. I'd give it all up again for you."

They say life begins after 40, but Cassie ain't feelin' it. Divorced and feeling trapped by her job, she wants to let loose for her friend's tropical beach wedding. She decides to let her hair down and get a little unpredictable. That's when she meets a handsome bartender, Wyatt.

Despite a few grey hairs, Wyatt's the liveliest man that Cassie has ever met. She knows that there's got to be more to his life story than just being a bartender, but this is just supposed to be a vacation fling. And after sunny days spent breaking all the rules on the beach together, Cassie realizes that nobody has ever listened to her the way that Wyatt does.

His carefree life is enviable, his kisses are intoxicating, and she can almost imagine a life with him. But all vacations come to an end. And when Cassie invites him to visit her hometown, Wyatt reveals that he can never go back. Not to her town. Not to America. Not to civilization.

Cassie leaves, confused and heartbroken, wondering just who she got herself involved with. Suddenly, her predictable life gets turned upside down when she sees her picture splashed across the Internet. And when the tabloids come looking for the mature woman who found the lost billionaire, she has no idea what to do...

...until he comes back.

Escape With Me: A Midlife Love Story

New York Times and USA Today Bestseller Krista Lakes is a thirtysomething who recently rediscovered her passion for writing. She is living happily ever after with her Prince Charming. Her first kid just started preschool and she is happy to welcome her second child into her life, continuing her "Happily Ever After"!

Thank you for supporting an indie author. Anything you can do, whether it be writing a review, or even simply telling a fellow reader that you enjoyed this, helps me out immensely. Thanks!

Krista would love to hear from you! Please contact her at Krista.Lakes@gmail.com or friend her on Facebook!

Further reading:

Bad Boys and Babies
    Family Doctor's Baby
    The Billionaire's Baby Arrangement
    Crime Boss Baby

Kinds of Love
    A Forever Kind of Love
    A Wonderful Kind of Love

An Endless Kind of Love

Billionaires and Brides
Yours Completely: A Cinderella Love Story
Yours Truly: A Cinderella Love Story
Yours Royally: A Cinderella Love Story

The "Kisses" series
Saltwater Kisses: A Billionaire Love Story
Kisses From Jack: The Other Side of Saltwater Kisses
Rainwater Kisses: A Billionaire Love Story
Champagne Kisses: A Timeless Love Story
Freshwater Kisses: A Billionaire Love Story
Sandcastle Kisses: A Billionaire Love Story
Hurricane Kisses: A Billionaire Love Story
Barefoot Kisses: A Billionaire Love Story
Sunrise Kisses: A Billionaire Love Story
Waterfall Kisses: A Billionaire Love Story
Island Kisses: A Billionaire Love Story

Other Novels
I Choose You: A Secret Billionaire Romance
His Every Desire: A Billionaire Seduction
Wolf Six's Salvation: A Shifter Love Story
Burned: A New Adult Love Story
Walking on Sunshine: A Sweet Summer Romance
An American Cinderella: A Royal Love Story
Mr. Darcy's Kiss: A Contemporary Pride and Prejudice

www.ingramcontent.com/pod-product-compliance
Lightning Source LLC
Chambersburg PA
CBHW061347190726
48288CB00005B/1627